PRAISE FOR
THE COWBOY SAYS I DO

"This is for certain, I say 'Ido' to reading Dylann Crush! What a rollicking fun ride as Bodie and Lacey team up to save their town and pretend their way to their own real happily ever after."
—Debbie Burns

"Crush sparkles in this small-town, friends-to-lovers contemporary, the first in her Tying the Knot in Texas series."
—*Publishers Weekly*

"*The Cowboy Says I Do* gets my highest recommendation."
—All About Romance

"This first in Crush's Tying the Knot in Texas series has southern charm, sizzling chemistry, and an adorable rescue dog."
—*Booklist*

Jove titles by Dylann Crush

THE COWBOY SAYS I DO
HER KIND OF COWBOY
CRAZY ABOUT A COWBOY

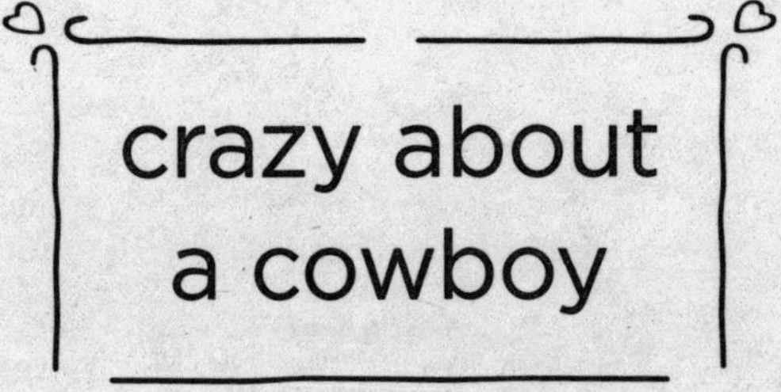

crazy about a cowboy

DYLANN CRUSH

JOVE
New York

A JOVE BOOK
Published by Berkley
An imprint of Penguin Random House LLC
penguinrandomhouse.com

Copyright © 2021 by Dylann Crush
Excerpt from *The Cowboy Says I Do* © 2020 by Dylann Crush
Penguin Random House supports copyright. Copyright fuels creativity, encourages diverse voices, promotes free speech, and creates a vibrant culture. Thank you for buying an authorized edition of this book and for complying with copyright laws by not reproducing, scanning, or distributing any part of it in any form without permission. You are supporting writers and allowing Penguin Random House to continue to publish books for every reader.

A JOVE BOOK, BERKLEY, and the BERKLEY & B colophon are registered trademarks of Penguin Random House LLC.

ISBN: 9780593197479

First Edition: May 2021

Printed in the United States of America
1 3 5 7 9 10 8 6 4 2

Book design by Gaelyn Galbreath

This is a work of fiction. Names, characters, places, and incidents either are the product of the author's imagination or are used fictitiously, and any resemblance to actual persons, living or dead, business establishments, events, or locales is entirely coincidental.

If you purchased this book without a cover, you should be aware that this book is stolen property. It was reported as "unsold and destroyed" to the publisher, and neither the author nor the publisher has received any payment for this "stripped book."

To my sister, Carrie,
one of the strongest,
most badass women I know.

one

Delilah Stone removed her rhinestone tiara as she ducked into the vintage trailer she'd been living in for the past few months. As the reigning Miss Lovin' Texas, her most pressing official duty was judging the state tourism board's search for the most romantic small town in Texas. Thirty days had been more than enough time to determine that the tiny town of East, which ironically happened to be located in the westernmost corner of the state, wasn't going to win. She'd already been to Hartwood, a charming little town located in the Hill Country and the clear favorite to take the title.

With only one more town to judge, she was looking forward to putting her time as Miss Lovin' Texas behind her. Living in the hot-pink branded trailer provided by the pageant's main sponsor was getting old. She just had to spend the next thirty days in Swynton—the final contender—before she could trade in the trailer for her condo and get back to pursuing something more meaningful than deciding which town would secure the title.

"Well, that was a nightmare." Delilah's manager, who also happened to be her mother, or "momager" in pageant terms, came in behind her and pulled the door shut.

"Two stops down, one to go." Delilah lifted her sash over her head and hung it in the tiny closet.

"Just think, a couple of months from now, and this will all be behind you." Her mother unfastened the eye hook at the back of Delilah's dress and slid the zipper down to where she could reach it. "Next time you might want to smile more and talk less."

"Thanks for the feedback, Stella." Delilah had been banished from calling her mother anything but her given name. God forbid someone actually mistake her mom for anything but her older sister—a game Delilah had grown tired of playing.

Her fingers closed around the zipper, and she stepped into the tiny bedroom area to change into something a little more comfortable and a lot less sparkly. Tonight's final farewell appearance marked the end of her time in East. Tomorrow they'd start the trek to the southeast Texas town of Swynton, where she'd spend the next month evaluating their efforts to win the title.

She'd be glad when this gig was up. She not only could use some time away from Stella but also was ready to move on to bigger and better things. Once she wrapped up her stay in Swynton, she'd just have one final appearance to make—the ceremony where the board would award the title to the most romantic small town in Texas.

At twenty-five, she was ready to retire from pageant life and use her connections to make a difference in the world. Some of her competitors might not believe in the causes they promoted on their personal platforms, but Delilah did. And once her current reign came to a glittering end, she had plans to put her money where her mouth was and start doing something to support her cause of empowering young girls, instead of just talking about it all the time.

She carefully slipped the glittery gown onto a hanger, then pulled on her dressing robe. As she slid a headband in place to start her long makeup removal routine, her cell rang.

"Want me to pick up for you?" Stella asked. Even with the door between the bedroom and the living area closed, it sounded like her mother was standing right next to her.

"I'll get it." Delilah moved through the trailer and reached for her phone. "Hello. Miss Lovin' Texas speaking."

"Good evening, Ms. Stone. It's Marty Plum. We've had a change of plans as to your travel itinerary tomorrow."

"Oh? What kind of change?" Delilah had spoken to the contest chair only a few times since she started her term.

Stella leaned against the counter next to her. "What's going on?"

Delilah shrugged. "I don't know yet," she whispered.

Mr. Plum cleared his throat. "Seems Swynton has been disqualified from the competition."

"Disqualified?" Delilah shot a glance to Stella. "What did they do?"

"That's right. They've been accused of bribing a member of the committee. We can't have any kind of scandal touch the competition, so we've taken them out of the running."

"I'm sorry to hear that." Delilah couldn't care less about Swynton, Texas. Didn't matter to her which town they sent her to, as long as she'd be done by the date her contract specified.

"What's happening?" Stella asked.

Delilah held up a finger. "Does that mean my judging obligations are complete? It's just between Hartwood and East?"

"Not exactly." Marty cleared his throat again. "The committee wants to let the runner-up town take Swynton's place. It's a fairly convenient swap since it's right across the river. Instead of spending thirty days in Swynton, we're going to have you spend the next month in Ido."

"Ido? Where's that?" Delilah had never heard of the town and as a lifelong pageant participant, she'd traveled back and forth across the great state of Texas more times than the Texas Rangers had in its heyday.

Stella whipped her head back and forth, turning her giant earrings into weapons. "No. You're not going there."

"I'm sorry, Mr. Plum. Could you hold for just a moment?" She put her hand over the mouthpiece and studied her mother. "What's in Ido?"

"It's where I grew up. You're not spending any amount of time in that place. I barely escaped alive, I'm not sending my only child back there. Traveling to Swynton was close enough. No, you can't do it."

"Ms. Stone, are you there?" Marty asked. "Is there a problem?"

"I'm still here." She motioned for her mother to sit down at the small dinette. "Can you please send over the information? I need some time to talk to my manager about the change of plans."

"Of course. E-mail okay?"

"That would be just fine. Thank you. I'll give you a call in the morning."

By the time Delilah disconnected, Stella sat at the fold-up table with her head in her hands. "They can't just trade out a town like that."

"What's the big deal? Whether I go to Swynton or Ido or Timbuktu, one of my official duties is judging their contest. I can't back out now." Stella was the one who'd insisted she sign up for the Miss Lovin' Texas pageant in the first place. Why the change of heart?

"I have such bad memories."

Delilah slid onto the bench seat across from her mom. "Whatever you ran from in Ido, Texas, is long gone. You don't have to come with me, you can go back to—"

"Not go with you?" Stella lifted her head, her blue eyes

taking on a haunted, wounded look. "You don't want me to travel with you anymore?"

"That's not what I said." Delilah couldn't win, not where her mother was concerned. If she wanted her to go with her, Stella would call her demanding. If she didn't want her to come, then she'd be insensitive. She'd navigated the tricky interpersonal relationship with her mother her whole life. "I want you to do what's best for you, even though I have to follow through on the commitment I made when I won this title."

Stella placed a hand over her heart. "If I'd have known they'd be sending you to Ido, I never would have encouraged you to enter that pageant."

Not wanting to argue, Delilah nodded. "This will be good though. You can head back to Dallas and keep things moving on our new cosmetics line while I serve out the rest of my sentence."

"Are you sure that's what you want to do?" Stella's frown switched into a hopeful smile. "We could still make a run for the big title. With your looks and my pageant know-how, we're a good team."

"We *have* made a good team, but weren't you the one who said I should quit while I'm ahead?" Winning a national-level title was her mother's dream, not hers. Even though they'd worked their tails off, winning local and regional competitions across the South, the big title had remained elusive.

"I know we agreed Miss Lovin' Texas would be your last pageant, but don't you want to try one more time?" Stella bit her lip, her forehead creased.

"You're going to give yourself wrinkles if you keep frowning," Delilah pointed out, tossing her mother's own wisdom right back in her lap.

Stella immediately relaxed her expression. "Are you sure your contract doesn't say anything about what happens if they switch locations on you at the last minute?"

"Nope. I'm pretty much at their mercy until we get through the final ceremony when they name the winner." Stella would know that if she actually read the contracts. But she tended to be more involved on the public side of things—picking out the dresses and offering unsolicited advice on makeup and hairstyle trends. Her mother might drive her crazy at times, but she never steered Delilah wrong when it came to appearances. She also had an amazing knack for business, hence the new line of cosmetics that she and Delilah would be launching after her reign came to an end. Delilah's mentor, Monique McDowell, the first Black woman to win multiple national titles, was also on board, and Delilah couldn't wait to get started.

Thankfully, Monique had stepped in early on in Delilah's pageant career and provided the guidance she'd been missing from her mother. Stella might have big dreams, but she lacked personal experience. Delilah had lost count of how many times she'd heard the story of how her mother chose love over pageant wins. How she'd sacrificed everything to get married and become a mother. Stella never actually came right out and said it, but Delilah had always gotten the sense that her mother thought she owed her a big win. She'd felt that way since the first time she'd stepped on a stage.

"I don't care what they say. It's ridiculous. They can't make you go to Ido." Stella pressed her lips together.

"Actually, they can, and it looks like they are." Delilah held out her phone. "Mr. Plum's new itinerary has me arriving on Friday in time for their kickoff celebration. That gives me three days to get there."

"Oh, honey, how are you going to manage all by yourself?" Stella's brow furrowed again.

Delilah pointed at her forehead. "Keep that up and you'll be taping your forehead while you sleep." Stella had often threatened to make Delilah sleep with clear tape holding her skin taut, saying it was a tried-and-true way to prevent fine lines and wrinkles.

"So, you'll go to Ido and I'll go back to Dallas?" Stella asked, her face devoid of any expression.

"I guess so. You said you had a lot of work to do on that line of cosmetics. What else were you looking into?" Delilah couldn't keep it all straight. Her mother had more projects in the works than the Texas Department of Transportation, and that was saying a lot.

Stella brightened. "Monique and I are finalizing with that cosmetics company on your signature line. Plus, we've got those fashion faux pas fixers in the works. Don't you worry, Texas won't forget Delilah Stone, even if you're no longer competing."

Staying in the public eye was her mother's dream, not Delilah's. But when Mama was happy, everyone else was happy so Delilah was content to let her mother work on whatever projects she wanted to. As long as it kept her busy and gave her something else besides her daughter to focus her overwhelming attention on, it was a win-win.

"I'll tell Mr. Plum to let Ido know they can expect me on Friday then."

Stella nodded, her attention already shifting away from the contest. "Do you think you can drop me at the airport on the way? I'll just take a flight back to Dallas. You'll be fine, won't you?"

"Absolutely." Delilah left her mother at the built-in dinette and resumed her nighttime routine. She loved her mother dearly but was eager for a break. They'd been traveling together for the past two months, and anyone who'd ever spent any time around Stella Stone would have agreed that was about two months too long.

Suddenly, having to spend the next thirty days in Ido didn't seem so bad. She'd have a bit of respite from the breakneck schedule she'd been keeping for the past several years. Without having to entertain her mother, she'd have plenty of time to think about what she wanted to do next, beyond the launch of all of the products Stella and Monique had orchestrated.

For the first time in a long time, the knot in Delilah's chest loosened just a smidge. Having to spend a month in Ido, Texas, might just be the best thing that had ever happened to her.

two

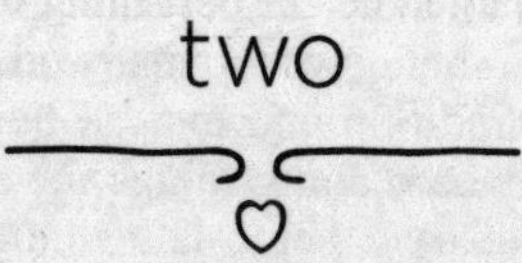

Jasper Taylor drew in a breath as he walked through what remained of his family's pecan orchard. The twister that blew through last month had skipped over their neighbor's cattle ranch but unleashed its wrath on Taylor Farms. Less than a quarter of the trees from their hundred-year-old orchard remained, not nearly enough to fulfill the orders they'd already committed to from this year's harvest.

"We're doomed." Jasper's dad, Frank, hung his head. "I shouldn't have taken out a loan against the farm. We're going to lose it all."

Jasper chewed on the inside of his cheek and tried to come up with a reassuring word. Truth was, they *were* doomed. Unless he could find a way to conjure pecans out of thin air, they weren't going to be able to dig themselves out this time.

"Your poor mama. She's going to skin me alive when she finds out what I've done." Dad ran a calloused hand behind his neck. "If only Colin were around. It's about time you two made up, don't you think?"

According to his parents, the absence of his older brother was the reason everything had gone to shit. Jasper had been tempted to tell them the truth on more than one occasion, but it would break their hearts. So instead he let them go on believing what they would while he tried to hold things together on his own.

"I might have an idea." Jasper hadn't wanted to bring it up yet. He'd been shot down too many times in the past for trying to buck tradition and expand beyond the family trade. But look where doing things the same had gotten them—wiped out by a fickle late summer storm. If he didn't figure out a way to literally save the family farm, there wouldn't be any traditions left to buck, because they'd be forced to sell their land and figure out a new way of life.

"Don't start spoutin' off about that woman's crazy wedding ideas again," Dad warned.

"Do you want to have to tell Mom you're moving the family into town?"

"She'd leave me." Dad sighed.

"She'd never leave you. But she might not talk to you for the rest of your lives." Jasper had seen his mama hold a grudge and it wasn't pretty. She still had trouble looking him in the eye, since she blamed him for Colin's departure.

"Tell me what you have in mind. I suppose it's worth a listen."

"Mayor Cherish said she's looking for complementary businesses to help expand Ido's hold on the wedding market. I told you years ago that people pay big bucks to rent out barns for wedding receptions. And we've got the oldest barn in the state of Texas, that ought to be good for—"

"You can't tell me some hoity-toity bride all dressed in white is going to want to say her vows while standing in a pile of horse shit." Dad shook his head.

"You're missing the point." His dad had almost run their business into the ground thanks to his narrow-minded ways. If he didn't come around to trying something new, they'd all suffer.

"What's the point then? Enlighten me." They'd stopped at the edge of the ring, where Jasper's twelve-year-old sister, Abby, was putting her favorite mare through her paces. Dad hooked the heel of his boot on the lowest fence board.

"We move the horses to the smaller barn and renovate the big one. You're right, no bride is going to want to use it like it is now. But with the insurance money we have coming in, we could use that to—"

"Have you lost your mind? That insurance money's got to buy trees to replace the ones we lost. What good is a pecan farm without pecan trees?"

Jasper tried to keep his cool. "You know it's going to take at least five years, probably seven or eight, to get those trees back to producing something we can sell. But if we revamp the barn, we could be making money hand over fist by next spring."

Dad shook his head. "That's crazy talk. Your mama would never go for such a crackpot idea."

Jasper's chest tightened. Now was his shot. "She thinks it might work."

"What?" Dad's eyes went wide, and his mouth hung open.

"I talked to Mayor Cherish about it last week, just to gauge her reaction. She thinks it's a great idea. Then I mentioned it to Mom."

"You went behind my back." Dad's voice dropped into a growl. "You talked to your mama, you visited with the mayor, all without saying a word to me?"

Jasper let out a long sigh. "Because I knew you wouldn't even consider it. But we've got to do something to make some money over the next few years. Even if we replant half the trees we lost, can't you try something else to supplement in the meantime?"

Dad rested his hands on the top rail of the fence and let

his head drop between his shoulders. "Over a hundred years. This farm's been operating under the Taylor name for four generations. I can't lose it."

"Then let me help you save it." Jasper clapped a hand on his dad's shoulder. "I only want what's best for all of us."

"If that's true, you'd best go find your brother and convince him to come back."

"Dad . . ." Jasper closed his eyes for a long beat, trying to battle away the tension in his jaw at the mention of his brother. He wished he had it in him to come clean, but it would make things so much worse. It was easier to let them believe what they wanted to.

"Whatever happened between the two of you, you're family." Dad squinted. "You can't avoid him forever."

Jasper nodded. "I know."

"I'm going to have to talk to your mama about this." Dad adjusted his hat and squared his shoulders.

"I understand." The phone in his back pocket vibrated. He reached for it and saw Mayor Cherish's number light up his screen. "Hey, it's the mayor. I ought to take this."

His dad didn't respond, so Jasper took several long strides toward the shade of one of the oldest pecan trees they had on the property and answered the call. "Hello?"

"Jasper, it's Lacey Cherish. Something's come up. Are you still interested in trying to make a go of it with your idea on using your barn for weddings?"

"I'm not quite sure yet." Jasper's chest tightened. "I mentioned it to Dad, and he needs some time to get used to the idea."

"Well, I'm in a bind. I just got word that the state tourism board gave us a spot to compete for the most romantic small town in Texas."

"That's great. But what does that have to do with turning the barn into a wedding venue?"

"I need someone to represent Ido as our hospitality

host . . . be the point of contact for the judge while she's here in town. Is that something you'd be able to do?"

"Oh, I don't know. I've got a lot to do around here. We still haven't cleaned everything up from the storm, and—"

"I'm in a real jam. We weren't supposed to be competing in this contest, but Swynton got disqualified and we got their spot. I don't have time to come up with another plan. If we can claim the title of the most romantic small town in Texas, we could increase the wedding business we've already got. It would give you a chance to really make a go of it with the barn idea."

Jasper sensed a golden opportunity within his grasp. Mayor Cherish was right. If Ido claimed the title, there would be a huge influx of tourists. Not only weddings, but they could do anniversary parties, maybe even corporate outings with trail rides. If he could turn things around and save their land, how could he refuse?

"What would you need me to do?"

"They're sending Miss Lovin' Texas over to judge. From what I understand, she'll live here in town for a month, and then they'll hold a big shindig in Houston in November where they'll announce the winner. We're the last stop. She's already been to Hartwood and East. What do you say? Will you be Ido's hospitality host?"

"You want me to entertain a beauty queen for a month?" His gut rolled. "There's got to be someone else better qualified for the job."

"I wish," Lacey muttered.

"What's that?"

"I wish we had time to find someone, but there's no one else. Believe me, I've tried to come up with ideas on who might be best to fill this role. You've got incentive. If Ido wins, you win. Plus, you can't argue that right now you've got the time."

No, he couldn't argue with that. Harvesttime was coming up and with 75 percent fewer trees to pick, not even the busiest time of year would keep him all that occupied.

"What would I have to do?"

"Easy peasy. Just shuttle her around and introduce her to the folks in town. Make sure she sees the best of Ido and gets to all the events on time. Should be a piece of cake."

A piece of cake. In his experience, most things folks thought would be a piece of cake ended up being more like a cake fight. He clenched his jaw, trying to think of another solution. But he'd spent the past month running through every scenario he could come up with to save the orchard. Turning the barn into some sort of event venue and taking advantage of the town's strategy to become the most romantic small town in Texas might be the best option. Maybe even the only option. But what did he know about romance?

"I'd be happy to pitch in, but I don't think I'm the right man for the job."

Lacey sighed. "Some help is better than none. Can you swing by my office this afternoon? We need to get started right away."

"Sure thing. I thought you said you were pretty busy this week with that big wedding coming up. Maybe we should wait until next week?" That would give his dad a chance to further warm up to the idea.

"We don't have time to spare. She'll be here Friday."

"Friday? As in the day after tomorrow?" His stomach flipped.

"Yes, Friday. We've got to put together some sort of kickoff event in less than forty-eight hours."

"Wow." Dammit. How was he going to convince his dad to get on board that fast? Dad was deliberate in his decisions. He took time to weigh the options and examine his moves from every angle before he committed to taking any kind of action. He'd never get behind an idea this wild in such a short time frame.

"Can I count on you?"

Jasper took in a deep breath. Helping the town would be the best way to help his family, even if Dad didn't see it that way yet.

"Let me get cleaned up, and I'll be over in a bit."

"Thanks, Jasper. I'll see you soon."

He ended the call and rejoined his dad by the fence.

"What did the mayor want?" Dad asked.

Jasper hooked his fingers over the top rail. "She asked if I wanted a job."

"What kind of job?"

"Seems Ido is in the running for most romantic small town in Texas and she needs a hospitality host."

Dad let out a deep laugh. "No offense, son, but I hope you turned her down. You don't really know much about either, do you?"

"What's that supposed to mean?"

"When's the last time you went on a date? Shouldn't someone who's in charge of romance and hospitality know something about one or the other?"

"I did turn her down, but told her I'd be willing to help. If Ido wins that title, it would mean a bunch of publicity for something like a wedding barn."

"Tell you what." Dad turned and faced him. The humor had faded from his eyes. "You and Lacey get that title for Ido and I'll let you try that wedding idea with the barn."

Jasper grinned. "You sure you want to make that deal?"

His dad thrust out his hand. "I'm sure, but how about you? If you fail, we're going to have to make some difficult decisions around here." He glanced to where Abby had slowed the mare to a walk. "Some of those horses we've got are worth quite a bit. I'm not afraid to make some hard decisions to do whatever it takes to save this place."

Jasper wrapped his hand around his dad's. "If all goes well, you won't have to."

three

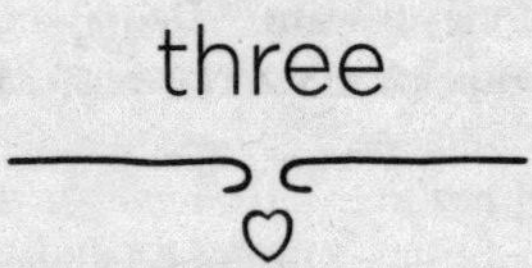

Delilah tapped her fingers on the steering wheel of the hot-pink, decked-out dually truck. She'd enjoyed the drive from East to Ido more than she expected. It was nice to have control of the radio and not have to bend to her mother's preferences when it came to where to stop for a meal, or even which gas station she thought would have the nicest bathroom. Freedom felt just fine to her.

Stella hadn't always been so overbearing. But since things had gotten a little rocky with the man Delilah had been sure would assume the role of stepfather number five, Stella had been more clingy than usual. Even insisted on going on the road together, which meant the two of them had to share space inside the tiny retro camper the tourism board had provided. It would be nice to have the place to herself for the next thirty days, even if she did have to spend it in another small Texas town vying for the title.

Maybe if the cosmetics line did well it would keep Stella busy enough that Delilah could put some effort into something with a little more meaning behind it. She'd always had a soft spot in her heart for the little girls who came to watch the pageants. They had stars in their eyes and hopes of winning a title of their own. What most of them didn't have was access to the kind of training and preparation that Monique had provided for her. But first, thirty days in Ido.

She glanced to the roadside sign welcoming her to town as she passed. It looked new based on the fresh piles of dirt sitting next to the posts that stuck out of the ground. Mr. Plum hadn't provided much background information on the town. He wanted her to evaluate each place based on her own personal experience, not go in with a bunch of preconceived ideas. As she navigated around the town square, looking for a place to park the truck and trailer she towed behind, she took her first real look at downtown Ido.

Seemed pleasant enough. The square took up about half a city block. Tall shade trees blocked the afternoon sun, and people sat on benches placed around the perimeter. A white gazebo stood in the center of it all. Chairs had been set up in front and a few people were working their way around the railing, fastening some sort of ribbon and flower clusters. Delilah pulled the truck in parallel to the sidewalk, taking up a handful of parking spots in front of city hall.

She'd used part of her per diem to stay in a hotel the night before so she could pull herself together and make a good first impression on the mayor and other representatives of the town. As she slid down from the running board of the truck, she adjusted her sash. Mr. Plum had made it clear she was representing the tourism board at all times, and needed to wear her sash anytime she was out in public. She pushed the heavy truck door closed behind her and set her gaze on the building in front of her.

She stepped onto the sidewalk and made her way to the stairs. As she did, someone came around the side of the building, a giant hose in his hand. Before she could get his attention, he shifted the direction of the sprayer. Icy cold droplets of water rained down on her, stopping her dead in her tracks. She opened her mouth to scream but closed it immediately as the water splashed across her face.

"Oh, shit!" The onslaught of water ceased as the man in front of her dropped the hose to the ground. "Cut the water! For fuck's sake, turn it off."

The hose continued to whip around, spraying water like a sprinkler. Delilah stood frozen in place on a drenched section of sidewalk, not knowing whether she should seek shelter behind the truck or try to race up the steps before the water sprayed over her again.

Too late. The hose had taken on a life of its own. Water shot out at every angle as the hose bounced along the grass. The man tried to step on it but slipped and fell. He climbed on top of it, wrestling it into submission as the gush of water came closer to her feet. She couldn't move. The end of the hose lifted, shooting a spray of frigid water straight up her skirt. He launched himself at the spigot, finally pinning it to the ground. The hose clenched in his hand, he sprawled across the sidewalk and squinted up at her.

"Please tell me you're not Delilah Stone."

She took a startled step back. From that angle he might very well be able to see right up her skirt. Her dripping-wet skirt. What was pageant protocol in a situation like this? Years of training and etiquette classes had left her unprepared. So she did what she imagined the reigning Miss Lovin' Texas should do in a moment like that—stepped over the man lying at her feet, straightened her sash, and proceeded up the steps of city hall.

The door had barely closed behind her when he followed her in. "I'm so sorry. Please, let me get you a towel."

"Is there a powder room nearby?" A drop of water ran down her cheek and she resisted the urge to swipe it away, lest she smear her favorite volumizing mascara.

"Right this way." The man gestured to the right. "I'm so sorry. I already said that, didn't I? I was trying to clean off the sidewalk for the kickoff event tonight. We've had a problem with pigeons shitting—I mean pooping—all over the square."

Delilah didn't care about pigeons or poop or anything beyond finding a place to pull herself together in private. "I understand."

"Bathroom's right here." His voice dropped as she put her palm on the door. "Are you sure I can't get you a towel or a change of clothes, or—"

"That's quite all right. I believe you've done enough." She pushed the door open and took refuge in the sanctity of the women's room. First things first, she checked under the stalls to make sure she was alone. It wouldn't do her any good to let someone get a bad first impression.

Satisfied she was the only person in the small space, she gritted her teeth and faced the mirror. Her once-loose waves stuck to her head in wet clumps. Black streaks ran down her cheeks and had dripped onto the white silk shell she'd slipped on under her blazer. And her sash. Delilah let out a soft groan. A few drops of diluted mascara had splashed onto her white satin sash. How the heck was she supposed to get that out? She reached into her purse for a stain wipe—one of the many items she carried in her small emergency bag.

As she dabbed at the black dots, the door to the bathroom opened and a woman walked in, a nervous smile pasted on her face.

"Hi, I'm Mayor Lacey Cherish. I heard you had some trouble outside of city hall."

Delilah turned toward the mayor. "Just a little run-in with your maintenance man. Nothing a stain wipe and a dryer won't fix."

"I'm so sorry." Lacey held a hand towel out to her.

"Thanks." Delilah pressed it onto her hair, trying to sop up the water that continued to drip onto the tile floor. "Accidents happen."

"Can I get you anything?"

"Oh, I'll be fine. Contrary to popular belief, pageant queens don't melt when they get doused with water." She tried to make light of the awkward situation. It wouldn't do any good for her to get off on the wrong foot with the mayor.

"Would you like to reschedule our meeting? We can move it back a little bit and give you a chance to settle in and get cleaned up."

The thought of getting the trailer situated and having a chance to compose herself tempted her to agree. But it was already after four, and she had to be ready for the kickoff event in just a few hours. "Why don't we go ahead and get the details out of the way? I'm going to need a little extra time to get ready for tonight, so I'd rather touch base now so I have the rest of the afternoon to get settled if that's okay."

"Of course. I'll give you a few minutes. Just head down the hall when you're ready. My office is at the end. You can't miss it."

"Thank you." Delilah met Lacey's gaze in the reflection of the mirror. "I'm going to run to the camper and grab a dry set of clothes. I'll be there in five."

Jasper ran his palms over his denim-clad thighs. Delilah Stone had been in town for less than five minutes and he'd already screwed up. How the hell would he explain to his dad that he'd managed to ruin Ido's run for the title before the judge even made it up the steps of city hall?

"What in the world happened?" Lacey entered her office, her cheeks flushed.

He jumped to his feet. "I don't know. I was cleaning the pigeon shit off the sidewalk and all of a sudden there she was."

"You didn't hear her? See her heading your way?"

Jasper shook his head. "I came around the corner and before I knew what was happening she was soaked through."

"Don't worry, you'll fix this." Lacey crossed her arms over her chest, her mouth set in a determined line.

"Me?" His stomach dipped. "How do you expect me to do that?"

"I need a hospitality host, and you owe me."

"Wait a sec. I said I was sorry and I meant it. But I don't think—"

The office door creaked open. Delilah Stone entered. She'd changed into dry clothes, but her hair still hung in damp curls, framing her heart-shaped face. He'd expected the beauty queen to be, well, beautiful. But *beautiful* was too dull a word to do justice to the gorgeous woman who'd just entered the mayor's office.

Lacey rounded the desk and moved toward the door. "Ms. Stone, welcome."

Jasper rose to his full height and drew in a breath. Then he forced what he hoped looked like a reassuring grin and turned it on Miss Lovin' Texas herself.

She might have been drenched from head to toe a few minutes ago, but she handled herself with the composure of a queen. Her spine ramrod straight, her face scrubbed free of any trace of makeup, she entered the office like she owned the place.

"We're thrilled to be hosting you as part of the Most Romantic Small Town in Texas competition." Lacey glanced toward him and he braced himself for the inevitable introduction. "I'd like you to meet Jasper Taylor, our hospitality host. He'll be your main point of contact while you're here in town."

Jasper shot a look to Lacey, who lifted one shoulder in a slight shrug. Great. He didn't want to undermine the mayor, even if she'd made an incorrect assumption that he'd changed his mind about taking on the role. He'd let it go for now. But once Ms. Stone left the office, he'd have to set Lacey straight.

"It's nice to meet you, Ms. Stone. I'm sorry about getting you all wet. Although I've gotta say, you look just as pretty soaked right through as you did when you won your title." He had to give major props to the beauty queen; she didn't flinch as she slid her hand against his.

Delilah glanced over to Lacey. What the heck was wrong with him? Based on how he was handling his interaction with Delilah, she'd probably never believe he actually held a degree in business and had aced his professional communications courses. For some reason his tongue seemed to get all hog-tied when facing the woman with the smoky green eyes who held the fate of Ido in her soft, delicate hands.

She slipped her fingers out of his grip and followed Lacey toward the desk. "It's my pleasure, Mr. Taylor."

"Oh, you can call me Jasper."

"It's my pleasure then, Jasper." The tight smile she gave him held more than a hint of frustration, making him think she'd rather slap him than have to rely on him for anything during her time in Ido. She probably thought Lacey was crazy for putting her trust in him. At least they were on the same page with regard to that.

"Jasper told me he was trying to get the square ready for our kickoff celebration tonight. It seems you happened to be in the wrong place at the wrong time. We hope you won't hold that against us."

"Of course not." Delilah's perfect pink lips split into a smile she directed at Lacey.

"Fantastic. Jasper, could you run through the schedule for tonight to make sure Ms. Stone knows what to expect?" Lacey clasped her hands in front of her and settled against the back of her chair.

"Sure." He pulled a small spiral notebook out of his back pocket. When he'd offered to help, he and Lacey had come up with a timeline for the kickoff celebration. "We plan on starting with the high school band. They've got a new number they've been working on for the homecoming game. Then we'll have Mayor Cherish say a few words to welcome you to town. Do you have something prepared that you'd like to say to the townspeople?"

"I'd love to thank everyone for their hospitality." Delilah crossed her left leg over her right, putting her slim ankle and hot-pink high heel directly in his line of vision.

His gaze snaked up her leg from her heel to a shapely calf. He tilted his head to the side, trying to shake off the uncomfortable warmth that suddenly flushed across his chest.

"Jasper?" Lacey prompted.

"Right." He dragged his attention away from Delilah's leg and skimmed his chicken-scratched notes. "Then we have time for a meet and greet. Just a chance for the townspeople to get to know you and for you to know them. We'll have cupcakes and cookies and maybe a little more music. Whole thing should only last about an hour. We figured you'd be tired after just getting to town so we didn't want to wear you out on your first night."

"That sounds just fine." Delilah graced him with a superficial smile. "Where would you like me to set up camp? I was told there would be a place for me to hook up my trailer to water and electricity?"

Lacey had put him in charge of that. Problem was, they didn't have any public campgrounds in the general vicinity. Not unless they wanted to put her up out at the state park forty-five minutes away.

"I've got two options for you. Either you can park in the lot of one of our local establishments, or my family would be happy to host you out at Taylor Farms."

"Taylor Farms?" Delilah asked. She turned her attention on him, her eyes sparking with just a hint of heat. "Didn't you say your last name was Taylor?"

"Yes." He fidgeted with the edge of the spiral notebook paper. "Unfortunately we don't have a public campground within city limits. But Helmut, the proprietor of the Burger Bonanza, offered up a spot in his back parking lot. Said he'd be willing to run water and power out so you'd be set. Otherwise my family owns land just outside of town, and I expect you'd be quite comfortable there as well."

Lacey must have sensed the need to intervene. "Either way, your comfort is our main concern."

Delilah glanced back and forth between them. "I'd love to get a real feel for the town. Perhaps somewhere more centrally located would be best."

"Absolutely." Jasper's chest loosened. Having her hunker down in the Burger Bonanza lot would be more than fine with him. After his rocky first impression, there was no telling how bad he might botch things if she parked her trailer on his land.

"Is there anything else we need to go over today?" Delilah asked.

"No, ma'am." As Jasper stood, he wiped his clammy palm across his jeans. "I can show you over to the Burger Bonanza and introduce you to the owner, Helmut Schmidt, if you'd like."

"Thank you, I'd appreciate it." Delilah got to her feet.

In heels she stood just a few inches shorter than him. He hadn't had a chance to fully appreciate Miss Lovin' Texas's physique between hosing her down and tracking her into city hall. She was slim, but not downright skinny. She'd changed into a different skirt that showed off her legs. Her shirt tucked in at her narrow waist and he couldn't help but notice the way her hips flared. Damn, that's all he needed was to have to spend the next thirty days with the blond bombshell. He'd probably end up with a chronic case of blue balls.

Lacey stood behind the desk. "I trust Jasper can take it from here. Don't hesitate to reach out if you need anything during your stay. We're thrilled to be considered for the title of most romantic small town in Texas. It would be a huge boost to our economy."

Delilah nodded. Jasper knew how important this was to Mayor Cherish—how important it was to the whole town, including his family's business. Even though they'd gotten off on a rather rocky foot, he'd do his best to ensure he got her settled without any further screwups. Then he'd come back to set Lacey straight. She had to find someone else to take the lead on this, at least if she wanted any chance of pulling it off.

"Right this way, Ms. Stone." Jasper gestured for her to walk ahead of him toward the door. As she moved past, he turned to give Mayor Cherish a look that begged her to let him off the hook.

But Lacey didn't flinch. She stood behind her desk, her arms crossed, a confident smile on her lips, as if to prove they were now in this together.

He wanted to shake some sense into her, but that would have to wait until later. So he pulled his baseball cap down over his brow and caught up to Delilah. The only way he was going to survive the next few hours was by catering to her every need.

four

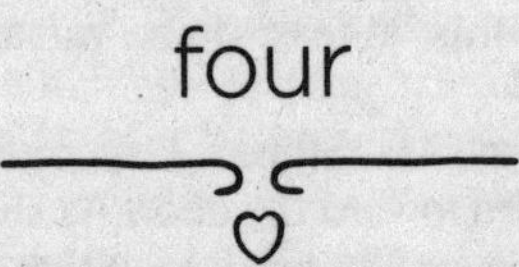

Delilah held herself together as she followed Jasper through the small downtown area. She'd already seen enough to convince her there was no way Ido would be able to compete with the likes of Hartwood. They may as well call the contest and award the title now. For a moment she let herself think back to her arrival. Even if the dense hospitality host hadn't soaked her through with a hose, it still wouldn't change her opinion of the tiny southeast Texas town.

He slowed and turned on his blinker as a big neon sign reading BURGER BONANZA came into view on her left. Thank goodness Stella wasn't with her now. Her mother would blow her top at the thought of living in a local dive's parking lot. Jasper pulled into a parking spot and directed her to the back corner of the empty lot. She brought the truck to a stop and killed the engine.

He met her as she climbed down from the truck. "How's it handle?"

"Excuse me?"

"The truck. Looks like it's got a Hemi under the hood." He patted the front side panel of the truck.

She moved toward the rear of the truck so she could disconnect the trailer. "I suppose it's all right."

"Here, let me help you with that." Jasper reached for the hitch.

Glad to have someone else willing to get their hands dirty, she stepped back and watched while he quickly unhitched the trailer and got it leveled. She hadn't given the man much more than a quick glance when they first met. Granted, he'd been standing behind the hose that drenched her, and then lying on the ground almost getting a good glimpse at her panties.

But now, as he knelt in front of her, she couldn't help but appreciate the way his muscles bulged under his T-shirt with the effort of getting her trailer situated. Strong hands made quick business of the lock. A well-worn baseball cap tried to tame his hair. It must have been a bit too long based on the way it curled up under the edges. Strong jaw, just a hint of scruff. Obviously he was the kind of man who didn't shy away from working with his hands.

She pulled her shirt away from her skin in an effort to get some air moving. The past two towns she'd worked with had assigned a slick public relations rep and a matronly mayor's wife as her contacts. In both cases, they'd been women. But man, Jasper was all man. He bent down in front of her to unhook the electrical, and she couldn't help but notice the formfitting jeans that clung to his assets.

"Do you think I can grab a glass of tea or something inside?" she asked. Even though it was already the last day of September, the heat hadn't let up its grip.

"I'll be done with this in just a minute." He stood, wiping his hands on a bandanna he'd pulled out of one of his pockets. "Why don't I take you inside and introduce you to

Helmut? I want to make sure I've got you all hooked up before I leave."

Hooked up. She had no business thinking about hookups or getting hooked up. Not while she was representing the Texas tourism board. Besides, Jasper Taylor wasn't her type. She preferred someone who knew how to wear a suit, who shaved at least once a day, who had the polish and professional mannerisms to handle any situation. Not a wall of muscle who seemed to have a penchant for four-letter words and a smile that had probably deprived many local women of their panties.

"Thank you." Delilah took the keys he handed back to her, and slipped them into her purse.

"Right this way." Jasper ambled toward the door to the restaurant. "Are you hungry? I wasn't sure if you'd had lunch yet or might be in the mood for a Banzai Burger."

"Oh, I'm a vegetarian." She smiled as he held the door open for her.

"A vegetarian?" His eyebrows lifted. "I wouldn't necessarily mention that to Helmut."

"And why's that?" She stopped at the hostess stand. It was like she'd stepped back to the early seventies. Fake wood paneling covered the walls. The flooring looked like the kind of commercial tile she'd had in her junior high lunchroom, and the light fixtures were a mix of orange and avocado green.

"Helmut doesn't understand some things."

"Being a vegetarian isn't exactly uncommon."

"Yeah, well, neither is global warming but he hasn't acknowledged that either." Jasper picked two menus from the stand. "Where would you like to sit? Best table in the house is in the kitchen."

"I'm fine, really." The smell of fried meat had pretty much killed her appetite when she walked in. If she could exchange some pleasantries with the owner, she'd be able to get settled in the trailer and start getting ready for the kickoff party tonight. "Can we see about getting my power and water hooked up? I ate when I stopped for gas and I don't have much of an appetite."

"Sure." Jasper put the menus back. "Wait here a sec?"

She nodded, more than willing to stay put.

He moved through the tables toward a set of swinging doors. Delilah used the opportunity to gather her bearings. Not a single customer sat in the dated restaurant. If this was the best they had to offer, there wasn't anything romantic about it at all.

"Ms. Stone." A bear of a man strutted toward her from the kitchen, followed by Jasper. "I'm Helmut Schmidt. It's a pleasure to meet you."

"The pleasure's all mine. Thank you so much for hosting me while I'm here in town." She forced a grin as he handed her a tall glass full of iced tea. She'd barely set it on the counter when he reached two heavily tattooed hands toward hers.

"Of course." His hands wrapped around hers as a smile spread over his lips. "I'm happy to help."

"Ms. Stone already pulled up in back. If you can show me where the electrical and water hookups are, I'll make sure she's set before I head back to the square. I've still got a few things to do before she joins us for the kickoff." Jasper used his thumb to point toward the parking lot.

Helmut nodded as he let go of her hands. "I'd be happy to. But first, have you eaten? Ido's known for my Banzai Burgers. I can fix up a platter with fried onions and a side of wings. You look like you could stand to put on a few pounds."

Delilah bristled. She was used to people making comments about her appearance—it came with the territory. But this was the first time someone had seemed so eager to fatten her up. "Thank you, but I ate on the road, besides, I'm a—"

"Little tired," Jasper interjected. "She needs to rest up to be ready for tonight."

She turned her glare on Jasper. "That's not—"

"The hookups?" Jasper asked.

"Of course." Helmut walked back through the restaurant to the kitchen.

Delilah grabbed her tea and followed. She glanced over her shoulder to where Jasper trailed behind them. "What was that about?"

"Can we hold off on telling him you don't eat meat? Maybe until you leave town again?"

"Are you serious?"

Jasper shrugged. "Unless you have some moral obligation to let everyone in town know. I think it would make things easier with Helmut. He has pretty strong feelings about the beef industry."

"Sure." She rolled her eyes. Nothing in Ido seemed to make sense. How did they even place fourth in the contest? So far, compared to the other two towns, they seemed the most backward, the most odd.

Jasper let out a breath. "Thanks. Now let's see what we need to do to get you a hookup."

She followed him out the back door and into the sun where Helmut stood, a long orange extension cord in hand.

"Hey, Jasper, we seem to have a problem."

Jasper wiped his bandanna across his forehead. Not even an hour into his unwanted new job as hospitality host, and he was already drowning. There was no way he'd be able to survive the next twenty-nine days as acting yes-man to the beauty queen. She was nice enough on the surface, but he'd already failed twice. First, because of the unfortunate circumstances surrounding their initial meeting. Next, because of his inability to get power rigged to her small camper trailer.

When Helmut said she could park in his lot, he didn't mention that the electrical on his restaurant hadn't been updated in over fifty years. As soon as they plugged the trailer in, the fuse blew, and the Burger Bonanza went dark. Now he had a pissed-off restaurant owner plus a bedraggled beauty queen on his hands. And both were looking to him for a fix.

"How about you grab your stuff and I can drive you out to my place so you can get ready for tonight?" Jasper turned to face Delilah. "I'd offer you a room at the Sleep Tight Inn but there's a big wedding this weekend and Lacey said they're all booked up."

"Your place?" She leveled him with a glare.

He shrugged. "Unless you want to go over to Lacey's. My place is closer, but I can run you out there if you'd rather. I'll get someone out here with a generator so you'll be set for later tonight but if you need electricity to get ready for the kickoff, my place might be your best bet."

"Fine. Let me get my things." She found the key on her key ring and moved toward the trailer.

Jasper took the opportunity to follow up on Helmut, who'd gone inside to check out his fuse box. "Figure it out?"

"No. Usually when I have a power surge, I just flip the breaker back but that's not working."

"You're probably not up to code." That was a massive understatement. Jasper hadn't ever seen the same combination of colored wires that Helmut's fuse box contained, and he'd been around plenty of old electrical boxes in some of the outbuildings on the farm. "I think your best bet is to get someone out here who knows what they're doing to take a look."

"But what about my restaurant? I'm supposed to be taking food over to the kickoff celebration."

Jasper let his head roll back as he sighed. "Ah, hell. What's left to do? We can't have a party without the refreshments."

"It was working fine until I plugged in that trailer. Maybe she's the one to blame. I've got half a mind to call the tourism board myself and have them send someone out here to check the electrical on that tacky camper."

Jasper reached out and gripped Helmut's shoulder. "That would be a surefire way to make sure we don't win that contest. You think they'll give an award to a town who accuses them of sabotage?"

Helmut scratched his chin. "What do you want me to do then?"

Jasper clasped his hands and slipped them over his head to rest behind his neck. He could think better when he walked, so he paced the small back room of the restaurant, trying to force some brilliant idea into his head. "Let me call Lacey. She'll know what to do."

"If you don't get me power in the next half hour, I may as well throw all the food I was planning on making away. Health department rules." Helmut shrugged and left Jasper standing alone, staring at the fried fuse box.

He dialed Lacey and held the phone to his ear. Better to call now than when he got in the truck with Delilah. She didn't need to know what was going on . . . he needed to keep things as seamless as he could.

"Hey, Lacey. Breaker blew out at Helmut's. You know anyone with a generator that can get out here ASAP so he doesn't lose all the food he's prepping for the party tonight?"

"What?"

He'd obviously caught her by surprise. "Yeah. When he plugged in Delilah's trailer his fuse box fried."

"Oh no. Where is she?"

"She's here. I'm going to run her back to my place so she can get ready for tonight. But we need to get the power back on."

"Right. Um, let me think for a minute." She clucked her tongue several times in rapid succession. "I bet the sheriff's department has something we can borrow until we can get someone out there to fix it. Let me call Bodie and I'll get back to you in a few minutes."

"Sounds good."

"And, Jasper?"

"Yes, ma'am?" He braced himself, waiting for the inevitable words. She was going to go off on him, he just knew it. Not even two hours into his role and he'd blown it. Literally.

"Is there anywhere else you can take her to get ready? The Phillips House won't work since we've got that big wedding, but I'm not sure your place is the best option."

She had a point. He wasn't too keen on offering his place to begin with. "Where would you like me to take her instead?"

"I don't know. My house is nuts right now with all the baby's gear and the wedding stuff. Maybe Zina's?"

"You want me to drive her all the way out there?"

"No, I guess not. Just, try not to scare her off, will you?"

"I'll do my best." Her lack of faith in him made him want to double down on his efforts. In that moment, a flash of inspiration struck. His aunt Suzy's was closer to town. She lived by herself since Uncle Gus had passed a few years ago. He could take Delilah there. Aunt Suzy wasn't exactly the world's best housekeeper, but it would be better than taking her back to his cabin. The only woman who'd ever visited him there was his mom.

Glad to have a firm plan, he fired off a text to Suzy, then tucked his phone back into his pocket and returned to the truck.

Delilah gripped a roller bag carry-on in one hand and a large hot-pink tackle box in the other. "I wasn't sure if you wanted me to follow you or if we should go together."

"Why don't you ride with me? My aunt Suzy's is closer to town and I think you'll be more comfortable there."

"Whatever you think is best. I just need access to a powder room and some electricity."

Jasper nodded. "I'll run you over there, then she can bring you to town when she comes for the kickoff." He glanced back at the pink pickup. "If you're sure you'd rather not drive yourself?"

"I'm liable to get lost on these backcountry roads. If you don't mind, I'll let you navigate."

"Sure. Here"—he reached for her bags—"let me toss these in the back."

"Oh, I'll hold on to this one if you don't mind." She let him take the carry-on but clasped the tackle box to her chest. "It's my makeup case."

He eyed the box as he slid her suitcase into the bed of the truck. "That's a lot of makeup."

She cocked her head and glanced from the case to him. "Comes with the territory."

"Let me get the door for you." Jasper moved past her to pull the pickup door open.

She climbed onto the running board and grabbed the handle to hoist herself into the passenger seat. He waited for her to get settled, then closed the door behind her. As he rounded the truck, he checked for a reply from Suzy. Thankfully, she said she'd be okay with having a little company.

"So how long have you lived in Ido?" Delilah had set her makeup box on the seat between them, like a bulky barrier reminding him to stay on his side of the cab.

"All my life. I've never lived anywhere else except the years I spent up in College Station."

"You're an Aggie?"

"Through and through. How about you?"

"I just finished up my undergrad through an online program at UT Austin." She leaned an elbow on the window frame. "What did you study?"

He grinned at the question. "Agriculture and business. Seemed like the best course of action. My family operates the largest commercial pecan orchard in Texas."

"Oh, I love pecan pie."

"What did you say?"

"Pecan pie." Her eyebrows squished together.

He shook his head. "It's pih-kahn, not pee-kahn. At least if you're a true Texan, that's how you'd pronounce it."

"Really?" Her arms crossed. "Says who?"

"Says everybody. At least everybody around these parts. Where are you from?"

She picked something from her shirt and dropped it on the floor mat. Hell, the last one to ride shotgun in his truck was probably Buster, the pit bull he'd adopted from For Pitties' Sake. The dog not only shed like a beast, he also had some major gastrointestinal issues.

"I've lived several places. California, Florida, Alabama to name a few."

"That explains it." Jasper navigated his truck onto the road, already counting the seconds until they got to Aunt Suzy's.

"Explains what?"

"Why you don't say the word 'pecan' right." His mouth quirked into a sideways grin. The beauty queen seemed a bit flustered. He kind of liked her better that way.

"I say it just fine."

Not wanting to cross the line between a little good-natured ribbing and totally pissing her off, he eased back on the teasing. "It is kind of cute the way you say it."

Her head jerked up and she met his gaze for a hot second before looking away.

"Just don't let the locals hear you," he advised. Especially not his dad. Dad would have no problem correcting her, and probably wouldn't mince any words in his approach.

As they neared Aunt Suzy's place, he tried to think of something else to say to bridge the awkward silence between them. "What made you want to run for Miss Lovin' Texas?"

She rested her chin in her palm. "My mother. She loves the thrill of a good title run."

"Oh yeah? Where is she now?"

"Back in Dallas. As soon as I'm done here, I'll join her. We're starting a new business that will help raise money for my mentor's nonprofit organization. She helps young girls learn what they need to know to compete in pageants."

For a second, he thought she was joking. That's all the world needed . . . more beauty queens. But the light in her eyes as she talked about it let him know she was serious.

"There's a big need for these girls to learn how to strut the runway in a swimsuit?" He couldn't help himself. Even as he asked the question, he imagined Lacey frowning at him and urging him to shut up and make nice.

"No. But there's a big need for girls to have access to the kind of training that can help them get ready for public speaking, to learn how to defend their beliefs, to build their confidence so they're not afraid to pursue their dreams."

"And a beauty pageant can do all that?" He should shut this line of conversation down. He'd already unintentionally insulted her—the one woman who might hold the future of Taylor Farms, and the whole damn town, in her hands.

"Yes, actually, it can. My entire platform is about empowering girls so they're not afraid to follow their dreams. When I'm done here, I'll be able to devote all of my time to raising money to do just that." The look in her eyes seemed to vacillate between heat and ice.

"I didn't realize a pageant could make that big of a difference." Best to back away slowly, so as not to further anger the woman sitting next to him. She might be sugar and spice and wrapped up in a gorgeous package with all the trimmings, but he could sense a fire burning deep down inside of her. No way did he want to be the one to ignite those flames.

He pulled into the long drive at Aunt Suzy's place. Her double-wide sat in a small clearing of live oaks and a few tall pecans. He used to love coming out here when Uncle Gus was alive. They'd spend all day in the saddle, checking the farthest corners of the orchard for his dad and filling their lungs full of fresh country air. Unfortunately, after Gus passed, Suzy couldn't keep up with the horses. She'd turned the outbuilding into her workspace. No telling what kinds of projects Aunt Suzy had in the works. He'd have to make sure to keep Delilah far away from there.

"Here we are." He eased the truck to a stop in front of his aunt's trailer.

Delilah peered through the windshield, her eyes wide.

Jasper tried to see his aunt's place with fresh eyes. He was used to her line of work but to a newcomer, especially someone who didn't spend much time in the country, the sight of Suzy's handiwork might be a little overwhelming.

Before he could admit that this had been a mistake, Suzy came out of the door and stood on the small stoop. She was dressed all in black, including the lace veil she wore over her head, obscuring her face.

Delilah glanced at him as she opened the door.

"Maybe you'd be more comfortable at my place instead."

Before Delilah could answer, Suzy came down the steps, waving her hand, her black glove whipping back and forth. "Hello, hello. Y'all are just in time."

Jasper closed his eyes for a long beat, wanting nothing more than to bang his head on the steering wheel. How could he have forgotten? The last day of September held special meaning for Aunt Suzy. It was the anniversary of James Dean's death. His aunt had always been a huge fan. How was he going to explain a tradition like that to Miss Lovin' Texas?

five

"It's so nice to meet you." Delilah held Jasper's aunt's hand in hers, the lace netting of the woman's gloves rough against her palm.

"The pleasure's all mine. Jasper said you need a place to get cleaned up. Come on in." Suzy held the trailer door open and gestured for Delilah to go inside.

"Aunt Suzy is a taxidermist by trade." Jasper gathered her bag from the truck bed and came to stand behind his aunt.

Delilah nodded as she entered the trailer. Eyes peered out at her from the walls. Her heart stopped. Her palms went clammy. Her vision went fuzzy. Deer and other woodland creatures she didn't even want to know the names of smiled, snarled, and frowned at her, their likenesses forever frozen in time.

"Aunt Suzy's won awards for her skills." Jasper's deep voice came from over her shoulder, drawing her attention away from the menagerie of animals whose eyes seemed to follow her.

"Is that right?" Delilah swallowed a lump of discomfort rising in her throat.

"Sure is. I've shown my work in several competitions. Even was featured as a centerfold in a big taxidermy magazine. I've got a copy right here." Suzy brushed past them, making her way to a small sitting area, where a coffee table held dozens of magazines.

Jasper leaned forward, his breath brushing her cheek. "I'm so sorry. I should have warned you."

Delilah closed her eyes for a moment at the contact. "It's fine. Your aunt seems like a lovely person." Lovely and just slightly off her rocker. But Delilah was a professional. She could keep her own feelings and emotions tucked deep down inside. She'd learned how to do that over the years, and that was something that no amount of pageant training could provide. Her ability to put up a front came from dealing with her mother's never-ending surprises.

"If you want to go, I can take you somewhere else to get ready," Jasper muttered.

She turned around, not prepared for how close he'd be in the small space. His nose might have brushed hers had she not stepped away.

"Ms. Stone." Jasper reached for her as her calves bumped into the bench of the dinette. She stumbled backward, his hand wrapping around her arm, holding her suspended even as her head tipped back. A bobcat snarled at her from above, its teeth bared, a glint of anger in its glassy eyes.

"Oh my." Her hand went to her chest and before she had a chance to register what was happening, she found herself chest to chest with Jasper Taylor.

"Are you okay?" One hand clasped her around the waist, the other held her arm . . . the arm that wedged between them . . . the only thing keeping her breasts from smooshing against the hard planes of his broad chest.

"I'm fine."

He set her upright and immediately released his grip. "I'm sorry. I didn't want you to get hurt."

Hot prickles danced across her cheeks. She averted her gaze, desperate to look anywhere but into the eyes of the man who'd just caught her by surprise. "Thank you, um, I think I might need some air."

"Of course." He stepped aside so she could get to the stoop.

In the bright afternoon sun, she took in a deep breath. She didn't belong in Ido any more than they deserved the title of most romantic small town in Texas. It was obvious. At least to her. And probably to Jasper Taylor as well.

"Here it is." Suzy joined her on the small wooden stoop, a magazine in her hands. "My first centerfold."

Delilah's gaze ran over the spread. Suzy sat in the middle of a virtual wonderland of stuffed animals. "That's really something."

"Those were the days." Suzy ran a gloved finger over the picture. "I suppose I ought to show you where you can get ready. Jasper said you don't have much time and that something went wrong with your trailer?"

"That's right." Relieved to be back on task, Delilah ran her palm over her skirt. "Could I possibly use your bathroom?"

"Of course. Let me show you where it is." Suzy reentered the trailer and Delilah followed.

Jasper had moved to the sitting area. His large frame barely seemed to fit in the small club chair. He made a move to stand as she reached for her makeup case.

"You need any help?" he asked.

"I've got it. I'll be a little while. Do you need to go take care of anything while I get ready?"

"I need to make sure everything's ready at the square." He frowned as he glanced down at his jeans. "And then get cleaned up myself."

"Oh, I'll make sure she gets to the party in time." Suzy

pulled on Jasper's hand. "You go take care of yourself and leave us girls to it."

Jasper glanced from Suzy to Delilah and back again, his brows drawing down to create a tiny furrow between them. "Are you sure?"

"Yes, I'm sure. But before you go, can we have a moment of silence?" Suzy took Jasper's hand in hers, then reached for Delilah's. "Go on, join hands, you two."

Delilah slowly reached out. Jasper's fingers closed around hers, sending a pulse of warmth up her arm.

He rolled his eyes and nudged his chin toward his aunt. "I failed to mention that September thirtieth is a special day to Aunt Suzy."

"Not just me. It's a big day for all of us Deaners." Suzy nodded.

"What's a Deaner?" Delilah was almost afraid to ask. For all she knew, it was a group of taxidermists who practiced some strange ritual on the last day of September.

"Fans of James Dean. He tragically lost his life on September thirtieth, and at five forty-five local time we share a moment of silence." Suzy glanced at the clock on the wall. A chipmunk popped out of a small log as a chime sounded. "If y'all will bow your heads."

Delilah snuck a look at Jasper, who appeared to clench his jaw before dropping his chin to his chest. She closed her eyes and focused on the way his hand felt in hers. That moment when he'd caught her . . . just thinking about it had her heartbeat ratcheting up and her pulse thundering through her ears.

Suzy squeezed her hand, then let it go. "Thank you. I normally honor him by myself. It's nice to have friends and family take part."

Jasper let her hand drop from his. "You sure you're okay riding to town with Suzy?"

His aunt dabbed a tissue under her eyes. "What do you think I'm going to do to her? Stuff her?"

Delilah gulped in a breath. It diverted down the wrong pipe and she coughed, sputtering in an attempt to catch her breath.

"Suzy, was that really necessary?" Jasper guided Delilah to the edge of the dinette bench. "You know she's joking, right?"

Nodding, Delilah pressed a hand to her chest, then cleared her throat. "Of course. We'll be fine. I'll see you at the kickoff."

He hesitated.

"Go on, get out of here. Leave us girls to get ready. Of course she knows I was joking." Suzy dismissed his concern with a wave of her hand. "Besides, I don't have the equipment to work on something her size out here. You know that."

Delilah bit her lip to keep from laughing. Hopeful that Suzy was just a tough old bird who liked to get a rise out of folks, she grinned up at Jasper. "Go on, Suzy and I will get along just fine."

He gave his aunt a final long look, and some unspoken message passed between them. Then he adjusted his baseball cap and grabbed his keys from where he set them on the counter. "You've got my number?"

Delilah nodded.

"Call me if you need anything?"

She nodded again.

"Anything."

"Got it." She stood and picked up her makeup case. "I'll see you in a bit."

"All right." He pressed a kiss to his aunt's temple, then turned and walked out the door.

Delilah waited as the truck engine turned over and the sound of his retreat crunched over the gravel drive. Suddenly the trailer seemed so much bigger without Jasper Taylor taking up all the space and sucking in all the air.

"Bathroom's right this way." Suzy covered the length of the trailer in just a few steps. "You can change in the bedroom if you'd like. You'll have more room in there."

"Thank you." Delilah smiled at the woman as she stepped inside the small bathroom.

"You're more than welcome. I'm always happy to help out my kinfolk. Any friend of Jasper's is a friend of mine."

"Oh, we're not exactly friends," Delilah tried to explain. "He's the hospitality host."

"We're all friends around here, sugar." Suzy propped her hands on her hips. "You need a towel to take a shower or anything?"

"No thank you. I'll just change into my kickoff outfit and redo my makeup."

"Suit yourself. You hungry? I can make you something to eat right quick before we have to go to the party."

"I'm fine, thanks." No telling what kind of meat Suzy might have sitting around in her freezer. The thought made Delilah's stomach roll.

"Best get to it then. I'll be ready whenever you are."

"Thank you." Delilah pulled the bathroom door shut behind her, enclosing herself in the small space. Two chipmunks sat on a log suspended above the toilet. She shook her head and focused on her reflection in the mirror.

Her arrival in Ido hadn't gone exactly as she anticipated. Hopefully the evening celebration would go well. She lost track of time as she brushed and dabbed and highlighted, her fingers expertly applying the makeup in a routine she'd perfected over the years.

Suzy said something, then a man's voice reverberated through the trailer.

A knock sounded on the bathroom door. "You about ready? We've got a visitor and he's got a special ride to get you to the party tonight."

Jasper checked his list once, twice, three times. This afternoon had been such a mess, tonight needed to go off without a hitch. They'd already pushed Delilah Stone to the edge. He could tell by the way her wild-eyed gaze had darted from beaver to bobcat at his aunt Suzy's place. If she fled before she had a chance to pass judgment on their tiny town, he'd never hear the end of it.

"You ready?" Lacey joined him in the gazebo, baby P in her arms.

"As ready as we'll ever be." He turned in a circle, doing one final check-in to make sure all was going according to the plan.

"You're sure Suzy will have her here in time?" Lacey didn't have the same unwavering faith in Suzy's abilities. In addition to working for the taxidermist, Suzy was the local florist. Up until Lacey started bringing in brides, his aunt mainly worked with the town's funeral parlor. But recently she'd been doing a whole lot of weddings, and never missed an opportunity to cross over between her two loves, sometimes working a small token of local wildlife into one of her bridal bouquets.

"The town's got a lot riding on this competition." Lacey bounced her son on her hip, even as she pinned Jasper in place with her glare.

"I know. So do I." He glanced toward his boots, the ones he'd polished to a shine. "That's why I don't think I'm the best person to act as hospitality host. If we don't pull this off, I don't know what we're going to do at the farm. Dad seems hell-bent on replanting, but it's going to take years for new trees to start producing."

"You may not be the best person, but you're my only option." Lacey shifted the baby and put a hand on his arm. "We're in this together. We'll make it work."

He shook his head.

"Unless you want me to offer the job to Suzy instead." Lacey shrugged.

His thoughts bounced back to Delilah's reactions at Suzy's place. He couldn't leave the fate of the town or the farm to his eccentric aunt.

"Fine." He let out a sigh. "I'll do it."

"I hoped you'd see things my way." Lacey gave him a confident grin, like she knew she had him over a barrel the whole time.

At that moment, a loud noise caught their attention. Sounded like a dozen Harleys headed their way, right through the center of town.

"What the heck is that?" Lacey's hand dropped, and she turned to face the incoming rumble.

Jasper walked to the edge of the gazebo, straining to catch a glimpse of what might be causing the noise.

A motorcycle turned the corner. Followed by another. And another. He put his hands to his temple. So help him, if his aunt had done what he suspected . . .

"Please tell me Suzy isn't involved in this?" Lacey's lips were set in a straight line, but her eyes went wide.

"I don't know." Jasper shook his head, his arms falling helplessly to his sides. He'd asked Suzy to make sure Delilah got to the event in one piece, but he should have specified how.

The local biker gang, if one could call it that, slowed as they reached the center of the square. Jasper jogged down the steps and over to the curb, each step taking him closer and closer to his downfall. He could feel it in his core. Lacey would fire him for this. Delilah would be traumatized and tear out of Ido faster than a cat in a room full of rocking chairs.

But when he reached the curb, he caught a glimpse of Delilah's wide grin. Her perfectly aligned, whiter-than-white smile hit him in the center of his chest. Helmut reached out and offered a hand, helping Delilah climb out of the low sidecar attached to his motorcycle and get her footing.

"What's going on?" Jasper directed the question to Suzy, who was in the process of climbing off the back of a bike.

"The boys showed up and wanted to give us a ride into town." She waddled, slightly bowlegged, joining him on the curb. "Your friend seemed up for the adventure, so here we are."

"Here you are?" Jasper muttered through clenched teeth. "Are you deliberately trying to send me into cardiac arrest today?"

"Settle down, we're just having a little fun." Suzy swatted at his shoulder.

Jasper turned away from his aunt, making a concerted effort to clear the frustration from his expression before facing Delilah. She stood on the curb, perfectly poised, not looking like she'd just ridden ten miles in the sidecar of a death trap on wheels.

"Are you okay?" Jasper reached her and took in her appearance. Her hair flowed over her shoulders in soft waves. The light yellow dress she wore practically glowed under the early evening sun. If she'd been traumatized by the ride into town, she was doing a damn good job of hiding it.

"Of course. Why wouldn't I be?" She peered up at him through full, dark lashes. His chest warmed at her attention.

"I just . . . I didn't realize my aunt would be riding in with her club."

"It's a gang, not a club, Jasper." Helmut approached, his fingers wrapped around the handles of Delilah's bags.

"Sorry, Helmut. Aren't you supposed to be doing the food?" Jasper glanced over to the tables under the gazebo.

"Sure am. Deputy Phillips brought that generator over, and the team should be showing up with the vittles any minute." He held up Delilah's bags. "Where do you want me to put these for you?"

"I'll take them." Jasper reached for the bags. "I'll just put them in my truck until after. I plan on running you back to your trailer when we're done here to make sure you get settled in okay."

"Thank you." Delilah nodded.

"I'm gonna show the guys where to park." Helmut gestured over his shoulder. "Then I'll start setting up."

"Great," Jasper said. "Be right back." He walked the short distance to his truck and locked Delilah's bags inside the cab. Delilah didn't look any worse for wear but what the hell had Suzy been thinking? From now on he'd have to keep a closer eye on the contest judge. He couldn't afford for her to get the wrong idea about Ido or, worse, get injured and hold it against them.

"So where do you want me?" Delilah joined him and they made their way to the gazebo together.

He could think of several responses, none of them particularly appropriate in the moment. So, he cleared his throat, chased away the illicit thoughts of Delilah underneath him, her tight yellow dress scrunched up above her thighs.

"We'll have you in the gazebo to start. Like I said earlier, the high school marching band will kick us off, then Mayor Cherish will say a few words. Since you want to say something, we'll have you go next. Then it's just a meet and greet. Should be pretty casual." He cast a glance her way.

She met his stride, even though he had no idea how anyone could walk in the tall heels she had on. "That sounds great. Your little town has been so welcoming so far."

So welcoming. Was that a genuine comment or was she in beauty queen mode? It was hard to tell. "About that ride to town," he started.

She turned to him, her eyes shining. "I've never ridden in a sidecar before. It was . . . fun."

"Fun?" His gaze roamed over her. How was she not covered in dust?

"Well, it would have been more enjoyable if they hadn't put a pop-up rain shelter over me until we hit the pavement. But I had to protect my hair." She ran a hand over her blond waves.

"A rain shelter?" He racked his brain, trying to figure out what his aunt had done. Didn't really matter now. What mattered was that Delilah had arrived, uninjured, apparently untraumatized, and ready to kick off the next thirty days.

"Your aunt is an interesting woman." Delilah smiled again and something inside him simmered.

He let out a laugh. "That's an understatement. I'm sorry if she got out of hand. I'll keep an eye on her."

"Ms. Stone." Lacey met them on the sidewalk, baby P squirming in her arms. "I'm so sorry about your trailer. I think we've got it sorted now. There shouldn't be any additional problems with your power."

"Thank you. Now who's this?" Delilah asked.

"This is baby P." Lacey juggled her son from one arm to the other. "It's time for dinner and he's not especially happy right now."

"Baby P?" Delilah cocked her head.

"We haven't agreed on a name quite yet," Lacey said. "But we're working on it."

Jasper bit back a grin. The kid would probably be walking before Lacey and her husband, Deputy Sheriff Bodie Phillips, came clean on a name. Rumor had it Bodie had flubbed the birth certificate and Lacey refused to tell anyone the kid's given name. Ten months old and the poor kid was still going by baby P.

"Jasper, can you take him for a minute? I want to walk Delilah around the square and ask a few questions."

He glanced to baby P and back to Lacey. She held her son out to him, and he didn't have a choice but to take the wriggling baby in his arms. "What kinds of questions? Should I come along?"

"Girl talk." Lacey scrunched her nose as she took Delilah's arm. "Just give us a few minutes, okay?"

He held baby P close to his chest as the women moved down the sidewalk. The baby's brow furrowed as he watched his mom and food source move farther away.

"Hey, little guy, she'll be back in a minute." Jasper bounced the kid in his arms, the same way he'd held his younger brothers and sister. It had been a while since one of his siblings was this little, but holding a baby was one of those life skills that automatically came back. He still remembered helping his mom with the younger kids.

Baby P reached up and grabbed ahold of his ear. Jasper grinned and blew a raspberry on the baby's neck, earning him a high-pitched series of giggles. Someday he'd have this for himself. A wife, a gaggle of kids. But not until he secured his future. He'd been through enough rough times with his folks to know that he wanted to be sure of his place in the world before he brought a kid into it or took on the responsibility of a wife.

He turned, swinging baby P around in his arms, and caught Bodie coming up the sidewalk.

"I thought I heard something familiar." Bodie held his arms out and baby P struggled to launch himself toward his dad. "Lacey around?"

Jasper relinquished the baby to Bodie. "She and Delilah are taking a stroll around the square for some girl talk."

"Girl talk, huh?" Bodie held his son against his deputy uniform. "Everything ready for tonight?"

"Seems to be. I'm surprised we were able to pull it together so fast."

"When my wife is on a mission, if you're standing in her way, it's best to move out of it."

"No kidding." Jasper had nothing but huge respect for the mayor. She'd single-handedly revamped the town, and he'd admired her efforts from afar. Now, being central to her continued plans to elevate their wedding operation, he had a different vantage point. Lacey would do whatever it took and expected nothing less of those who'd pledged to help her.

"Good luck tonight. Let me know if you see anything strange going on, will you?" Bodie asked.

Jasper nodded. "Strange like how?"

Bodie shook his head. "I heard Swynton was supposed to be up for this award but got disqualified. They don't usually take kindly to a perceived slight."

Jasper's gut clenched. "You think the whole town of Swynton's going to turn up and try to steal the show?" That's all he needed.

"No, nothing like that. Buck might have operated that way, but Mayor Monroe is a lot more subtle."

Jasper remembered the controversy between the ex-mayor of Swynton and Bodie's family. Since Troy Monroe had been elected mayor of their neighboring town, the rivalry had simmered down a bit. "Is Adeline still battling Mayor Cherish for brides?"

"Yeah. She slowed down for a while but now that her daddy's taken over as mayor, she's back at it. I told Lacey she needed to sit down and have it out with Adeline, but with the baby and now this"—Bodie rolled his eyes—"there hasn't been much time. You ought to know better than anyone what Adeline is capable of."

Jasper hated to admit it, but unfortunately, he did know Adeline better than most.

"Just let me know if you see anything odd. We need this win. All of us." Bodie tickled baby P under the chin and earned a series of giggles.

They did need this win. Whether Jasper liked it or not, he'd hooked his family's future to the fate of the town.

But he knew something the rest of them didn't . . . not Bodie, not Mayor Cherish, not meddling Adeline Monroe-Hawk . . . this wasn't the first time he'd had to put it all on the line to save his family. And if he had any say in it, the Taylor family wouldn't go down without a fight.

six

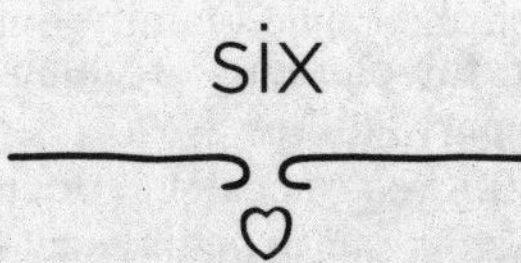

"Thank you for your hospitality. I'm looking forward to getting to know all of you and spending time in your romantic town." Delilah gave the crowd her biggest, brightest smile as she wrapped up her short speech and gazed out over the small group assembled in front of the gazebo.

"Thank you, Ms. Stone." Mayor Cherish stepped next to her. "We're excited to have you here and can't wait to show you the best Ido has to offer." Lacey nodded toward the tables set up to the side. "If you'd all like to join us for some refreshments, I think we're ready to get the welcome party started."

The crowd erupted into polite applause. Lacey flipped the switch on the mic, then turned toward Delilah.

"That went well. I know you're probably tired from traveling and ready to settle in for the night. Do you mind sticking around for a little bit to mingle before Jasper runs you back to your trailer?"

"I was planning on it." Delilah tried to find Jasper in the crowd. He stood a head taller than most people, so it didn't take her long. Her stomach warmed as he met her gaze. His lips quirked into a grin and she found herself smiling back before she regained her composure and turned her attention back to the mayor.

"Great." Lacey took her son in her arms from a man who'd joined them in the gazebo. "Have you met my husband yet?"

"I haven't had the pleasure." Delilah took the man's hand in hers. "Deputy Phillips, isn't it?"

"That's right. But you can call me Bodie." He shook her hand, then released it and tipped his hat her way. "We're thrilled to have you with us, Ms. Stone."

"Call me Delilah, please."

"Will do." He handed her a card. "You have any trouble during your stay, just let me know."

"Thank you, I will." She slipped his card into the small clutch she held in her hand.

"I've got to go change the baby. Bodie, can you introduce Delilah around and make sure she gets one of Helmut's cupcakes?" Lacey bounced the baby on her hip. "I'll catch up to you in just a bit."

"I'd be happy to," Jasper said as he came up the steps.

"Great. I'm going to walk around the perimeter and make sure everything is in order." Bodie tipped his hat again. "See you later, Ms. Stone."

Delilah nodded at Lacey and Bodie before turning her attention on Jasper. "So, there you are."

"Here I am." He gave her a lopsided grin that made her pulse tick up. "Ready to meet the good people of Ido?"

"I suppose so." She wrapped her hand around the arm he offered and let him lead her down the steps.

"What do you think of the town so far?" Jasper asked.

She breathed in the scent of just-popped kettle corn mixed with the smell of fresh-cut grass. "I think it's charming."

"Really?"

"Why do you sound so surprised?" They meandered past a large fountain as they made their way toward the tables full of refreshments, where most of the people congregated.

Jasper shook his head. "Sorry, I don't mean to act surprised. This is my first go-round as a hospitality host, so I'm not sure how we stack up against the other towns you've visited."

Delilah went through the motions of locking her lips with a fake key and tossing it to the side. "I'm not at liberty to say."

"I get it. I'm sure part of your job is to stay impartial and not give out info on your other stops."

"That's right." The same thing happened in East. They'd tried to pump her for info on how her time had gone in Hartwood. It wouldn't be fair to share details that might give one town an edge over another, not even at the request of the charming hospitality host.

"Well I bet they didn't have melt-in-your-mouth cupcakes like Helmut makes in the other places you visited." Jasper stopped at the edge of a table that had been packed full of cupcakes a few minutes ago. "Care for a sample?"

Helmut ambled over, his leather biker jacket replaced by a pristine white chef's apron. "Ms. Stone, what can I get you? Red velvet? Chocolate decadence? Vanilla bean?"

She tilted her head and looked up at Jasper. "Which one's your favorite?"

"Mine?" His eyes widened. "They're all good. But I've got to admit, I'm pretty partial to the chocolate bourbon pecan pie cupcake. Helmut uses pecans straight from my family's orchard for those."

Her stomach growled, reminding her she hadn't had anything for dinner. "That sounds wonderful. Do you have any of those?"

Helmut shook his head. "Not tonight. But I'll bake a special batch for you when I get my next delivery of pecans from Taylor Farms."

"I'm going to hold you to that." Delilah tapped a finger

against her lip as she looked over the other choices. She could gain ten pounds just by inhaling the sweet smell of sugar and chocolate. "Let's go classic. How about vanilla bean?"

"Fantastic choice." Helmut placed a white cupcake with white frosting onto a paper plate. "Here you go. Enjoy."

"Hey, don't I get one, too?" Jasper asked.

Helmut nodded toward the paper plates. "You've got two hands."

Jasper let out a laugh and reached for a chocolate cupcake.

"What do you think?" Helmut waited, his palms braced on the table, a tiny hint of vulnerability showing in his kind green eyes.

"Oh, you want me to try it now?"

He nodded.

She peeled back the paper and took a nibble. The perfect blend of vanilla and sweetness exploded on her tongue and she had to restrain herself from literally inhaling the rest of the cupcake in one bite.

"Good, isn't it?" Jasper's brows raised.

"Mmm. Delicious." She nodded, relishing the first taste of refined sugar she'd allowed herself in the past two weeks.

Helmut seemed pleased with her reaction. "Plenty more where that came from. Feel free to help yourself to any of the flavors."

"Thank you." She broke off another small bite and popped it into her mouth.

Jasper's plate was empty.

"Did you already eat your cupcake?"

"Yeah. I'm a sucker for sweets. Would you like to meet some of the other folks involved in the wedding business here in Ido?" he asked.

"Sure. But is there somewhere I can get rid of this first?"

His brow scrunched, making him look a little confused as to why anyone would pass on such deliciousness. "You don't like it?"

"I love it. That's why I need to get rid of it. I'm on a strict no-sugar diet. How else do you think I fit into all of these gowns?" She cocked a hip and his gaze flickered down, past her waist. Her cheeks warmed as the hint of humor in his eyes gave way to something darker.

He shook his head as he took her plate, folding the cupcake inside, and walked to the edge of the crowd. "It's a damn shame to waste a cupcake."

"You can finish it if you don't want to waste it." She wouldn't blow her diet just to make him feel good.

"It's all right. Just don't let Helmut know. He might look like a badass on the back of his bike, but he's a big softy. Now, let me introduce you around."

They approached a circle of people who seemed deep in conversation. "Zina, Alex, meet Miss Lovin' Texas, Delilah Stone. She'll be spending the next month here."

"Nice to meet you." Delilah shook hands with both.

"Zina runs the For Pitties' Sake pit bull rescue and Alex here is going to be the best vet in town when he finishes his degree."

Delilah couldn't help but notice the familiar warmth between them. The way Alex's eyes softened as he looked at the woman next to him or the way she tucked herself against his side. Someday she hoped she'd have the chance to find a man to share that kind of bond with her.

"I read something about the pit bull shelter. What a great cause."

"Unfortunately, it's necessary around here." Zina shook her head. "We seem to be a dumping ground for unwanted pit bulls."

"I think it's wonderful that you've got a place for them to go. I'm a huge proponent of supporting the underdog." Delilah smiled. "I'd love to tour the shelter while I'm here."

Zina glanced at Jasper. "That would be great."

"I'm sure we can find a time. Zina runs a fantastic program over there." Jasper's chin tipped up. "She's even started working with a veterans' support group to train dogs to help soldiers acclimate to life outside the military."

"Really?" Delilah arched a brow. She made a mental note to spend some time getting to know the pit bull rescue director. Zina could be a good ally since they both had a vested interest in helping others.

"She's amazing." Alex turned a wide smile on the woman next to him. "We actually met while working on the dog rescue together."

"I think it was more because of the penguins, wouldn't you say?" Zina smiled up at him.

"Penguins?" Delilah narrowed her eyes.

"It's a long story." Jasper nodded toward an area where a small band had set up. "I promised the band I'd introduce them if you don't mind. It's their first time to meet a reigning pageant queen."

"Of course." Delilah tucked her arm into the crook of his elbow. "It was so nice to meet both of you."

Zina and Alex nodded as Jasper led her toward the band. "I'll check with Zina to find out when a good time would be to visit. She's amazing with those dogs."

"I'd like that, thanks."

"In fact, I adopted my dog from For Pitties' Sake last year."

"I love dogs. I've never had a chance to have one because I travel so much, but once this trip is over, I'm hoping to get one of my own." Her mother never would have let her get a dog, even if they hadn't spent most of their time running from pageant to pageant. In Stella's eyes, dogs were slobbery, hairy, filthy animals that belonged outside. As she pictured her mother surrounded by pit bulls, she let out a soft laugh.

"What's so funny?" Jasper asked.

"Just picturing my mom's reaction if I came home with a rescue dog. She's pretty particular."

"I don't know what life would be like without a dog.

We've always had at least one or two running around the orchard. They keep the goat in line."

"You have a goat?"

"A goat, chickens, couple of dogs."

"What's the goat's name?"

"Tie Dye." He glanced down at her. "There's a story behind that."

"I'd expect nothing less with a name like Tie Dye. Are you going to tell me how the goat got that name?"

"Later. Right now I'd like you to meet the Wicked Washboarders, our very own eclectic bluegrass-country-polka band." He reached out to shake hands with an older man who held a strange-looking musical instrument in his hands. "Kirby, meet Delilah Stone, the reigning Miss Lovin' Texas."

Kirby took his cowboy hat off his head and bent into a low bow. "The pleasure's all mine, Ms. Stone. The fellas and I were about to get started on our set. I do hope you'll stick around to watch for a bit."

"Just a few minutes," Jasper said. "Ms. Stone's been traveling all day, so I promised her an early night."

"I'd love to." Delilah's gaze swept over the variety of instruments they'd set up.

"All right then." Jasper pointed to a few round tables occupying the perimeter of a small dance area. "Should we grab a seat before the music starts?"

"You let us know if you have any special requests." Kirby nodded before turning his attention back to tuning a few strings.

Delilah let Jasper lead her over to the table. "What kind of instrument does he play?"

"Kirby hasn't met an instrument he can't coax a tune from, but that's a steel guitar. Don't you like country music?"

She bit her lip, not wanting to admit that the last time she'd listened to country was probably at a high school dance.

"You're kidding me." Jasper grinned. "Please tell me you know how to two-step?"

"Of course." She smiled at his good-natured ribbing.

"Whew. I thought for a second there we might have to vote you out and get a new judge. Hey, would you like a lemonade?"

"Maybe just a water instead?"

"You got it. I'll be back in a second. Save my seat?"

Delilah nodded and watched Jasper walk back toward the refreshment table. It was odd having such a good-looking, charming hospitality host. They'd gotten off to a rocky start but there was no denying their involvement had taken a turn toward something much more pleasant. She'd have to do her best not to mix business with pleasure. It wouldn't do her any good to let her attraction to Ido's main man get in the way of her doing her job.

No good at all.

"How's it going?" Lacey snatched him by the arm as he approached the refreshment table.

"Good. She met Zina and Alex. And I introduced her to Kirby, too. I think she wants to tour For Pitties' Sake while she's here. Maybe she can help us spread the word about the rescue."

There had to be some benefit to catering to the beauty queen's every need for the next month. Especially if Ido didn't waltz away with the title. He'd done some research on the two other towns in the brief amount of time he'd had between his talk with Lacey and Delilah's arrival. Hartwood oozed romance from every street corner. They had a huge Valentine's celebration every year and a wine trail that catered to long couples' weekends and picture-perfect wedding settings.

East wasn't quite as polished. Their website spoke to

romantic dude ranch stays and communing with nature in the state park that bordered the town. Jasper was fairly sure Ido could put on a better show than East, but was still struggling to figure out a way to best Hartwood.

"Have you given any more thought to our big event?" Lacey asked.

"I've been trying. It's not like I've had a lot of time."

"None of us have. I wish we'd had more notice. How about playing up the Fall Festival this year?" She snagged a cup of lemonade and tried to keep it away from the grabby hands of baby P.

"That would work. I was thinking we could make it bigger. Maybe add a pumpkin thing where we float lit-up pumpkins down the river?" He'd been trying to come up with an idea that would foster community spirit and show Ido in a romantic light. "Do you have any themed weddings coming up in the next month?"

Lacey's brow furrowed. "I'll go through the reservations again. The only thing that comes to mind is the bride who wants to build her whole wedding around butterflies. She even sent over boxes of caterpillars. Thinks they ought to turn into butterflies before her wedding, and she wants us to release them all right after they take their vows."

"That sounds kind of cool. Let me see what I can come up with to work with that."

"Really?" Lacey turned a questioning eye his way. "I suppose butterflies are kind of romantic."

"Doesn't matter what you think. It just matters what Ms. Stone thinks."

Lacey shrugged. "That's true."

He glanced over at Delilah, who sat clapping her hands along with the music coming from Kirby's steel guitar. As he reached for a cup of water for her and a cup of fresh-squeezed lemonade for himself, Lacey bumped him with her hip.

"Who's that?"

"Who's who?"

"Sitting down next to our judge. Please tell me that's not Adeline." Her eyes narrowed.

Jasper followed her gaze. Adeline took the seat opposite Delilah at the two-top table. She reached over and shook hands. Then bent her head toward Miss Lovin' Texas like she was about to divulge world secrets.

"Jasper, we've got to get over there and find out what's going on. We can't have Adeline messing with our chance to win." Lacey drained the rest of her lemonade and tossed her cup in the trash. "Let's go."

He covered the short distance to the table with Lacey on his heels. "Here's your water."

"Thank you." Delilah wrapped her hand around the red plastic cup.

"Jasper. Lacey." Adeline nodded, making her short bob swing. "I was just telling Delilah how disappointed we were to be out of the running. We all know Swynton is a much more romantic place to spend some time."

"Maybe if y'all hadn't cheated you'd still be up for consideration." Lacey lifted a shoulder.

"We didn't do anything wrong. And I'm going to prove it." Adeline got up from her seat. "Ms. Stone, if you'd like to experience some real Texas hospitality, you let me know. We have a gorgeous bed-and-breakfast right downtown that would be happy to host you during your stay."

Something jabbed into his shin. Jasper winced and bent down to rub his hand over the spot. As he glanced up at Lacey, she made her eyes go wide and nudged her chin toward the dance floor. What was that supposed to mean?

"The music is lovely, isn't it?" Lacey asked. "Are you much of a dancer, Ms. Stone?" Again, with the tilt of the head toward the dance floor.

"I've taken some variety of dance classes most of my life. But mainly to help with posture. Definitely not to perform." Delilah turned her upper body to glance at the couples twirling around the dance floor.

"Would you like to dance?" Jasper asked, finally connecting the dots on what Lacey was trying to get him to do.

"I'd love to. Will you excuse us?" She stood and took a step in front of him.

He put his hand at the small of her back and guided her toward the small clearing they'd set up for dancing, praying he wouldn't make a fool out of himself. Lacey hadn't mentioned dancing as a requirement of taking on the role of hospitality host. He hadn't led a woman around a dance floor in a long time.

"Sorry about that." He clasped Delilah's hand in his and put his arm around her waist. She smelled like every happy memory he'd ever had—a mixture of lemons and bright summer days. Who could have imagined someone could bottle up the scent of joy?

"I'm used to women getting territorial. Comes with competing in pageants." Her hand rested lightly on his shoulder.

He wanted to pull her close and let himself breathe her in, one long breath at a time. But they were only on day one. He had twenty-nine more days of being subjected to the sunshine of Delilah Stone. Best not ruin it all the first night.

"Adeline doesn't like to lose."

"I gathered." She smiled. "No one really likes to lose though, do they?"

From this close he could catch the way the light sparkled in her smoky green eyes. "I suppose not."

"The way a person handles a loss can tell you quite a bit about them, don't you think?"

Jasper thought back to the year his high school football team lost the division title to Swynton. Some of the guys wanted to head across the river and interfere with their parade. Coach had pretty much told them the same thing.

Winning was great, but showing that you could handle a loss said more about a person's character.

"I think you're right." He lifted his hand from her waist and twirled her around before nestling her against his chest.

"Where did you learn how to dance so well?"

"You'll laugh if I tell you."

"No, I won't. I promise." She crossed her heart with her fingertip.

He had to tear his gaze away from the spot where her finger connected with her chest. "My aunt Suzy used to make me take her to the Friday night fish fry down at the VFW. They always had music playing after dinner and my uncle Gus refused to dance with her, so she paid me."

Delilah's eyes widened and her lips quirked up. "How old were you?"

"Middle school. Probably thirteen or fourteen. Dancing with Aunt Suzy paid better than helping my dad around the orchard. Plus, it got me out of the house for a little while. Gave me something to do besides go looking for trouble."

"You don't seem like much of a troublemaker." Her hand tightened on his shoulder.

He hadn't been much of a troublemaker at all. Not like his older brother. Thinking about Colin was one way to wring the fun out of a night.

"You okay?" Delilah's voice drew him back to the present.

"Yeah. It's getting late though. You ready to turn in for the night? Tomorrow's a big day . . . your first day in town."

She let her hand fall from his shoulder. He immediately missed her touch. He offered his elbow and she wrapped her hand around it as he led her back to the table, where Adeline and Lacey were caught in some kind of a glare-down.

Lacey looked up as they approached. "Jasper, would you like to walk Adeline to her truck? I want to make sure she doesn't have any trouble finding her way out of town."

"I was just leaving." Adeline pushed the chair back from the table. "It was nice to meet you, Ms. Stone."

Delilah's lips curved into a tight smile. "It was nice to meet you, too, and I can assure you, I'm quite comfortable here in Ido."

Score one for the beauty queen. Jasper gestured for Adeline to walk ahead of him. He didn't dare touch her. Men had been turned to stone in her presence for far less. "Shall we?"

"We wouldn't make you park in the back of a greasy burger joint if you were our guest." Adeline backed away, her cheeks flushing.

Jasper wondered how Adeline knew where Delilah's trailer had been set up. He didn't know what she was up to, but he was concerned about her next move. Adeline wasn't a woman who liked to lose. He'd heard stories about her recent rivalry with Mayor Cherish. She'd even started up her own wedding-planning business across the river in an effort to beat out Lacey when she'd transformed the town. She wouldn't let anything stand in her way of besting her old rival, even if it meant trashing Swynton in the process.

"Does your dad know you're out here causing trouble?" Jasper muttered as the two of them walked away from the crowd.

"Who do you think told me what was going on over here?" She turned on him, her hands clamped to her hips. "Y'all don't deserve this title. You don't even deserve to be in the running, and I'm going to see to it that you don't have a snowball's chance in hell of bringing home the win."

"Snowball's chance in hell, huh?" Jasper gritted his teeth.

"That's right. You disagree?"

"I'd say if anyone has a snowball's chance in hell of winning this title it would be the town who managed to create a whole winter wonderland wedding last summer, wouldn't you?"

Adeline let out a huff. "We'll see about that. I'd suggest you keep your eyes and ears open, Jasper."

"And why's that?" He could handle a little friendly across-the-river competition, but if Adeline wanted to start slinging threats, she'd best be prepared for the fallout.

"Because I'm going to be waiting for you to screw up. And when you do, I'll be there to turn Miss Lovin' Texas's eye where it belongs—on Swynton."

Jasper waited until he was sure Adeline had gotten in her truck and was well on her way to hauling ass back across the river before he rejoined Delilah. He wouldn't put it past Adeline to stoop to low levels to turn things her way. It wouldn't be the first time she'd tried to derail him. He was already unsure enough about his involvement in this crazy competition. Knowing Adeline would be waiting for him to slip up put an extra heaping helping of pressure on his already overburdened shoulders.

"Sorry about that." He stepped to the table where Lacey had engaged Delilah in what appeared to be some lighthearted conversation.

"Did Ms. Monroe-Hawk make it to her truck okay?" Lacey smiled, her halfhearted grin barely covering her disdain for Adeline's antics.

"Seems so. Ms. Stone, I know you've had a long day. Are you ready to go?"

"I would like to turn in early. What's on the agenda for tomorrow?" Delilah glanced back and forth between him and Lacey.

Hell, he had no idea what her schedule entailed. All he knew was that he was the one who'd be ferrying her around and making sure she got the most picture-perfect impressions of life in their little town.

Lacey pulled a thick binder out of her diaper bag. "I've taken the liberty of putting it all in here. I'm hosting an intimate brunch with the ladies' group tomorrow morning to let you settle in and get your bearings. Then Jasper will take you on a tour of town in the afternoon. Ortega's has planned a special dinner tomorrow night."

"That sounds lovely." Delilah stood and pushed her chair back in. "I look forward to seeing you tomorrow."

Lacey held baby P's hand in hers and waved. "Have a good night."

Jasper gestured for Delilah to go ahead of him. One night down, twenty-nine more to go.

seven

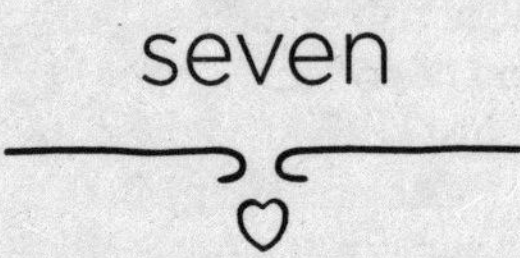

The next morning Delilah woke to an odd smell. She checked to make sure the windows were closed, and flipped the small portable air conditioner on high to circulate the air. It didn't help.

She peeked through the pink-and-white-gingham curtains toward the back of the Burger Bonanza. The parking lot was full, at least a dozen pickup trucks parked in a giant circle, and Helmut stood in the center of them all, in front of a huge contraption. Smoke poured from the sides as he lifted the lid. What in the world was going on?

She didn't dare leave the trailer without looking her Miss Lovin' Texas best. By the time she showered and got herself fixed up, half the trucks had left the lot. Jasper wouldn't be picking her up for another thirty minutes, so she pulled her sash on over her head and pushed the door open wide.

"Good morning." Helmut lifted a spatula in a wave. "Fine day we've got in store for us."

Delilah slid her sunglasses on, trying to shield her eyes from the bright sun. "Good morning. Is there a party going on?"

"You could say that." Helmut gestured to the men who remained. Most of them sat in camping chairs, forming a lopsided circle around him. "Once a month we get together for Smoker Saturdays. Today's your lucky day, Ms. Stone. Care for some fresh smoked catfish for breakfast?"

Her stomach pitched. "No thank you. I'm headed to a brunch Mayor Cherish organized. Is there somewhere I can grab a quick cup of coffee?"

"Of course. Just head inside and Jojo will help you out."

"Thank you." She pressed her hand against her stomach and crossed the parking lot, taking care to give Helmut and his giant smoker a wide berth. By the time she reached the door to the restaurant, the smell of mesquite and fish seemed to coat her in a fine layer. Maybe she should take Jasper up on his offer to move the trailer outside of town. Otherwise she might put off the good folks of Ido by sheer smell alone.

"There you are." Jasper smiled as he rose from his perch on a stool at the counter.

The sight of him made her heart beat faster. She'd enjoyed spending time with him the night before, especially learning more about his family and getting a chance to nestle against his chest on the dance floor.

"I came in search of coffee." She slid onto the stool next to him.

"Jojo, can we get a coffee for Ms. Stone?" he asked.

The waitress nodded and poured her a cup.

"Please call me Delilah. And are you early or am I running late?"

"We've got some time before we head over to Lacey's." He leaned an elbow on the counter and focused his warm brownish-green eyes on her while Jojo filled a cup. "Everything go okay last night?"

"It was fine." It usually took her a few nights in a new place before she could sleep through the night. Last night she'd fallen asleep as soon as her head hit the pillow, but woken up around two to the sound of a couple of dogs getting into it in the lot behind the restaurant.

"Just fine?" Jasper eyed her over the rim of his mug. "Nobody bothered you, did they?"

"Oh, no. Nothing like that. I think there were a couple of stray dogs nosing around. That's all."

"You sure you don't want to move out to the country? It would be a hell of a lot quieter."

And a hell of a lot closer to him. Not that it would be a problem. Jasper was polite and charismatic and definitely knew his way around a dance floor, but she wasn't interested in him like that. She didn't plan to get involved with a man until she and Stella had the new business established. After she got through the contest and her time as Miss Lovin' Texas was up, of course.

"I think I'll be fine here. The catfish thing is only one day, right?"

Jasper chuckled as he set down his mug. "Once a month. Sorry about that. I completely forgot to warn you."

"That's okay. Hopefully, my hair hasn't absorbed the smell. It was pretty strong when I woke up this morning."

Jasper leaned close, invading her personal space, and nudged his nose into her hair. Her skin pebbled at the unexpected gesture, and time seemed to stand still as he took in a long breath.

"I think you're good." He sat up, finished his coffee, and pulled out his wallet.

"No fish smell?"

"Not even close."

She held a hunk of hair to her nose and took in a whiff. "Are you sure?"

He swiveled on his stool to face her and put a hand on her shoulder. An awareness thrummed through her, making her chest tighten. The feeling only increased as his face drew close to hers. She kept her gaze on his lips, bracing herself as the tip of his tongue poked out. Her lips parted and her eyes drifted closed. He was going to kiss her; she could feel it in the marrow of her bones.

But then his nose nudged into her hair again, his breath warm on her ear. "You smell like lemons. And something flowery."

"Lavender," she whispered, her hand coming up to circle his wrist.

"Mmm." He inhaled. "Yeah, lavender."

"Ahem." Jojo cleared her throat, and they broke contact. "You need change?"

"No, we're good." Jasper's hand dropped and he faced forward, his eyes on the handwritten tab. "Lacey's expecting you. Are you ready to get going?"

Delilah nodded, not trusting herself to speak. Her reaction to Jasper's touch had caught her off guard. And she wasn't a woman who dealt well with surprises. Seemed like he didn't want to acknowledge the heat that had sparked between them, so neither would she.

"Let me go lock up the trailer. Can I meet you by your truck?"

He rubbed a palm across the back of his neck. "Sure. I'll meet you outside in a few."

Good. She'd have a few minutes to pull herself together.

"Thanks, Jojo." Jasper got up from his stool and headed toward the back of the restaurant.

Delilah sat there for a long moment, trying to collect herself.

"You want more coffee?" Jojo cocked a hip against the counter, the pot of coffee in hand.

"No, thank you." She reached for her purse and slung the strap over her shoulder as she stood.

"He's a real catch, that one." Jojo looped her finger through the mugs and lifted them off the counter.

"Who, Jasper?"

"That's right. Poor guy got dumped pretty hard a couple of years ago. Everyone expected them to get married but then she showed up in town, a new fiancé in tow. If you ask me, I'm surprised he agreed to work on the wedding stuff. But then again, no one asks me anything, so there you go."

"Who would do such a thing?"

Jojo shrugged. "Someone not in their right mind. But I suppose that's one way to describe Adeline Monroe."

Delilah made a career out of keeping her emotions in check. But when Jojo dropped Adeline's name, her jaw might as well have dropped to the floor. "Jasper used to date Adeline?"

"You didn't hear it from me." Jojo disappeared through the swinging doors leading to the kitchen.

Delilah didn't want to be standing there when Jasper came back, so she made a dash toward the door. The crowd in the parking lot had doubled again. She returned Helmut's wave as she made her way to the trailer.

By the time Jasper had pulled around to pick her up, she'd freshened up.

"You ready to meet the ladies of Ido?" Jasper rounded the truck to open the door for her.

"Is that what brunch is about?" she asked.

"I'm afraid so. Lacey hosts them once a month in an effort to stay in their good graces. She'd never hear the end of it if she deprived them of being some of the first to welcome you to town."

Delilah had an inkling of what to expect. She'd been speaking at women's groups and luncheons since she'd won her first big title. As her mother used to tell her all the time, "It's not what you know, it's *who* you know." She shouldn't be surprised that Mayor Cherish was using her visit to impress some of her constituents.

"You ever get tired of it?" Jasper pulled out of the parking lot, leaving Helmut and his giant smoker behind. The air coming into the truck cab changed and the smell of the fresh outdoors tickled her nose.

"Tired of what?"

He glanced over at her before turning his attention back onto the road. "People using you."

She let out a long breath. "Comes with the territory, I suppose. Besides, isn't that what we all do?"

"What do you mean by that?" His hands tightened on the steering wheel, and she looked away.

"We all use each other in some way. Call it networking, or mentoring, or collaborating. But I think most people rely on others for a lot of their success."

"I suppose."

"Haven't you ever used someone else to get ahead?"

"Not that I'm aware of."

"Well then, that makes you different than any man I've ever met." She settled against the back of her seat, taking the tiniest bit of pleasure at the slight shock on his face.

Jasper didn't say anything else until he brought the truck to a stop in front of a sprawling country home. A narrow porch stretched the entire length of the front, complete with two big rocking chairs and a miniature kid-sized one where Lacey's son would probably sit someday.

"You ready for this?" he asked.

"As ready as I'll ever be." She gave him a smile that was supposed to hold all of the confidence she didn't feel as she climbed down from the truck and stepped onto the stamped concrete sidewalk.

The front door opened wide and Lacey stood just inside. "There you are. Welcome."

"Thank you so much for having me."

"My pleasure. Come on in, everyone's so excited to meet you." Lacey held out a hand and Delilah took it. "Hey, Jasper. Why don't you come back in a couple of hours to pick her up?"

"You got it, boss." He lifted his hand to wave.

Delilah glanced back as the door shut behind her, a small part of her wishing she were spending the morning with Jasper instead of being subjected to the fine ladies of Ido.

* * *

After Jasper left Delilah in Lacey's care, he headed into town. He wanted to check on the power and water hookups at Helmut's to make sure there wouldn't be any additional issues. So far the generator Bodie provided had been working, but Helmut had someone coming out to take a look at the wiring. As he passed through the square on his way to the Burger Bonanza, his phone rang.

He hadn't talked to his aunt Suzy since last night when she'd delivered Delilah to the kickoff event in a sidecar. "Hey, did you have fun last night?"

"You heard from your brother lately?"

"Which one?"

"Colin."

His heart lurched. "No, why?"

As far as he knew, his brother was playing by the rules they'd set up. Rules they both agreed to the last time they'd seen each other in person.

"I've got a feeling." Suzy let out a long-drawn-out breath. "I swear I saw his ghost while I was leaving the feed store over in Swynton."

"Last I heard he was up in Amarillo. You really think it was him?" That's all he needed was Colin coming back, especially right now. Nothing good ever came from him showing his face around town.

"I don't know, but if it wasn't him, he has one hell of a doppelgänger."

"Did you try to talk to him?"

"No. I was loading my truck when I saw him drive by. Had to stop and get some of that fox pee they sell. Damn rabbits are eating all of my fall spinach."

The tightness in his chest eased. "So, you're not sure it was actually him?"

"Well, no. But it nearly gave me a heart attack. You don't think he'd actually be stupid enough to come back, do you?"

"I don't know." He didn't want to try to guess what Colin might do. He'd been wrong so many times in the past when he'd tried to anticipate his older brother's moves. "I've got a little time. Maybe I'll swing through Swynton and see if I can spot him. What was he driving?"

"A truck. A big black Chevy with a gun rack in the window. You sure you don't want to talk to Deputy Phillips or the sheriff? They're better equipped to handle him."

"No." Maybe if he'd made the decision to turn Colin in years ago, it would make sense to call the police. But how could he get them involved now without implicating himself? Having his parents believe Colin left because of a fight between brothers was a hell of a lot easier than letting them know what had really happened. He'd only confessed things to Suzy when she'd overheard him threatening his brother. But he'd sworn her to silence and would continue to handle it on his own. If Colin had the balls to come back to town, it could only mean one thing. He wanted something.

"I don't feel right about this," Suzy said.

Jasper cleared his throat and swallowed the regret he'd carried with him for bringing his aunt into his confidence in the first place. "Everything will be fine. Thanks for letting me know. I'll check it out and get back to you."

"While you're over there, why don't you have a chat with your old girlfriend? Rumor has it she's been making waves about Swynton being disqualified from that contest." Suzy clucked her tongue. "Never did figure out what you saw in that girl."

He never really knew what he saw in Adeline Monroe either. But back in high school, when she was head of the cheerleading squad and he was the starting quarterback, it had seemed so much more cut-and-dried. They were supposed to go together, everyone said so, and he convinced himself everyone was right. At least until they left for college and she forgot about the promises they'd made each other and came home with a fiancé. Truth was, she'd done him a huge favor, but it sure hadn't felt that way at the time.

"I'll talk to her."

"Be careful there, too. I'm not sure who's more dangerous—your brother or Adeline with a chip on her shoulder."

He broke the tension with a chuckle. "I can handle Adeline."

"For your sake, I sure hope so. Take care now."

"You too, Suzy." He disconnected and swung the truck around in a wide U-turn. If Colin was over in Swynton, he needed to know.

An hour later he'd gone up and down the main streets with a dozen sightings of a black Chevy with a gun rack. He'd figured it would be a lost cause based on the generic description but had to see for himself. With time running out before he had to go pick up Lacey, he decided to swing by Adeline's place before he headed back across the river.

She didn't look a bit surprised to find him standing on the other side of her front door. As his gaze drifted over her, his aunt's words rattled through his head. What exactly *had* he seen in Adeline? Whatever it was, it was long gone now.

"Jasper Taylor. To what do I owe this honor?" She stuck her head through the crack in the door, not bothering to invite him inside.

"What's going on? Rumor has it you've been spouting off all over about how Ido doesn't have a right to be competing in the state tourism board contest."

She rolled her eyes. "Don't believe everything you hear. But in this case, it's true. Y'all don't deserve it. Swynton won fair and square."

"And then cheated. It's not our fault you got yourselves disqualified."

"I didn't know anything about anyone cheating. Somebody did that on their own. Daddy doesn't condone that kind of behavior and never would have asked someone to reach out on Swynton's behalf." With her hand clamped to her hip and a fire burning in her eyes, he almost believed her.

"What's done is done. If you've got a problem with the contest, take it up with the committee."

"I tried. They didn't care. And now we're paying the price." Her lower lip stuck out, a move he'd actually found cute at one point in his misguided youth.

"It's a silly contest, Adeline. Let it go."

"I can't. You know better than anyone that Swynton is a more romantic place. That's why we spent all of our time on this side of the river when we used to go out. You do remember that, don't you?" She flashed a grin.

"As I recall, didn't you try to get married over in Ido last year? Speaking of, is your husband home? I haven't had the pleasure of actually meeting the man yet."

Adeline's smile flipped upside down into a nasty frown. "I only tried to get married there to help them. But now Swynton has its own wedding venue. And sooner or later the state tourism board will realize their mistake."

"I don't know what you're thinking about doing, but whatever it is, don't."

"Or what? You don't scare me, Jasper. I know you're nothing but a big ol' pussycat under all that brawn." She pushed her finger into his chest.

"Consider yourself warned." He backed away and tipped his hat. "Have a good day, Mrs. Hawk."

Her eyes narrowed and she opened her mouth like she wanted to say something, but slammed the door instead.

Jasper wasn't sure whether he should consider the visit a success or not. But she'd been warned twice now. If she didn't back off, he'd be willing to take things to the next level. He had to win that title. It was the only way to fix things, to make things right for his family.

Eager to get back across the river, he pressed on the gas, happy to put some distance between him and Swynton.

By the time he got back to Lacey's, Delilah was sitting on the porch, a big glass of sweet tea in her hand. His mouth watered at the sight, so when Lacey asked if he'd like to set a spell and stay for a glass of tea, he didn't hesitate to accept.

"How did it go?" He lowered himself into a chair as his gaze drifted over Delilah's long legs. She'd propped them up on a footstool next to him.

"It was fun. Brunch was delicious and I enjoyed getting to know some of the ladies of Ido." She turned a weary smile his way.

"You ever get tired of smiling?" he asked.

A furrow creased the area between her brows. "Why do you ask?"

"Just seems like it would be hard to always be 'on' like that. No matter what's going on, you just smile and wave."

"Are you saying I don't have feelings?"

"No, that's not what I mean at all. I'm sure you have feelings." He didn't mean to offend the woman, just wondered how she did it. "I'm just curious about how you can bury your own feelings and pretend like everything's okay all the time. Don't you ever feel like frowning?"

She let out a laugh. "My mother says it takes more muscles to frown than it does to smile."

"Is that true?" He leaned forward, resting his forearms on his thighs.

"I don't know. She's always telling me things like that. Doesn't want me to get any premature wrinkles." She bit her lower lip with her teeth like she'd just divulged a state secret.

"I think you'd look just as pretty with a wrinkle or two." Where did that come from? Now he was the one who wanted to clamp his mouth shut.

But she grinned. "Why, Mr. Taylor, you say the nicest things."

He couldn't help but laugh. "Yeah, right. Telling ladies how great they'd look with wrinkles has always been one of my best pickup lines."

"What's your best pickup line?" Lacey asked as she came out onto the porch.

"Nothing. I'm just putting my foot in my mouth like always." Jasper reached for the tea Lacey handed him. "Thank you."

"You're welcome. I had a call from Mrs. Winegate while I was in the house. She wanted to tell me how much she enjoyed meeting you this morning." Lacey smiled at Delilah. "I hope she didn't pester you too much about her daughter."

"She was lovely." Delilah took a sip of tea.

"What happened?" Jasper asked.

"She's interested in getting her daughter into some pageants." Lacey set her glass down on the table. "She's not the only one, either. I heard at least half a dozen women asking about how to get their daughters started."

"I don't mind." Delilah's lips curved up at the edges and Jasper found himself captivated by the different types of smiles she had at her disposal. With a simple tilt of her mouth, her whole face changed. "I've thought about starting a program for girls who want to get into pageants. I was lucky enough to find a mentor early on, but most girls aren't as fortunate."

"Maybe you could chat with them while you're here in town," Lacey suggested.

Delilah's eyes took on a bit of a shine. "I'd love that."

Jasper sat mesmerized, studying the contours of Delilah's face . . . the way her cheeks flushed when she was happy, the spark that lit up her eyes at Lacey's suggestion.

"Jasper?" Lacey toed him in the shin.

"Huh?" He swung his head to meet her gaze.

"I asked if you'd be willing to set something up? You can use the Phillips House as a meeting location. Maybe week after next? I've got that big wedding this weekend and another one the next, but we've got openings after that."

"Sure."

"Great, it's settled then." Lacey nodded.

"Wait, what am I setting up?"

"Pageant lessons for the local girls."

He glanced back and forth from Delilah to Lacey to Delilah again. How did he miss that? He'd started off by saying he'd help Lacey with the contest and somehow found himself in charge. Now he'd agreed to coordinate pageant training? If his brothers found out, they'd definitely demand he hand over his man card.

But the look on Delilah's face might make it worth the sacrifice. Her lips had split into the biggest smile he'd seen from her yet. One that showed off all her teeth. The kind of grin that would leave his cheeks aching. So, he did what any hot-blooded man would do at the sight of something so lovely. He beamed back at her and swallowed his pride.

"Great. I'm looking forward to it."

eight

Delilah groaned and rubbed her hand over her belly. What she wouldn't give for a sunken bathtub right now. She'd stuffed herself full of delicious food at the dinner at the Mexican restaurant in town and was paying the price. That's what happened when she trained her stomach not to expect more than a few bites at a time and then blew it all by gorging on the buffet. But how could she resist? The veggie fajitas had been so tasty, the deep-fried ice cream, divine. If her mother could see her now . . .

As if Stella could sense her misbehavior, her phone pinged with an incoming text.

> You still up?
> Of course.

Her mother knew she never fell asleep before midnight, no matter how hard she tried. Within moments, the phone rang. Delilah rolled over and answered.

"Hello?"

"I had a sense you'd still be awake. How's Miss Lovin' Texas doing?" Stella's voice rang out, the cheerfulness making Delilah's stomach pangs worsen.

"I'm fine. What are you still doing awake?"

"I'm too excited to sleep. Monique and I met with the cosmetics rep this morning and they had some amazing new ideas for us. I think you're going to be pleased." Nothing got Stella excited like the prospect of making money.

"I'm sure they're great."

"The publicity firm wants to do a photo shoot. I went ahead and scheduled it week after next in Ido."

"Oh, I can't do that."

"Why not? They gave me some new samples. I'll drive them down myself. Franco said he'd be willing to travel, just for you. We'll be in and out in two days, three tops."

"I don't think that's such a good idea." The thought of having to squeeze into anything beyond a loose nightshirt made her stomach cramp.

Stella tsked. "Of course it's a good idea. We've got no time to waste. If we want to soft launch before the holiday season, we've got to get the marketing materials done."

She was right. "Fine. Just let me know when and where. I'll be there."

"That's my girl."

Her girl. Seemed like she was only her mother's "girl" when she agreed to do everything Stella wanted. Delilah reached behind her to plump her pillow as her mother prattled on about the level of shimmer in the new blush. As she settled her head against the pillow, something crawled over her hand. She shrieked, leaping off the narrow bed and hitting her head on the cabinet above as she jumped to her feet.

"Delilah?" Her mother's voice came from where the phone had landed, facedown on the floor, next to a giant cricket that stood rubbing its gangly legs together.

She shook off the shivers racing up and down her limbs. Just a cricket. No big deal. Crickets didn't even bite. She'd just grab something to scoot her phone away from it, then shoo it out the door.

Fumbling, she managed to make her way to the kitchen area, where she whipped open the narrow drawer that held a small assortment of kitchen utensils. A dozen, maybe two dozen, crickets crawled over the spatulas and silverware. Delilah screamed and slammed the drawer shut.

"What's going on?" Stella's muffled voice came from the floor.

"Hold on a sec. There's a bug." Delilah knew it was irrational, but she'd always had a fear of creepy-crawly things. Up to that point she hadn't had any trouble with the trailer beyond a random ant or mosquito. She opened the closet door and grappled for the broom. It clattered against the countertop but, thankfully, was cricket-free.

Delilah tiptoed closer to where her phone had landed. If she stretched, she might be able to reach it with the broom and sweep it close enough that she could grab it without having to get close to the cricket. The bug in question sat on the ground, rubbing its front legs together in all of its dark, glossy glory. She shrieked as she pulled the broom back, causing her phone to skitter across the floor of the trailer and disappear under the table.

Bending down, she reached a hand under the table to retrieve her phone, only to touch something undeniably crickety instead. She let out a scream that probably could have woken the dead in at least four surrounding counties, and exploded out of the trailer into the parking lot.

It was empty, thankfully. Smoker Saturday had ended several hours ago, although the scent of fish lingered in the air. The neon lights from the Burger Bonanza sign burned bright although the windows were dark. Helmut and the staff had gone home hours ago. Which meant she was standing in a deserted parking lot.

In her nightgown.

Alone.

She glanced down at her bare feet. It's not like she'd be able to walk somewhere to get help. What was she going to say? "I'm too chicken to enter my trailer because it's full of crickets"?

Embarrassed at her own ridiculousness, she poked her head back into the trailer. "Stella?"

No answer.

Either her mother had hung up or the call had been disconnected when her phone flew across the floor. She could do this. It was just a few bugs. Bugs that didn't even bite.

She waited a few minutes, letting her pulse slow. Then, grabbing the handle on the outside of the trailer, she lifted a bare foot to the step. Those crickets were more scared of her than she was of them. That's what her dad used to tell her. Her eyes teared up at the memory of her dad. She could still picture the humor in his eyes and see the whisper of a smile as he used to toss her into the air and catch her over and over again. He wouldn't be afraid of a few harmless crickets.

Emboldened, she entered the trailer. The broom rested against the counter and she reached for the handle. She'd just sweep those helpless crickets out into the fresh air. No problem. She lifted the broom, preparing to do just that, when something landed on her shoulder.

All thoughts of peacefully coexisting shattered. She whipped around and raced down the steps, flinging herself through the door and right into a hard, broad chest.

"You okay?" Jasper wrapped his arms around her, drawing her tight against him, her breasts smashed against his pecs.

She wasn't sure what to be more mortified about . . . her irrational fear of some harmless crickets or the fact she was standing half-naked and braless in the very public parking lot of the Burger Bonanza, chest to chest with Jasper Taylor.

"I'm fine. What are you doing here?" She pulled back, thought better of letting him see her in her skimpy nightgown, and crossed her arms over her chest.

"Your manager called. Said it was an emergency and you were being attacked." Jasper's gaze flicked over her like he was checking her for injuries. His hair stuck out in all directions, and he looked like he'd just woken up.

"I'm sorry. I was on the phone with my mom when a cricket attacked me."

His brow furrowed and the edge of his mouth ticked up. "You were attacked by a cricket?"

"Not just one. There's a whole army of them in there." She pointed to the door of the trailer.

"An army of crickets attacked you?"

"Well, not really attacked. I mean, I'm sure it wasn't a premeditated move on their part." She kept her palms over her breasts, aware of how absolutely ridiculous she sounded.

"Do you mind if I take a look?" He bit back a smile.

"By all means, please." She nudged her chin toward the door. "But be careful. They're everywhere."

"I'll keep that in mind." He disappeared through the small door and she waited for some confirmation that she hadn't overreacted, that her trailer hadn't been caught up in some cricket swarm of biblical proportions.

A few minutes later, Jasper came out, her phone in his hand.

"Well?"

"Looks like you've got a bunch of crickets in your trailer."

She blew out a breath, sending the hair that had fallen in front of her face sailing. "Thank you. I actually made it that far on my own. How are you going to get rid of them?"

"I'm not."

"What do you mean, you're not?"

He glanced at his watch. "It's almost one. I'll come back in the morning and deal with it when it's light out."

"But I can't sleep here tonight."

"I'm not asking you to. Come on, I'll take you back to my place."

Her eyes went wide, just about bugging out of her head

like the crazy-eyed cricket who'd started the whole mess. "I can't go back to your place."

"You have another suggestion?" He cocked his hip and ran a hand through his unruly hair. "If you want to call someone else, I'd be happy to run you somewhere. I imagine Lacey's asleep. Suzy's probably still up. You want me to see if she can put you up tonight?"

The idea of sleeping on Suzy's couch, underneath the watchful eye of that menacing bobcat, was enough for her to seize Jasper's offer. "No, I don't want to bother her."

"It's settled then." He shrugged off his button-down shirt and handed it to her. "Here, put this on."

She shook her head even as she took in the sight of how his white undershirt molded to his muscular chest. "I don't need your shirt."

"You sure about that?" His gaze raked over her, from her feet, up her legs, pausing at her chest before landing on her face.

A shiver raced through her that had little to do with the cool night air and a whole lot to do with the way his fingers twitched like he wanted to reach out and touch her. Her nipples perked, and she clamped her arms even tighter against her middle.

"Fine." She snagged the shirt out of his hand and shoved her arms through the sleeves. His scent overwhelmed her. A hint of campfire mingled with the muskiness of a hot-blooded man. When was the last time she'd worn a man's shirt? The intimacy of the moment threatened to make her knees weak.

"You want to grab anything from inside?" He tore his gaze away from her face, and the heat between them cooled by a few degrees.

As much as she'd love to go back in and pack a few things, she didn't dare.

His tone softened. "If you tell me what you need, I'll go in and get it for you."

"I'd love a change of clothes. And maybe my toothbrush."

"Why don't you sit in the truck and warm up. I'll be back in a sec." He took a step toward the trailer. "Where are your keys? I'll lock it up."

"On the hook just inside the door." Her cheeks flushed as she climbed into the cab of his truck and watched him go back inside. She should be able to handle a few bugs. It's not like she needed a man to rescue her from a couple of crickets. As the ridiculousness of the situation settled around her, she debated whether to go back in and relieve Jasper of his bug-fighting duties.

But then she pulled the collar of his shirt up to her cheeks. Her heart warmed as she imagined his arms wrapped around her instead of his shirtsleeves. Her desire to stand up for herself and prove she could take care of herself warred with her need to sit in the warm cab of his truck and let someone take care of a problem for her for a change.

As she sank even deeper into the passenger seat, his shirt drawn up around her ears, she decided she'd let someone else look out for her. Just this once. And if he happened to be a buff, hazel-eyed cowboy who looked like a Greek god, well what was the harm in that?

A change of clothes. Jasper pulled open a drawer of the built-in dresser. Surely she had a pair of jeans and a T-shirt sitting around. Faced with a drawer full of ladies' unmentionables in a rainbow of colors, he slammed the drawer shut. Fuck. Seeing Delilah's panties folded up in neat little squares shouldn't send a bolt of heat straight to his dick. But it did.

He could only imagine what seeing one of the lacy thongs on her actual backside would do to him. On second thought, it would be a really bad idea to imagine that. He'd shoved the drawer closed but it did nothing to wipe the image out of his head.

Great, now he was snooping around her private things with a raging hard-on. Frustrated by his lack of self-control, he grabbed a handful of items from each drawer and shoved them in a plastic shopping bag he'd found under the sink. He flipped off the lights and grabbed the keys off the hook.

Taking in a few deep breaths, he tried to clamp down on the budding attraction to the disheveled beauty queen. He didn't need any more complications in his life. And adding a woman to the mix would definitely constitute a complication. After his relationship with Adeline imploded, he'd promised himself that he wouldn't get played by a woman again. Not even if she looked like an angel who'd come straight down from heaven.

Satisfied he'd gotten himself under control enough to face her again, he locked the trailer and stalked back to his truck. "I didn't know what to grab, so I just threw some of your stuff into a bag."

She held it in her lap, tight against her stomach. "Thank you."

"You're welcome."

"I'm sorry about tonight. My mother shouldn't have called you. I could have taken care of things myself."

He eyed her across the dimly lit cab. "Your manager is your mother?"

"Yes." She let out a breathy sigh.

"That's got to be interesting." He shifted into gear, eager to get her back to his place so he could get her settled and put a little distance between them.

Her arms tightened around her middle. "Don't you work with your family?"

Damn, he'd gone and pissed her off . . . again. "Sure, but that's different."

"How so?" Her back pressed against the door like she wanted to get as far away from him as possible in the small space they shared.

"I don't know. We work the land. Everyone does an

equal share. We're building something we can leave behind for future generations."

"Oh, I get it." Her head rolled back against the headrest.

"What?" He'd barely said anything. What could she possibly "get"?

"Sounds like you don't respect my vocation."

Whoa. "Come again?" He sensed dangerous territory ahead. Not to mention, her mom's call had dragged him out of a deep sleep, so he wasn't operating at 100 percent.

"You think working the land is more meaningful than what I'm doing." She turned her head and gazed out the window.

"I never said anything like that." He'd been around enough women to know there was no easy way out of this kind of conversation. "I'm sure what you're doing is an admirable use of your time."

"That's right. A portion of the money we raise on the cosmetics line is going to my mentor's nonprofit and will help young girls."

"That's great."

"It is." She nodded to herself.

He wanted to laugh at the stubborn set of her shoulders, but that would only get her all riled up again. Best to focus on things he had control of. "I'll head back to the trailer tomorrow and see what I can do about your cricket problem."

"Thank you. I'd appreciate that."

"In the meantime, I think it might be best if you stayed at the big house with my parents." That was the most reasonable option. The safest option based on how his body seemed to react to her.

She swiveled her head to face him. "Just for tonight though, right?"

"Maybe a few nights. If I have to do a bug bomb you'll probably want to stay out of the trailer for a few days."

"Okay."

Her acceptance surprised him. She didn't seem like the

kind of woman who agreed to anything easily. "You have any brothers or sisters?"

"No, just me and my mom. My dad left when I was three."

"It's been just you two the whole time?"

"Not exactly. I've had a few stepfathers along the way. But none of them had kids, so I've never had any stepsiblings. How about you?"

He paused, wondering how best to answer. Should he tell her the truth or try to downplay the number of Taylors she'd wake up to in the morning? "I've got a handful of them."

"What, like five?" Her eyes widened.

"Yeah, plus two." He shifted his gaze back and forth between her and the dark road ahead.

"Seven? You have seven brothers and sisters?" Her palm splayed over her heart.

"It is what it is."

"Where do you fall in the lineup?"

"I'm second."

"From the top or the bottom?"

"From the top. My older brother took off a couple of years ago. We don't talk about him much." Even saying the words out loud made his heart squeeze tight.

"I'm sorry."

"It is what it is with that, too. Colin's the oldest. Then I've got five younger brothers and one sister."

"Your poor mother. Where does everyone live?"

"Some still live at home. Some in town. My youngest brother, Noah, is away at college." It would take too long to run through the details. He pulled the truck around the gravel drive and eased it to a stop in front of his parents' place. "We're here."

Delilah peered through the windshield at the two-story white farmhouse where generations of Taylors had been born and raised. "I can't go in there now and wake everyone up."

"They're used to it. Everyone comes and goes at all hours."

"But I don't want their first impression of me to be like this." She glanced down.

"I've got a place down the road if you want to stay there instead." *Say no.* It would be safer for her to stay with his parents. Not that he worried about stepping out of line, but having her that close, that vulnerable, might threaten the fragile hold he had on his attraction.

"What would people think?" Her eyes betrayed her nerves.

"Honestly? I don't know that anyone would find out. And even if they did, it's not like we'd have anything to hide."

"I really don't want to disturb your family. It's late, and I'm in no kind of shape for a proper introduction."

He didn't bother to waste breath telling her the idea of "proper" didn't fit in with his family in any way, shape, or form. "It's settled then. We're going back to my place."

"If you think that's best."

"I do." But best for whom? If someone did catch sight of them, would he risk having Ido disqualified? He shook his head. It was late. Her trailer was uninhabitable. No one could argue with him over that. Being around Delilah was making him paranoid.

Ten minutes later he'd introduced her to Buster and given her the tour of his one-bedroom cabin, which sat on the edge of his family's land. She padded behind him on bare feet since he hadn't thought to grab her a pair of shoes.

"Why don't you take the bedroom? You'll have more privacy, and I wouldn't feel right with you sleeping out here on the couch." He moved to the linen closet and grabbed a set of clean sheets.

"I'm so sorry about all of this." She hadn't loosened her grip on the front of the shirt he'd given her since they'd walked in the door except to give Buster a scratch on the head. And she looked damn good with his favorite flannel button-down wrapped around her.

"It's fine. Let me go remake the bed so you can get—"

Her fingers wrapped around his arm and a burst of heat stunned him into silence at the contact.

"Don't worry about the sheets. I've been enough of a nuisance. Thank you for your hospitality." Those green eyes peered up at him through long, thick lashes.

He felt dangerously close to doing something he shouldn't. He wanted to pull her against him, brush her tousled blond waves away from her face, and find out if she tasted as sweet as she looked.

Instead, he cleared his throat. "My room's probably a bit of a mess."

"I'm sure it's fine. I appreciate it. Thank you." She stood on tiptoe to press a kiss against his cheek.

He closed his eyes as her lips met that day's scruff. Clenching his hands into fists, he held the stack of sheets to the side, afraid to move. His cheek burned where she'd kissed him, like she'd seared him with her lips.

Every cell in his body ached for more.

She dropped back onto her feet, lowering herself by a few inches. He opened his eyes, meeting her gaze. What he saw there made him want to throw caution to the brush pile and let it burn. The heat racing through his limbs ignited parts of him that had been numb for years.

"Delilah." Her name drifted from his lips on a whisper, like a prayer.

She rose back onto her tiptoes, her lips inches from his.

He held himself in check, fighting the urge to claim her with every ounce of his self-control.

Then she pressed her lips to his. His control shattered like the empty beer bottles he and Colin used as target practice when they were kids. He dropped the sheets, wrapped his arms around her, tangled his hands in her hair, and gave in.

nine

Delilah couldn't believe what she'd started. She had no idea a simple kiss could release the kind of passion that flooded through her as she met Jasper kiss for kiss. His tongue slid against hers, his hands cupped the back of her head, cradling it as he took the kiss even deeper. She gripped his biceps with her hands, trying not to lose herself completely.

He pulled away first, nudging his nose against hers. "You okay?"

Words escaped her. Not only was she incapable of forming a cohesive sentence, but she'd lost all ability to speak. Her knees knocked together as she looked for somewhere to sit before she lost the use of her legs.

Jasper's arm went around her back and he guided her toward the couch.

"I'm fine." She drew in a deep breath. No matter how she tried, she couldn't escape his scent. She wasn't even sure she wanted to.

He held on to her until she'd settled on the cushion of the overstuffed couch. "You sure you're all right?"

Telling the truth would only make the situation worse, so she lied. "I'm absolutely fine."

"Can I get you a glass of water? Something to eat?" He stood next to the couch, his fingers kneading the back of his neck.

She needed to process what had just happened . . . the way the world shifted when their lips met . . . the way his kiss made her want to throw away all of her inhibitions and do unspeakable things with the cowboy in front of her.

"Delilah?" The way his voice caressed her name made her want to shrug off his shirt and pull him down onto the couch next to her.

But she couldn't. She shook her head, trying to rid herself of the heated images running through her mind. Getting involved with Jasper would be a bad idea. An epically bad idea. Her days in Ido were numbered. Twenty-eight more, to be exact. And then she'd be headed back to Dallas to make her fortune in private labeled cosmetics and fashion accessories.

Things could be worse. Thanks to her inherited good looks and Stella's business sense, she had something waiting for her on the other side of her pageant career. A lot of girls she knew couldn't say the same. It wasn't worth risking her future for a temporary fling with Jasper Taylor. No matter how those hazel eyes might wordlessly beg her to throw caution to the wind.

"I ought to get to bed. Don't we have something scheduled tomorrow?"

His shoulders rose and fell as he let out a long-drawn-out breath like he was relieved she'd given him an out. She'd been the one to initiate the kiss. He'd probably been trying to figure out a gentle way to let her down.

"I'll have to check the binder. I think there's a tour of a local vineyard in the afternoon, but nothing in the morning. It's Sunday. My family usually goes to church together, but I might beg off from that tomorrow."

What kind of guest would she be if she didn't accompany them to church? "I'd love to join you if you go."

His eyes widened.

"Unless you think it's not a good idea." Why was she so off-kilter? She hadn't felt so out of place in Hartwood or East. Of course, she hadn't been an unwanted houseguest in either location. Plus, she'd had Stella to keep her company.

"Why don't we talk about it in the morning? I think we could both use a decent night's sleep."

"Of course." She wasn't thinking. How could she think when he was standing so close? Sucking in all the air? "I'd be happy to take the couch."

"You take the bedroom. I insist."

He didn't look like he wanted to be challenged so she nodded. "Okay. Thank you."

He held out a hand and helped her up. "Let me know if you need anything else."

Besides him lying next to her? She shook her head, outraged at the way her body seemed to crave the connection with his. Reluctantly, she let his hand go. "See you in the morning."

"Good night." He stood in the short hallway as she entered his bedroom . . . *his bedroom* . . . alone.

She pressed the door closed behind her and leaned against it, trying to catch her breath. The man knew how to kiss, that was for sure. Her legs still wobbled, and she wasn't sure when she might be capable of putting one steady foot in front of the other. Maybe never if Jasper Taylor was around.

He'd flipped the switch on a lamp sitting on the nightstand during the short tour. She hadn't taken a good look at the bedroom though. Now that she was in his space, she soaked it in.

The rough log walls and dark green and navy quilt agreed with him. This was a man's room. A flat-screen television sat on a dresser across from the bed. The nightstand

and lamp were the only other furniture. The absence of a woman's touch made her heart skip a beat.

She thumped her chest with her fist. It shouldn't matter that there were no obvious signs that a woman had been there. Whatever heat had passed between her and Jasper had to end with that kiss.

That toe-curling, goose bump–producing, panty-melting kiss.

She flung herself down on the bed and pulled a pillow to her chest. What the heck did the man bathe in? One whiff of his pillow, and her hormones leapt to high alert. It was like he'd covered everything in his bedroom in pheromones.

The clock on his nightstand told her it was way too late to engage in her favorite game of what-if. What if she and Jasper had a fling while she was in town? What if he laid another one of those kisses on her? What if she went out into the living room and curled against him on the couch?

Groaning, she reached for the switch on the lamp and flicked it off. With the room shrouded in darkness, his scent grew even stronger. She inhaled, pretending the shirt she'd wrapped herself in was his embrace instead.

Light filtered in through a crack in the curtain. Delilah woke to something warm and wet slathering her face. She tried to swat it away, but it kept coming back. She cracked her eyelid just in time to catch a slobbery swipe of tongue to her cheek.

"Buster!" Jasper's voice came through the doorway and the dog stopped, cocked its head, and jumped onto the bed.

"Good morning, Buster." She pulled the cotton blanket up to her chin, trying to protect herself from the onslaught of doggie love. His entire backside wagged back and forth with his tail. "Are you supposed to be in here?"

He turned a few circles on top of the quilt, then collapsed into a heap against her side. The door creaked open and Delilah glanced over. Jasper peeked through the crack in the doorway.

"Buster, get out of there," he whispered.

Buster looked at him, lifted his leg, and licked at his privates. Delilah stifled a giggle.

"You awake?" Jasper asked, swinging the door wide.

"Your dog woke me." She squinted at the clock. Eleven o'clock? Flinging the covers off, she swung her legs over the side of the bed. "Why in the world did you let me sleep so late?"

His gaze raked over her bare legs, reminding her of the events of the night before. Her stomach clenched, her core warmed. She pulled the covers against her chest.

"It's okay. You missed church, but you don't have to be anywhere until this afternoon. I checked Lacey's binder."

That should have made her feel better. But all it did was make her think of obscene ways they could pass the time. She'd hoped a good night's sleep would cure her of her attraction. But as she swept a finger across her lips, she could still feel the way his lips had pressed on hers the night before.

"If you want to get dressed, we can pick up breakfast on our way over to take care of the cricket situation." His lips curved up.

"Sure. Just give me a few minutes?" He looked like he'd already showered and shaved. For a split second she let herself remember the way his whiskers had felt against her skin.

"Take as long as you need. Do you want me to get him out of here?" He gestured toward the dog, who'd spread out from his initial tight circle and now sprawled across half of the king-sized bed.

"He's fine. I didn't notice it last night, but what happened to his ear?"

Jasper tilted his head as his smile faded. "He's a rescue. Zina thinks he might have been part of a dog-fighting ring at one point. A lot of the pit bulls she gets at the rescue come from that kind of background."

Her brow furrowed and her lips turned down. "That's awful. Why do so many dogs seem to come from dogfighting rings around here?"

He ran a hand over Buster's belly. The dog flopped over on his side and let his tongue loll out of his mouth in pure ecstasy. "Deputy Phillips has been tracking a mobile dogfighting ring for a couple of years. Every time they think they're getting close, it moves out of the area and pops up somewhere else."

"That's terrible." Delilah ran her palm over the dog's stomach, earning her a series of tail whaps.

"He likes you." Jasper grinned, his smile warming her soul.

She scratched a little harder and Buster moaned. "He doesn't know any better."

"He's actually a really good judge of character." Jasper retreated through the open door and back into the hall. "I'm going to run up to the house to see if my dad's got anything to take care of your crickets. I set a clean towel out for you on the bathroom counter, and coffee's on."

"Thank you." Delilah wasn't used to anyone catering to her. Usually she was the one trying to make things easier for Stella, always soothing her mother's rattled nerves. It was nice to be on the receiving end for a change.

Jasper pulled the door closed behind him. She stretched her arms over her head as her gaze traveled around the room. It had been dark last night, but now, with the soft light coming through the curtain, she could get a better look. She'd been right about there not being any sign of a woman's presence. It shouldn't have made her feel better, but it did. After that blistering kiss last night, she was going to have a hard time thinking about Jasper Taylor in a strictly platonic fashion. Her pulse kicked up as she remembered how his lips had felt on hers.

Getting involved with the hospitality host wasn't a good idea. She'd only be in town for a month. And she wasn't about to throw herself into a no-strings-attached fling. She'd be better off bottling up all that heat and saving it for when she got back to Dallas and got settled. Then she'd have plenty of time to find someone who checked off all her boxes.

She gave Buster a final scratch on his stomach, then rolled out of bed. The day had already gotten away from her. She had places to go and people to see. Not to mention an attraction to squelch.

Jasper wasn't sure what to expect when he entered his place again. When he left, Delilah had been curled up in his bed, snuggling with his dog. It didn't surprise him that Buster had taken to her right away. As far as he could tell, Delilah had spent her whole life winning people over. It was literally her job. He'd best remember that and not try to find any deeper meaning in that kiss she laid on him last night. He wasn't about to get used by another gorgeous woman with an ulterior motive. For a half a second, he thought of Adeline. She couldn't have been responsible for the crickets in Delilah's trailer, could she?

He knew from experience that Adeline wouldn't let anything stop her from getting what she wanted. And she wanted the title of most romantic small town in Texas. But sabotaging the judge's trailer wouldn't win her any points. Besides, Adeline didn't do bugs. Someone else had to be behind it. Whoever it was, they'd better stop at a relatively harmless prank. Keeping Delilah safe fell under his umbrella of responsibility. For better or for worse, she was in his care, and he'd make damn sure no harm came to her under his watch.

"I'm back," he called out as he opened the front door. The last thing he needed was to surprise her and find her walking around naked. Seeing her in that flimsy, see-through nightie had already ensured he'd never be able to look at her the same again. Not now that he had a pretty good idea of the curves underneath those fancy skirts and dresses she seemed to favor.

"In the kitchen," Delilah answered.

Buster bounded over to greet him. "Hey, boy. Have you been good for Delilah?"

She stood in the doorway that led from the living room into the kitchen, a spatula in her hand. "He's been fabulous. I wish he could talk though. Would have saved me some time trying to figure out where you keep everything."

"Are you cooking?" So that's what he smelled. He'd noticed it when he came in the door, but figured she'd sprayed some sort of perfume or air freshener.

"Pancakes. Would have cut up some fruit to go along with it, but your refrigerator is empty." She turned to head back into the kitchen. "Time to flip. You want any?"

He glanced down at Buster. "What's going on?"

The dog didn't answer, just cocked his head one way and then the next.

"I couldn't find any maple syrup so you can have peanut butter or honey on top." With her back to him, she stood at the stovetop and worked the spatula in her hand.

"You didn't have to do this." He leaned against the counter, enjoying the way her hips moved as she flipped flapjacks.

"I know you said we could go out but look at me." She turned, pointing to her clothes. "I hope you don't mind I borrowed a shirt and some shorts."

He hadn't even noticed when he walked in, but she was wearing one of his college T-shirts and a pair of his athletic shorts. "Where are the clothes I grabbed for you?"

Her face flushed before she twirled back around to face the stove. "I'm not sure it would be appropriate for me to go out in public in any of them. Seems you were in a hurry and only grabbed things from my lingerie drawers."

Shit. He scrubbed a hand over his eyes. The image of Delilah's lacy underthings had been seared on his brain.

And now she knew he'd had his hands in her drawers. Dammit. Her dresser drawers. "Sorry about that."

"It's okay. I figured breakfast was the least I could do to thank you for your late-night rescue." She opened the cabinet next to the stove. "Where do you keep your plates?"

He moved to her other side and pulled two plates from the cabinet. "Here you go."

"Thanks." She piled a tall stack of pancakes onto a plate and handed it to him, then flipped one onto her plate before walking over to the table.

"Is that all you're having?"

She rubbed a hand over her stomach. "I ate way too much last night at that restaurant."

"Yeah, Ortega's does an amazing job." He pulled up a chair next to hers. "There's another place over past Swynton that has the best cheese enchiladas. I'll have to take you there while you're in town."

"I'd like that."

"Me, too." Before he drove himself crazy trying to figure out if he'd just asked her out on a date or if she'd accepted as a friend, he slid the first bite of pancake into his mouth. Delicious. "This is great."

"It would be better if you had a stocked pantry. Don't you ever eat at home?"

"Not often. I usually grab dinner up at the house or stop and pick something up. Do you like to cook?"

She cut off a small bite with the side of her fork. "I love it. But I haven't had very many opportunities lately."

"That trailer doesn't have much of a kitchen."

Nodding, she slipped the bite into her mouth, and for a moment he focused on those soft, full lips.

"Well, you're welcome to cook in my kitchen whenever you want." He shrugged. "I'll even stock the pantry if you tell me what you need."

Her eyebrows lifted. "Careful what you offer. I might just take you up on that."

"I hope you do."

A look passed between them that made his pulse tick up. A hint of heat sparked in her eyes, making him want to pull her into his lap and pick up where they'd left off the night before. He forced himself to shut it down.

"You're on. I figure I owe you something for taking care of the cricket problem. If you're serious about letting me use your kitchen, I'd love to make you dinner one night this week."

His stomach rolled as he thought about Delilah moving around his kitchen with the same kind of ease she'd shown this morning. So much for keeping his distance. He could do it, though. She might look like a goddess, but he could keep himself under control.

"That sounds great. Now what do you want to do about your wardrobe?"

"You don't think I should go out in public like this?" She laughed as she looked down at his *Gig 'Em* shirt.

"I think you look great." He wasn't lying about that. Her hair was piled on top of her head, still damp from her shower. She didn't have a trace of makeup on her flawless skin, and if he'd run into her in public, he never would have guessed she was the reigning Miss Lovin' Texas. "You should wear makeup less often."

"I'm not sure how to take that." Her fork stabbed another bite. "Are you trying to say I look bad with makeup on?"

Now he'd stepped in it. "No, you look just fine with makeup."

"I must not do a good job with it though if you think I look better without it."

"That's not what I meant at all. I was trying to pay you a compliment. You don't need all of that crap on your face or those sparkly, glittery dresses to look beautiful. I think you're gorgeous just the way you are. Right here. Right now. With me." He let his fork clatter to his plate.

Her eyes went wide. "I was just teasing, Jasper. Thank you for saying that. Most people forget there's something beyond the Miss Lovin' Texas sash. I appreciate you noticing."

He didn't want to acknowledge the vulnerability. "I grabbed some stuff from my dad and I'm going to run over to the trailer now. Do you want to come with me so you can pick out some clothes?"

"Yes, thank you." She gathered their empty plates and took them to the sink.

"I'll clean up when we get back. Come on, I'll run you by the house and you can borrow something more appropriate from my mom or sister."

"Oh, I couldn't." Her mouth twisted into a frown. "Can't we just sneak back so I can grab something quick?"

"Not on a Sunday. Helmut does a full brunch buffet at the Burger Bonanza. You show up looking like that and tongues will start wagging."

"Okay then. I guess I don't have much of a choice."

Less than fifteen minutes later Jasper finished introductions. His mom had been in a flat-out tizzy since he'd walked through the door with Delilah on his heels. But then she and his twelve-year-old sister, Abby, took Delilah upstairs and promised they'd find her something appropriate. At least something she could wear long enough to get back to the parking lot and pick up some of her own things.

"She spent the night at your place?" his brother Lucas asked.

"That's what I said."

"Anything happen?" Lucas arched a brow.

"Nothing like you're thinking." Jasper settled onto the couch while he waited for the women to finish upstairs.

"You had a woman like that at your place last night and nothing happened?" Lucas bounced his daughter, Maggie, on his hip. He and Maggie had been living at the house for the past two years. Ever since Lucas's one-night stand, aka Maggie's mother, took off.

"Out of all the people in this family, aren't you the one who should be cautioning me about getting carried away?" Jasper held out his arms and Maggie launched herself at him. His niece might not have a mother in her life, but she was absolutely cherished by her daddy, her grandparents, and the rest of the family.

"I miss women," Lucas admitted as he lowered himself into their dad's favorite recliner.

"You're not dead, you know. You should ask someone out."

"Who? Nobody I know wants to go out with someone who comes with a built-in family. Not at my age."

Jasper held on to Maggie's hands as she sat on top of his boot and commanded him in her giggly two-year-old way: "Bounce."

He grinned as he gently bounced his leg up and down. She laughed, the high-pitched giggles like music to his ears. Lucas was trying to make the best out of a rotten situation. A one-night stand that left him with a lifelong commitment to an adorable little girl.

"Don't give up. There's someone out there for you."

"You ever listen to your own advice?" Lucas's gaze shot to the steps. "She's here for what? A month?"

"Not going to go there." Jasper shook his head.

"Sounds like a wasted opportunity if you ask me."

"Good thing no one's asking." Jasper bounced Maggie high enough to grab her in his arms. "Don't you have to work today?"

"I'm going. Hey, are you really trying to get Dad to turn the big barn into some kind of wedding place?"

"I sure am. He said if we could win the title of most romantic small town in Texas, he'd give me his blessing. We've got to do something to keep our heads above water until we can plant and harvest some new trees." He hoped his dad would keep his word.

Lucas shifted to the edge of his seat. "If we do, does that mean I can give up my job in town and come back to work here?"

"Hopefully."

"Well let me know if you need help. I'll do what I can to make sure I don't have to leave Maggie for so long every day."

"If you have any ideas on how to make things romantic, feel free to share. Mayor Cherish needs me to plan some big event before the judging period is over. So far all I've got is an idea to work on something around the Fall Festival."

"Apples and pumpkins aren't romantic." Lucas slapped his baseball cap against his leg as he stood. "If only Colin were here . . . he was always the ladies' man."

Jasper tried not to react. Everyone seemed to think Colin was the answer to their prayers. It wasn't his place to tell them the truth. "Yeah. If only . . ."

"Hey, can you keep an eye on Mags until Mom's done? They're going to the apple orchard later on today."

"You got it." Jasper tickled Maggie under the chin.

"See you later, bug." Lucas pressed a kiss to the top of his daughter's head. "You know I wouldn't change a thing, right?"

"I know." His brother might have messed up, but a Taylor always made things right. That was one mantra that had been ingrained in all of them by their parents. And Jasper would do right by Delilah. Which meant sticking to the plan of carting her around Ido, making sure they stayed on schedule, and not letting himself think of her as anything but the contest judge he'd agreed to work with.

No matter what.

ten

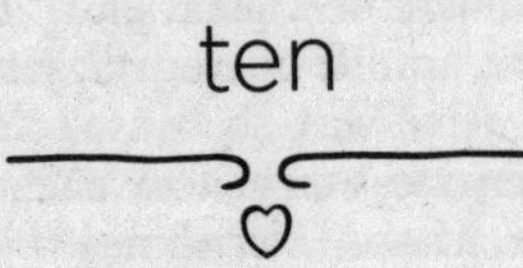

"Thank you so much." Delilah shook hands with the vineyard owners, then the head winemaker, then a whole slew of others whose names and jobs had all jumbled together in her head. As long as she kept smiling, maybe they wouldn't notice that she'd lost track of who did what and who was related to whom.

She and Jasper had been given the royal treatment: a full tour of the vineyard, a step-by-step walk-through of the wine-making process, and a private tasting of every varietal the small local vineyard produced. Her cheeks hurt from smiling, and she might be just the slightest bit tipsy from all the wine. She'd tried to take tiny sips but didn't want to offend anyone, so she'd tried a little sample of everything.

"Ready to go?" Jasper asked.

"I am." She slid off the tall stool and grabbed the edge of the table to steady herself.

"You okay?" Immediately, he was by her side, his arm behind her.

"Of course. I've just been sitting for so long." She summoned a reassuring smile.

"Okay." He leaned close, his breath warm against her ear. "But maybe you want to take my arm on the way back to the truck? Just in case two hours of sipping wine might have messed with your balance a bit?"

"I think that might be a good idea." She wrapped her fingers around the arm he offered, grateful to him for not making a scene. Truth was, she wasn't much of a drinker. A nice glass of wine every now and then or a fresh-squeezed vodka lemonade sometimes hit the spot. But she didn't like to feel out of control, not when so many people were always watching. She'd seen pageant winners taken down for a lot less than a drunken night on the town. Her reputation was everything, and with the cosmetics line coming out soon, Stella kept reminding her that her behavior needed to remain beyond reproach.

Jasper opened the truck door for her. "Here you go."

"Thank you." She pulled her feet in as he closed the door behind her. Such a gentleman. He might live in the country, but he had better manners than most of the big-city men she'd gone out with. If only they lived a little closer, maybe she'd be willing to take a chance on the cowboy with the impeccable manners and the big heart.

He climbed into the cab and fired up the engine. "I hope you don't mind, but while we were at the vineyard, I asked my dad to move your trailer over to our land."

"What?" She clicked her seat belt in place and pressed on her stomach, which had started feeling a little woozy with that bit of news. "Why did you do that?"

His strong hands gripped the steering wheel, navigating the truck onto the two-lane road. "I think it'll be safer having you parked close by."

"You think someone put crickets in the camper on purpose?" She'd suspected as much, but who would have it out for her? So far everyone in town seemed happy to have her there.

"I'm not sure, but I'd rather be safe than sorry. I had them park it up by the main house." He glanced over, his teeth scraping against his lower lip. Made her think about how those full lips had claimed hers last night. Suddenly the intimate cab of his truck heated up. She lowered her window a crack, trying to get some fresh air.

"Thank you." She met his gaze for a hot second, then looked away. At least she wouldn't be sleeping at his place. If people found out she'd spent the night, no doubt the small-town gossip mill would start churning out the rumors. She might have spent most of her life in big cities, but the pageant community seemed enough like a small town that she could imagine how it would play out.

They didn't talk much on the way back. By the time they reached his family's home she was ready for a quick bite to eat and the chance to change out of her dress. Her trailer sat in the shade of a giant tree, about a hundred yards from the house. Someone had set up a big umbrella and a few camping chairs outside the door.

"Did your dad do this, too?" Delilah asked.

"That looks like my mom's work. Don't get me wrong, my dad's a good one to have in a crisis, but he's not used to hosting guests."

"That was so sweet of them."

"They've got their moments."

"Is it safe to go inside? I'd love to change." She was used to spending her days in heels, but trekking through the vineyard had taken a lot more effort than a typical meet and greet. A pair of flats and some jeans waited for her somewhere inside the trailer.

"Not yet. That bug bomb we set off said to keep the area clear for at least twenty-four hours." Jasper came around to help her down from the cab.

She didn't need assistance but still took his hand. "Well, shoot. Can I get a room at that hotel for tonight?"

He led her up the sidewalk and opened the front door. "I believe my mom took care of that, too. You're bunking with Abby tonight if that's okay with you."

Bunking with his little sister? Her heart skittered around in her chest like a pat of butter on a hot skillet. She swallowed hard. "I'd appreciate it."

"Good. Let me show you where we put your things." He gestured to the steps leading to the second floor. Jasper held out a hand and Delilah took it, taking her time on the stairs.

They entered a long hallway at the top. Half a dozen doors on her right and another few on her left. He turned to the right. "Abby's room is this way."

Noises came from behind a couple of the doors, but the one at the end of the hall sat wide open.

"Hey, Abby. Delilah's here. Can you show her where she's sleeping tonight?"

"Sure." Abby got up and wrapped Delilah in a hug. "You have no idea how nice it is to have a girl around for a change."

"She's been praying for this her whole life." Jasper laughed and gave Delilah an apologetic smile. "Abby, go easy on her. You're going to scare her away."

"I don't scare that easily." Delilah gave the girl a squeeze before stepping back. "I've never shared a room before. You'll have to fill me in on the rules."

"I've got a trundle." Abby pointed to a set of drawers under her bed. "Mom told me to put clean sheets on earlier. Are you staying for dinner?"

"Oh"—Delilah glanced to Jasper—"I don't know."

"Yes, she's staying for dinner." Jasper nodded toward his sister. "I'm going to take a look at the trailer and make sure it's hooked up right. Can you entertain Delilah until it's time to eat?"

"Of course." Abby pointed to where Delilah's bag sat on

the floor. "If you want to change clothes, I can introduce you to Tie Dye."

"Tie Dye? That's the goat, right?" Delilah glanced to Jasper, but he just stood there with his lips quirked up.

"Yep. Jasper found him tangled up in some barbed wire and brought him home. Nobody claimed him so he stayed," Abby said.

"Why do you call him Tie Dye?" Delilah asked. Seemed like a strange name for a pet, especially a goat.

"I'm sure she'll tell you all about it on the way down to the pasture. You all right here?" Jasper leaned against the doorframe.

"We'll be fine." She gave him a smile that held a lot more confidence than she felt. Spending time around a large family hadn't been part of her plans. She was used to being on her own, although the amount of time she spent around Stella made it seem like they lived together sometimes.

"All right then. I'll see you later." Jasper disappeared down the hall, and for a moment she wished she were going with him.

"Want to see my lizard?" Abby asked.

"I'm sorry, your what?" Delilah turned around to find the girl holding out a scaly critter that took up the majority of her forearm. Instinctively, she jumped back a couple of feet, bumping her arm against a dresser.

"Are you okay?" Abby came close, the lizard still on her arm.

"I'm fine. You caught me off guard, that's all." She'd never seen a creature like that so close up before. "Who do you have there?"

"This is Sly. He actually likes crickets. We should have let him loose in your trailer. I bet he'd eat them all." Abby stretched her arm out. "You want to hold him?"

"Um, maybe later. Right now, I'd love to change if you can show me where the bathroom is." Delilah skirted around Abby and Sly, her eye on her bag.

"Second door on the right. Do you want me to show you?"

"I think I can manage finding it on my own." She rummaged through her bag, locating a pair of jeans and a long-sleeve shirt. "I'll be back in a few minutes."

Abby nodded, her attention focused on her pet. Delilah left the bedroom and turned to the right. She entered the bathroom and shut the door behind her, breathing in a sigh of relief as the lock clicked into place. Finally, she could let her guard down for a few minutes and figure out what she needed to do next. Ever since she'd stepped foot in Ido, things had veered off course. Her time in Hartwood and East had gone strictly by the book. They'd paraded her around local events and left her to herself for the most part in between.

But being in Ido, she felt totally immersed in the day-to-day life of the town. She'd never intended on staying at someone's home, much less the one of the man who was responsible for her welfare while she was in town. Not to mention pulling his entire family in on it. She was totally out of her element. No amount of pageant training had prepared her for joining the family of her hospitality host. They all seemed nice enough, but she'd never had much in the way of family. Just her and Stella and sometimes her mother's latest boyfriend or husband. They never lasted long.

Delilah took her time changing her clothes, taking advantage of the solitary space for as long as she could. She'd asked Stella once about why she never seemed able to settle down. Her mom answered her with a sadness in her eyes Delilah had never seen before, and said something about having lost her chance at happiness when she chose to walk away.

When she was younger, Delilah would have given just about anything to have a sister. When that didn't work out, she opened up to being okay with a brother instead, figuring maybe she'd been too picky with her request. But Stella kept moving between men, and no siblings ever showed up.

Spending time with Jasper's family would be good for her. She'd figure out what she'd been missing by being an only child.

As she nodded to herself, doing her best to convince herself to get back out there, someone pounded on the bathroom door.

"Get out of there, asswipe. You know I've got to clean up before dinner."

Delilah gasped and grabbed onto the counter. "I'll be out in a second."

The pounding stopped. "Abby?"

"No, this is Delilah. I'm just finishing up."

Another voice joined the first in the hall. Muffled voices argued with each other and she wondered if she should hide out until they left or open the door and get it over with.

"What are y'all doing?" Abby's voice joined the mix. "Come on out, Delilah."

She cracked open the door and peered through. Three men stood in the hall, each one of them bigger and broader than the next.

Abby held out a hand. A hand free of Sly the lizard. "It's okay. These are my brothers. Davis, Trent, and Mitchell, meet Miss Lovin' Texas, Delilah Stone."

Jasper made sure the trailer was level, then checked and rechecked the connections. He couldn't afford to have anything else go wrong for Delilah. The fact Lacey hadn't chewed him out yet for letting Delilah's trailer get overrun with crickets meant it was just a matter of time.

Her laugh pealed out over the sound of his dad mowing a section of the orchard. Turning, he caught sight of her and Abby moving toward the pasture. She'd changed into a pair of jeans. He did a double take, surprised the woman owned something made of denim. Her hair flowed wild and free, blowing over her shoulders in the late afternoon breeze.

Abby said something and Delilah laughed again. The sound of her happiness brought a smile to his face. He kept an eye on the two of them until they disappeared around the back of the barn.

"Who the hell is that?" An arm whacked him across the stomach.

Jasper spun around.

Three of his brothers faced him, their arms crossed over their chests. "You want to tell us who Trent almost walked in on in the bathroom?"

Jasper's hands clenched into fists, a sense of protectiveness washing over him. "You better not have walked in on her."

"He didn't." Mitchell gave Trent a little push forward. "But he wishes he did."

Jasper silenced the growl that threatened to escape his lips. "She's a guest. And she's judging that contest. Don't piss her off, she might be the only chance we have at keeping the orchard."

"You're not kidding." Davis let his arms drop to his sides. "Dad said something about a family meeting tomorrow night. Is that what he wants to talk about? Are we really at risk of losing the orchard?"

"No." Jasper huffed out a breath. He shouldn't have said anything. No need to drag his younger brothers into this. At least not until he figured out what their next step ought to be.

"Then why did you say that?" Mitchell asked.

"Did Dad really say he wants to talk tomorrow night?" Jasper brushed his hands against his jeans. His dad hadn't said anything to him about a family meeting.

"Yeah." Mitchell leaned against the side of the trailer. "What's up with this eyesore?"

Everything had happened so fast, Jasper hadn't filled his brothers in on his new role. "This belongs to Miss Lovin' Texas, otherwise known as Delilah Stone, otherwise known as the woman who's joining us for dinner and staying over, at least for tonight."

"So, Abby was telling the truth." Davis shook his head. "What the hell have you gotten yourself involved in?"

Jasper rolled his shoulders under the weight of their collective gaze. "Mayor Cherish needed someone to pitch in last minute, so she asked me to be Ido's hospitality host. Ms. Stone is in town to judge our efforts to be voted the most romantic town in Texas."

The three of them stood in silence for a long beat. Then the laughs started.

"Just stay out of her way." He gathered his tools and started to make his way back to the garage.

"Wait." Davis grabbed for his arm. Out of all of his brothers, Davis was the most likely to end up working a desk job. His ability to analyze a situation far surpassed the other Taylor brothers. "What's in it for us?"

"What could possibly be in it for us?" Mitchell asked. "Jasper doesn't know shit about being romantic. The mayor should have given the job to Tie Dye instead."

Trent almost bent all the way over as he cracked up.

But Davis pressed on. "There's got to be something in it for the farm. What's your angle?"

Jasper slung an arm around his brother's shoulder. "Mayor Cherish said if we can get Ido named the most romantic town in Texas, we'll be an even more desirable wedding destination."

Davis nodded. "And?"

"Well"—Jasper pulled his arm back—"if we can snag that title we'll have even more weddings coming to town. Mayor Cherish is looking for other complementary businesses and I thought if we could spruce up the barn—"

"It would be the perfect place to hold a wedding." Davis turned to him, his eyes bright. "What did Dad say?"

"He thinks it's a stupid idea. But if we spend the insurance money fixing up the barn, we can host weddings and trail rides and other events to tide us over until the new trees we plant start producing."

"That's genius." Davis nodded, the wheels in his head probably spinning out of control with the possibilities.

"Would you be on board with an idea like that?" Jasper elbowed his brother.

"Yeah. Hell yeah." At twenty-four, Davis had already graduated from college but was having a hard time finding a job nearby that would put his engineering degree to good use. It was only a matter of time before he'd make the decision to move away. Maybe if they could build up a big enough business, he wouldn't have to.

"Does that mean you're up for helping me?" Jasper asked.

"I'm in." He motioned for Trent and Mitchell to come closer. "What do we need to do?"

"I've got to keep an eye on Delilah, and make sure there's no doubt in her mind that we're the most romantic town in Texas. Lacey wants me to pull together a big event."

"Like what?" Davis asked.

"That's just it, I don't know. Something that reeks of romance. Like a big Valentine's party, but in October. Got any ideas?" Colin might be the ladies' man, but Davis was definitely better at seeing a project through. Suddenly, a light bulb went off in Jasper's head. "I think I've got something."

"What?" Davis shot him some side-eye. None of the Taylor brothers were known for being super in touch with their softer side.

"What if we built a trail kind of thing? Then we can have people stop and take pictures in super-romantic spots."

"Like what? The only place in town that might be considered somewhat romantic is the kissing cove down by the river." Davis squinted, making his eyes scrunch up, like kissing someone was the worst possible thing that could happen.

"We'd have to make them up. Like a tunnel full of those

white lights. You know, the kind they string around town during the holidays. Maybe have an arbor or something. Just lots of little romantic spots around town where people can pause and sneak a kiss." Jasper executed a neck roll as he tried to think of something romantic.

"I don't know. If that's all you've got . . . Christmas lights . . . we're going to need some more help." Mitchell wasn't on board. Jasper could tell by his scowl.

"I'll ask Lacey. And maybe I can try to get some info out of Delilah." Jasper shifted his weight from one foot to the other. "What if we all keep the conversation around romantic stuff during dinner? We're bound to get some ideas."

"If you think it will help, I'm game." Davis lifted a shoulder.

Mitchell and Trent shrugged and nodded as well.

"Good. I'm going to go check on Delilah and make sure Tie Dye hasn't chewed her up yet."

"Sounds good." Davis tapped him on the arm with his fist as Jasper walked by. "You know what would be really cool?"

"What's that?"

"If Colin was around to pitch in. Out of all of us, he's probably the one who'd have the best ideas."

Jasper's gut pitched. "Yeah, it's too bad Colin's not around."

"We'll manage without him though. That's what family does." Davis joined the other two while Jasper forced air into his lungs. If Colin was around . . . He very well might be. But as much as his brothers might think Colin had all the answers, Jasper was the only one who knew how dangerous it would be to bring their oldest brother back into the fold.

Before he let himself travel too far down the path of regret, he shook it off. He hadn't heard another word about Colin being back in town, and if his brother knew what was good for him, he'd stay far, far away.

Jasper heard Delilah before he saw her. Her laugh reached his ears, a high-pitched musical melody that put a smile on his face. It only grew bigger when he stepped around the barn. Tie Dye stood on the top of the fence line, nibbling at Delilah's hair.

"Get down off of there." He rushed toward the goat, who startled and fell off the fence into a pile of hay. "Abby, I thought you were looking out for her."

"You know how Tie Dye gets." Abby crossed her arms over her chest. "He's just saying hi."

"She doesn't need a haircut." He turned his attention toward Delilah. "You okay?"

"I'm fine." She patted down her hair.

"Sorry about that. Damn goat's got a mind of his own." He glanced toward Tie Dye, who'd recovered and stood nibbling on a huge carrot that Abby must have given him.

"At least now I know where he got his name." Delilah's lips spread into a grin as she looked back toward the goat.

"Abby filled you in, huh?"

"Sure did." Abby shrugged. "You'd think the color would be gone by now, but it's just faded a little."

Jasper shook his head. "Silly goat. You should have seen the inside of my truck after I brought him home. That's some strong dye."

"How do you think he got mixed up in it in the first place?" Delilah turned her gaze on him, sparking that same spot in his lower belly that always seemed to light up under her focused attention.

"There's a place in town that does fabric dyeing for a linen company. My guess is he was poking around for something to eat and got himself mixed up in it." Jasper let out a chuckle. "He's one of a kind though."

"That he is." Delilah held out her hand and the ornery goat trotted over, knocking his horns against the fence as she scratched behind his colorful ears.

As they shared the quiet moment, a bell began to clang.

"Time for dinner." Abby's gaze darted back and forth between him and Delilah. "Want to race to the house?"

"You go ahead." Jasper waved her on. His little sister had been running cross-country track for the past two years. Wouldn't do him any good to get bested by her while he tried to run half a mile in cowboy boots.

Abby took off, leaving him alone with Delilah.

"She's great." Delilah gave Tie Dye a final scratch, then began the walk back to the house.

Jasper fell into step next to her. "She's a tough cookie. Mom and Dad thought they were done, then eight years later Abby showed up. She puts up with a lot having so many older brothers."

"I can't imagine having one sibling, much less seven." She glanced over. "What's it like to be one of the oldest?"

He let the question sink in. How could he explain the sense of responsibility he felt toward his younger brothers and sister? Toward his parents and even Aunt Suzy to make sure things stayed all right? Instead of telling her the truth, he kept it light.

"It's not bad. I figure it's my job to break in my parents, right?"

Her lips twitched up in a hint of a smile. "It's a lot of work though, too, isn't it? I've heard older siblings feel responsible for their younger brothers and sisters. Not that I would know anything about that."

"Stick around and Abby will probably claim you as the older sister she's always wanted." He could think of a few ways he wouldn't mind claiming her as well. But those feelings were far from brotherly, and he'd rather swallow his own tongue than admit them.

"She did ask me for some advice on makeup. Do you think your mom would be okay with me showing her a few things?"

"I imagine it would be all right, but Abby ought to check to make sure. I don't know what age the makeup restriction gets lifted in our house, seeing as Abby's the first one it applies to."

Delilah wrapped her fingers around his arm, the gesture so natural after escorting her around the vineyard that he wondered if she even realized she'd done it. She might have been stomping around the pasture with his sister, but she still smelled like sunshine and lemons. He'd have to keep reminding himself to not get used to this. Three days into his monthlong stint and he was already having a hard time remembering what life was like before Delilah Stone.

eleven

Delilah bowed her head along with the Taylors as Jasper's dad said the blessing. She was grateful for the few moments of quiet. Ever since she and Jasper returned to the house, it had been nothing but chaos. On one hand, the way the brothers jostled one another around and flung insults back and forth made her yearn for a big family. On the other, no one seemed able to get a word in, so everyone shouted. Seemed like whoever could yell the loudest got the final say. She didn't know how they all made it through the day without recurring headaches. Kind of like the one throbbing behind her temples as she took the bowl of salad Jasper passed her.

"Do you have any brothers or sisters, Ms. Stone?" Mrs. Taylor asked.

"She's an only child," Abby answered. "I bet she never had to share a bathroom with a bunch of stinky boys growing up."

"Abby, let Ms. Stone answer for herself," Mrs. Taylor chastised.

Abby's cheeks flushed. "Sorry, Mom."

"Please, all of you, call me Delilah." She didn't need the extra layer of formality, especially not after witnessing a burping contest as a couple of Jasper's brothers finished setting the table. "And Abby is correct. Unfortunately, I don't have any brothers or sisters."

Delilah took the plate of homemade fried chicken and passed it to her left.

"Don't you like chicken?" Abby asked, her fingers wrapped around a drumstick.

Jasper wiped his mouth with his napkin before slipping it back in his lap. "She's a vegetarian."

"Oh, honey, you should have said something." Mrs. Taylor pushed back from the table. "I'm sure I've got something I can whip up for you."

"There's plenty here to choose from." Delilah crumpled the napkin in her lap, hating how her choice in diet made other people feel responsible. "I'm used to making do with what I've got, and this salad looks delicious."

"It's okay, Mom. If she's hungry later, I'll build a fire out back and stuff her full of s'mores." Jasper nodded to his mother.

"I wish you'd said something, Jasper." His mom scooted her chair back in, then eyed him over the rim of her sweet tea.

Delilah didn't want to cause a scene. "I'm really quite fine, but thank you so much for offering."

"Do you eat fish?" Davis asked. She remembered his name, but hadn't been able to keep the others straight yet.

"No, no fish."

"How about eggs?" another one of the boys asked.

"No, dumbass," the brother with the buzz cut said. "An egg is a baby chicken. If she doesn't eat meat, she doesn't eat eggs either."

"We've got a wonderful farmers' market that sets up every Friday morning on the town square," Mrs. Taylor said. "Jasper, you ought to add that to your list of places to take Delilah."

"That sounds great." Delilah helped herself to some of the green beans being passed around the table.

"What other places are you going to visit while you're here?" Abby asked. "Can you come talk at my school?"

Jasper eyed his little sister. "What would you want her to talk about?"

"I've done seminars for girls on ways to empower each other. If your school would be interested in something like that, I'd love to take part." The few times she'd been asked to speak to preteens and tweens, she'd enjoyed it. She'd experienced her own fair share of the "mean girls" at her school and used her pageant platform as an effort to spread kindness and understanding.

Abby bounced up and down on her chair. "Can I ask my teacher, Mom?"

"Of course, if Delilah's sure she doesn't mind."

Delilah shook her head. "It would be my pleasure."

"Where else are you going to go while you're here? You're supposed to visit places that are romantic, right?" Davis asked.

"That's right." Delilah glanced to Jasper. "But I don't get to decide. It's up to your town to show me the places all of you think are romantic."

"Well, there's the cove down by the river," Davis said.

Buzz Cut joined in. "There's also the Sunday night movie on the side of the Hamptons' barn. That's got to be pretty romantic since I saw Mitchell mashing lips with a certain brunette there a few weeks ago."

Mitchell's cheeks flamed red, and Delilah felt sorry for him for a moment but also a bit relieved since now she'd been able to deduce that Buzz Cut's name was Trent. "Do they have it every Sunday night?"

"Most of the time," Davis said. "They're planning on showing some cheesy chick flick tonight, aren't they, Mom?"

"As soon as the sun goes down, which this time of year seems to be getting earlier each week"—Mrs. Taylor grinned at Delilah—"they alternate between showing family films and lighthearted comedies more appropriate for an older crowd."

"You didn't mention that to me." Delilah turned her gaze on Jasper.

"I haven't had a chance yet. Besides, I wasn't sure if you'd want to sit outside on the ground and watch an old movie."

"Sounds like the perfect way to wrap up the weekend." She stabbed another green bean with her fork. Whatever Mrs. Taylor had used for seasoning was delicious. She made a mental note to ask her later when they had a few minutes alone.

"All right, let's do it." Jasper shrugged as his brothers laughed.

"If you think that's romantic, you ought to check out the apple wine festival, too." Mr. Taylor had been quiet most of the meal so it surprised Delilah when he piped up. "That's where Ann and I met. Seems like only yesterday."

"Yesterday plus thirty-five years," Mrs. Taylor said.

Delilah looked on as Jasper's parents shared a tender glance. That right there was what romance was all about. Falling even more in love with someone after being together thirty-five years. That's what she was holding out for . . . the kind of relationship she wanted in her own life.

The rest of the meal passed with good-natured ribbing among the brothers and reminders from Mr. Taylor about chores for the coming week. She hadn't had the opportunity to ask Jasper about his family's business, but it appeared all of them were involved in the pecan orchard to some degree. He'd mentioned the tornado that passed through the month before, and she wondered how much of their business had been lost. Whatever had happened, they seemed to be in good spirits. The fact they had one another must have helped a lot. What would it be like to be surrounded by family? To know that someone always had your back, no matter what was going on?

Hopefully she'd find out for herself someday.

Dinner didn't end until Jasper and his brothers had emptied every platter of the delicious homemade meal Mrs. Taylor had made. When they were done, Delilah pushed back from the table and started to clear the dishes.

"Oh, you don't have to help with that, you're a guest." Mrs. Taylor took the platter from her hands as she entered the kitchen.

"Thank you for dinner, it was wonderful." Delilah stood by the counter while Mrs. Taylor rinsed plates and began to stack them into the dishwasher. "Can I help clean up?"

"If you want to, although it's not necessary. I've got these boys trained to help around the house." As she spoke, Mitchell and Davis came into the kitchen with their arms full of dirty dishes.

"We've got this, Mom. Why don't you and Delilah go relax on the porch for a few minutes," Davis suggested.

Mrs. Taylor arched a brow. "Now that's not an offer that comes around very often. Let's take advantage." She scooped up little Maggie, then linked her arm with Delilah's and led her to two of the rocking chairs that sat on the large wraparound front porch.

Delilah settled into one of them, catching a glimpse of Jasper clearing the table through the dining room window. She didn't want to admit to herself how much she enjoyed spending time with his family. They were a little overwhelming as a whole, but even she could see the love and respect they held for one another.

"Do I get to sit with you, too?" Abby sprang through the front door and grabbed the arms of another rocker.

"Of course, sweet girl. Us women need to stick together

around here, don't we?" Mrs. Taylor ran her hand over her daughter's dark brown hair as she bounced her granddaughter on her knee.

"Will you really come speak at my school?" Abby asked.

"As long as it's okay with your teacher," Delilah promised. "If you want to check tomorrow, I'd be happy to set up a time if she says yes."

Abby clapped her hands together. "That would be so much fun. Dad's been in to talk about pecans, but no one really paid too much attention."

Mrs. Taylor let out a laugh. "I'm sure they'll find Delilah's presentation more interesting and relevant."

"Hey, Mom, Delilah said she'd teach me to put on makeup, too. Can I try?"

Delilah glanced to Mrs. Taylor. "Only if it's okay with your mom, remember?"

"I think that would be fine. Poor Abby doesn't get much girl time with all these boys around. I keep hoping one of them will settle down and find someone special so we'll have another woman in the group, but so far . . ." She shook her head.

"Jasper used to bring Adeline around a lot," Abby said.

Her mother's head shot up. "Let's not talk about that right now."

"Oh, sorry." Abby frowned for a moment, then began to rock her chair back and forth. "I hoped Lucas would get married when we found out Amanda was going to have a baby, but then she left."

Mrs. Taylor put her hand over her daughter's. "Lucas will find someone. Right now he needs to focus on Maggie."

At the sound of her name, Maggie squirmed and reached for Abby. Her aunt picked her up and held the little girl on her lap while she rocked back and forth. Delilah saw the love in Mrs. Taylor's eyes and wondered if her own mother had ever looked at her the way Jasper's mom now looked at her daughter and granddaughter.

Before she let herself get too wrapped up in her own thoughts, Jasper came through the door and onto the porch.

"If you want to get a good spot for the movie, we probably ought to head over."

Abby turned to Jasper. "Can I come with you?"

"You've got school tomorrow," Mrs. Taylor said.

Abby opened her mouth to protest but one look from her mom made her snap her jaw shut.

Mrs. Taylor turned a kind smile to Delilah. "Y'all have a good time."

"Thanks again for dinner. It was wonderful." Delilah stood and joined Jasper at the edge of the steps.

"Don't worry about waking anyone up when you get back. We're used to everyone coming and going at all hours. I'll leave the lights on and the door will be unlocked."

"Thank you." Delilah still wasn't sure about staying over and sharing a room with Abby, but with her camper still being de-cricketed, she didn't have much of a choice.

"Shall we?" Jasper offered his arm.

"Sure." She took it, letting him lead her down the steps and to the truck.

He opened the door for her and slid a cooler in the back.

"What's in the cooler?"

"You can't watch a movie without refreshments."

"Are any of your brothers going to be joining us?"

"I sure as hell hope not, but I figured we could take Buster if you don't mind."

She held back a laugh at the pained expression on his face. His brothers might tease, but as she was learning, that seemed to be what siblings did best.

"I'd love to have Buster join us." Abby, Mrs. Taylor, and even Maggie waved until they disappeared from view. Delilah took in a deep breath and tried to look forward to the evening ahead. Lying on a blanket with Jasper. In the dark. What could possibly go wrong?

* * *

It seemed like forever since Jasper had been to the Sunday night movie at the Hampton barn. He tried to remember exactly how long it had been and what movie had been playing. A hazy flashback of Adeline and him watching an eighties rom-com came to mind. He pushed that memory out of his head before thinking about Adeline ruined the whole evening.

Delilah held the blanket he'd grabbed in one hand and Buster's leash in the other while he carried the cooler. He wanted to find a spot far enough away so she wouldn't feel like everyone was watching her. Speak of the devil. Adeline perched on a blanket next to a thin man with a receding hairline. Could that be her husband?

She glanced up as they passed, her eyes narrowed.

Jasper pretended like he didn't see her and meandered through a sea of blankets until he reached a spot far away.

"How's this?" He stopped at the edge of the small group of moviegoers.

"It's fine with me."

He set the cooler down and took the blanket from her. Every time he tried to spread it out, Buster leaped up and grabbed an edge in his teeth.

"Cut it out, Buster. If you let me get the blanket down, you'll have a place to sit." The scolding must have worked since Buster plopped down on his butt and huffed out a breath.

"Let me help." Delilah grabbed the opposite corners and together they stretched the blanket out and laid it down.

"Thanks." Jasper motioned to the dog. "There you go, bud. Pick your spot."

The damn dog walked in a circle, first one way, then the next, before plopping down in the middle of the blanket.

"Wow. So much for sharing," Jasper said.

Delilah settled on the other side of the dog. "He hogs the bed, too, doesn't he?"

"You've just got to be tough and show him who's boss." Jasper patted his leg, trying to get the dog to get up and move over. On second thought, maybe it was best with Buster sitting between them. He'd spent all day trying to figure out how to put a muzzle on the attraction he'd been feeling for Miss Lovin' Texas. Having Buster play chaperone might be the best thing that could happen this evening. At least with the big lug between them, Jasper couldn't accidentally touch her.

The one time he didn't want the dog to obey instructions, Buster leapt to his feet and sat down right in front of Jasper. Now he'd look like a total dumbass if he made him lie back down where he'd been.

"Aren't you a good boy." Delilah gave him a good, long scratch behind the ear.

"Sorry if my family was a little much tonight."

She glanced over at him, the corners of her mouth already turning up. "They were a riot. I can't imagine what the holidays are like at your house. It's got to be utter chaos."

Nodding, he chuckled to himself. Utter chaos with a major side of dysfunction. "Funny thing is, I've never known anything else. I can't remember when it was just Colin and me, so my earliest memories are of all us boys. When I think about the damage we've done over the years . . ."

"What's the worst trouble y'all got into?"

"Hmm. I'm going to have to think about that one. But I do remember a few times we almost lost our heads."

"Your poor mama. What did you do?"

"You really want me to divulge those kinds of family secrets?" He laughed at the way her eyes lit up. "Well, I remember one time Colin talked me into sneaking out in the middle of the night. My aunt Suzy had bought a new horse, and everyone said we weren't old enough to ride him. Colin wanted to prove them wrong, so we snuck into her barn, and saddled him up."

"What happened?"

"My uncle thought someone was breaking into the barn, so he fired his shotgun into the air. Damn horse spooked and took off like the devil himself was hot on his trail."

"And you and Colin?"

Jasper could recall the sound of the wind whipping past his ears as he gripped his brother's back. "Held on for dear life until we got to the edge of the property line and the horse bucked us off before he cleared the fence."

"Were you hurt?"

Jasper pushed his sleeve up and exposed a long, faded scar on his forearm. "Shattered two bones in my arm. Colin walked away without a scratch."

"You were lucky."

"I suppose we were."

"What happened to the horse?"

"A neighbor found him stomping through their field the next day and brought him home. Aunt Suzy was the only one who could ride him after that." Jasper shook his head at the memory. He and Colin had been two of a kind back then. At least until he stopped letting his older brother talk him into causing trouble. Now they couldn't be more different if they tried.

Delilah let her hand rest on Buster's head and adjusted her position on the blanket. Buster must not have been satisfied with the interruption in attention and scooted himself over to where his head and half of his upper body draped over Delilah's lap. Then he let out a loud rush of gas.

"Get off of her." Jasper reached for the dog's collar.

"He's okay." Delilah laughed and gave him the sweetest smile as she ran her hand down the length of Buster's side as far as she could reach.

Buster eyed him like he was rubbing in the fact he was getting a full-body massage while Jasper didn't even get to hold her hand.

"Want something to drink?" He leaned toward the cooler. "They've also got popcorn for sale if you want some fresh-popped kettle corn."

"I'll take a drink, but I don't think I could eat another bite."

"Wine or lemonade?" Jasper held up a bottle of white wine he'd nabbed from his parents' refrigerator.

"Just lemonade tonight. That wine from earlier made me sleepy." She gave him a lazy grin as Buster rolled over onto his other side between them.

Jasper popped the top off a lemonade and handed it to her as the opening credits to the movie started to play.

Two minutes in and the film shut down. The lights flipped on around the perimeter and Mr. Hampton called out from the small shed where they kept the projector. "Sorry, folks. There's a problem with the film. Sit tight and we'll see if we can fix it."

"Does this happen often?" Delilah took a swig of lemonade.

"Not that I know of." In all the years he'd been watching movies at the Hampton barn, he couldn't remember a time when the film had been bad. They'd had to cancel for weather, but never for a mechanical failure. "I'll go see what's going on."

He left Buster and Delilah on the blanket and made his way to the shed. Other folks had started packing up their things and heading toward their cars. Great. His first night to try to make a good impression on his own with Delilah, and look what happened.

"Y'all need some help?" He leaned in through the open doorway of the shed.

Mr. Hampton turned, pieces of film in his hands. "Somebody cut the film."

"You sure about that?" Jasper eyed the pieces of filmstrip in the older man's hands.

"I don't know how else to explain it."

Jasper groaned. "I've got Miss Lovin' Texas here tonight. I was trying to show her the romantic side of Ido."

"I heard about that contest." Mr. Hampton glanced toward the dispersing crowd. "Can you give me a few minutes? I'll see if I have anything in the garage I can put on tonight. I'd hate for her to not get to experience a movie under the stars."

"Absolutely." Jasper clasped a hand to the man's shoulder. "Thanks."

He made his way back to the blanket, searching for Adeline along the way. She must have gone. Bailing at the first sign of trouble had always been her style. At least half of the audience had left, making it feel a whole lot more intimate as a black-and-white film began to play. *Casablanca.* This one had to have come from the vault. He'd only seen it once, a long, long time ago when Aunt Suzy tricked him into watching it with her. He leaned back, ready to enjoy the show.

There was something about being outside, sitting on a blanket under the clear Texas sky, that made him consider what it would feel like to pull Delilah next to him and wrap himself around her. While the movie held her captive, he kept his gaze trained on her.

Too soon, it was over. The lights surrounding the seating area turned on as the final credits rolled. The remaining people stood and gathered their things before heading to their vehicles.

Delilah didn't move right away. For a moment Jasper wondered if she'd fallen asleep. He sat up, leaning toward her.

She angled her face away from him and ran her finger under her eye.

"Are you crying?" He put a hand on her arm—the first

time he'd allowed himself to touch her since they sat down on the blanket together.

Smiling, she faced him. "It's silly. I've seen this movie a half dozen times. But it always gets me."

"Come here." He put his arm over her shoulder and pulled her into his side.

"I understand why they can't be together. But what if they could? What if Rick and Ilsa turned their back on convention and ran off together?"

"Then it wouldn't be *Casablanca*." He lifted his other shoulder in a half shrug. "The story resonates with so many people because of the sacrifice. If he threw her husband under the bus and ran off with her, it wouldn't be a classic."

"But do you think she'll ever be happy without him?" Delilah turned her face toward him and it took everything he had not to lift his finger to her cheek and wipe away the trace of her tears.

"I don't know."

"If I found a love like that, I wouldn't be able to walk away." The firmness of her voice surprised him.

"What if he lived on the other side of the world? Say an apartment in Paris. Would you give up everything you have here to follow him?"

"They have internet in Paris. I could still run my business from there."

"What if he lived on a remote island? Maybe he raises sheep in New Zealand or something? No internet, no cell phone service. Would you follow him there?"

Her forehead furrowed. "If we had a love as strong as Rick and Ilsa's, I suppose I wouldn't have a choice."

"Hmmm." He nodded.

"What, you disagree?" The tears had stopped, and her jaw now held a hint of the stubbornness he'd seen in her before.

"I don't think it's that simple." He held out a hand and

helped her to her feet. The other moviegoers had left by then, leaving them alone with the Hamptons. Jasper folded up the blanket and clipped a leash on Buster, who seemed eager to help with the cleanup effort.

"What's not simple about that? She loves him, he loves her."

"Yeah, but sometimes other things get in the way. Things too important to overlook. I mean, in the movie, there's a war going on. No matter how much they love each other, he has to put her safety and his own responsibilities above everything else." Jasper set the blanket on top of the cooler and held out Buster's leash. "Can you hold him for a minute? I want to give the Hamptons a hand."

Delilah took the leash but joined him when he bent down and began to clean up the lawn. The sight of the beauty queen picking up discarded popcorn buckets and empty soft drink cans made him do a double take.

"I've got this. You can go wait in the truck with Buster if you want."

She shrugged. "I don't mind. Besides, what's that saying about many hands make for less work?"

"'Many hands make for light work.' My grandma used to say that all the time." He grabbed a trash can from the edge of the clearing and rolled it to the middle. "Here, you can toss that stuff in here."

"Thanks for your help, Jasper." Mr. Hampton walked over and threw some trash into the barrel. "We can handle the rest. You young folks go on and enjoy the rest of your evening."

Jasper cast a glance around the space. They'd gathered almost everything. "Thanks for another great movie night, Mr. Hampton."

"I really enjoyed it." Delilah gave the older man a smile.

His eyes lit up at her attention. "Edna and I met at the movies. Of course, back then, a night at the theater only cost you about a dollar, including popcorn. We like to do what we can to provide an opportunity for other folks to experience the same kind of magic that brought us together."

Jasper couldn't believe he hadn't thought to make introductions. "Mr. Hampton, meet Delilah Stone. She's the reigning Miss Lovin' Texas and is in town to consider Ido for the title of most romantic small town in Texas."

"Is that so?" Mr. Hampton nodded. "Edna, come meet the woman who's going to fall in love here in Ido."

Jasper's cheeks heated and he shot a glance to Delilah. The comment hadn't rattled her at all. The glimpse he'd had of her vulnerable side had been replaced by the smiling, friendly demeanor she seemed to be able to slide on at will.

"It's so nice to meet both of you. I'd shake your hands, but I've been picking up trash. How long have you been hosting Sunday night movie nights?"

A glance passed between the Hamptons. "Oh, I'd say maybe about, what, twenty-five years?" Mr. Hampton said.

Mrs. Hampton nodded her agreement. "Maybe thirty. It's so nice to give young folks a place to spend an affordable evening out. We show family movies, too. So many of the couples who used to come here on dates now bring their kids. It's a wonderful tradition."

"I had a fantastic time tonight. Thank you for having me." She gave them another grin.

"We ought to be on our way." Jasper moved the trash can back to the edge of the clearing. He met up with Delilah by the passenger side of the truck. "Did you have a good time?"

She nodded as she squirted some hand sanitizer in her hand. "Here, take some of this."

"What all do you have in that purse? You're like a Boy Scout. Aren't they the ones who are always prepared?"

"Do you want some or not?"

He held out his palm, then rubbed the hand sanitizer between his hands. "There. Now I'm ready for anything."

"Anything?" she asked, a sly smile spreading across her lips.

twelve

"What exactly do you have in mind?" Jasper sat behind the wheel, looking at her like he could see past the front she put on for everyone else, like he could see straight through to her core.

"I don't know. That lemonade you gave me must have been full of sugar. I was pretty tired when we got here, but I think I'd have trouble falling asleep if you dropped me back at the house now." That was mostly true. What she really wanted was the chance to spend more time with him.

"So you're looking for a way to burn off some of that energy?" His eyes might have sparkled a little. Or maybe it was the light hitting him at just the right angle. It could have been wishful thinking, but she felt like he was flirting with her a bit.

"Sure. Do you have any ideas?" She flirted right back. That kiss they'd shared the night before had left her in a worthless state. The more she thought about it, the more she felt completely unfulfilled. The kiss itself had been remarkable. But it had also cracked open a longing she couldn't seem to shake. Lying next to Jasper through the movie, even with a dog the size of Buster between them, had only increased her inexplicable need.

"We could"—he checked his phone for the time—"head over to the bar in Swynton for a drink. They're serving for another couple of hours."

"Isn't that pretty far out of the way?"

His shoulders rolled. "Well, yeah. But it's not like I've got to get you somewhere super early tomorrow."

"If that's what you want to do."

He studied her for a long beat. "I've got another idea."

"Uh-oh. What kind of idea?"

"It's a surprise." He fired up the engine and headed back the way they came. Keeping one hand on the wheel, he fiddled with the radio dial with the other. "What kind of music do you like?"

"I'm flexible."

He settled on a country station. "You sure are accommodating tonight."

"What's that supposed to mean?" Buster's nose nudged into her arm. Technically he was sitting in the back seat, although he'd been working his way onto the console.

"Get back, Buster." Jasper rested his elbow between them, forcing Buster to retreat to the back seat again. "He's used to riding shotgun."

"I feel so special. You've given me priority seating over your dog." Delilah let out a soft laugh. Maybe it was the sugar in the lemonade. Or maybe it was spending the evening watching one of the most romantic movies of all time, knowing she was sitting next to the best kisser she'd ever met. Whatever it was, something had loosened her grip on her self-control. She'd shed the weight of her public persona. For some reason when she was alone with Jasper, she felt like she didn't have to put on airs or worry about what he would think of her.

"You should feel special. You're the first woman to displace

Buster to the back seat. Not even Abby gets to ride up front when he's in the truck." Jasper reached back and ruffled the dog's fur, earning him a few long swipes of wet dog kisses.

Delilah smiled to herself. Jasper had just confirmed there wasn't another woman in his life. She'd assumed as much after spending the night at his place. But having him confirm that she was the first woman to displace the dog convinced her he wasn't dating around. That definitely made her feel better about planting that humdinger of a kiss on him the night before.

They passed the turn off to Taylor Farms and drove down the blacktop a few more miles. Jasper kept his eyes on the road, humming along every once in a while to the soft sounds coming from the radio. She was content to let her head rest against the doorframe and enjoy the chance to study him under the cover of the dark cab.

Finally, he turned on the blinker and slowed. They hadn't passed another vehicle in at least ten minutes. If it were someone besides Jasper, she might be a little concerned about heading out to the middle of nowhere. But in the short time they'd known each other, he'd shown her he was a gentleman.

The truck bounced onto a narrow dirt road. "Careful, it's a little rough here."

"Where in the world are you taking me?" Tall grass rose up on either side of the truck, almost high enough to reach the windows.

He shot her a glance, his lips quirked up in a grin. "You'll see."

Her fingers wrapped tight around the handle over her head, and she tried to anticipate the worst of the bumps. They passed through a stand of scrubby trees, and just when she was about to ask him to turn back, he stopped.

He cut the lights and killed the engine. "We're here."

She looked through the windshield. The truck sat on top

of a bluff. Off in the distance the lights of the town twinkled. "Is that Ido?"

"Yep." He scooted closer. "See the dark section between the lights?"

She nodded.

"That's the river. The lights on the other side are coming from Swynton."

"It's beautiful."

"If you think that's great, come with me." He got out of the truck, and Buster hopped over the seat to follow.

Delilah checked out the window. They'd left the tall grass behind when they passed through the trees, but she was careful to watch her step. With her luck she'd set her foot down on a snake, or maybe even something way worse.

Jasper had climbed into the bed of the truck. "You want to come up?"

She slid her hand in his, and he pulled her up onto the tailgate. "Where's Buster?"

"Off checking out all the smells. He won't go far." Jasper spread out the blanket they'd used when they watched the movie. "Have a seat."

"What are you up to?" She sat down, keeping an eye on him while he opened the cooler and retrieved the bottle of wine. He poured them each a plastic cup full, then handed her one.

"Sorry about the lack of glassware." He clunked his cup against hers.

"What are we doing out here?" The sound of crickets surrounded them. She couldn't help but worry a little bit about one of them jumping into the truck bed. Just thinking about the other night gave her a shiver.

He leaned back, propping himself up on an elbow. "Do I make you nervous?"

She wrinkled her brow. What was he getting at? "Why do you ask?"

"Do you always have to answer a question with a question?"

"I don't do that." The wide grin he gave her made her reconsider. "Do I?"

"You just did it again. Come here." He motioned for her to scoot closer to him.

"Why did you ask if you make me nervous?" She slid over a few inches.

He groaned. "Sometimes I don't know what to do with you."

"What about the other times?" She'd skipped ahead to full-on flirt mode. Seeing him a little flustered, a little out of his element, was a bit of a turn-on.

"The other times I want to . . ." His gaze slid from her eyes to focus on her mouth.

"What?" she whispered.

He cupped her cheek with his palm, then ran the pad of his thumb over her lower lip. The contact sent a wave of warmth over her.

She opened her mouth, giving his thumb the slightest nip with her teeth. His eyes widened and before she had a chance to tease him about his reaction, his lips were on hers.

He pulled her down next to him as he stretched out. She registered the hardness of the truck bed against her hip, even through the blanket. Then she didn't register anything at all, except for the heat of his tongue sliding into her mouth.

If she could pause time and spend the rest of eternity kissing Jasper Taylor, she'd do it in a heartbeat. He'd perfected the art of kissing.

By the time she pulled away to catch her breath, his hands had found their way under her shirt and scorched the skin over her ribs. "Is this what you brought me out here for?"

He shook his head, his nose nudging against her neck. "Look up."

"What am I looking for?" She rolled onto her back, and looked up at the clear, dark sky. Thousands of pinpricks of light dotted the blackness above. "Oh, wow. The stars."

His fingers twined with hers and he brought her hand to his lips. "They're beautiful, aren't they?"

"I never knew there were so many."

"You've got to get far enough away from town to be able to see them. We got lucky with no clouds tonight."

They lay there for several minutes, looking up at the sky, the crickets playing a symphony around them. A flash of light streaked across the darkness.

"Did you see that?" She squeezed his hand.

"A shooting star. You know you're supposed to make a wish now, right?"

She took in a shaky breath. "What would you wish for?"

"It's not my star. I don't get a wish." He flipped onto his side to face her and propped his arm up to rest his cheek on his palm. "The question is, what are you going to wish for?"

"I don't know." She hadn't wished on a star in years. The last time she had, it hadn't come true. That was before she figured out that wishing on stars didn't have enough magic to bring her dad back into her life.

"Go on, make a wish." Jasper let their clasped hands rest on her stomach. "You don't have to tell me what you wish for."

"I guess I don't believe in wishing on shooting stars."

"That's a shame. Everyone knows wishing on a shooting star works."

She shook her head.

"What if I can prove it?"

"How exactly are you going to do that?"

"Hold on, and I'll show you." He rolled onto his back, staring up at the sky. A few minutes passed before he lifted his arm and pointed. "See that? I'm calling that one."

"You're crazy." She shook her head, wondering how he planned to make his point.

"I'm making my wish right now." He closed his eyes, his lips moving without making a sound.

"So . . . what did you wish for?" She nestled into his side, her curiosity piqued. What would a man like Jasper Taylor want bad enough to wish for on a shooting star?

"I can't tell you or it won't come true."

She let out a soft laugh. "Then how are you going to prove it to me?"

"Come here." His hand tangled in her hair as he drew her face close to his.

Her stomach clenched in anticipation. She knew what was coming. But no amount of bracing herself could prepare her for the way she felt when their lips touched. Saying it rocked her world seemed so cliché, but was the most accurate description she could come up with. Kissing Jasper literally scrambled her brain, crisscrossed all her internal wiring, and made her yearn for things so incredibly beyond her reach.

Jasper took the kiss deeper, his hands exploring as eagerly as his tongue. His fingers slipped under the hem of her shirt again, racing up and down her ribs.

A deep ache pulsed between her thighs. She wanted him. Wanted him like she'd never ached for anyone before. But she wasn't the kind of woman who would toss reason out the door for the fleeting passion of a magical moment.

Or at least she hadn't been in the past.

With Jasper, she wasn't sure who she was. He made her want to do things she'd never dared to imagine.

His hand paused when he reached the underwire of her bra. "We can stop whenever you want."

Stop. Why would she want to stop? She never wanted to stop feeling the kind of feelings he stirred up. She shook her head.

"Delilah. I don't want us to do anything you'd regret. I get the sense you're not the kind of woman who's into one-night stands. But I also know you're leaving in a few weeks.

And dammit, there's something going on between us. Something I can't explain, but it's something I've never felt before."

She nodded. That was how she felt, too. And in that moment, nothing else seemed to matter. She reached between them and put her hand on his, gliding it under the cup of her bra.

His fingers smoothed over her skin, tentative at first. Then his lips were back on hers and he reached behind her to work on the clasp.

She'd never wanted anything as much as she wanted to feel his hands on her skin. He pushed her shirt up and released her bra, then cupped a breast in each hand, his thumbs working over her nipples. She couldn't help but let out a little sigh. "So good."

He gently rolled her onto her back, then lowered his head toward her chest. His tongue swirled over one breast before he switched to the other.

Her body burned for his touch. But even the heat from his mouth wasn't enough. She wanted . . . no, she needed . . . more.

Her skin felt like satin under his rough palms. Her body tasted like a mix of sweetness and salt. Not even the brush of cooler evening air could tamp down the heat between them. Looking at her, her chest bare in the dim light of the moon, his heart beat so fast and strong it seemed like it might thump right out of his chest. Jasper wanted to savor each kiss, each flick of his tongue against her skin. But something deep within him urged him on.

She must have felt it, too. Her hands roamed over his shoulders, down his chest, working their way under his shirt. When her palms met his skin, he hissed in a breath. Even the way she touched him turned him on. Her fingers danced over his abs, pressed against his pecs, and gripped his shoulders. He didn't know if he should put a stop to things or see how far it would go.

Then her fingers came to rest on his belt buckle. If she breached the waistband of his jeans, he might not be able to hold back. Reluctantly, he shifted next to her, and took her hands in his.

"What's wrong?" The concern in her eyes nearly undid him.

"Nothing. Nothing at all." He licked his lips, the taste of her still on his tongue. "We don't have to do this."

"Do you not want to?" A wrinkle bisected her brow.

"Hell, yes, I want to." He'd been attracted to her since the first day he met her. The day he almost hosed her off the steps of city hall. And even though they hadn't known each other very long, he felt like he'd known her all of his life. Or maybe even in another life. Being around her was like experiencing a deep sense of déjà vu. Over and over again.

He'd heard people say they fell in love at first sight. But he'd always dismissed it as complete bullshit. How could he fall for someone he didn't even know? But there was no other way to describe the way he felt about Delilah. Like he knew her on some deep, otherworldly level, even though they didn't know the trivial things about each other yet.

All of those thoughts created a traffic jam in his brain. How could he get involved with her when she'd be leaving in such a short time? How could he not? Would he spend the rest of his life wondering what might have been if he didn't have the balls to take a chance?

She leaned over him, her hair creating a curtain around their faces. "What are you thinking about right now?"

"You sure you want to know?"

Her hair moved as she nodded, tickling his chest.

Now or never. "I'm thinking how amazing it would feel to make love to you."

She didn't react, not even the slightest quirk of her lips or scrunch of her nose.

Great. He'd decided to be honest and she'd turned to stone. Time to dial it down. Way down. He was about to sit up, chalk up the whole stargazing thing to an epically bad idea. But then her palm on his chest pushed him back.

"I don't do one-night stands."

"I get it. That's not what I want from this."

"I don't do no-string flings."

"I get that, too."

"But I can't say no to you." She nipped at her bottom lip with her teeth—a move that made him desperate for her.

He laid her back on the blanket and slid her jeans down her legs. The blanket was big enough that he was able to pull half of it over them, trapping them inside. She finished what she'd started with his belt buckle and before he could voice any rational thought as to why this was a bad idea, her hands found his cock.

He pulled the one condom he'd carried around for forever out of his wallet and she helped slide it into place. Then, with the eyes of a million stars looking down on them, he hovered over her. He tried to commit each detail of her face to memory: the curve of her lips, the arch of her brows, the emotion in her eyes. Then he lowered himself into her, losing himself in the slick heat between her legs.

Her hands gripped his shoulders as her hips met his. They moved to some internal rhythm that both of them knew by heart. He slipped a finger between them, circling that bundle of nerves that would drive her over the edge. With a moan, she clenched around him. Every part of him wanted to take her faster and harder but he didn't want her to lose her momentum. So he kept it steady, increasing the pressure of his finger a fraction more each time he pulled back.

"You feel so good, Delilah. Like you were made for me."

For half a heartbeat he wondered if she had been. They didn't make sense on paper. The polished beauty queen and the farmer's son. But he'd never been one to take things at surface value. And she was so much more than what met the eye.

Her fingers gripped his shoulders even tighter. She was close, he could tell by the way her hips moved, grinding against him, like she was at the edge and about to fall over, throw herself into it, give herself over to him completely. Her head tipped back, her brow furrowed in concentration. She was so fucking beautiful it almost hurt to look at her.

He focused on her eyes, willing her to open them up and meet his gaze. Like she could sense his silent request, she gazed up at him as her body stilled, clenched around him. He continued to move, so far gone he couldn't stop if he wanted to. And as she gazed up at him, the reflection of a million stars in her eyes, he joined her.

After they floated back down to earth, he held her tight against his chest, running his fingers lightly up and down her side. "I feel like I could lie here forever with you."

She reached up and pressed a kiss to his scruffy cheek. "Wouldn't your family wonder where you are?"

"They'd probably miss you before they'd miss me. You've made quite an impression on everyone."

"Don't be silly. I can tell how much they love you." She lifted the blanket and tossed it to the side. "Are you as hot as I am? I feel like I just ran a marathon."

He leaned over and blew cool air on the bare skin of her back. "You're definitely much, much hotter than I am."

"Stop." She let out a giggle that shifted to a snort. "Oh no, now you know my deepest, darkest secret."

"That you snort when you laugh?" It had to be the cutest thing he'd ever heard. He reached out to tickle her, trying to get her to do it again.

"Don't. It's so embarrassing. I don't know where I get that laugh. My mom would never make such an unladylike noise, and I don't remember my dad ever sounding like a hog in heat."

He laughed, making her cheek bounce up and down against his chest. "Trust me, you don't sound like a hog in heat. If you don't believe me, there are some wild boars out by Aunt Suzy's property I can introduce you to."

"Now that sounds super romantic. I didn't get that experience in Hartwood or East."

He could have used that opening to ask her what kind of experience she did have. Her defenses were down. She might say something that would give Ido an edge. Damn that stupid contest. He was grateful that it led her to him, but he didn't want it to come between them. But how could it not when he'd just violated the one rule he'd promised himself he wouldn't break?

"I should probably get you back." He brushed her hair away from her cheek.

"Do we have to?" She closed her eyes and pressed her cheek into his palm.

"Unless we want them sending out a search party. I don't know that anyone would care too much if I went missing, but I'm sure they'd come out looking for you."

"I'd miss you if you went missing."

"You might change your mind after you see what kinds of plans we've got in store over the next couple of weeks."

"Really? Do I get to partake in another stargazing night with the local hospitality host?"

"About the contest . . . I feel like we should keep it under wraps if we're going to be seeing each other on a personal level." He waited to see how she'd respond.

"Are we going to be seeing each other on a personal level?"

"I'd like to."

"I'm not sure that there's anything in my contract that specifically states I can't date my local contact." She gazed up at him, a hint of hope in her eyes.

"I'm not sure I feel right about it."

"You don't think I can be impartial?"

"If you can be impartial after that"—he gestured between them—"then it obviously wasn't as good for you as it was for me."

Even in the dim light of the moon he could see a flush race over her cheeks. "I suppose we could agree not to see each other again. In a nonprofessional capacity, that is."

"I'd rather keep doing this," Jasper admitted. "If that's what you want."

She tugged her lower lip into her mouth. "It is."

He felt like jumping to his feet and executing a few fist pumps into the air. But he was naked. With the woman he'd been waiting for nestled in his arms. So, he settled for letting a wide grin spread over his lips as he bent down to kiss her again.

By the time they got half-dressed, kissed a bit more, finished their cups of wine, kissed some more, and finally settled in the cab of the truck, Buster hadn't returned. Jasper put his fingers to his mouth and let out a low whistle that usually had the dog racing to his side.

Several minutes passed and finally, Buster loped over the crest of the hill, his tongue lolling out of his mouth.

Jasper climbed out and moved his seat forward so the dog could get in the back. "What the hell did you get into out there?"

Buster hopped into the truck, his tail wagging, his entire head covered in burrs.

"He looks like he had a good time." Delilah swiped away a sloppy wet kiss Buster managed to surprise her with.

"He won't think that when he's getting a bath tomorrow." Jasper got back behind the wheel and started the truck.

"Hey." Delilah put her hand on his arm, her touch already so familiar.

"What?"

"When are you going to tell me what you wished for? You said you could prove that wishing on a shooting star worked. How will I know if your wish came true?"

He turned to face her, the taste of her still on his lips. "It already did."

thirteen

Delilah tiptoed into Abby's room and pulled the door closed behind her. She might have spent a magical evening with Jasper, but she wasn't quite ready to announce it to the whole wide world. By the time she'd changed into her pajamas and got settled on the trundle bed, she couldn't fall asleep. The night's events kept playing through her head like a loop stuck on repeat.

She'd been in Ido for just over forty-eight hours, but she already felt like she was part of the town. Even more disturbing, she felt like she was becoming part of the Taylor family, which might make it hard to stay impartial when it came time to make her recommendations to the contest committee. If Jasper resigned as the hospitality host, she might not feel so conflicted.

As she wrestled with herself, trying to get comfortable, her phone vibrated. Stella's picture lit up the screen. Why did her mother only call late at night? She dismissed the call, figuring her mother would call back in the morning. But then her phone vibrated again. Stella wasn't the kind of person to give up, not when she needed something. So, Delilah pulled the blanket around her shoulders and crept out of the room. By the time she made it downstairs and out onto the porch, her mother had hung up and called back twice.

"Hello?" Delilah answered as she pulled the front door closed behind her, then slipped into a rocker on the porch.

"Were you asleep?" Stella asked.

"Not yet. Is something wrong?"

"Walter and I broke up." Her mother sniffled. "I don't know what I'm going to do."

Delilah let out a sigh. The dramatic rise and fall of her mother's love life never seemed to end. "You're probably better off without him."

"He was my last chance at a happily-ever-after. I'll never find true love now, not at my age." When her mother got like this, it was better to stay quiet and offer emotional support than try to get her to face reality. Delilah had learned that lesson too many times to count.

"I'm sorry. He doesn't know what he's missing."

"I wish you were here. How am I supposed to get through this without you?" Stella had a history of relying on Delilah to help her through the series of breakups.

"I wish I was, too. But you'll manage. You're a beautiful, strong, brave woman."

"If I'm so beautiful, why did he leave me?" Stella moaned.

Delilah pulled the blanket tighter around her shoulders. "I'm sure it's him, not you."

"He said I was too demanding. Can you believe that? Me? Too demanding?"

It wouldn't do any good to tell the truth, not in a situation like this. "That's crazy. See? He doesn't deserve you."

"That's right. I feel so alone right now. Can you come home for a few days?"

"You know I can't do that. How would it look if I left now? When all of this is over, I'll be back."

The muffled sound of Stella blowing her nose came through the phone. "One more pageant, sweetheart? Can we do one more run for the big title?"

Delilah hated that her mother seemed to use her to make herself feel better. But it had been just the two of them for so long. What was she supposed to say? They'd talked about this more than once. The Miss Lovin' Texas pageant was supposed to be her last. She didn't want to be one of those pageant queens who didn't know when it was time to move on.

"Can we talk about it when I get home?" If she could put Stella off for a few weeks, it might buy her some time.

"But I'm feeling so low. It would give me something to look forward to if I knew we had another competition coming up."

"It's late. How about we pick this up again tomorrow? You need to get some rest and I've got a full schedule."

"I saw your post on social media. I can't believe they had you traipsing around grapevines in that gorgeous dress. And did you really go to a movie and sit in the dirt tonight?"

Part of Delilah's job was to keep her social media updated with pictures and posts of her experience with the contest. Of course Stella would be stalking her accounts. "It was fun. I learned a lot about wine this afternoon and the movie was . . ."

"What?" Stella asked.

Delilah tried to think of a way to sum up the feelings she had about sitting next to Jasper on a blanket as Humphrey Bogart and Ingrid Bergman fought against the love between them on the side of an antique barn. "It was nice."

"Hmpf." Stella's voice hardened. "When you get back home you won't have time to take part in ridiculous stunts like that." Delilah didn't want to open up a whole other can of worms by telling her mother how much she'd enjoyed her time so far in Ido.

"Did that cowboy with the deep voice take care of that little cricket that was bothering you?"

"It's a work in progress." Her mother would freak out if she knew Delilah had spent the night at Jasper's, or that she was currently staying at his family's home. And she'd lose her shit completely if she knew what had gone on in the back of Jasper's truck bed. "I need to get some sleep. I'll give you a call tomorrow. How does that sound?"

Stella sniffled. "It's been good hearing your voice. You get a good night's sleep. I'll try to find something on TV to distract myself."

Usually Delilah would offer to stay up and talk to her mother. Maybe even stay on the line while Stella fell asleep. But the events of the past few days had worn her out. "I'll talk to you tomorrow. Good night."

She pressed the button to end the call. The wind rustled the leaves high in the trees and she sat in silence, letting her conversation with her mother play back through her head. She was about to get up and go back inside when something moved in the darkness. The Taylor property was out in the country, but not so isolated that she worried about wild animals. Whatever it was came closer. She stood, ready to make a dash for the front door if necessary.

A bell jangled. She'd heard that sound, pretty recently too. Tie Dye, the colorful goat, meandered into the clearing. He didn't appear to feel out of place at all, even though it was well past midnight.

"What are you doing out here?" she whispered.

He came close enough to nibble on the edge of the blanket. Delilah didn't know much about goats, but Abby said Tie Dye was a crafty guy and sometimes worked his way out of the gate. She could call Jasper, but she didn't want to bother him. Maybe she could just return the goat to his pen without bothering any of the Taylors.

They'd been so kind to her, the least she could do was to take care of putting the goat back. But how would she get him to stay on the porch while she ran upstairs to throw on her jeans? She glanced back and forth from where she gripped Tie Dye's collar to the door. There wasn't anything nearby to secure him with. But there was a pair of tall cowboy boots sitting just outside the front door. She shoved a bare foot into one and then the other. Pulling the blanket tight over her shoulders, she led the goat off the porch and down the path she and Abby had walked earlier that day.

Tie Dye willingly followed as he continued to chew on the edge of the blanket. She didn't dare jerk it away. If she did, she wasn't sure he'd follow her. They got to the edge of his pen and he balked, raising up on his hind legs and pawing at the air. She held tight to his collar while she worked the latch of the gate. Holding it open with one foot, she tried to coax the goat into the pen.

"Come on, buddy. It's too late to be out gallivanting."

He settled, falling back on all fours and she pulled him through. The gate slammed shut, the two parts of the latch clanging together so loud she winced. Tie Dye reared back again but instead of catching air, one of his front hooves collided with her cheek.

Pain exploded across the right side of her face. Her hands went to her cheek as she raced to the fence line, away from Tie Dye's reach. The side of her face throbbed like the time she'd been struck below the eye by a flying stiletto during the Miss Potato Princess contest when she was fourteen. She'd ended up with a bruise on her cheek and had to withdraw from the competition. Based on how her cheekbone throbbed, she was afraid she might have suffered a fate far worse.

Hobbling toward the gate, she tossed a look back at Tie Dye. He stood chomping on the blanket that had fallen off her shoulders, unaware of the injury she'd just sustained. No wonder Jasper said he was a pain in the ass. She made sure to clasp the gate behind her. Her injury would be for nothing if he got loose again. Then she wrapped her arms around her middle and walked as fast as she could back to the big house. Why did she ever allow herself to think she might be able to make a wild place like this her home?

Jasper stopped the truck on the gravel drive. His older brother, Colin, sat on the edge of the porch. Squinting through the windshield, he tried to confirm what he saw was real and not a figment of a bad dream.

"I wondered how long it might take you to show up." Colin stood and shuffled his feet, drawing Jasper's attention to the custom-made boots their dad had given him on his last birthday they'd celebrated together. That had been three years ago. Had it really been that long since he'd set eyes on his older brother?

Jasper moved toward the porch with Buster right behind him. Where the hell had Colin come from? What was he doing creeping around when he'd promised to stay far away? "What do you want?"

Buster crouched down, letting out a low growl.

"Hey, buddy. It's okay." Jasper reached out to calm the dog.

"I'm in trouble, bro." Colin shook his head and winced. He held a rag to his arm. "I need some help."

"We had a deal. You aren't supposed to come around here again." Jasper shot a glance at the door. Thank goodness he'd locked it for a change.

"I'm telling you I need help," Colin said, repeating himself. "I didn't know where else to go."

"What's wrong with your arm?"

"I cut myself. Can you stitch me up real quick? Like you used to?" Hazel eyes, the same as Jasper's, stared at him from under the brim of Colin's hat.

"I haven't done that in years. If you need help, you should go to the hospital."

"You know I can't do that." Colin's jaw clenched as he tightened his grip on his arm.

Jasper looked for a truck or car. "How did you get here?"

"I had someone drop me off."

"Great. So not only did you come back after you swore to stay away, but now your asshole friends have been here, too?" Jasper thrust his hands through his hair. He had to get Colin out of there, and fast. Before Dad or one of his brothers came by. "Let's go inside. I'll put on a pot of coffee and we'll figure out a way to get you out of here before someone sees you."

"I don't want to stay away anymore. I'm ready to come home." Colin didn't move, but stayed as still as one of the beams holding up the porch.

The fact his brother had the balls to stand there after everything he'd put the family through made Jasper see nothing but red. "Get your ass in the house or I'll call the sheriff's department. I've got enough info on you to put you away for a good long time. Is that the way you want this to go down?"

"No. I need to figure out what to do."

"Don't say another word until you're sitting at my kitchen table." Jasper cast a glance around, not trusting his brother that he didn't have someone watching them from the woods. How had the best night of his life suddenly turned into the worst?

Colin shuffled his feet, eventually following Jasper through the front door. "Can you leave the dog outside?"

Buster had followed them in, continuing to growl.

"I've never seen him act like this." Jasper glanced back at his brother, then motioned for Buster to go out front. He grabbed a clean rag and tossed it at his brother, then threw a pot of coffee on to brew. By the time they finally sat down at the table, two fresh-brewed mugs of coffee between them, he gritted his teeth and gave his older brother a long, hard glare.

"Show me what you did to your arm and tell me what the hell you're doing back." He'd pulled the small sewing kit his mom had given him from a drawer. It had been a good long while since he or Colin had stitched each other up, not that either one of them had ever been very good at it.

Colin lowered his arm, revealing a deep gash on the underside of his forearm. "I didn't mean for things to go this way."

"How did you manage to cut yourself?" The edges of the wound were jagged, not like he'd sliced it clean with a knife.

"Doesn't matter. Can you put a couple of stitches in?"

"I can try but it's going to hurt like a bitch."

"Good. I deserve it." Colin dabbed at the cut and tipped his chin toward the cabinet where Jasper kept his whiskey. "Got a shot I can use to dull the pain a bit?"

Jasper grabbed a bottle along with a short tumbler.

Colin's hand shook as he downed the shot. He nodded and Jasper cleaned out the wound, less concerned about being gentle than he was about making sure he wiped away all of the blood.

"Shit." Colin made a fist with his other hand and bit down on his lip.

"Change your mind about going to the hospital?" Jasper asked.

"No. Keep going. I need help."

Jasper gave a slight shake of the head. "Tried that once. As you'll recall, it didn't go so well."

"It's the dog-fighting ring. At first all they wanted me to do was move some money for them. But it's gotten out of hand. Folks come in from all over. Big names, Jasper. I'm trying to get out, but I'm in too deep."

"Don't tell me you were stupid enough to go back to them after the last time I bailed you out of trouble."

"I tried to get a job somewhere else. Nobody wanted to hire a guy with a record. What was I supposed to do?"

"Uh, stay clean, keep your nose out of trouble—you could have started with that." Jasper squinted as he threaded the needle he'd soaked in whiskey. Why now? Why did Colin have to show up when they had so many things riding on getting Ido named the most romantic small town in Texas?

"I tried." He reached for his mug and took a gulp of coffee.

"What the hell do you want me to do?" Jasper knotted the thread. "Dad's struggling to hang on to the orchard. The whole town's trying to schmooze a beauty queen who's here to judge the Most Romantic Small Town in Texas contest. I've kind of got my hands full already without taking on your bullshit as well."

"I'm sorry. I should have been here for you." Colin scrubbed a hand over his face.

Jasper took in a breath through his nose. "Here comes the sting."

He pierced Colin's skin with the needle, taking his time to try to make the stitches as even as he could. As much as he wanted to help his brother, he'd been there done that so many times he could have written a sad country song about it. Colin never wanted to change his ways; he just wanted help getting himself out of whatever hot water he found himself in. As soon as the problem was solved, he'd make all kinds of promises he never intended to keep, then go back to his old ways.

When Jasper finished, he'd put twenty-two stitches in his brother's arm. He tied off the thread and cut it. "Not quite as good as new, but it will do."

"Thanks. And for what it's worth, it's going to be different this time." Colin glanced up. Something odd shone in his eyes. For the first time in a long while, Jasper found himself wanting to believe his brother.

"Hypothetically speaking, what the hell would you need me to do?" Jasper asked as he cleaned off the needle and tucked everything back into the case.

"I'm ready to talk to Bodie. Tell him everything I know so he can finally catch those sick bastards. They're planning something big at the end of the month. I'm not sure of the details yet, but I'm willing to find out." Colin's gaze didn't waver. Either he meant it, or he'd gotten a hell of a lot better at bullshitting people.

"You're telling me if I call Deputy Phillips and have him meet us somewhere, you're ready to spill the beans on the whole operation?"

"That's right."

"What about Mom and Dad?"

"What did you tell them before?"

"I told them we had a fight. That you said as long as I was here, you wouldn't set foot in the state of Texas again."

"And they believed you?" Colin asked.

"Unlike you, I haven't spent my whole life lying to them, so I guess they figured I meant what I said."

"I didn't mean for it to turn out this way." Colin's head hung low.

Jasper had no doubt his brother meant it, at least for the moment. But what would he do when Bodie showed up, ready to take a statement? "If you're serious about me calling Deputy Phillips, I'll do it."

Colin glanced up and ran a hand over his face. "Can we do it tomorrow? I haven't slept in two days. Let me catch some shut-eye, then we'll call him when I wake up?"

"Give me your boots."

"What?" Colin squinted at him.

"I can't take the risk that you're going to wake up and

bolt out of here." Jasper didn't know much about how his brother had been spending his time over the past few years. But if he knew anything about him, he knew there was no way Colin would leave his handmade, custom boots behind, no matter what kind of trouble he was in.

"You're an ass," Colin said, already pulling a boot from his foot. "Can I crash here for a bit?"

"Sure. But I don't want Mom or Dad to know you're back, not until you talk to Bodie and figure out what's going to happen."

"That's fair." Colin leaned over and set his boots next to Jasper's chair. "How's everyone been?"

"All right. Twister took out most of the orchard in August. We're trying to rebuild. Might focus on turning the barn into an event center while we replant." It was no use reminding his brother if he'd made different choices, he'd know how things were because he'd be part of making decisions.

"Dad's heart doing okay?"

"Yep. Mom's still forcing him to eat more greens and less red meat."

"I bet that's going over well."

For half a second, the brothers shared a laugh. Reminded Jasper of the good ol' days, when the two of them used to shoot the shit over a beer or two every now and then. But that was before . . . before Colin had torn the whole family apart.

"You can take the bedroom. I've got to get up early anyway." Jasper drained his coffee and set the cup in the sink. Then he reached down and picked up Colin's boots. "You don't mind if I keep these close, do you?"

"Suit yourself." Colin stood, a little unsteady on his feet. Looked like he couldn't keep his eyes open. "Thanks, bro."

Jasper took one last look at the older brother he used to idolize as Colin shuffled past him on the way to the bedroom. When they were younger, Jasper didn't just think

Colin hung the moon, he thought he'd hung all the stars in the sky as well. It was hard to watch someone he admired take a bad turn. But here they were. And it was up to Colin to figure out which direction he wanted to take from there.

That's what would matter.

fourteen

Jasper finished up his early morning chores around the barn and was eager to set eyes on Delilah. After Colin had crashed, Jasper had lain awake for hours, trying to convince himself the time they'd spent stargazing in the back of his truck hadn't just been a dream.

As he entered his mom's big country kitchen, he caught sight of Delilah sitting on a stool at the kitchen counter. She cupped her chin in her hand and had a cup of coffee sitting in front of her while she chatted with his mom.

"Good morning." He wanted to greet her with a hot-blooded kiss. But seeing as how he didn't know if she had any regrets in the bright light of day, he grabbed a mug of coffee and slid onto the stool next to her.

"If you say so." She turned to face him, and he realized she hadn't been resting her chin in her hands but had been holding a bag of frozen sweet peas to her cheek.

"What happened?" He swiveled to face her, his hands reaching for her face.

"I got in a fight with your goat."

"Tie Dye?" He'd never known the goat to be aggressive. He also had no idea when she would have found the time between when he dropped her off at the house and now to be in the goat's presence. "When did that happen?"

"Last night. My mother called and I stepped onto the porch, so I didn't disturb anyone. Tie Dye came up and I figured he got out of his pen, so I thought I'd be helpful and take him back." She pulled the peas away from her cheek. "He caught me with his foot when the gate clanged shut."

Jasper felt like someone had run him over with a combine. The shiner Delilah sported on her right eye rivaled several of the ones he'd earned from fistfights over the years. "Are you okay?"

She managed a shaky smile. "As long as you don't need any photo ops in the near future."

"I'm so sorry. Mom, isn't there something we can do? Do you have any rib eyes in the freezer?"

His mother shook her head as she prepped something to toss into the slow cooker for dinner. "Ice is the best thing."

"I'll be fine." Delilah put the peas back on her cheek. "I've never had an actual black eye before. I suppose it's like a rite of passage for some, isn't it?"

"With seven boys, it's more like a way of life." Mom slid a plate of toast in front of Delilah. "Here you go, sugar."

"Thank you." Delilah took a sip of coffee. "Please tell me we don't have any appearances today. I don't know if they'd take too well to me showing up with a black eye."

"I'll move some things around. You sure you're okay?" He wanted to do something, anything, to help. But she shook her head and took a bite of toast.

"This is fabulous, Mrs. Taylor. Did you make the jelly yourself?"

His mom's face shone with pride. "Homemade preserves. They won first place at the Fall Festival last year.

You're going to enjoy all of the festivities. Don't you think so, Jasper?"

"Yeah, you sure will." The Fall Festival. That reminded him, he needed to call Lacey and see what she thought about the ideas he'd talked about with his brothers. But first, maybe he could switch up Delilah's schedule and send her out to Zina's for the day.

"I can't wait," Delilah said.

"Do you mind if I step out and make a few calls?"

Delilah waved a hand, her mouth full of another bite of his mom's homemade preserves.

He slid his phone out of his back pocket and pulled up Zina's number. If Delilah went out to tour the dog rescue, it would give him some time to help his dad work on the orchard. Seemed like they'd never get all of the trees cleaned up from the storm.

When he returned to the kitchen, his mom had gone upstairs. "It's all set. Zina's expecting you after lunch."

"Great. I'm looking forward to seeing what kind of place she has out there."

He sat down next to her. "I'm really sorry about your eye."

"It's fine."

"I wish there was something I could do to make you feel better."

She tilted her head. "There might be one thing I can think of."

"What's that?" He took her hands.

"Maybe if you kissed it . . ."

He didn't need any more encouragement than that. After a quick glance around to make sure they wouldn't get caught, he pressed a gentle kiss to her cheek. "Is that better?"

"Mmm. Not quite yet."

"Let me try again." He kissed her lips next, a perfectly polite peck that quickly turned into more.

The front door opened, and they broke apart. "Jasper, are you coming?"

"Be there in a minute," he yelled. "That's Mitchell. They're waiting on me to come help in the orchard."

"You should go then." She nodded but the look in her eyes made him think she didn't mean it.

"Will you be okay until lunchtime?" He didn't want to leave her there, but he also didn't want her tramping around in the orchard with him and the guys.

"I'll be fine. I offered to help your mom with some stuff in the kitchen." She put her hands on his shoulders and gave him one more kiss. "I'm a big girl. You know I can take care of myself."

"Yeah. I get that. But I'd much rather you let me do it." He left before he gave in to temptation, already looking forward to the next time he'd see her.

Finally, as Jasper was about to take a break to satisfy the rumbling of his empty stomach, Dad called for a rest. Mom was headed down the path from the house to the orchard, her arms full of whatever she'd made for lunch. Buster raced ahead of her, his tail wagging, his head bounding above the long grass that framed the path on either side. Jasper reached down to pet him, causing Buster's tail to wag at a frenzied pace. Then he looked up, his gaze catching on Delilah.

She had her hair piled on top of her head and wore a curve-hugging T-shirt and a pair of jeans that could have been painted on. His stomach clenched, then rolled, then gave way to a warmth that radiated out from his core.

"We brought lunch." Mom held the big picnic basket in her hands.

His brothers abandoned their tasks, drawn by the smell of barbecued chicken and fresh-baked biscuits. Delilah held a bowl of salad. He walked over, hyperaware of the smile on her face, feeling pretty damn proud of himself for being the one who'd put it there.

"Hey." He sidled up next to her, not trusting himself not to touch her.

"Hey, yourself." She set the bowl down on a table his dad had set up. "Hungry for some lunch?"

"More like hungry for you," he mumbled close to her ear, low enough that only she could hear him.

"Looks like y'all made some good progress." Mom finished setting out the lunch spread.

"We sure did." Dad went to stand next to her. "I think we might finish up this week or next."

While his family filled their plates and talked about all of the things still left to do, Jasper grabbed Delilah's hand. "Come with me?"

She nodded, taking his hand and letting him lead her down the path and closer to the creek. He needed to get her alone, away from the prying eyes of his brothers. He needed to get a taste of her, pull her against him, and let her kiss away the worries he couldn't talk about yet.

Not even to her.

"You'd better get back up there and eat something if you want to keep your strength up for this afternoon." Delilah pressed another kiss against Jasper's lips. They'd been making out down by the creek for the past twenty minutes. Surely his dad would send one of his brothers to look for them if they didn't join the others soon.

"I don't need food. All I need is fresh air, sunshine, and you." He gave her another smile before capturing her mouth with his again.

She wasn't ready to admit it, but she felt the exact same way. Last night had been amazing. Something in her had shifted, like he'd connected with a part of herself she hadn't known about. With Jasper's encouragement, she felt like she could do anything, be everything she dreamed about. He made her a better person. And they'd only spent one night together. The best was yet to come.

"I don't think you'll be able to survive on only air, sunshine, and me." She smiled against his mouth.

It didn't stop him from continuing to kiss her, his lips landing on her cheek, her nose, her forehead. "You're such a downer."

"Me? I'm the downer?" She laughed as she pushed to her feet. "Come on, you've got work to do and I'm supposed to tour the dog rescue."

"You'll have a good time with Zina." He stood, then stepping in front of her, he lowered his nose to lightly tap against hers. "You want to have dinner together tonight?"

"Did you buy groceries? Can I cook at your place?"

He took a step back. "No, I haven't had a chance to do that yet. How about I take you out for those amazing cheese enchiladas instead?"

"Or"—she turned around and pulled his arms around her—"we can go to the store, then head back to your place. Dinner and dessert?"

"I don't think I'll be done in time tonight. But we can grab whatever you need from the store tomorrow. Sound good?" He pressed a kiss to the top of her head, then slid his arms away from her grasp. "We'd better get back before they come looking for us."

"Okay." She brushed off the bottom of her jeans, a little confused by his reaction. Last night he seemed like he'd been into her. Like totally into her. Had she misread the signals? Was she trying too hard? Things had been so easy between them. Maybe they'd been too easy. She followed him back to where the others had finished lunch and had already begun working again.

"There you are." Mrs. Taylor gestured toward the empty bowl of salad. "I don't know what you put in that salad, but

I'm going to need the recipe for the dressing. I've never seen my boys eat so many vegetables so quickly."

Delilah summoned a smile. "I'll be happy to jot it down for you when we get back to the house."

She helped Mrs. Taylor clear the dishes and repack the basket. Before she turned to head back, she scanned the area for Jasper. He must have moved to a different section of the orchard. Disappointed she wasn't going to get a chance to say good-bye, she filled her arms with dishes and set off for the house.

After she'd helped Mrs. Taylor clean up the kitchen, she grabbed the directions Jasper had drawn out for her and headed for the bright pink truck. She'd spent so much time with Jasper since she'd been in town. Getting out on her own for a bit would be good for her. At least that's what she told herself the whole way to For Pitties' Sake.

Zina must have heard her coming up the drive. Several dogs occupied the outdoor kennel runs and they greeted her as she climbed down from the truck.

"Hi, I'm glad you could make it this afternoon." Zina held her arms open. "What happened to your eye?"

"Just a late-night run-in with a crazy goat." Delilah gave her a hug, then stepped back to check out the building and surrounding area. A single-story house sat a few hundred yards away. But the shelter occupied its own building. Dozens of chain-link dog kennels protruded from the side of the building. "Thanks for the invitation. This is a great space."

"Thanks to Alex and his dad. Let me show you inside first. Maybe these dogs will quiet down a bit if we head inside." Zina opened the door and held it while Delilah stepped into the space. "It's not much, but it's everything we need, and at least it's not falling apart around me."

Delilah lifted her brows. "Does that happen a lot around here? Buildings falling down?"

"No." Zina let out a laugh. "But that's kind of how Alex and I met. He tried to check a leak on the roof of my old building and ended up falling through. The whole building was condemned, but it all worked out."

"How?"

"What's that?" Zina tilted her head.

"How did it work out after he had your building condemned?" Didn't sound like the start to a perfect relationship.

"Oh, well, it's a long story. We ended up having to move the dog rescue into the wedding warehouse for a bit. But then Alex was training penguins for that winter wonderland wedding, and—"

"Penguins? Real penguins?"

"That's right. Lacey will go to any and all lengths to make sure the brides who book their weddings in Ido get the wedding of their dreams." Zina rolled her eyes. "It can get to be a bit much. I'm assuming you've heard about the upcoming butterfly wedding?"

Delilah smiled. "Yes, Lacey mentioned it's coming up soon."

"She's good at what she does though, and she's single-handedly saving the town." Zina clucked her tongue. "Don't tell her what I said. She told me to be nice today."

"The two of you seem like you're pretty close." Delilah wondered what it would be like to have a close female friend. The closest thing she had was Stella, who didn't really count. Monique had been a good friend, although she was more of a mentor. Not the kind of friend Delilah would call if she wanted to whine about her love life.

"We've been friends since junior high. No matter how crazy things get around here, I've got her back and she's got mine." Zina pointed to a door. "You want to tour the offices before we go back to meet the dogs?"

"That would be great."

"We've got a training session going on, but we can peek in on them." Zina led the way and Delilah followed. "Since we moved the rescue out here, we've been able to add some additional services. Alex's grandpa's been volunteering with a program that works with veterans to pair them with service dogs."

"That's fabulous." Delilah peered through the window into a large area with a concrete floor. A half dozen dogs worked one-on-one with their handlers.

"It really is. It's a win-win. So many of our dogs are abandoned or surrendered. We've found a lot of our service members feel the same way. Seeing them build a bond with each other is an amazing thing." Zina motioned for Delilah to move on. "We've even done some work with kids from the community."

"Oh? What kind of work?" Delilah was always looking for ideas on how to further her platform.

Zina peeked through the window of the door to their right. "Good. One of our trainers is here. I'll introduce you."

Delilah followed her into a medium-sized room where a man sat at a desk, his pen flying over the page in front of him.

"Hey, Zeb, got a sec?" A dog lying at the man's feet lifted his head.

Zeb turned around in his chair. "What's up?"

"This is Delilah. She's the current Miss Lovin' Texas and I'm showing her around the rescue. I told her about the program we're working on that pairs youth with the dogs."

Zeb nodded. "It's been working well so far. The kids get a chance to work with the animals and the dogs get the opportunity to socialize and learn some good behaviors. Some of these kids feel so out of control. It's cool to watch them learn how to control their own emotions."

"What happens to the dogs? Do the kids get to adopt them?" Delilah asked.

"If possible. But their home environment doesn't always

allow that. Some of these kids live in apartments or mobile homes that don't allow pittie mixes." Zeb glanced toward Zina. "But my sister's working on trying to change some of that."

"You're siblings." Delilah felt so stupid for not noticing that sooner. The high cheekbones were the same, and so were the brown eyes.

Zeb grinned. "I don't like to advertise it."

"I'm not that bad, am I?" Zina gave her brother a playful punch to the shoulder.

"Nah." He leaned down and patted his thigh. The dog who'd been lying at his feet got up then sat down next to him. "This is Semper. He's the reason we started the program."

"Can I pet him?" Delilah asked.

Zeb nodded.

She reached her hand out to the dog. Semper sniffed, then glanced up at Zeb, who nodded at him. The dog nudged his head under her hand.

"He likes you," Zeb said.

"Want to meet some of the other dogs?" Zina asked.

Delilah nodded. "It was nice to meet you, Zeb."

"Nice to meet you, too." He called Semper back to his side.

Zina led her back to the main room, then through a door to the back of the building. "Zeb and Semper are proof that the programs we're putting in place work."

"Was he in the military?"

"We both were. He came home with debilitating PTSD. I feel like Semper is the only reason I have my brother back."

"Do you think the same kind of training you're doing with the teenage boys would work to empower girls?" Delilah's head spun with ideas. Maybe that would be a way to work directly with the girls she wanted to help.

"Absolutely. I mean, it depends on your goals. But we've

seen incredible progress with some of the kids we've been working with. Zeb takes a van full of dogs into the city twice a week and runs classes at a local park. Some of these kids have been through hell and back. Working with the dogs teaches them how to build empathy and gain confidence. A dog won't respond to a handler who's out of control. I've seen kids start with nothing and end up working their way through school, getting jobs, and turning their backs on the bad influences that landed them in trouble in the first place."

"I'm working with my mentor on putting some programming together to empower young girls. I don't know if there's a place for training dogs somewhere in there, but I figured it wouldn't hurt to ask."

"Are you working locally? I'm sure we could partner on an initiative."

"I'm not sure." Delilah's current plans involved moving back to Dallas at the conclusion of her term as Miss Lovin' Texas. That was about as far from local as she could get. But Zina's testimony had given her plenty to think about.

"Have you ever had a dog?" Zina asked.

"No. I never had a chance. We moved around so much as I was growing up."

"That's too bad." Zina leaned down and opened the kennel of a shy light brown dog. "This here is Chantilly. She was surrendered a few weeks ago when her owners found out she was pregnant."

"When is she due?" Delilah ran a hand over the dog's head, pausing to scratch behind her ears.

"Another six to eight weeks. We've had a lot of puppies born at the rescue." Zina shook her head. "It's a damn shame what some of these poor creatures go through."

Delilah spent the rest of the afternoon helping out around the shelter. She fed the dogs, worked with a few of the newer rescues on how to walk on a leash, and spent plenty of time being smothered in warm, wet doggie kisses. By the time she checked her phone, it was almost dinnertime.

"You want to stay for dinner?" Zina asked.

"Thanks, but I've got plans." At least she thought she did. She wasn't sure where she and Jasper had left things. Last night had been magical, but he'd been a little distant that morning and disappeared before she could say goodbye after lunch. For a moment she wondered if he'd changed his mind about getting involved. But that was silly. She didn't have any reason to doubt him.

"If you want to come back and visit, you're welcome anytime." Zina walked her to the parking lot, where Delilah's obnoxious pink truck sat in the shade.

"Thank you so much. I may take you up on that if I can come up with a way to work the dog training into the program I'm putting together."

"Like I said, I'm happy to help." Zina pulled her in for a hug. "Any friend of Lacey's is a friend of mine."

Delilah waved through the windshield as she drove away. Friends. She could easily be friends with a woman like Zina. Lacey, too.

For the first time in a long time she let herself imagine what it would be like to settle down somewhere. Somewhere she could be herself and stop worrying about putting on a front or keeping up appearances. Moving back to Dallas and working side by side with Stella every day wouldn't provide that kind of environment. Could she find that somewhere else? Somewhere like Ido?

As she pondered her future, her phone lit up. Jasper. "Hello?"

"Hey, sorry about earlier. If you're up for grabbing a bite, I'd love to take you out."

"I'd like that."

He told her he'd pick her up at her camper in forty-five

minutes and she disconnected. They'd be far enough from Ido tonight that she wouldn't have to wear her sash. She and Jasper could be two people out on a date.

Just a guy and a girl who might kind of like each other sharing a meal.

fifteen

Jasper scrubbed a towel over his hair as he stepped out of the shower. Looked like Colin had gotten up earlier, raided the fridge, and was now passed out again in his bed. He and his brother were going to have to have a heart-to-heart soon. But right now, Colin needed sleep more than anything. He looked like shit. Shit that had been run over a few times. Besides, he wasn't going anywhere without his boots, and Jasper didn't want to let his brother's unwelcome arrival get between what had started up with him and Delilah.

By the time he'd tiptoed into the bedroom and pulled on some clean clothes, Colin stirred.

"Hey." Colin swung his legs over the side of the bed. "Where are you off to looking so spruced up?"

"Dinner."

Colin ran a hand over his belly. "I'm starving. Want to pick me up something while you're there?"

Jasper shoved an arm through his sleeve. "Not really. Are you ready to talk to Bodie?"

Colin let his head drop. "I changed my mind. Just give me my boots back, and I'll be on my way."

"That's how you want to play it?" Jasper asked. "You show up here, a gash in your arm, and now that you're fixed up, you want to pretend like everything's fine again?"

"Look"—Colin stood and stretched his arms over his head—"I was in a jam. You helped me out, and now I'll be on my way."

"I'm not going to continue to protect you."

"Is that what you call it?" Colin smirked. "No offense, little bro, but not even you can protect me from the bogeymen I'm involved with now."

"It doesn't have to be this way, you know. I can help."

"Help what? I'm not going back to jail. I can't." His gaze changed. Something dark passed through. Colin stepped into the jeans he'd shed when he crawled into Jasper's bed the night before. "I'd rather die than go back to prison."

"What if it didn't come to that? Let me talk to Bodie. We'll figure something out." Jasper hadn't planned on seeing his brother again. But now that he was here, how could he turn him away without trying to help?

He thought he was helping by taking the blame for Colin's absence. He'd rather have his parents think that he and Colin had a falling-out than break his mom's heart by telling her he'd gone to jail. He thought he was protecting everyone. But now he knew he couldn't spend his life trying to fix everything for everyone. It was impossible. And sooner or later, the lies he told, even if he'd told them with good intentions, were going to catch up to him.

"I don't think Bodie's going to want to hear what I have to say. At least not enough to keep me from going back to jail." Colin cocked his head. "Any chance I can bum a clean shirt off of you?"

"Yeah, take what you want." It was clear Colin wasn't going to accept his help. Maybe he could appeal to his buried sense of family. "Hey, did you hear Lucas has a kid now?"

Colin picked a shirt from the drawer and tugged it on over his head. "No shit?"

"Maggie. She's almost three. Mom's planning a birthday party for her next month. If you stick around—"

"Cut it out. You know I can't do that. Just give me my boots and I'll be gone before you get back from dinner with that hot beauty queen you've been banging."

"What the hell are you talking about?" Jasper gripped the doorframe.

"You talk in your sleep." Colin looked around the floor, probably trying to locate his boots.

"Wait until I get back from dinner. We can talk."

"I don't need to talk, I need to get out of here."

"That's not what you said last night. Not when you showed up with your arm messed up, and—"

"Forget it. I was messed up last night. Didn't know what the hell I was saying."

"You sure about that? Because you said something about there being a big event coming up. Whatever you and the scum you're hanging out with have going on, it better not interfere with Lacey's plans."

"I'm outta here." Colin gave up looking for his boots and headed for the front door.

Jasper took in a deep breath, his heart pounding in his chest like a jackhammer that had spun out of control. He waited a few moments, figuring he and Colin could use a minute or two to calm down.

After he'd taken a few deep breaths, he walked out the front door just in time to see Colin pull the passenger side door of a giant black truck closed. The tires spun on the gravel and the truck fishtailed down the drive.

Jasper slapped his palm on his thigh. "Dammit."

His brother was gone, and it was all his fault . . . again.

Not even the promise of Delilah waiting for him to pick her up for dinner could put a smile on his face. Why did he have to be so good at ruining everything?

Ten minutes later he tried to paste on a grin as Delilah got settled in the front seat of his truck. She was full of smiles and smelled like she'd been soaking in strawberry lemonade all day. Hoping her good mood would rub off on him, he got behind the wheel and started toward the restaurant.

As he drove past fields that had just been harvested, she filled him in about her visit with Zina. Her eyes sparkled with excitement over some new idea she'd come up with. Seemed she and Zina had spent a lot of time talking about the programs they'd put in place at For Pitties' Sake. Delilah wondered if the girls she wanted to work with might benefit from the same types of options.

"After talking to Zina and Zeb, it hit me. Maybe pairing the girls I'd love to support with rescue dogs would help them build up confidence."

"Yeah, that sounds good." Jasper drummed his thumb against the steering wheel, his mind half-engaged with listening to Delilah and half wondering where Colin might have gone.

"You okay?" Her fingers brushed his arm.

He caught her hand in his and let them rest on his thigh. "Sorry. I'm a bit distracted."

"I can tell. What's going on? Is something on your mind?"

"It's nothing." He tried to placate her with a smile.

She didn't smile back. "You've been off today."

"Just some family stuff. I had a rough talk with one of my brothers. He's in a bit of a bind and I'm not sure what's going to happen." He didn't want to drag Delilah into the mess with his brother. Even though they'd taken things to a whole new level, he still had to be careful about oversharing. She needed to view the town in the best light possible if Ido had any chance at all of being named the most romantic small town in Texas.

"You know, it's never too late to do the right thing." She lifted a shoulder. "Not sure if that helps, but it's one of the principles I try to live by."

"Thanks. I'll pass that along." He lifted their hands to his lips and kissed the back of her hand. "There's just been a lot on my mind. Work on the orchard is going well though."

"That's good. Your mom said you've got a lot to do still. I figured I could be in charge of my own schedule over the next few days to give you a chance to get caught up."

He let their hands rest on his thigh. "I don't mind driving you to events."

"I know. But with everything you've got going on, it might be easier. Plus, the sooner you get the orchard cleaned up, the more time we'll have to spend together, isn't that right?"

She looked so happy at the idea, he didn't want to ruin it. But somehow the thought of spending the next few days without her put an even bigger damper on his mood. "If that's what you want to do."

"Good. Now that's settled, give me the scoop on the assisted living facility on the outskirts of town. Lacey has me scheduled to be the hostess at their fall dance this week." She reached out and adjusted the vent. "I think it's great they're still encouraging romance, but how romantic can it be if they're cramming it in between lunch and the afternoon nap hour?"

Jasper had skimmed the big binder Lacey gave him. She had Delilah booked with events at places he'd never even heard of, and he'd been a lifelong resident of Ido. "Tell me where else she has you going."

"Well, there's the Sweetest Day bake and take. Jojo is going to be teaching a cupcake-baking class and I'm her assistant. We'll be making cupcakes and candy for people to take home to their sweethearts."

"Mmm. I could get on board with that." Jasper licked his lips. "I still owe you that chocolate bourbon pecan pie cupcake. I should be able to drop some pecans off at Helmut's this week, so I'll ask him to make up a batch."

Listening to Delilah go on and on about all of the romantic things she'd be doing during her time in town made him wish the two of them didn't have to downplay their attraction. He'd love nothing more than to be able to take her out to dinner somewhere in town, not sneak off to the Mexican restaurant two towns over so they wouldn't be recognized.

"Here we are." He turned in to the parking lot. At least tonight they'd be able to hold hands and not have to pretend he was nothing more than her driver.

"Hey, isn't that Helmut's bike?" Delilah pointed out the window.

A line of Harleys sat in front of the restaurant. Either Helmut was dining in tonight or someone had stolen his motorcycle. He was the only person Jasper knew who drove around with a sidecar. So much for having a night away from prying eyes.

"Well, we might not be able to treat this like a date, but at least they have amazing enchiladas." He rubbed his thumb over the back of her hand.

Delilah gave him a wistful smile as he got out of the truck and went around to open her door. "Maybe one of these days we'll be able to go out to dinner without it being a show."

"Maybe if I quit as your hospitality host, that day would come a whole lot sooner." Jasper held the door as she brushed past him and entered the restaurant. With so little time together, he needed to decide. What was more important . . . making sure she saw the most romantic side of Ido, or having the freedom to make sure she saw the most romantic side of him?

Delilah spent the next week and a half calling bingo numbers at the ladies' luncheon, decorating the sidewalks around the town square by drawing hearts with the local day care kids, and leading a small group of Abby's classmates in some basic pageant-training classes.

She'd been having an absolute blast, except for having to save the kid who'd shoved a piece of chalk up his nose. They'd managed to avoid a trip to the emergency room thanks to the set of tweezers in various sizes and shapes that she carried in her emergency kit.

While Jasper spent his days working on the orchard with his brothers, she'd been given the royal treatment by the town. Kirby even took her on a tour in his custom limo.

She was blown away by the hospitality the townspeople had shown her, but there was one man she didn't seem to get enough of . . . Jasper. If absence made the heart grow fonder, she felt like she could have been head over heels for the hazel-eyed cowboy by now.

The last time they'd been together she hoped they would have a chance to see what it would be like to be on a real date. But that dream had been dashed to bits when she realized they'd never be able to get far enough away from Ido to completely avoid the residents.

Delilah had started to wonder if she'd imagined the attraction between them. Maybe she and Jasper were destined to just be friends. But then she remembered the way it felt to have his lips on hers, to feel him moving inside her. Which is why she decided to take matters into her own hands and surprise him with a homemade dinner.

She'd gone to the farmers' market his mom had mentioned and picked up some fall vegetables. He never seemed to lock his front door so she let herself in and got to work in the kitchen.

"Hey, Buster." The dog didn't even bark when she entered. He probably remembered that the last time she was there she'd fed him bits of pancake straight from the griddle.

As she chopped peppers and peeled carrots, feeling more and more comfortable in Jasper's house, making herself right at home in his kitchen, she let herself imagine what it might be like if they ended up together.

A lightness filled her chest, and she danced around the kitchen as she searched for a can opener for the beans she wanted to add to her vegetarian chili. Finally, with it simmering on the stove, the smell of cumin and chili powder lingering in the air, she sat down at the kitchen table.

"You know what would really surprise Jasper?"

Buster laid his head on her lap and she scratched behind his ear.

"I wonder if he still has that bag of my lingerie somewhere." The dog tilted his head to the side and swiped his tongue across her hand.

"Let's go check." She got up, wondering where exactly she'd left the plastic bag of underwear Jasper had accidentally grabbed the first night they spent together. He'd been so embarrassed that the tips of his ears had turned pink.

Wanting to make the night extra, extra, extra special, she located a pair of pink lacy panties and one of her matching flimsy nighties. When Jasper came home, she'd be waiting with dinner and dessert.

As she secured the ties on her hips into tiny pink bows, her phone rang. Maybe Jasper was calling to tell her he was on his way home and wanted to see her tonight.

"Hi there," she answered, not even trying to contain her giddiness knowing she'd be seeing him soon.

"Hey, how's your day been going?" Hearing his voice sent goose bumps racing down her arms.

"Good. But it's better now that I'm talking to you. Are you still working out in the orchard?"

"Actually, I'm headed home now."

Heat simmered in her belly. "Oh? Do you have plans tonight or are we going to get to spend some time together?"

"That depends." His voice dropped, so low she had to strain to hear him. "There's nothing I'd like better than to have you to myself."

"Mmm. That would be nice." She stood up and thrust out her chest.

"But . . ."

But? She hadn't counted on a but.

"I forgot it's my turn to host poker night. Some of the guys are coming over and if you want to join us, you're more than welcome to. I'd beg off but Bodie called and said he was already on his way over."

The door creaked. Delilah turned toward the noise as Buster trotted over to investigate.

"Delilah?" Jasper asked.

At the same time a male voice called out from the door. "Jasper? You home?"

"What was that?" Jasper asked.

Delilah glanced toward the pot bubbling on the stove. She reached out and flipped the dial to simmer.

"Delilah? Where are you?" Jasper asked again.

Footsteps sounded on the wooden floorboards by the door. They were coming closer. Any second whoever it was would enter the kitchen and find her standing by the stove in a pink baby doll nightie and a matching pair of panties.

So she did the only rational thing she could when faced with an impossible situation. She turned toward the door leading from the kitchen to the backyard, and fled.

sixteen

Jasper dialed Lacey's number as he paced along his parents' front porch. He'd had it. After being thwarted multiple times over the past two weeks in his attempts to spend some private time with Delilah, he was ready to resign as hospitality host.

He'd been biding his time, assuming he'd figure out how to balance his duty to the town with his attraction to the contest judge, but when he came across Delilah the other night, sprinting back to her trailer in see-through lingerie, he'd lost it. Something had to change.

By the time he got past Lacey's assistant, he'd almost worn a path in the floorboards from the tense pacing. He didn't want to quit on her, but he also didn't want to give up seeing Delilah. It had become obvious he couldn't do both.

"Lacey Cherish speaking."

"Mayor Cherish, it's Jasper Taylor."

"Hi, Jasper. How's our resident contest judge on this fine Monday morning? I heard you took her to the movie at the

Hampton barn last weekend. Nice touch. I remember going out there with Bodie a few times before baby P was born."

"Yeah, about the contest."

"Don't tell me you ran her off. I've got enough going on today, I can't take any more bad news."

He tried to spill it out, just dump a whole breath full of words about how he couldn't be her hospitality host anymore. But instead, he asked, "What's wrong?"

"I'm in a heap of trouble and I need help."

"What now?"

"I swear someone's out to get us. The butterfly wedding is this weekend."

"That's right." Hopefully Delilah's black eye would be gone by then or at least faded enough that she could hide it with makeup.

Lacey let out a groan. "We don't have butterflies. Someone let them all loose last night. That bride is going to show up and all we're going to have to release is a few giant moths. I need help."

Jasper ran a hand through his hair. "What happened? I thought you had them tucked away in a tent in the warehouse or something."

"I did. But someone snuck in and unzipped it. There are a few in the warehouse but most of them have flown away. They're probably halfway to Mexico by now. Are your brothers around?"

Jasper clenched his jaw. He didn't know what a cutthroat business weddings could be before he took on the role of hospitality host. "A few of them. What can we do to help?"

"I don't want to alert the bride yet, not if we can figure out a way to replace the butterflies that were set loose. Do you think you and your brothers might be able to rustle some up for me?"

His heart stopped. For a long moment, he waited for it to start up again. Finally, he thumped the middle of his chest. "You want us to do what?"

"I've got some nets I picked up from Coop down at the feed store. I need as many people as possible to catch butterflies. I don't care what kind. Just as many as you can. Bring them to the warehouse."

"You got it. I'll call Suzy and see if she can get her club to pitch in as well."

"Thanks. You're a lifesaver."

"We'll do what we can."

"I've got a few more calls to make. I'll be at the warehouse after four this afternoon if you want to bring me whatever you can find."

"See you then." Jasper stood there for a second, letting her crazy request sink in. Butterflies. What was his world coming to?

He wandered back into the kitchen. His mom had finished making breakfast and his dad sat at the head of the table, about to dig into his scrambled eggs.

"Hey, Mayor Cherish just called. She's got a favor to ask if any of you have some time today." Jasper's stomach growled at the smell of a homemade breakfast. He'd been working for a few hours already and had burned through the protein bar and cup of coffee he'd fixed himself when he woke up. But no time for that now, not with a mission from the mayor.

"What's up?" Lucas diced up a banana and slid it onto the tray of Maggie's high chair.

"Lacey's got that butterfly wedding this weekend and someone let all the butterflies loose." Jasper reached for his mug of coffee that had cooled on the counter.

"You sure you want to get wrapped up in that?" Dad held a piece of bacon in his hands. "Butterflies? That's asinine."

"She's hoping we can catch enough to replace the ones that got away." Jasper let his gaze linger on Trent, Mitchell, and Lucas. Davis was probably still in bed, and Abby had already left for choir practice, then school.

"I can't help, I've got to open the store," Trent said.

Lucas shook his head. "My shift starts at nine and Mom's watching Mags."

Jasper took in a slow breath through his nose as he eyed Mitchell.

"Dad needs me to take a look at some equipment if we want to be able to harvest the pecans we've got left." Mitchell lifted a shoulder. "Sorry."

"I'll help." Delilah peered up at him, her eyes shining bright, the bruise on her cheek faded to a lighter shade of purple.

"Are you sure you're up for it?" He winced as his gaze drifted over her.

"Of course. I don't have anything going on today. What else am I going to do?"

With a sinking feeling in his gut, he wrapped a hand around his coffee and lifted it to his lips. "All right then. Let's go hunt some butterflies."

Three hours later Jasper slipped another huge monarch butterfly into the netted hamper his mother had given him. They'd been hunting butterflies all morning and had collected only a fraction of the number Lacey started with.

"How many does that make?" he asked Delilah. She was in charge of keeping the hamper closed so they didn't lose any.

"Around thirty maybe?" Delilah guessed. "I lost count when Buster knocked the hamper over and we had to recapture some of the ones that got away."

"That's it?"

Delilah had on a bright yellow sweater. She looked like a sunflower standing against the backdrop of some fields that had been left to compost. The butterflies seemed to flock to her, probably drawn in by the color of her sweater.

"Hold still." Jasper gently plucked a few more butterflies

from her sleeve and slipped them into the hamper. "At this rate we won't have enough to make much of an impact."

"What are butterflies attracted to?" Delilah asked.

"I don't know. I've never tried to find them on purpose before."

She pulled out her phone and typed on the screen. "Looks like they love milkweed. Is there any of that growing around here?"

"Hey, Aunt Suzy," Jasper called to his aunt, who'd joined them with a few of her biker friends. "Isn't there some nursery around here that specializes in local plants?"

"There sure is." Suzy nodded. "That place out east of town. I think it's called Milkweed Gardens, or something like that."

"Perfect. Delilah, why don't you and I head over and see if it's worth pursuing. Suzy and Helmut, you stay here and if we think you need to come over, I'll give you call." Delilah had already started to move toward his truck when Jasper caught up. "Thanks for pitching in with this."

"Of course. What else was I going to do today? Sit around while the rest of you went on a mad dash to try to collect butterflies? Besides, this is fun. It's not every day I get to learn how to track down monarchs."

"But your eye." Finally, far enough away for the others to notice, Jasper cupped her cheek with his palm.

"It's fine. Don't worry about me. Right now I'm only thinking about butterflies."

He nodded. "Hopefully we'll find enough to make it work. I hate to think about that poor bride."

"You put on quite a front, don't you?"

He turned to find her studying him. "What do you mean by that?"

"Nothing, really. I'm just surprised that a guy like you cares so much about how a stranger might feel." She tucked a leg underneath her while a teasing smile played across her lips.

Jasper shifted his gaze to the road ahead. "I don't want Lacey to have to deal with the fallout."

"Right."

"What? Is it that strange that a guy would be concerned about a friend?"

"Nope. Not strange at all."

He glanced over and caught her biting back a grin. "Are you saying men shouldn't think about other people's feelings?"

"Not at all." She faced him, her green eyes shining. "I'm saying it's refreshing to see someone who's not afraid to show he cares."

Jasper blew out a breath. "Great. Now you're making me out to sound like a softhearted wuss."

Her fingers brushed his arm. "That's not what I meant at all. I think it's nice that you care so much. Not everyone has the ability to put themselves in someone else's place and consider how they feel. That's all."

He wasn't sure if he should take her observation as a compliment. "How about we focus more on finding butterflies and less on my emotional intelligence?"

Her grin spread wider. "Sounds like a plan."

Ten minutes later he'd pulled up in front of the milkweed farm. It was a mom-and-pop operation well outside town limits. They focused on cultivating native plants and operated an organic produce market.

Jasper entered the small building, Delilah right behind him. He explained the situation to the owners, and they directed him to a spot along a stretch of a narrow creek where the milkweed flourished. Hundreds of butterflies flitted from one plant to the next. Jasper gathered the nets from the back of the truck and handed one to Delilah.

"Have you ever seen anything like this?"

The look on her face told him she hadn't. Her good eye sparkled as a butterfly landed on her shoulder. "It's beautiful."

Another one came to rest on her nose. Her eyes crossed. He snapped a quick picture with his phone.

"Don't you dare share that with anyone." She tried to look stern but with a butterfly on her head, one on her nose, and several more dotting her shirt, he couldn't take her seriously.

"Pinkie promise." He held out his hand and she looped her pinkie finger around his.

"You've got one on your head." Her gaze rested above his face. "I think we need a selfie of this. No one's going to believe it." She pressed against him, turning her bruised cheek to his chest, and snapped a pic as they both smiled into the camera.

"Let's get to work." He gently ushered butterfly after butterfly into the net, then transferred them into another one of the hampers his mom had provided.

Delilah helped, the smile on her face not faltering once. "Look, there are a bunch of them over here."

Jasper glanced over just in time to see her foot slip on a rock near the creek. "Careful!"

She went down, her ass landing in a deep patch of mud. Her mouth opened in surprise, but nothing came out.

"Are you okay?" He rushed over and held out a hand.

Delilah rubbed at her backside. "That hurt. I think I'm going to have a bruise on my backside for life from that."

"You need some ice?" He should have warned her earlier. It could be slick by the water. Now she was injured—again—and this time there was no doubt it was all his fault. "I'm sorry. I should have warned you."

"Warned me about what? That mud can be slippery?" She reached out so he could help her up. "I'm a grown-ass woman. I ought to know better."

He pulled her to her feet, and she tried to steady herself by grabbing a fistful of his shirt.

"Oh no. I'm sorry. Now I've gone and got you all muddy,

too." She stared at the center of his chest where she'd gripped the fabric, leaving a crinkled, muddy spot.

"I'll survive. You sure you're okay?" He held her upper arm, trying to make sure she didn't slip again. "You've got some mud on your cheek."

She swiped a hand across her nose, running it over her cheek. "Better?"

"You actually made it worse." He let go of her arm to wipe the mud away. As he did, she took a step forward.

She went down again, grabbing his arm as she did. Before he had a chance to gain his footing, they both landed. Him on his back, her splayed over his chest, her breasts pressing against him.

She gasped like she'd had the wind knocked out of her. "You okay?"

Like a crab, he scuttled backward, trying to get to a position where he could make sure she wasn't hurt. She rolled over onto her back, her face smeared with mud. A deep laugh rumbled through her chest.

"You should see your face." She pushed herself to a seated position and wiped a palm across his cheek. "Oh no, I made it worse."

Seeing her there, her hair matted with mud, one eye bright with humor, her cheeks flushed underneath the dirt, did something to his insides. It was like the image of perfection she presented to the world had melted away, leaving the real Delilah exposed, for his eyes only.

His arm looped around her shoulders and he lowered his face toward hers. The desire to kiss her consumed him. He fought it, knowing it could make things harder. But the heat inside him turned all of his reservations to ash.

Her smile faded as she realized his intent. A conversation seemed to flow between them even though neither one of them said a word. He lifted a brow. She gave a slight nod. He touched his lips to hers.

Everything faded away, leaving the two of them in a vacuum that seemed to transcend time and space. He stopped trying to fight it and leaned in.

Delilah couldn't believe the storm of emotions swirling around inside her. They were covered in mud. Her hip ached like she'd fallen flat on her ass on a rock the size of Texas. Her cheek still smarted from her run-in with the goat. But butterflies danced around them as Jasper claimed her mouth with his, over and over again.

She didn't want to stop. She couldn't. It was like she'd shrivel up and die if they broke the connection. Her body ached for him, like his kiss could make her whole.

Gasping, she pulled back, just enough to fill her lungs with air. "Wow."

He touched his forehead to hers, his chest heaving just as hard as her own. "I second that. Wow."

They stayed like that for a long beat, foreheads pressed together, their breaths slowing in unison.

"I'm sorry, Delilah. I didn't mean to take advantage."

She put her palms on his chest and gave a slight push. "Take advantage? Is that what you think you're doing here?"

He shook his head. "We haven't had a chance to talk about the other night yet. I don't know how to explain what I'm feeling."

"Then don't."

His eyes crinkled at the edges and a furrow bisected his brow. "Don't?"

"No. Don't try to explain it. Let it be. Just let yourself feel it." Her palm caressed his cheek. She didn't know how to explain her feelings, either. They'd snuck up on her, slowly taken over, and left her reeling. She hadn't planned on falling for Jasper Taylor. They barely knew each other.

But something in her recognized something in him, and she was drawn to the man.

No, *drawn* wasn't a strong enough word. *Drawn* gave the impression she could choose whether or not to give in. But there was no choice happening. Deep in her core, she knew they were meant to be together. The only thing she didn't have a clue about was how long it was going to last.

He got up then helped her to her feet, leading her away from the muddy bank of the creek. "If your manager could see you now . . ."

She didn't even try to stop the smile from spreading across her mouth. "She'd die. Literally have a heart attack right here."

"I'm not done talking about what's happening with us." His jaw set. He had a serious side to him. That was one of his many attractive attributes. He wasn't the kind of man who just wanted to get into her pants. She knew the type. They looked at her as a conquest. Like nailing a beauty queen was something they could cross off their bucket list and spend the rest of their lives bragging about to their friends. Sometimes she could spot a man like that from a mile away. Other times they were more difficult to weed out. But something always gave them away.

Jasper was different. She could tell he was just as apprehensive about their growing connection as she was. He wouldn't be the type to string her along and fake it just long enough to get her in his bed. He was the real deal. That might be what scared her the most.

"What time do we need to get these butterflies to the wedding site?"

He glanced at his phone, which had surprisingly survived the fall and the mud. "Damn. We've only got another hour."

"Let's do it." She picked up the net from where it had fallen on the ground.

"I've got to get a picture of you first. Do you mind?"

She laughed. "May as well. As long as you get my good side and can promise me it won't make its way to social media."

"You've got my word on that." He held up his phone and snapped a pic of the two of them beaming at the camera. "Do you want to get cleaned up? I can run you back to the house, then come back with some of the guys, and—"

"You think I'm going to melt under all of this dirt?" She gathered her hair in one hand, then pulled an elastic out of her pocket. "In case you haven't figured it out just yet, I'm tougher than I look."

His mouth quirked into a lopsided smile. "You look pretty damn tough right now."

"Ido is definitely putting me through the ringer. But I can handle it."

"All right then. Let's catch some butterflies."

For the next forty-five minutes they did just that. By the time Jasper pulled into the parking lot at the wedding venue, they had hundreds, if not a thousand, colorful butterflies in their possession.

"You want to wait in the truck while I drop these off?" he asked.

She'd tried to clean herself up a bit on the drive over, but hadn't been able to make much progress with the amount of dried mud caked to her face, her neck, and her clothes. At least it covered up a little bit of the bruising that had started to fade on her cheek.

"That might be for the best." Her mother would pitch the epitome of all tizzies if someone snapped a picture of her in all of her bruised, muddy glory.

She waited in the cab of the truck while Jasper carefully carried the butterflies into the warehouse. A handful of other folks they'd been working with earlier did the same. It looked like Lacey might be off the hook and the butterfly crisis avoided. All thanks to the town coming together to save the day.

Jasper returned, a huge grin on his face. "I think they might have more butterflies than they started with."

"That's great. You really came through."

He turned a heated gaze on her. "Not just me. Everyone who could, spent some time pitching in. That's what we do around here."

She nodded, happy to be a part of the effort, at least while she was in town.

"Let's get back and get cleaned up. Lacey invited us both to the wedding on Saturday. I can't wait to see what it looks like when they release all of those butterflies."

"Me, too." She leaned across the seat and pulled him close. "Thanks for taking me with you today."

"Thanks for going with me." He pressed a quick kiss to her cheek. "We probably ought to get out of here. I don't want people to see us together and think I'm trying to sway the vote."

Delilah immediately retreated to her side of the cab. "You're right. I don't know why I didn't think about that."

"Hey"—he gave her hand a squeeze—"it's okay. We just have to be careful. I tried to tell Lacey I didn't want the host job anymore but she was so upset about the butterflies, I didn't have a chance. Now that it's all taken care of, I'll give her a call tomorrow."

She nodded but inside, her chest pinched tight. She'd spent her whole life in some sort of spotlight. But today she'd forgotten about that. Let the emotion of the moment flood over her, and hadn't thought about who might be watching. She'd have to be more careful, not only for her own sake, but for Jasper's as well. If the contest committee thought she was getting involved on a personal level with the town, they'd probably remove her as a judge and maybe even disqualify Ido from the running. She couldn't be the cause of that.

"Maybe we ought to put a halt to this"—she gestured to the space between them—"at least while I'm in town. I don't want people to think my judgment will be compromised or anything."

"I said I'd resign as the host."

"But I don't want anyone to get the wrong idea." A tiny sliver cracked her heart at the thought of shutting things down with Jasper. But she couldn't risk the fate of his hometown on a few kisses or a night of pleasure.

"If that's what you want to do . . ."

That's not what she wanted to do. What she wanted was to lose herself in Jasper's arms, forget who she was for as long as she could, and give the connection between them freedom to see where it might lead. But for his sake, for the town's sake, for her own sake, she didn't say that. Instead, she nodded. "I think it's for the best."

"Okay then." Jasper shifted into gear and moved back onto the road, his jaw tight, his shoulders tense.

She could feel the shift in his energy, like he'd constructed an invisible wall between them. As much as she ached to reach out to him, to tear it down, she didn't. Sometimes she had to put others first. That was a lesson that had been ingrained in her through her entire life. She was about to tell Jasper just that when movement caught her eye. She leaned forward, trying to convince herself what she was seeing wasn't what she thought. That the whirlwind on heels heading directly toward them wasn't who she feared.

"You okay?" Jasper's hand landed on her arm. "Delilah?"

"Delilah Francine Stone. What on God's green earth have you gotten yourself into?" Stella, in all of her designer-clad glory, approached. Storm clouds of fury gathered in her eyes as her gaze swept over the mud-spattered truck.

Delilah's stomach twisted itself into a giant knot. "Stella. What are you doing here?"

Her mother stopped when she reached the passenger window. "I wanted to surprise you and hand deliver those samples myself." The clipped, tense tone of Stella's voice sliced through Delilah like a hot knife passing through a stick of butter.

Trying to defuse the situation, Delilah gestured toward Jasper. "Stella, meet the hospitality host, Jasper Taylor. Jasper, this is my mother and manager, Stella Stone."

"It's nice to meet you, ma'am." Jasper tilted his chin toward her mother.

Stella's lips curled, her disgust for the entire situation so thinly veiled that Jasper would have to be blind not to see it. "I wish I could say the same, Mr. Taylor. Are you the reason my daughter's been shirking her duties as Miss Lovin' Texas?"

"I'm sorry?" Jasper's brow crinkled. "Your daughter's been doing a fine job while she's been in town."

Delilah met his smile with a tentative one of her own. She wanted to reach up and caress his cheek for trying to stick up for her in front of her mother. But she knew Stella better than anyone, and Jasper had no idea what he was up against.

"A fine job?" Stella took a step closer, not daring to get close enough to risk her designer suit brushing up against the dirty truck. "I don't know what the hell's been going on down here for the past week, but you need to get my daughter out of here. Now."

"Stella!" Delilah appreciated where her mother was coming from. Reputation and public persona meant everything. But what she'd been experiencing in Ido was bigger than that.

Stella turned her steely gaze on Delilah next. "If you want to see this contest through, you'd better get yourself cleaned up. Now. I'll catch up to you after I've had a chance to finish my talk with the mayor."

Jasper gave her hand a squeeze. "Actually, I think Stella's right."

Delilah opened her mouth to try to talk some sense into both of them. "But—"

"I'm glad we can agree. At least on my daughter's well-being." The look Stella gave Jasper could have taken down a weaker man.

But Jasper held her gaze. "Delilah's happiness and safety have always been my top concern."

"Then get her the hell out of here before someone sees her like this," Stella muttered, her jaw clenched tight.

Jasper started the truck and backed out of the parking spot.

"Don't I get a say in this?" Delilah asked. Since when did Jasper and Stella have enough in common that they'd gang up against her? "What are you doing?"

"I'm getting you out of here before someone takes advantage of the situation and snaps a picture of you that will haunt you forever."

As much as she wanted to argue with that, it was the best thing to do. And now it looked like she had her mother on her hands. Any chance of seeing where things might go with Jasper disappeared.

seventeen

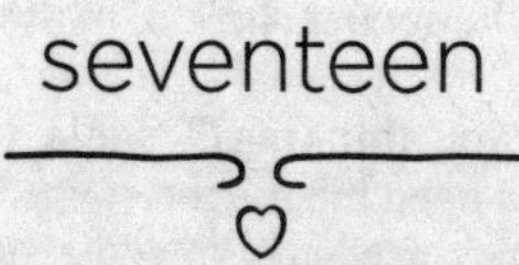

Delilah got herself cleaned up and moved her things back into the trailer. She was grateful to the Taylor family for hosting her, but now with Stella in town, she needed to get back to her own space. At least her mom had found a room at the local motel. She wasn't sure she could stomach sharing the trailer right now—not with how disappointed Stella seemed.

She'd gotten used to riding shotgun with Jasper, maybe too used to it. Pulling into the motel parking lot in her hot-pink contest truck, she realized how much she missed him chauffeuring her around. Based on their conversation earlier, she probably wouldn't get another chance. He seemed pretty sure about ending whatever had started between them. Even though she'd been the one to say it was the right thing to do, it wasn't going to be easy.

Before she could exit the truck, Stella stormed out of her motel room. "I need a drink. Please tell me there's somewhere in town where I can get something stronger than a beer."

Delilah hadn't been to many places, but she remembered Jasper talking about a bar over in Swynton. "I think I might know of a place."

"Take me there. I need a cosmo with top shelf if I'm going to survive the night."

Delilah did as she was told. Any minute Stella would start in on her. The sooner she did, the sooner it would be over.

"What were you thinking?" Stella yanked the visor down and flipped open the mirror.

"I wasn't. Lacey needed help and everyone pitched in. There's a big wedding this weekend with butterflies, and—"

"And it's none of your concern." Stella lined her lips, then filled them in with her signature color. "What happened to your face?"

Delilah checked the rearview mirror. She'd done a halfway-decent job of covering the bruise with some of the heavy pancake makeup Monique had taught her how to apply. "You won't believe me if I tell you."

"Try me." The visor snapped shut.

"I got kicked by a goat."

"Try me again." Stella scowled.

"That's the truth. I was trying to put him back in his pen and he got spooked." She glanced at her reflection again. "At least the bruising has faded."

"I told you I booked Franco to come and take pictures for the cosmetics line."

"That's right." Delilah's shoulders slumped and she tilted her head back against the headrest. "I'm sure he can edit out my black eye. He's a god behind the camera."

Stella pursed her lips. Franco had been her find and Delilah knew she was pretty proud of herself for securing his services. He didn't come cheap, but he was one of the most talented photographers she'd ever worked with.

"He might be able to make you look presentable in editing, but what are you going to do about your appearances?

I should have known better than to let you come here by yourself."

Gripping the steering wheel tight with both hands, Delilah took in a breath. "I'm twenty-five years old. I should be able to do some things on my own, don't you think?"

Stella gasped, then reached into her purse and pulled out a tissue to swab at her cheeks. "All of the sacrifices I made for your career, and this is the thanks I get?"

Not now. Delilah clenched her jaw. She'd seen a glimpse of the woman she might be if she was able to get out from under Stella's thumb. And she liked her. She'd had more fun chasing butterflies and rolling around in the mud with Jasper than she'd had in a good long while.

Stella pulled the visor down to check the mirror again. "Now I've gone and messed up my mascara. Maybe we should just go back to the motel."

"No." Delilah reached out and rested her hand on her mother's arm. "You're here and I think we both need some cheering up. Let's grab a bite and you can fill me in on the progress you've made on the cosmetics line."

"I'd like that." Stella nodded, her lower lip jutting out in a tiny pout. "I've missed you."

"We've only been apart a couple of weeks."

"I know. But with Walter leaving me and all of the work I've been putting in on the business . . ."

"It's been hard." Delilah patted her arm. "I appreciate all of the time you've been working on this. I hope you know that."

"Of course." Stella moved her arm and gave Delilah's hand a squeeze. "You're my baby girl. I'd do anything for you."

Anything but let Delilah live her own life. Delilah squeezed back. She thought once she was done with her reign as Miss Lovin' Texas, Stella might find something else to focus on. But now it seemed like she'd never be free.

She could see her entire life laid out before her. She and

Stella would do the cosmetics line together. Then they'd move into the fashion faux pas business. Pretty soon Stella would want to shift into a clothing line or restaurants or pageant dolls or who knew what else. But it was clear as day that if Delilah wanted the freedom to live her own life, she needed to start setting some boundaries.

As they drove down the main street of Swynton, she kept her eyes peeled for a place that looked like it served something besides bar food and beer. A sign outlined with twinkle lights caught her eye.

"How about this? It looks cute." Delilah eyed the charming restaurant. It sat a little way back from the main road, close to the river.

"It sure looks better than that burger place we passed before we drove over that bridge." Stella grimaced.

Delilah wanted to tell her that the burger place was owned by a very nice man named Helmut. And even though she didn't appreciate some of his marketing tactics like Smoker Saturdays, he'd given up his day to catch butterflies for a complete stranger. That was the kind of community Delilah wanted to live in. Those were the kind of people she wanted to hang out with. But words like that would fall on deaf ears if she tried to explain all of that to her mother.

They entered the restaurant and were immediately seated next to a wall of windows overlooking the river. Stella ordered her cosmo with Grey Goose and Delilah waited for a sign as to what kind of mood she might be in.

"I told you I brought those samples." Stella dipped into her oversized bag and pulled out a few compacts. "I want you to try this blush. It's absolutely gorgeous on. Go ahead, try it."

Delilah looked around at the other diners. "I'm not going to put on makeup at the dinner table. I'll try it when I get back tonight."

"Take it to the bathroom. You need to see how easy it

goes on. Just the perfect amount of shimmer." Stella pressed the blush into her hands. "Go."

It wasn't worth getting into an argument over so Delilah pushed back from the table and made her way to the powder room. Standing up to Stella over something so silly as trying a blush would have been an easy place to start setting boundaries. But her mother looked so sad when she talked about her breakup with Walter. Being firm could wait until tomorrow.

By the time she got back to the table, Stella had downed half of her drink. "What do you think? It's fantastic, isn't it?"

"It's great." Delilah took a sip of her white wine. It reminded her of the wine she'd shared with Jasper after the movie. For a moment she let herself remember what it had felt like to gaze up into his eyes with the glittering night sky spread out above them.

"Monique thinks we've got a winner. We're so close to making it happen. How does it feel to have all of your dreams coming true?"

Delilah stared into her glass. All of her dreams? What did Stella know about her dreams? Before she could answer, someone touched her on the shoulder.

"Delilah?"

She turned toward the woman's voice. Bright red hair, teased way beyond its natural height, stuck out from Jasper's aunt's head. "Oh, hi, Suzy."

"I thought that was you. I'm just about to head out but wanted to make sure I stopped over to say hello." Suzy stood there, her eyes full of kindness. "What are you doing all the way over here in Swynton?"

"We're just grabbing a bite. Suzy, this is my mother, Stella Stone. Stella, Suzy is Jasper's aunt. She's been a huge help since I've been here."

Stella blinked a few times in rapid succession, her telltale sign of annoyance. Then she nodded, like a queen greeting a commoner. “How nice to meet you.”

“Stella?” Suzy’s brow wrinkled underneath her teased bangs. “Are you from around here?”

“She grew up in Bellsview.” Delilah didn’t mean to speak for her mother, but Stella looked like she wanted to crawl under the table and hide.

“Stella.” Suzy said her mother’s name like she was trying to work out where she’d heard it before. “Is Stone your maiden name?”

“It’s my only name.” Stella regained her composure and polished off her drink. “We don’t want to keep you.”

“I’m not in a hurry. It’s card night over at Helmut’s. Those boys will be grateful if I’m a little late. None of them know I taught myself how to count cards, so I always end up coming home with the jackpot.”

Stella reached for her glass and sucked the rest of her drink through the stirrer straw. A loud slurping noise made Delilah turn to look at her mother. Her eyes were wide, and her cheeks had gone white.

“Are you okay?” Delilah asked.

Stella reached for Delilah’s wine and downed it in one gulp. It was so out of character, Delilah just sat there, frozen in place. She’d never seen her mother so unnerved before.

“Gardner, that’s right.” Suzy’s face lit up like she’d just won the lottery. “I tell you, my mind doesn’t hold on to information like it used to. Why, just the other day I was telling Helmut—”

Stella closed her eyes, her hand shaking so hard that the wineglass clattered as she set it down on the table.

“What’s going on?” Delilah asked.

“Oh.” Suzy’s eyes widened. Her eyebrows shot up so high they disappeared under her bangs. “I’d better be going. It was so nice to see you. And nice to meet you, Estelle.”

"It's Stella," Delilah corrected Suzy, thinking she must have misheard her say Stella's name the first time.

Suzy gave her a tight-lipped smile. "Sorry. Nice to meet you, Stella." Then she turned and fled toward the door.

Delilah's gaze bounced from Suzy's hasty retreat to her mother, whose face had taken on the same color as the light gray tablecloth. "Do you know her?"

"Darling, it's been a long day. Can you ask them to change our order to takeout? I'm not feeling well, and I'd really like to get back to the motel so I can lie down. I'll wait for you in the car."

"Of course." Delilah flagged down the server as Stella casually made her way toward the door. While she waited for the food, Delilah pulled out her phone and skimmed through the pictures she'd taken since she'd been in Ido. Her and Jasper at the kickoff celebration. Jasper watching the movie at the barn. The two of them catching butterflies. If she ever needed a reason to stand up to her mother, maybe this was it.

The server brought their food and Delilah slid her phone back into her purse. She and Stella needed to have a talk. Her mother wouldn't take it well, but it was time to set some boundaries. She had every intention of doing just that when she got to the truck. But Stella wasn't inside.

"Stella?" Delilah set the bag in the truck and turned to scan the parking lot.

An old El Camino sat a few spaces away. The windows were fogged and the person sitting in the driver's seat was waving his or her hands around. Other than that, the parking lot was quiet. Delilah was about to return to the restaurant to see if Stella had gone back in to use the restroom. But then the passenger door of the El Camino opened. Stella got out, her eyes wild, her cheeks full of smeared mascara.

"Mom. What's going on?" Delilah rushed toward her

mother as the car reversed out of the spot and pulled away. "Who were you talking to?"

"It doesn't matter." Stella gripped her arm. "Let's go."

"Not until you tell me what's happening. Was that Suzy?"

"Yes." Stella wiped at her cheek. "We actually knew each other once upon a time."

eighteen

After he'd dropped Delilah off at the trailer, Jasper went for a drive. He felt like he was at a crossroads. He either needed to shut down what was going on with him and Delilah and focus on saving the family farm, or give his all to convince her they belonged together. His desire to have something for himself for a change battled with his lifelong habit of putting his family first. And with Colin back in the picture, how could he turn his back on the people who'd raised him? The people who'd loved him through thick and thin?

He couldn't.

If it came down to making a choice, and he prayed it wouldn't, he couldn't set the needs of his family aside. So, he drove back to the big house, grateful Delilah's truck wasn't parked in the drive. It was time to get serious about turning up the romance in Ido. And lucky for him, he had access to four committed helpers.

Mom was setting dinner on the table as he walked in the door. "Jasper. Come join us. I made enough chicken-fried steak to feed an army."

"Don't mind if I do." He took his regular spot at the table, surrounded by his parents, his brothers, Abby, and even little Maggie. This was where he belonged. He'd been a fool to ever think he could let something else take priority.

They passed bowls full of mashed potatoes and gravy, platters of fried okra and buttermilk biscuits. When everyone had filled their plates, Jasper looked around.

"I've got an idea for the contest and I'm going to need some help." He waited for someone to be the first to respond.

"I'll help." Abby gave him a sweet smile. His little sister was always ready to pitch in.

"That would be great. I'm sure we can use a bit of a feminine touch to smooth things over when I'm done."

"What exactly do you have in mind, son?" Dad wiped his mouth with a napkin and set his forearms on the table.

"Lacey's been after me to come up with some big romantic event to wrap up Delilah's time in Ido." Jasper leaned against the back of his chair.

"I can think of a way to send her on her way." Trent waggled his eyebrows.

"Cut it out." Davis elbowed Trent in the gut. "Jasper's right. If we don't get that title, we could very well lose this farm. Whatever you need, I'm with you."

"Thanks." Jasper nodded at Davis. He was the most logical. Jasper knew he'd be on board.

"Even if Ido wins the title, that's no guarantee we'll be able to make a go of it as a wedding barn," Dad said. "Now I know I promised that if you somehow convinced that beauty queen that there's love to be found here in our little corner of Texas, that I'd let you try out your crazy plan. I've been going over the numbers and Jasper's right. If we want to stay here, in this house that's been in our family for four generations, work the land our ancestors first planted over a hundred years ago, then we need to do something."

Mom's chair legs scraped on the hardwood as she pushed

back from the table. "Is that what we're up against, Frank? We might lose this place?"

"I pray it doesn't come to that." His dad hung his head. "Right now, it looks like Jasper's idea is our best bet."

Mom stood, covered her mouth with her hand, and rushed out of the kitchen.

Jasper's stomach tightened. He was tempted to go after her, but Dad beat him to it.

"I'm going to go calm your mother down. But I'm asking you boys to listen to your older brother." He put a hand on Jasper's shoulder as he walked by. "Whatever you need, son, we'll do it."

With the weight of his family's fate pressing down on him, Jasper nodded. As his dad went after Mom, he turned his attention to his brothers. "So here's what I think we should do."

The next day Jasper woke from a restless night spent tossing and turning. He got up to start a pot of coffee, his mind already spinning with all the plans he and his younger brothers had talked about late into the night.

While he waited for the coffee to brew, Jasper scrubbed his hand over the scruff on his chin. He was glad he didn't have to deal with Colin and his shit, but knowing he was out there, somewhere close by, sure did mess with his head. But he didn't have time to worry about Colin now. His brother had made his own bed, and eventually he'd have to lie in it.

He and the other Taylor men were starting on their plan today. Jasper would join them later, but first he had to take Delilah up to the school. She'd set up a time to speak with Abby's class and he'd promised to be there. The text she sent late last night said she'd spent the night at the Sleep Tight Inn with her mom but would be back by the time he needed to pick her up.

He wasn't looking forward to the conversation they needed to have. Every time they got together, he seemed to forget all the reasons why he shouldn't get involved. But now, after getting his entire family on board the crazy train he'd proposed, he had to draw a hard line in the sand. One he couldn't let himself cross, no matter how much he wanted to.

She was sitting on the steps of the trailer when he pulled up. As he brought the truck to a stop, she got to her feet and gave him a sweet smile that made him instantly reconsider his resolve. He fought back the urge to pull her into his arms and press a kiss to those full lips. Instead, he leaned over and opened her door for her.

"Good morning." She hopped into the cab, her sash hanging across her chest.

"Hey. How did things go with your mom last night?"

"Just great. She overindulged in a mix of vodka and white wine. I got to hold her hair back while she puked up the overpriced dinner I bought her over in Swynton."

"I'm sorry I asked."

"It's fine." She clipped her seat belt in place. "She'll apologize later, and we'll pretend it never happened. We have a somewhat complicated relationship."

"Are you all right?" Against his better judgment, he reached out and put his hand on hers.

The lips he wanted to kiss spread into a tight smile. "I will be. We saw Suzy at the restaurant. Seems she and my mother knew each other once upon a time but as usual, Stella doesn't want to talk about anything from the past. Do you think I could follow up with your aunt sometime?"

"I'll text you her number. I know she's got a big order this week. Some museum in Texarkana flooded and needs their stuffed beaver display remounted. But I'm sure she'd love to talk to you."

"Good. Now, onto bigger and more exciting things. Is Abby looking forward to me coming to her school today?"

He put his hands back on the wheel. "That's all she wanted to talk about last night."

"She's a great kid."

"She sure is."

"I hope I live up to her expectations."

"I don't think you'll have any problem with that. As long as she gets to tell everyone you slept on her trundle bed while your trailer was being de-cricketed, she'll be in seventh heaven."

Delilah let out a laugh. "Ah, the naivete of youth."

The mood in the truck lightened and by the time they arrived at the middle school, Delilah seemed to be in better spirits. He introduced her to the office staff, some of them the same faces he'd seen on a daily basis when he'd attended school there. They were early, so Delilah asked if she could head over to Abby's science class. The last time he'd been inside the walls of the junior high he'd been a student himself. Somehow the building felt like it had shrunk over the years. The lockers seemed narrower. The ceilings seemed lower. Although, the smell of teenage body odor and ammonia was the same.

He held the door and they slipped into the back of the classroom. The teacher was talking about recessive genes. Jasper vaguely recalled studying the same topic, led by the same teacher, all those years ago.

Abby turned around, spotting them leaning against the back wall. She bounced up and down in her seat, and Jasper could feel her excitement like it was a tangible cloud of bubbles, hanging in the air over her head. Finally, the bell rang, and she sprang from her desk.

Delilah was ready and had a hug waiting for her after she skipped to the back of the room.

"I'm so glad you're here." Abby bounced on her feet like she couldn't stand still.

"What are you learning about?" Delilah asked, her gaze flicking to the whiteboard.

"Nothing exciting. Just what kind of eye color two parents might have. Like Mom and Dad both have brown eyes so the odds of their kids having brown eyes, too, is really high. What color eyes do your parents have?"

"Oh. Um, my mom's eyes are blue and my dad . . ." Delilah's forehead furrowed. "I'm pretty sure his were brown. Isn't that odd? I haven't thought about it in so long, I'm not sure I remember."

Abby checked the whiteboard. "He must not have been brown. If your mom's are blue and his were brown, the chance of you having green eyes would be, like, zero percent."

Delilah peered at the board. "Maybe they were green. I feel awful I can't remember. I'm going to have to check when I get back. Otherwise it will drive me crazy."

"But not now." Abby grabbed her hand. "I can't wait for you to meet my friends. Are you ready?"

"Of course. Show me where to go."

Jasper followed as his sister half led, half tugged Delilah to the auditorium, where the student body had gathered. The principal introduced her, and Delilah took the stage. He stood to the side as she launched into a speech talking about how she'd been bullied as a middle schooler. He'd planned on stepping out to check in with his brothers, but he got sucked into listening to her talk about what it felt like not to belong. He never would have guessed she'd been teased as a kid. The woman was drop-dead gorgeous. But she'd struggled with depression and major anxiety as a teen.

Hell, he wasn't female, or a middle schooler, and her words still inspired him. When she finished her speech, she opened it up for questions and he took that opportunity to step into the hall. While he'd been spellbound by Delilah, he'd missed three calls from Lacey and one from Delilah's mom. With a sense of trepidation, he dialed Lacey first. If something was going on, he'd rather hear it from her than have to deal directly with Delilah's mother.

"There you are. I've been trying to reach you." Lacey didn't even bother saying hello.

Jasper braced himself for something bad. "What's going on?"

"We've got a problem. I just sent you a text with a screenshot."

"Hold on a sec." Jasper pulled his phone away from his ear and opened his texts. An image of Delilah and her mother sitting at a table filled his screen. "I don't get it."

"Do you see where they are?" Lacey asked.

"A restaurant?" Jasper zoomed in on the photo. Looked like the inside of that place over in Swynton. His heart dipped. "When was this taken?"

"Last night. And Adeline is having a heyday telling everyone that Ido can't come up with anything good enough to feed Miss Lovin' Texas, so she had to go to Swynton for dinner."

Jasper let out a soft chuckle. "Come on, Lacey. That's ridiculous."

"Maybe to you and me. But not to Adeline. Where were you last night? Were you with them? Please tell me you didn't take them across the river to Franklin's for a special dinner or something."

"No, I was at home. Delilah's mother showed up and surprised her, and they must have gone out for a bite. Maybe she wanted privacy since everyone here in town knows who she is."

"Well, everyone in Swynton now knows who she is, too, and they're not wasting any time sharing their side of things. Can you please gently remind Miss Lovin' Texas about the longstanding rivalry between the two towns?"

"I think you're making a bigger deal out of this than—"

"They mentioned it on the local radio station. I fully expect it to get picked up by the paper, too. If there's anything she needs, anything at all, you're her contact. If she wants takeout from Franklin's, that's fine. But please don't let her cross the river again."

"Okay." Students began to file out of the auditorium doors. "I've got to go. Don't worry, I'll handle this."

He hung up and waited for a break in the mass exodus so he could get inside. Just when he seemed to make progress in one area, something else popped up that needed his attention. With a little less than two weeks until Delilah's time in Ido came to an end, he needed to make sure she experienced the best they had to offer, while keeping his heart out of the equation.

"Thanks again for talking to the students today." The principal shook Delilah's hand one more time. Finally, Jasper was able to take her by the elbow and lead her through the front doors out of the school.

"That seemed to go well." She carefully slid her sunglasses into place. She'd been able to cover up the bruise well enough, but it was still tender. "What do you think?"

"I think your talk was amazing. Were you really bullied in middle school like that?"

She let out a breath. "Sure was. I looked like a stork. All legs, big teeth. I towered over most of the boys and the girls all hated me because I did pageants."

"I never would have guessed."

"That's why I want to do something that helps young women. Through my training with the pageant community, and especially Monique, I learned that feeling good about myself had to come from inside. If you wait for other people to give you external validation, you're wasting your time." She pulled out her phone as she got settled in the front seat of the truck.

"Hey, I talked to Lacey while you were answering questions."

"Anything I need to know about? Is something wrong?" Delilah lifted her gaze to meet his.

He glanced to his feet. "I guess someone snapped a picture of you and your mom out at dinner last night."

She turned her attention back to her phone. "Oh no. Why is my picture plastered across the home page of the Swynton town website?"

"It's Adeline. She's saying you couldn't find something decent for dinner, so you had to turn to Swynton instead."

"That's ridiculous. We only ended up there because my mother wanted a drink and I remembered you saying something about there being a bar over in Swynton."

"So, it's my fault?"

He might have meant it as a joke, but she didn't take it that way. "It's no one's fault. Why is it such a big deal if we grabbed dinner somewhere?"

Jasper rolled his shoulders back. "In case you haven't noticed, Adeline's got a bit of a sore loser complex going on. I think she'll take every opportunity she has to discredit Ido."

"And my mother's request for a top-shelf cosmo has put us in the center of a turf war?" She wanted to ask if that was all it was, or if his past dealings with Adeline had anything to do with the rivalry between them.

"Looks like it."

"I'm sorry. I had no idea she'd spin it that way."

"Lacey was hoping that you might be able to stick to Ido's side of the river while you're here. Just to avoid giving Adeline any future ammunition." He squinted at her, like he was uncomfortable making the request.

"Of course." She reached out to give his arm an encouraging squeeze. "I'm sorry I didn't think about that."

"If you need anything, just let me know."

"I will. You've done so much already. Between your family and you carting me around everywhere . . ." She wanted to say something that would communicate how much she'd enjoyed her time with him. But before she had a chance to come up with something more eloquent, her phone rang. "It's Stella."

"Go ahead." He shut the door and walked around the truck.

"Hello?"

"Where are you?" Stella asked, her voice just shy of a high-pitched panic.

"I'm leaving the middle school. I had a talk scheduled here this morning."

Stella had been sleeping off her late-night wine and whine fest when Delilah left earlier that morning. Which meant Delilah hadn't had a chance to grill her mother about the weird run-in with Suzy. All she'd managed to get out of Stella last night was that she knew Suzy from way back when. After that, Stella refused to talk about it.

With everything else going on, Delilah was willing to give her mother a pass. But only for a day. Two at the most. She'd never seen Stella act so strangely. There was something going on, something her mother didn't want to tell her about, which made it even more important that she figure it out soon.

"When is Franco going to be in town?" Delilah asked.

"This afternoon. He messaged me an address of some warehouse he found to set up his shoot. I need you to meet me there in half an hour."

"Okay. What do I need to bring for wardrobe?"

"I've got it. He wants you all in white so we can focus on the makeup. We could use some muscle, so bring that cowboy with you." Stella seemed to be back to her old self, barking orders like she hadn't spent most of the night before in the fetal position on the bathroom floor.

"I don't know that Jasper will be up for it." Delilah peeked at his profile from the corner of her eye.

"Whatever you need, I'm there." He nudged his chin her direction.

With a shrug, she put the phone back to her ear. "He'll be there. We'll see you in a bit."

"What was that all about?" Jasper asked.

"Stella said they might need some help moving Franco's equipment. Do you have anything going on this afternoon?"

"Nope. Where you go, I go."

Delilah returned the smile, wishing that could be true forever. Her phone pinged with an incoming text. "Crap on a cracker."

"What is it?"

"Stella just texted me the address where we're supposed to meet the photographer."

"And?"

"It's in Swynton."

Franco wasn't thrilled about the last-minute change in plans. Delilah could tell by the exaggerated air-kisses he gave her when they met up at Lacey's wedding warehouse. Thankfully, Jasper had been able to coordinate with the mayor, and they had access to the space as long as they needed it.

"What's all this?" Franco stood at the edge of the screened-in tent where the butterflies flitted around a bunch of potted perennials that Lacey must have brought in for them. "You didn't tell me this place came with built-in props."

"Those are very important butterflies." Jasper stepped between Franco and the zippered front of the tent. "They're already promised to a bride for her wedding this weekend."

"That's a shame." Franco swayed, his hands moving through the air as graceful as always.

"I'm picturing you all in white with hundreds of butterflies resting on your dress."

"Why don't we get the shots Monique suggested first? If we have time, maybe we can talk about incorporating some of your other ideas." Delilah stood behind Franco and shook her head at Jasper. There was no way she'd let the photographer wipe out the butterfly collection. Not after it had cost her a bruised hip to gather most of them.

"Fine." Franco shifted into "go mode," which meant he started bossing everyone around. "Delilah, go get ready. Stella, I'm going to need you to pitch in with styling today since I don't have my assistant."

"Can I do something to help?" Jasper asked.

"Sure. Can you grab my lights from the back of my SUV? Just be careful with them." Franco tossed his keys to Jasper.

Delilah changed, then spent the next two hours pursing her lips, thrusting out her hips, and letting Stella and Franco move her arms and legs into a variety of poses.

While Franco reviewed the shots, she took the opportunity to grab a bottle of water and check in on Jasper. "How are you holding up?"

"I had no idea getting a picture for an ad could take this long. Isn't it just one shot?"

"You should see what happens when we're doing press for a pageant." She slid a straw into her bottle of water so she could take a sip without messing up her makeup. "If there's something else you need to do, you don't have to stick around."

Jasper stood from where he'd been leaning up against the table. "I told Lacey I wouldn't let you out of my sight. I guess you're stuck with me."

She could think of a million things that would be much worse but couldn't come up with a single one that would be better than having Jasper by her side.

"If you think it's been rough up to this point, just wait. He's barely getting going. We've had some sessions that have lasted fourteen, fifteen hours." She dabbed at her cheeks and forehead with one of the blotting paper samples Stella had brought.

Jasper took a swallow from his own bottle of water. "Do you like it?"

"What?"

"I don't know. Getting your picture taken? Wearing a couple of inches of makeup on your face?"

She set her bottle back on the table. No one had ever asked her how she felt about modeling or being photographed before. It was just one of those things that was expected. If you were into the pageant scene, you knew you'd have to sit for photos and subject yourself to all the prep work that went along with it.

"Ready for you again, D." Franco snapped his fingers.

Delilah immediately startled. "I've got to get back. We'll probably be at this for a few more hours. Are you sure you want to stick around?"

"Where you go, I go." He flipped a chair around, then straddled it, leaning an elbow on the back and resting his chin in his hands.

"You don't have to look so excited about it. I'd hate for you to be bored all evening. Want me to see if Franco wants to get a few shots of you?" She flashed him a teasing smile.

"Hell no." He took a playful swat at her backside as she moved away.

Franco had her pose, pout, and posture until her cheeks ached from smiling. Then he had her do some serious shots as well. It was after ten when he finally decided he had enough. Jasper helped break down the equipment and pack it into the back of Franco's SUV. Not even Stella had the energy left in her to argue about anything.

When they were done, Jasper carried her bag out to the truck. Stella said she was too tired to be sad, so Delilah appeared to have the night off from trying to make her mother feel better about herself.

She climbed into the front seat of Jasper's truck and tried to keep her eyes open for the relatively short drive back to Taylor Farms.

"When do we get to see the pictures?" Jasper asked.

"I probably won't see them until they're edited and Stella has the marketing company place them somewhere." She'd outgrown the excitement of seeing her picture on a page a long time ago.

"Why do you do it?"

"Do what?"

"You can't tell me you enjoyed that."

She pressed her back against the door. "It's complicated."

"What's complicated?"

"It's just not as simple as whether I enjoy it or not. Sometimes you have to do things because they're part of your job description. I bet you don't always enjoy the work you have to do around the orchard." She studied him in the dim light from the dash.

His jaw set in a firm line. "No, but I enjoy knowing that the work I do is for a greater good."

"So is this. We're going to be able to donate a portion of the proceeds to the nonprofit group Monique started. I might not like having my picture taken for ten hours straight, but if the end goal is to raise money to help other girls so they don't have to go through the same things I did when I was their age, then it's worth it to me."

"How much of the proceeds are going to the cause?" Jasper glanced over at her.

She didn't want to answer. Not because she didn't know, but because that had been a sticking point between her and Stella. Her mother wanted to donate the bare minimum. She reasoned that the cosmetics line would be their only source of income. If they were the ones putting in all the work, why should they give up any of the profits?

But Delilah refused to have her name or brand associated with a company that would only give the bare minimum. After days of arguing, they'd finally settled on 12.5 percent. The number was far below the 20 percent mark that Delilah had wanted, but also quite a bit higher than Stella's initial offer of five.

Jasper shot another look her way. "I don't want to upset you. It's just that I feel like I saw two different people today. When you spoke to those kids at Abby's school, it was like you lit up inside. And I'm telling you, they hung on every word."

She grinned as she thought about how it felt to stand up there and share her story. So many girls came up to her after and thanked her for not being afraid to open up.

"Then this afternoon, it was like you closed up. That light I saw in you earlier went out." He reached for her hand. "It just makes me wonder. Is donating a percentage of the profits going to be enough to make you light up inside?"

When Jasper pulled up in front of Delilah's trailer, she didn't wait for him to come around and open her door. He barely caught up to her as she slid her key in the lock.

"Want me to take a look around before you go in?" Ever since the night of the crickets, he'd worried that Adeline or one of her minions would find something equally vile to unleash. So far the only thing he'd found in one of his searches was a giant moth.

"It's okay. We've both had a long day. I'm sure you'll hear the scream if I come across anything that's not supposed to be here." She let her hand linger on the door handle. "Besides, don't you need to get home to let Buster out?"

"I asked Abby to go over when I figured we'd be late." With him on the ground and Delilah standing on the second step, they almost stood eye to eye.

"What's on the agenda for the rest of the week?"

"The butterfly wedding is on Saturday. Do you still want to go?"

"Of course." Her lips turned up in a weak smile. She had

to be exhausted after the last twenty-four hours. But he didn't want to let her go without making sure he hadn't said or done something to add to whatever made her shoulders slump forward and had taken a little bit of the shine from her eyes.

"About earlier . . ."

Her head tilted, like she was studying him under the dim light coming from the moon. "What about it?"

How could he sum up everything he wanted to say in a few short words? "I just want you to be happy."

She nodded, her head moving up and down so slightly that he squinted to make sure he hadn't imagined it in the semidarkness.

"I appreciate that. And I am happy. Or at least I will be when I can finally start doing something that makes a difference." She set a hand on his shoulder. "Thanks for being there today."

"My pleasure." He picked up her hand and brought it to his lips. "I'll see you tomorrow then."

"Tomorrow."

She ducked inside the camper and he stood there for several minutes, trying to decide if he should go after her. It was so obvious to him that she needed to start putting herself first and figure out what would make her happy instead of sacrificing everything for her mother. She'd probably been doing it her whole life. The irony of that wasn't lost on him. He'd been doing the same thing to some degree.

It made him wonder . . . would she ever be able to truly give herself to someone, or would she always be holding something back?

nineteen

"Are you coming to check out the wedding venue or not?" Delilah only had about an hour before she'd agreed to swing back to Taylor Farms and help Abby do her hair. Jasper's sister had been invited to sing during the ceremony and he and Delilah had promised to take her. After the all-day fiasco with Franco, Stella had sunk back into a funk. Delilah tried to prod her mother into getting ready, but if she wasn't going to budge, Delilah wouldn't let it keep her from the commitment she'd made.

"Just go without me." Stella waved a hand in the air and held it to her forehead, her palm facing out. "I'll be fine here by myself."

"That's it. You're being ridiculous." Delilah hadn't dared to use that sharp a tone with her mother before.

Stella must have realized it, too. She sat up on the bed and let her hand fall away. "I'm not being ridiculous. I've had my heart broken."

"You and Walter dated for what . . . four months?" Delilah rummaged through the dozen or more dresses her mother had hung in the small closet of the motel room. "Is your heart really broken or are you just lonely?"

"He told me he loved me. I thought he was going to propose over the holidays." Stella shifted to the edge of the bed and flung her feet over the side.

Delilah picked out a long, flowy light blue dress that would match her mother's eyes. "Here, wear this. You're going with me and that's final."

"I don't know why you're so worked up about this wedding," Stella grumbled but took the hanger from Delilah as she passed her on the way to the bathroom.

"It's important to me. Jasper and Suzy and so many others pulled together in a crisis to come through for a complete stranger. I want to see her reaction when they let the butterflies loose." And she wanted to see it with Jasper. In the past several weeks he'd become such an important part of her life. She hadn't quite decided what she was going to do when her time in Ido came to an end.

"I don't know why you're so wrapped up in all of these people's problems. You'll be heading home in another week. Won't it be nice to get back on track with your own career?"

If Delilah hadn't figured out how she felt about Jasper, she wasn't about to try to explain it to her mother. "Sure. Once the gala is over it will be good to be able to focus on the cosmetics line and stay in one place for a while. I was thinking when I get back to Dallas, about maybe getting a dog."

"A dog?" Stella stuck her head through the doorway, a lip liner in hand. "Don't be silly. You don't want to worry about dog hair all the time, do you?"

"There are some breeds that don't shed. Maybe something small to keep me company."

"Darling, you don't need a dog to do that. That's why you have me." Stella finished filling in her lips with a deep pink stain. "There. I think you're right. Getting back out there is the best way to get over a broken heart. Not that there are any eligible men worth considering here in Ido, but at least I can practice my social game tonight."

Delilah didn't bother wasting breath on trying to reason with her. It wouldn't do any good. Stella was set in her ways and didn't take well to change. Especially when it wasn't her idea. She thought back to touring the dog rescue. All of those sad eyes staring up her, looking for love, looking for someone to see the value and worth they still carried inside.

She recognized herself in their gazes. She'd been waiting her whole life for someone to see the worth and value she carried. Beyond the satin sash and perfectly plucked brows. While she waited for Stella to pull on her body shaper and wiggle into her dress, Delilah scrolled through the pictures on her phone again, something she'd taken to doing more often than she wanted to admit.

Jasper covered in butterflies. Jasper sitting on a blanket in the back of his truck bed. Jasper covered in mud. The smile on his face tugged at something deep down inside. Like a thread leftover from when she'd wrapped her heart up tight. He seemed to be the only one who'd been able to unravel any of it.

Stella came out of the bathroom, ready to go. "All right. Let's get this over with."

"You look really pretty today." Delilah meant it. Her mother had been beautiful once. Not that she wasn't still a very attractive woman. But there was a hardness to her now that Delilah didn't remember from when she'd been younger.

"Thank you." Stella offered a rare smile—the kind that actually reached her eyes and went deeper than the surface.

"What was your wedding day like? Do you remember?" They rarely talked about Delilah's dad. Stella always said it was too painful. As soon as she asked the question, a pang of regret twisted through her stomach. "Sorry, you don't have to answer that."

But in a rare moment of openness, Stella reached for her

wallet and pulled out a small photo. She and Delilah's dad stared into the camera. Her dad had a huge smile on his face, the one she remembered from her childhood. But her mother's lips barely tipped up at the corners. There was a sadness in her eyes.

Delilah searched her father's face. Brown eyes, that's right. How could she have forgotten? The memory of him kneeling down in front of her and helping her with her shoes flooded her brain. He'd looked up at her, those deep, dark brown eyes shining with love.

"Why did Daddy leave?" She'd asked the question over the years, more times than she could count, but Stella always put her off with a flippant remark. She'd say things like "We were too much to handle" or "He wasn't man enough to take care of us," and Delilah never pressed.

"I told you, sweetheart, he couldn't handle being a husband and a dad." Stella slipped the picture back into her clutch. "It was good while it lasted, but it wasn't meant to be. When you start on shaky ground, there's not much there to build a solid foundation."

That was the most information Delilah had ever been able to squeeze out of her mother. Maybe they'd reached a new point in their relationship. Now that Delilah would be retiring from the pageant scene, perhaps Stella was ready to open up a bit.

"You don't want to keep everyone waiting." Just like that, the old Stella was back. "I hope you're going to do something with your hair. It looks so much better when you pull it up. Let everyone see your beautiful face."

Delilah grimaced as her mother brushed her hair back from her cheeks.

"I'd planned on wearing it down today." She didn't add that Jasper liked it down. Stella had made her feelings about small-town life, and especially small-town men, pretty clear. If she had any inkling that her daughter had gotten so involved with a local cowboy, she'd blow her top.

"You'll wear it up." With that, her mother opened the door and stepped into the early afternoon sunlight. "I'm going to go track down that mayor before she gets too busy at the wedding. I'll meet you there."

Jasper sucked in a breath as he stepped onto the porch where Delilah sat in the rocker next to Abby. She had on a low-cut, flowery dress that accentuated her bust. Her hair was piled on top of her head in a mass of curls, but she'd left several tendrils loose that framed her face and drew his attention to her slender neck. All of the reasons he'd come up with in the shower as to why he shouldn't kiss her again seemed to disappear.

"You look beautiful." He delivered the compliment with a shy grin, not sure how she'd take it after their talk a few nights before.

"Thank you!" Abby got to her feet and twirled, sending her skirt billowing out around her. "Delilah did my hair. French braids."

Jasper shifted his gaze to his baby sister. She looked beautiful, too, although she hadn't exactly been the target of his compliment. "It looks really nice."

"Can you tell I have on lip gloss?" Abby stepped in front of him and pursed her lips. "Delilah showed me how to put it on."

"Does Mom know you're wearing makeup?"

"Yes." Abby drew the word out. "Of course, I asked her first. Do I look older?"

Jasper shook his head. They were entering new territory if Abby was going to start wearing makeup and worrying about looking like a woman instead of a girl. He pulled her into his side. "You'll always be Little Bug to me."

"Stop it, Jasper. You're messing up my braids." She pushed on his chest, but her grin let him know that she didn't mind the affection.

"Y'all ready to go?"

Abby ran to the door. "Hold on, I need to tell Mom we're leaving."

As she dashed into the house, Jasper's gaze slid to Delilah. His pulse ticked up as she stood and smoothed her palm over her dress.

"You look amazing."

She smiled, her eyes holding just a trace of something he couldn't identify. "Thank you. You look pretty good yourself."

"Thanks." He'd had to borrow a suit from his brother Trent since he'd burned his only pair of suit pants with the iron earlier. The jacket was a smidge tight in the shoulders, but he figured that would be a good thing. It would prevent him from being able to ask Delilah to dance to a slow song.

"About the other night . . . ," Delilah began.

But then Abby burst through the door again, barreling past them on the way to the truck. "Mom said to have fun and to have me home before eleven."

"She might be a little excited about singing at the wedding." Delilah picked up her purse.

"A little?" Jasper chuckled. "She's been waiting for this all month. Do we need to swing by and pick up your mom?"

"I thought we were going to ride together but she decided she wanted to stop in and talk to Lacey before everything starts. Something about getting more exposure on Ido's social media." Delilah shook her head. "Who knows what she's got up her sleeve this time."

"Okay then." Jasper gestured toward the steps. "Let's go."

Jasper hadn't attended a wedding at the Phillips House venue since Lacey tied the knot with Bodie a couple of years back. That wedding hadn't gone as planned and he hadn't had a reason to go to any of the others they'd held since. He'd heard about what went on out there between the historic house they'd turned into an event center and the giant warehouse on the property that had been repurposed as a blank slate, ready for whatever dream wedding a potential bride could come up with.

For the butterfly wedding, they'd rented giant white tents. The wedding was going to be held outside, in the beautifully landscaped grounds, then the butterflies would be released before the guests moved into the tents for the reception. He wanted to pay extra-special attention in case he got any ideas for the wedding barn, although he couldn't imagine holding events on a grand scale like this.

Lacey didn't want to miss a single opportunity to showcase Ido in a romantic light, so she met them at the front door when Jasper arrived with Delilah on his arm.

"I'm so glad you could make it." Lacey pressed an air-kiss to both of Delilah's cheeks. "Come on in. Let me show you around before the festivities start."

"Are you sure we're not crashing the wedding?" Delilah asked.

"Don't be silly. The bride said she'd be honored to have you here."

Delilah let out a breath. "I just wanted to check. Oh, and have you seen my mother?"

Lacey shook her head. "She was here earlier but I haven't seen her for a little while. Do we need to wait for her before I give you a tour?"

"No, she'll catch up if she's interested."

Jasper hadn't been inside the Phillips House since Lacey had gathered several of the local business owners to discuss her plans of turning their little town into a wedding destination. The whole house had been redone, restored to what he imagined was its original glory.

"This is amazing." Delilah voiced the same reaction he felt. "How long did it take to renovate this space?"

"A few months. We were on a bit of a time crunch." Lacey walked through the lower level, pointing out pieces that were original to the house. By the time she led them through the two upper levels, the wedding party had arrived and taken over the second-floor bedrooms to make final preparations.

"How many weddings have you had here so far?" Delilah asked.

"Too many to count." Lacey stopped by the front door. "I can look it up and get you that information if you need it."

"I was just curious. But it might be fun to share that on social media. Gives you some legitimacy if you've got the numbers to back up your claim of being the most romantic place in Texas to tie the knot."

"Wait, you're posting about your experience in town on your social media accounts?" Jasper asked.

"She's got her own hashtag for the contest and everything." Lacey squinted at him. "I thought you knew about that."

"No, I'm pretty sure I didn't." Not that it mattered much. Jasper didn't even have any of those online accounts. He had no need to tell the world what he planned to eat for dinner or how he felt about social issues. If someone wanted to know, he'd rather have a face-to-face conversation.

"Well, you ought to check it out." Lacey held out her phone. A recent post from Delilah featured a picture of the Hampton barn, where they'd watched that movie a few weeks ago, and had over five thousand likes.

He blinked hard, and the number grew by ten. If and when they did move forward with the wedding barn idea, he'd need to get up to speed on all of that. He almost groaned at the amount of work ahead of him. Maybe Delilah would be willing to help him get started since she obviously knew a lot about it.

"I've got to go check on the wedding party." Lacey tucked her phone back into the pocket of her dress. "Y'all feel free to head outside and find a place to sit. We should be starting in just a little while."

"Thank you so much for the tour. I'd love to walk around

outside and get some pictures of the gardens." Delilah looked up at him.

"Sure, let's do that." He held the door for her, breathing in a whiff of her perfume as she passed by.

"I can see why so many couples choose Ido for their wedding." Delilah turned right at the bottom of the steps, taking the path that led to the garden where the wedding would be held.

"Lacey's done a fantastic job. She pretty much saved the town by coming up with the idea of focusing on weddings."

"I read something about that in the information Mr. Plum gave me. Ido used to be known for a big stationery company, didn't it?"

"That's right." Jasper walked under an arbor covered in some sort of climbing vine. No need to get into the scandal surrounding the downfall of the Phillips family business. He turned the conversation. "It sounds like you're pretty good at that social media thing."

She leaned over to snap a photo of a butterfly resting on a large orange bloom. "It comes with the territory. One of my responsibilities with this contest is to post pictures of my experiences. Hopefully, it will make more people aware of what each town has to offer."

"That's smart." He nodded, wishing he could ask for help with putting together some ideas for the wedding barn. But he wasn't ready to talk to her about that quite yet. He still wanted to keep it to himself so she wouldn't be swayed one way or another when it came time to make her decision.

"I've also started ramping up the marketing for the new company Stella and I are working on . . . the one I told you about with my mentor, Monique. Stella hired a publicity company to do the launch and everything, but I'm handling the day-to-day posts."

"I wouldn't even know how to get started."

She turned to him and put a hand on his arm. He could feel the weight of her touch, even through the layers of his long-sleeve dress shirt and the suit jacket. "I'm sure you could figure it out, it's not that hard."

"Thanks." He stopped himself from sliding his hand into hers and pulling her close.

As Delilah moved around the garden, snapping pictures of flowers and groups of smiling wedding guests, the music began to play. "Should we find some seats?"

"You pick."

"We're not really part of the official guest list. Let's stand at the back." She headed toward an out-of-the-way area behind the rows of chairs.

Jasper followed, his chest burning as he watched the gentle sway of her hips. His fingers tingled with the memory of having his hands on those curves not that long ago.

She stopped at a bench that had been set up at the edge of a path that wound through the garden. "How about here?"

"Works for me." He waited for her to get settled, then took a seat next to her, his hip brushing hers on the narrow bench.

"What a gorgeous dress." Delilah smiled as the bride took a spot behind her bridesmaids. "She looks so happy."

Jasper glanced from the nervous excitement on the bride's face to see the calm, confident stance of the groom, who waited for her at the end of the aisle. Delilah gripped his arm as the last bridesmaid trailed past them. The crowd stood for the bride, and the swell of the wedding march began.

He couldn't help himself. His fingers found Delilah's and tangled with hers.

She gave his hand a squeeze as the couple took their places under a wooden arbor covered in flowers. The officiant asked the guests to be seated. Delilah didn't break their grip. Not while the couple said their vows. Not when the tiny ring bearer handed over a satin pillow. Not when the couple kissed for the first time as man and wife.

Jasper had been to a fair number of weddings in his life,

but for some reason he seemed to watch this one unfold through new eyes. Instead of witnessing a couple of strangers pledge their love to each other until death, he couldn't help but wonder how it might feel to be the one standing there, in front of his own friends and family. Vowing his love to one woman for the rest of his life.

Then he looked down at the woman next to him. She met his gaze with an emotionally charged look of her own.

twenty

Delilah tried to hold back the wave of emotion as she met Jasper's gaze. She had no right to picture the tall, ruggedly handsome man next to her standing in front of her, holding her hand, and promising to love, honor, and cherish her for the rest of their lives. But for some reason, she did. Jasper had thrown a wrench in her carefully constructed plans. A wrench that she wanted to grab onto and never let go.

"It's time for the butterflies," he reminded her. His voice had gone soft.

Reluctantly, she shifted her gaze away from his in time to see a horde of butterflies emerge from a stand of shrubs behind the arbor. They rose into the air, their wings fluttering against a backdrop of the late afternoon Texas sky.

Delilah squeezed his hand tighter. "They're beautiful."

"So are you." His warm breath brushed her cheek as he leaned closer to whisper into her ear.

A chill raced through her and she turned her head, almost causing them to bump noses.

He pulled away and tilted his head back. "There they go.

How many hours did we spend collecting butterflies? And they're gone in a blink of an eye."

"Some things don't have to take a long time to make a lasting impression." Her lungs filled as she drew in a breath.

One side of his mouth ticked up. "Is that so?"

She nodded, realizing the unspoken understanding between them. Maybe that was all this would be. A moment of attraction they'd both recognize before realizing it wasn't meant to be.

As the last of the butterflies fluttered away, Abby's voice rose over the crowd. She sang a sweet song about finding the love of a lifetime as the bride and groom walked back down the aisle.

"Your sister has a gorgeous voice." The crowd began to leave their seats and Delilah let her fingers fall from his.

Jasper took a half step to his left, putting a breath of distance between them. "Yeah, she sure does."

The song wrapped up and the guests milled around the patio, some of them already starting to make their way over to the tent where the reception would take place.

"Shall we?" Jasper stood and buttoned his suit jacket, then offered her his arm.

They started for the tents on the other side of the property, until Delilah came to an abrupt stop.

"There you are." She could have picked Jasper's aunt Suzy out of any size crowd. Her bright red hair had been tamed into a bun at the nape of her neck. A set of jeweled clips held the sides in place. Were those frogs?

"Suzy." Jasper stopped and let go of Delilah's arm to greet his aunt. "Did you do the flowers today?"

"Sure did." Suzy beamed. "Just wait until you see the bouquets on the head table. I used some branches from my own property as the base. Lacey wouldn't let me use real butterflies at the reception. She said she had to draw the line there and it wouldn't be sanitary since there'd be so much food around. Sometimes I don't think that woman understands that there shouldn't be lines when it comes to appreciating art."

"She probably didn't want butterflies landing in their dinner." Jasper's brows rose as he glanced at Delilah over the top of his aunt's head.

"Do you think we could chat for a few minutes?" Delilah asked Suzy.

"Oh, yes. I've been meaning to talk to you." Suzy took Delilah's arm. "Jasper, can we have a second?"

"Sure. I need to check on Abby. I'll meet y'all back here in a few minutes?"

Suzy waved him away, already tugging Delilah to the bench they'd just vacated. "I wanted to apologize about that run-in with your mama. Seems like I had her mixed up with someone else. You know, my eyesight's just not what it used to be."

Delilah squinted at her. One of the rhinestone frogs in Suzy's hair had caught the sun and sent a bright array of sparkles dancing at the edge of her vision. "But I saw you and my mother talking in the front seat of your car. And then she said she used to know you a long time ago."

"She did?" Suzy's hand went to her heart.

"I don't understand. Were you in school together?"

"Oh, honey, your mama was a few years behind me. But I remember her well."

"Were you friends?" Delilah wondered how Suzy would have known her mother. They didn't seem like they were the type that would have much in common. As much as Delilah enjoyed Suzy's unconventional ways, Stella didn't have the same attitude when it came to expanding her social circle.

"We weren't really friends. Did Estelle, I mean, Stella, say anything about it?"

"No. There's something she's not telling me, and I have no idea what it is." Stella had never provided any detail about her childhood days. All she'd said was her parents didn't support her decision to marry her father so they lost touch. Stella had shut them out of her life and never looked back. Not even when she and Delilah's dad divorced.

Delilah had always wanted to learn more about her family, more about her past, but the memories were too painful for her mother to talk about, so she'd left it alone.

"I think it's best you ask your mama about it. Whatever it is she's not willing to talk about, it's her story to share." Suzy nodded, more to herself than anything else. "Now, we've got a party to get to. Are you going to cut a rug with my nephew? He sure looks handsome when he gets all gussied up, doesn't he?"

Delilah wanted to press the issue, but looked up in time to see Jasper making his way toward them, Abby by his side. "He sure does."

"Take care, hon." Suzy stood and wrapped her in a hug, the faint scent of formaldehyde lingering as she released her grip.

"Did you hear my song, Delilah?" Abby's excitement was contagious. "I get to sing another one at the reception. I can't wait to taste the cake. Jojo made it and promised me she'd save me a piece with extra frosting."

"Well then, what are we waiting for?" Delilah linked her arm with Abby's, a safer choice than subjecting herself to Jasper's charms, and they made their way toward the huge white tents.

Giant, colorful butterflies hung from the ceiling on clear filament. It made it look like butterflies danced all around them. Soft lights had been strung around the edges, making the inside of the tent glow. She'd never seen anything like it.

"I see Jojo over there." Abby released her arm. "I'm going to go say hi and make sure she remembers about the cake."

Delilah laughed as Abby sprinted across the dance floor,

headed toward the cake table on the other side. "Where does she get her energy?"

"I bet you were like that when you were her age," Jasper said.

"No." Delilah tried to remember what she'd been like at twelve years old. She'd won several titles by then. Stella had decided that her pageant career took top priority over settling down somewhere, and they'd moved all over the state of Texas and even spent time in Louisiana and Georgia in Stella's quest for Delilah to win one of the bigger titles.

"Are you sure about that? You strike me as someone who probably loved having a chance to dress up and go to parties."

"Back then I probably would have preferred to stay home, learn how to ride a horse, and hang out with my friends. The pageants and parties were fun sometimes, but I missed out on a lot by always being on the move."

"I guess I assumed that's what you wanted."

"Oh, I did. The first time I won a title, my mom was so proud. She said she'd always wanted to compete but then she met my dad and fell in love. I felt like I was giving her a second chance to realize her dreams."

"What about your dreams?"

"What about them?" She shrugged. She'd lost sight of what she wanted a long time ago. When she realized winning pageants made her mom smile again, she set out to do just that. It got to the point where Stella's dreams had blended with her own, and she couldn't tell what she really wanted anymore.

"The business you're building with your mom and your mentor . . ."

"Monique."

"Right, Monique. Is that something you believe in?"

"Of course." But it was so much more complicated than that. She'd used her platform to speak about empowering young girls. So many times in the pageant world she'd seen the girls who had the big budgets use their experience to intimidate the girls who couldn't afford to hire coaches and consultants. The business she was building with Monique and Stella would be her way of supporting girls who couldn't afford to compete at those levels.

"Sounds like there's a *but* there," Jasper said.

She'd already crossed the line with Jasper. What difference would it make if she came clean about her reservations? "Giving money toward causes that will empower young girls is great. But I'd love to be more involved. When I talk to those girls, get to look in their eyes and tell them about my own experiences, that's what fills my soul."

"Then why aren't you doing that?"

He made it sound so easy, so simple. "What do I tell Stella? 'I know I said I wanted to run the business with you, but I've decided I just want to hang out with teenagers instead'?"

"Well, yeah, for starters. Can't you do both?"

"I don't think there's enough time in the day. My mother's shifted from entering me into pageants to having me do appearances everywhere. She thinks I need to be the face of the brand. That doesn't give me time to be the company spokesperson and spend my days running an actual program."

"I guess I don't see why you can't make it work. My dad always told me if you want something bad enough, you'll find a way to make it happen."

"Is that what you're doing?" She was tired of everyone plying her with advice. "Have you always wanted to run a pecan orchard?"

He glanced down at her, his eyes taking on a hint of hurt. "No. But my dream is making sure my family's legacy carries on. The pecan orchard has been in my family since my great-great-great-grandfather came over from England and settled on that piece of land. I can't stand to see my dad lose it. Hell, if we lost the pecan orchard, it would put most of us out of a job. Trent runs the retail store. Mitchell spends most of his time fixing the equipment. Lucas only took a part-time job in town to make ends meet since that tornado came through. If I can give us a chance to rebuild, it would save everything."

Delilah couldn't bear to hold his gaze. "We're not so different then, you and me."

"How's that?"

"Your dream is to keep the orchard going for your family. Mine's to save my own."

"It shouldn't be your job to make your mother happy, Delilah."

"Did you want some punch? I'm going to go grab a beverage." She didn't want to have this conversation with him. Not now, not ever. The relationship between her and Stella had been set in stone from the time she'd won her first sash. Jasper couldn't understand that. How could she expect him to when she barely understood it herself?

He shook his head. "No thanks. I'm going to go check on Lacey and see if she needs help with anything."

"All right then. I'll see you later."

She walked away first, heading toward the bar in the opposite corner of the tent. And as much as she wanted to, she didn't allow herself to look back.

Jasper stayed to the edge of the crowd. The wedding party was from Arkansas, so the only local folk were the people busing tables, manning the bar, and making sure everyone had a good time. Lacey had outdone herself. Again. By tomorrow there'd be talk of the great butterfly hunt, and another heartwarming story about how the town had joined forces to save another bride's happy day.

As he looked around the tent, he couldn't help but wonder if he was making a mistake by strong-arming his parents into following his idea of a wedding barn. What did he and his brothers know about weddings? Hell, what did they know about love? He'd struck out the one and only time he'd tried to commit to a woman for more than a few dates.

None of his brothers had settled down yet. Lucas was the one who'd come closest, and even then, he'd skipped the whole romance part and found himself raising a daughter as a single dad. Maybe the Taylor brothers were destined to stay single. They'd all live together in the big farmhouse while they worked to create happily-ever-afters for strangers.

He shook his head. Damn, he was turning into a sap. He might be hopeless but at least his younger brothers still had a shot. And God only knew what Colin was up to. He didn't want to think about his older brother tonight. No one else had mentioned seeing him around town. Maybe he'd decided to clear out. The last thing his family needed was to have him show up again.

As he stood at the edge of the crowd, taking it all in, Delilah caught his eye. She was spinning around the dance floor in the arms of a stranger . . . a tall guy decked out in a tailored suit. Jasper didn't like the way the guy's eyes roamed over her bare shoulders. Didn't like the way his hand rested a little too low at the small of her back. His stomach clenched as the music shifted into a slow song and the asshole pulled her in close.

Before he realized what he was doing, he made his way to the center of the dance floor, tapped the jerk on the shoulder, and asked to cut in. Delilah nodded her agreement and the stranger released his grip and slunk away.

"Was he bothering you?" Jasper asked, his pulse slowing now that he had her in his arms.

"No, he was a nice guy. His cousin got married and he came all the way from Nashville to be here." Her fingers pressed into his shoulder and he shifted to pull her even tighter against his chest.

"Looked like he might be holding you a little too tight." The suit jacket stretched and a few threads might have snapped as Jasper swayed to the music with her in his arms.

She bit down on her bottom lip. Almost like she was trying to prevent herself from smiling.

"What?" He angled his head down. "Was he?"

"Not as tight as you're holding me now." She tossed her head back and met his gaze.

His attraction sparked at the sight of her smooth, slender neck. He wanted to run his tongue along it, nip at the spot where her neck gave way to her shoulder, and slip the thin straps of her dress away.

"I want to apologize for earlier." He smoothed his palm over the small of her back, enjoying the way it made her breath come just a smidge faster.

"No apology necessary."

"Then I'll do it for me. I'm sorry. I shouldn't have pushed you about your mom."

"It's fine. I know she has boundary issues. It's something I've been working on for years, and will probably spend the rest of my life trying to sort out."

He slowly spun her around, using the opportunity to slide his foot between hers. "Well, for what it's worth, I don't know what that's like. I apologize if I made you feel uncomfortable."

"It's fine, Jasper." His name rolled off her tongue in a breathy exhale.

He did a half-assed job of suppressing a groan.

"You okay?"

"Say my name again."

Her brow furrowed. "Jasper?"

"No. Like you did before."

The edges of her mouth tipped up into the slightest of grins. "Why?"

He leaned close. Close enough he could breathe in his fill of that damn perfume. "Because it drives me crazy."

She pulled back and glanced around the dance floor. "I thought we weren't going to go there?"

"I can't help it." His gaze drilled into hers. "I saw you dancing with that guy and I couldn't think of a single reason why he should get to enjoy having you in his arms while I deprive myself of the very same thing."

"Oh, Jasper."

"Yeah, like that. I love it when you say my name just like that."

She grinned. "I didn't mean to say your name in a certain way. That's just how it came out."

"Look, Delilah. I don't know what this is or where it's going, but I can't stop myself from wanting you."

"Wanting me how, exactly?" Her eyes sparkled. He'd bet his best pair of boots that she knew exactly what he meant.

He dipped her low as the song came to an end. "I want you in every way possible."

Her fingers gripped his biceps even though there was no chance he'd let go. "Is that an invitation?"

"Hell, I don't know." He set her upright, pulling her against his chest. "Call it what you want, but I call it the truth. I've wanted you since the first day I set eyes on you, Delilah Stone."

"Well then." She let her hands fall from his shoulders. "We probably ought to drop your sister at home so I can explore that truth a little."

His belly burned with anticipation. They'd been flirting around the combustible attraction between them for the better part of the past two weeks. Would she regret giving in to it again?

She twined her fingers with his and gave them a squeeze. "I need to say good-bye to Lacey before we go, and see if I can locate my mother."

"I'll find Abby and meet you by the truck?"

"That sounds good." She lifted her gaze and gave him a shy glance. "I'll see you in a few minutes."

Their fingers slid apart as she moved toward the edge of the crowd, where Lacey surveyed her domain. He scanned the interior of the tent, on the lookout for Abby. He needed to get her home before he let himself have too much time to think about what might happen with Delilah.

A half hour later Abby slid out of the small back seat. "Thanks for the ride, Jasper. That was so much fun."

He nodded to his sister as Delilah handed her the extra piece of cake Jojo had boxed up. "Don't forget this."

"Think Mom will let me have cake for breakfast?" Abby asked.

"I say what Mom doesn't know won't hurt her." He waited for Abby to make her way up the steps and disappear inside the house. It wasn't quite eleven, pretty early to turn in on a Saturday night. "Do you want to take a drive?"

"Or we could watch a movie," Delilah said.

Seemed neither one of them was brave enough to make reference to the heated moment they'd shared while dancing.

"A movie sounds good. Why don't I drop you off, then run home and change?"

"That works."

Before he could walk around to open her door for her, she met him at the steps of the camper. "You've got your key?"

"Right here." She slid it into the lock.

"I'll see you in a few."

She nodded, disappearing inside.

Jasper got back in the truck and drove the short distance to his place. As he slipped off his brother's suit and hung it in the closet, he let his mind wander. Were they really going to go all in? Yes, they'd given in to the attraction before, but the stakes were higher now.

Buster followed him from room to room, not used to being left behind.

"Bud, this is a one-man job." Jasper ruffled the fur behind his ear and gave him a soup bone he'd been saving. "This ought to keep you busy for a while."

As Buster settled on the living room floor with his bone, Jasper slipped through the front door. He tossed his keys from one hand to the next. It would probably be best to leave his truck here and walk back up to the camper. No reason to give anyone something to speculate about. Based on the way he and Delilah had held each other close while they danced, anyone who'd seen them might already suspect there was a fair amount of heat between them. But he wouldn't compromise her reputation as the contest judge, so he set off on foot.

She opened the door to the camper in a pair of cropped yoga pants and a T-shirt. He preferred the flimsy nightie he'd seen her in before, but he wasn't about to admit it. He'd take her however she was, as long as she would be his.

"Come on in. I can make some popcorn if you want."

"That's okay. I'm not here for the popcorn."

"What movie do you want to watch?" She picked up a remote and gestured to the tiny seating area that doubled as a kitchen.

"I'm not here for a movie, either."

She sucked in a breath and scraped her teeth over her bottom lip. "Want a soda?"

He shook his head.

Her palms slid up his chest, her fingers clasping together behind his neck. "What is it you're here for then?"

"I think you know." Walking her back toward the bedroom area, he slipped his arms around her waist, his hands holding on to her hips. "You okay with this?"

Her nod against his chest gave him the final bit of encouragement he needed. As the backs of her legs reached the edge of the bed, he lowered her down. She didn't let go of him, but pulled him on top of her. For half a second, neither one of them moved. Then he tentatively touched his mouth to hers.

twenty-one

Delilah couldn't get close enough to Jasper. His warmth, his heat, his scent surrounded her, but still it wasn't enough. He propped himself up on an elbow as he took the kiss deeper. Heat flooded through her, making her blood feel more like lava racing through her veins.

His hands were everywhere . . . her hair, her hips, her skin. Everywhere he touched, his fingers seemed to sear her skin. And still, she couldn't get enough.

This man, the way he treated her, the way he cherished her . . . made her hungry for him in a way she hadn't ached for anyone before. Her entire body was on fire.

He nipped at her lips and sucked on her tongue. She tried to pull him tighter against her but there was nowhere else to go. He leaned over her, trying to keep his weight balanced on his arm, preventing himself from crushing her.

Her fingers found their way under his shirt. He was hard in the places she was soft, making her realize how perfectly they complemented each other.

She worked his shirt up his abs, over his pecs. With one fluid motion he reached behind his neck and pulled it off. For a moment she just let herself stare. The last time she saw his naked chest they'd been bathed in moonlight. But now, under the warm light of the lamp attached to the camper wall, she feasted her gaze on him.

His body had been chiseled by hard work, not like the guy she'd dated who worked on each individual muscle group with precision at his high-priced gym. Jasper had earned every square inch of rock-hard muscle with manual labor. Knowing that made her even hotter for him, if that was even possible. She was already soaked, ready to take things to the next level and push them past the point of no return.

His lips trailed kisses over her neck. Then he focused on that spot behind her ear he seemed to favor. The one that drove her wild. If he kept that up she might come before he even touched her below the waist. Although, thankfully, his fingers seemed to be heading that way. He breached the waistband of her yoga pants. She shifted her hips in an attempt to urge him on. Every part of her ached for him.

Finally, his palm rested below her belly button. A finger slipped beyond the thin elastic of her lacy panties. She moaned as he slid a finger into her curls, zeroing in on her need. At the contact, she bucked her hips, writhing against him. He teased her to the brink of her release, backing off every time she got too close.

Trying to get even, she fumbled with the waistband of his pants. Her hand slipped underneath, running over his sculpted ass. He flexed, his muscles moving underneath her hand.

"Do you want me to stop?" he muttered against her ear.

She couldn't even form words, she was too far gone. So, she violently shook her head from side to side.

He pulled back, shed his sweats, and eased her yoga pants down her legs.

"Come here." He reached for her, sliding his hands under her shirt.

She hadn't put a bra on when she changed, so his fingers moved up her ribs, then paused as he realized he had unfettered access. His touch was tentative at first. His thumb grazed one nipple, then the other.

In a move she hadn't seen coming, he lowered his head, running his tongue between her breasts, then sucking a nipple into a hard point before he blew out a warm breath. Her skin pebbled immediately, and he turned his attention to her other breast.

She barely had time to catch her breath before his fingers were back at her entrance. With one hand he coaxed her toward a climax, his touch sending her higher and higher. With his other, he unrolled a condom that had appeared out of nowhere, his hand wrapping around his length.

"Wait." She barely forced the word out.

He stopped, his gaze searching hers. "Are you okay? Do you want to stop?"

"Absolutely not." She scooted out from under him and guided him to lie on his back. "I want to be on top."

He settled on his back, and she lowered herself onto him. She had to pause as she became accustomed to the way he filled her. But he couldn't stay still. His hips moved to a slow, glorious rhythm. His palms cupped her breasts, his thumbs playing over her nipples. She lifted her hips up, then slowly lowered them, again and again.

His mouth found hers as the first waves of pleasure hit. She grabbed for the cabinet above the bed, trying to get a little leverage. He clamped one hand on her hip, while the other tangled in her hair. The pace increased. She gripped the cabinet with both hands.

Jasper thrust his hips up, and she held on. And then she crashed. She seemed to stretch out, suspended in time and space. Then plummeted, faster and faster into a free fall spin. A shriek pierced the silence. It was her. Jasper pulled her down, his own body straining to reach a climax. She let go of the cabinet and made a move to collapse on his chest.

A horrible cracking noise filled the camper, then the cabinet above their heads separated from the wall. Jasper held her to his chest, rolling out of the way as it landed on the bed, inches from where their heads had been just moments before.

Her chest heaved and a sheen of sweat covered her skin. Jasper's hair stuck out all over and he propped himself up, his gaze searching hers.

"You okay?"

She glanced up where the cabinet had been. "We broke my camper."

His lips spread into a grin. "No, you broke your camper."

"How am I going to explain that?" She curled into him, not willing to let their time together be interrupted, not even if the walls were coming down around them.

He ran a finger down the center of her breastbone, causing her skin to pebble, all the way down to her toes. "You could tell them the truth."

"That I yanked the cabinet off the wall in the throes of passion?"

"Throes of passion, huh? That sounds pretty intense."

"Was it?"

"What? Intense?"

She nodded.

"It was fantastic." He rolled off the bed and picked up the cabinet. "We should figure out where to put this. I don't want anything to get in the way next time."

"Um, next time?"

"That's right. You don't have anything on the schedule tomorrow. I figured we could stay up all night and watch the sunrise together."

"And what's your family going to think?"

"What they don't know won't hurt them."

* * *

Jasper didn't leave Delilah's trailer until the first streaks of pink bled across the sky. He wanted to wake up with her in his arms, to be the first thing she saw when she opened up her beautiful green eyes. But he also wasn't ready to take their connection public. If folks found out they were getting together, the contest committee might pull her from the judging. She couldn't afford any negative publicity, and Lacey would strangle him if he threatened Ido's chance at a win.

So, he gathered his things, pulled his sweats up over his hips, and shoved his feet into his sneakers. Delilah hadn't moved. Her cheek rested on the pillow they'd shared. Her hair fell over her face, almost covering her eyes. He wanted to reach over and brush it back but didn't dare risk waking her. With a final kiss to her cheek, he cracked open the door of the camper and tried to quietly make his way down the steps.

Today he needed to put the final details in motion for the Fall Festival. He'd asked his brothers to block out their calendars and was pleasantly surprised when he showed up at the big house and everyone was ready to go. His mom wouldn't let them head out on empty stomachs so as they filled their bellies with scrambled eggs, biscuits and gravy, and homemade sausage links, he divvied up tasks.

"Trent and Mitchell, you work on the site down by the kissing cove. Lucas and Davis, I want the two of you to take on the tunnel of lights." He checked items on the list he'd made up, making sure he didn't miss anything.

"What do I get to do?" Abby grabbed the last sausage link before Trent could snag it. She was getting to be pretty fast thanks to battling her brothers.

"You can come with me, Little Bug. We're going to set up an arbor." Jasper skimmed his own chicken scratch. "Once we all finish the station we're at, we'll meet up and finish the other two. Got it?"

"You really think this is going to work?" His mother returned to the table with a pot of coffee.

"We won't know unless we try, isn't that right?" Jasper slipped the last bite of his breakfast into his mouth, then cleared his place from the table. "We're leaving in five."

He loaded the dishes in the sink into the dishwasher while he waited for his brothers and Abby to gather their things. As he scraped plates into the trash can, he wondered if Delilah had woken up yet. She'd told him her mother would be heading back to Dallas the next day, so she wanted to spend some time with her before she left. Which was perfect since he didn't want her to find out about the surprise he'd been planning.

And she'd promised not to leave the town limits so he wouldn't get into any more hot water with Lacey. They'd made it this far. If he could hang on for another week without any major crises, Ido might have a decent shot at coming in first.

"I'm ready to go." Abby came into the kitchen, her excitement at being included in the plans obvious by the wide grin on her face.

"Let's hit it then." Jasper grabbed his keys and the plans he'd drawn out. He'd spent a few hours over the past week in his dad's workshop. All he needed to do was put the arbor together and then train those climbing vines he'd picked up from Milkweed Gardens.

It took him a little longer than he'd anticipated to piece together the arbor. Abby was an eager helper but lacked the upper-body strength to carry any of the larger pieces by herself, so he spent just as much time carting the wood over to the site as he did actually putting anything together.

When they'd finished, they both stood back and gazed upon their accomplishment.

"It's really pretty, Jasper." Abby walked underneath. "You know what would make this a million times better though?"

His heart dropped into his stomach. "What?"

"A swing." She ran her hand over the latticed side. "You could hang one right from the middle. Just think how romantic it would be if you kissed Delilah here while you're sitting next to her on a swing built for two."

"What are you talking about?" He might have had a little trouble keeping his attraction for Delilah under wraps, but he hadn't been so careless that he expected his twelve-year-old sister to figure it out.

"I know you like her." Her smile was more of a smirk.

"And just how do you know that?" He narrowed his eyes.

She giggled. "Because you look at her like you want to kiss her."

"Is that so?"

"Yes. Kind of like this." She smooshed her lips up and made kissy noises.

Jasper laughed as he grabbed her around the waist, swinging her around until the kissy noises turned to shrieks of laughter.

"Put me down."

He stopped spinning and they both stumbled, dizzy from the game they'd played when she was younger and used to beg him to spin her for what seemed like hours at a time.

Her hand landed on his arm and she struggled to catch her breath from laughing so hard. "I still think you like her."

Since when had his baby sister become so astute? His mouth ticked up on one side. "You know what?"

"What?"

"I think you might be right."

She clapped her hands together while she jumped up and down. "I knew it. Does she like you, too? Are you going to get married?"

"Slow down." Jasper put his finger to his mouth. "And shush before someone hears you."

Abby drew her lips into her mouth and clamped down, making her look like she'd lost all her teeth.

"She might like me back a little. But nobody should know. At least until the contest is over, okay?"

Abby nodded, still unable to stand completely still.

"Don't make me regret telling you. You've got to keep this between us."

Her head nodded up and down.

"You think we need to add a swing, huh?" He let out a sigh as he shook his head. Abby had a point. If they were going to bill the Pucker-Up Path as a main feature of the Fall Festival this year, adding a swing would definitely provide the right touch.

"So, do you like her like her or just like her?" Abby asked, her hands clasped together while she waited for him to respond.

"We're done discussing my love life." He couldn't believe he'd even shared as much as he had. But it wasn't like he had anyone else to talk to about matters of the heart. He and Colin used to confide in each other. But like everything else, that was ruined when his brother turned his back on everyone.

"Let's get these vines planted and then I'll see about adding a swing if I have time before the festival starts. Sound good?"

Abby grinned as she nodded her head.

"You can talk again now. As long as you keep it down."

"Okay. I'm so excited. Do you think Delilah will wear a dress like the bride from the wedding yesterday when you get married? Are you going to move into town? Can I pick out the flavor on your cake? Jojo said she really wants to try to make one with lemon frosting, and I know you like lemons. Or at least you used to because Mom said one time you used all her lemons to make lemonade, and I . . ."

Jasper tuned her out. He had to if he wanted to get the rest of his to-do list done. When they'd finished planting the vines and running them through the holes in the lattice arbor, he sent a group text to check on his brothers. Everyone had finished their stations. Eager to wrap things up and get back to Delilah, he packed up the truck and headed to their meeting point.

twenty-two

Delilah was ready for Stella to head home. She needed the next week without her mother around to figure out how she felt about everything, especially Jasper. But before Stella left, Delilah was determined to get to the bottom of whatever secret she'd been keeping.

She pulled up in front of the motel, expecting she'd have to humor her mother into a late brunch before she had to hit the road for the drive home. But as she brought the truck to a stop, Stella came out of the door like she'd been waiting.

"Good morning." Stella slid into the front seat, her fingers wrapped around a book. Or maybe it was a photo album.

"What do you have there?" Delilah asked.

"My high school yearbook. It's not my copy. God only knows where my things ended up after I left home, but I borrowed it from someone I reconnected with at the wedding last night."

"Do I get to see?" Delilah's fingers itched to flip through

the pages, as if she could find answers from her mother's past somewhere inside.

Stella slid her dark sunglasses into place. "I need coffee first. Lots and lots of coffee."

"I know just the spot." Delilah didn't press things until after Jojo had shown them to a table in the back at the Burger Bonanza. Jasper hadn't been joking when he said the place got busy on the weekends. Delilah might not be able to eat much off the menu since there were very few vegetarian options, but the coffee was strong, hot, and never ending.

"Where the hell have you brought me now?" Stella slid into the booth with her hands in the air, like she was afraid to touch anything.

"I've been told they serve an amazing breakfast here on Sunday mornings. I thought you might like to eat something substantial before you drive back."

Stella pulled an antibacterial wipe from the pack in her purse and ran it over the table. "Here, do your side, too."

"That's not necessary. I happen to know the owner and he runs a pretty tight ship." The decor might look like it was from the past, but she'd seen Jojo go through her cleaning routine on more than one occasion and even if the tabletops were avocado green, Delilah had no doubt they were sparkling clean.

Jojo stopped by with two empty mugs and a carafe of coffee. She jotted down their orders and headed back to the kitchen, leaving Delilah to face her mother.

"Can I see your yearbook?" Delilah held out her hand, expecting Stella to slide it across the table.

Instead, her mother held it close to her heart. "There are some things I haven't told you about my past."

Duh. Stella couldn't be so obtuse that she didn't realize Delilah knew there was something missing. "Now would be a fine time to share them."

Stella's jaw set and she passed the book over. "I just want you to know that everything I've ever done was for your own protection."

Delilah frowned as she opened the front cover and began to flip through the pages. "Is this your senior year?"

Stella dumped three creamers into her coffee and slowly stirred. "Yes."

Delilah scanned the pictures, locating her mother on the page that showed the homecoming court taking the field during halftime at the football game. Her heart squeezed as she read the caption. "You didn't tell me you were on the homecoming court."

Stella swallowed and focused on a spot just over Delilah's right shoulder. "It was a beautiful dress."

The next page showed pictures from the dance. Stella stood onstage, a crown sitting lopsided on her head, her arm wrapped around the handsome man next to her. Both of them beamed into the camera.

"Who's this?" Delilah asked. The man had his arm wrapped possessively around Stella's side. His eyes looked familiar. Such an odd shade of green. She shifted her gaze from the picture to Stella and back again. "'Homecoming queen Estelle Gardner and her king Helmut Schmidt'? You went to homecoming with Helmut?"

Stella's face paled.

"Mom? Did you used to date him?" Delilah glanced over her shoulder where Helmut had just come out of the kitchen.

Clasping her hand to her mouth, Stella slid from the booth, colliding with Jojo, who'd stopped by to deliver the veggie egg-substitute omelet Delilah had ordered along with Stella's platter of biscuits, gravy, and grits. Dishes crashed to the floor, gravy splattered Stella's blouse, and a glass of orange juice dumped directly into Delilah's lap.

Silence descended on the restaurant. Helmut turned his gaze their way. "What the hell was that?"

"Just a spill. Don't have a coronary." Jojo set the tray down on the table and began to collect pieces of broken plates and glasses.

Helmut peered over at them from behind the counter. He squinted, making his eyes crinkle. "Estelle?"

Stella didn't respond, just stood there with her eyes almost closed, her body frozen.

Delilah slid out of the booth, her brain working double time to try to sort through the information overload in her head.

"Helmut?" She zeroed in on the man standing behind the counter. He bore little resemblance to the slim eighteen-year-old in the photographs. His head was shaved, he'd put on at least fifty pounds of muscle, and his arms were now covered in tattoos. Delilah hadn't paid much attention to them before, but now her gaze skimmed over the eagle on his forearm, the American flag peeking out from the V-neck T-shirt he seemed to favor when he worked behind the grill, and the curly script covering his arm. She could make out a swirly *E* followed by an *s* and a *t* before it disappeared into the sleeve of his shirt.

"Oh my God." Delilah turned back to Stella. "Oh my God. What's going on here? Did you two date? Is he the reason Daddy left?"

Stella finally moved. She gathered her purse and tossed a twenty onto the table. "Delilah, I'm not feeling well, please take me back to the motel."

"No." Delilah crossed her arms over her chest. Her pants might be soaked but she wasn't going anywhere. "Not until you tell me what's going on."

Stella glanced around and Delilah tried to see the world through her mother's cool blue eyes—the diners staring at them, Jojo continuing to pick up shards of glass from the floor, and Helmut, who stayed behind the counter, his eyes wide, his mouth hanging open. Just like he'd seen a ghost.

"This is neither the time nor the place." Stella slid her

purse strap over her shoulder and made a beeline for the door.

"Don't walk away from me, Mom." But her cries fell on deaf ears. Stella's ears. With her mother nearing the door, Delilah lost it. She needed to know the truth. She deserved it and it was time her mother finally confronted whatever had driven her away from Bellsview. "Stella Stone, did you have an affair with Helmut Schmidt?"

Stella held her head high and turned around. Her eyes were so cold Delilah shivered as her mother's gaze swept over her. "Don't talk about that man like that. He's your father."

"I don't understand." Delilah cupped her chin in her hand and stirred another spoonful of calorie-free sweetener into her already-sweetened sweet tea. "How could she do this to me? To us?"

Helmut sat across the table from her, a cup of coffee in front of him. "I'm sure she had her reasons. I can only imagine what she must have been going through."

"Well, I can't." Delilah took a long draw through her straw. "All these years. Why would she lie?"

"She was alone." Helmut shrugged. "I shipped out to basic training the day after our high school graduation. After my time at Fort Benning I was on a plane to the Middle East. Her parents never wanted us to be together. I wrote to her every day, but then the letters started coming back."

"Why wouldn't she tell you she was pregnant?" Delilah had never pretended to understand her mother's motives, but there had to have been some reason behind her decision to leave her hometown.

"What was I going to do? It would have been a couple of years before I could have come back and married her. If only I'd known." Helmut put his head in his hands and those huge shoulders shook.

Delilah reached across the table and tried to convey some comfort through her touch. "Everything was a lie."

"I know one thing that can't be a lie." Helmut looked up at her, and she felt like she was looking into her own gaze. How had she not noticed his eyes were the same exact shape and color as her own?

"What's that? Not that it will make me feel any better or give me any reason to forgive her."

"She must love you very, very much, and that's not an easy thing for her. Your grandparents, her parents, were so strict with her. I know they loved her in their own way, but they never showed it. I think that's one of the reasons she fell for me." He lifted one shoulder in a half shrug. "I'm a hugger."

So many emotions bubbled up inside, all Delilah wanted to do was take some space. She needed to go somewhere where she could sort through her feelings. About Stella, the father she'd never known, and more.

She needed Jasper. He was the one she wanted to talk to, to bare her heart and soul to. But she'd sent him a couple of texts already and he hadn't responded. He'd said something about being tied up all day making preparations for the Fall Festival.

She didn't want to go back to her empty trailer. She sure as hell didn't want to go after her mother.

"I've got to get back to the kitchen." Helmut tapped his hands on the table. "I don't know how this works, but could I maybe call you sometime? I'd love to get to know you better."

"Of course." She might be unsure about where things would go with her mother, but she'd never turn down the chance to get to know her family.

"Can I get a hug?" He stood, towering over the booth. He looked so out of place, the tatted Army vet with a sheepish smile.

"I'd like that." She buried herself in his arms, trying to

breathe through her mouth since the scent of fried onions and fish clung to him. That might take a little getting used to, but she'd gladly suffer through a year full of Smoker Saturdays for the chance to get to know her dad.

Helmut returned to behind the counter and Delilah was about to get up to leave when the woman sitting in the booth next to her cleared her throat.

"Rough day?" Adeline twisted around, peering over the back of the booth.

"I don't want to talk about it." That's all Delilah needed was Adeline using her personal drama to cause another stink online.

Adeline slid out of her booth and onto the seat across from Delilah. "Sorry, I couldn't help but overhear."

"And I'm sure my personal family drama will be all over Swynton's website within the next fifteen minutes."

"Hey, even I have some lines I won't cross." Adeline shook her head and refilled her coffee mug with the carafe in the middle of the table.

"No offense, but that's not what I heard." Delilah studied the woman sitting across the table. "What are you even doing here? I thought you were too good to come slumming over in Ido?"

"I never said that. Swynton's for sure more romantic. But Helmut makes the best pineapple milkshakes in the world."

"You're having a pineapple milkshake for breakfast?" Delilah sat up straighter and caught a glimpse of a tall, empty glass sitting on the table next to them.

"Hubby and I had a fight. It was stupid, really."

Delilah wondered what would constitute a fight in Adeline's world. "What happened?"

"Well, seeing you here, representing the Miss Lovin' Texas pageant, it made me wonder about competing in a pageant, too. Not like I want to go up against you personally—"

"Don't worry about that. My pageant days are over." Delilah shook her head. If her experience today had taught her anything, it was that she was done putting her mother's needs before her own. It was time for her to step back and start doing something for herself.

"Roman doesn't think we can afford it. I read somewhere the pageant dresses can cost up to a few thousand dollars. Is that true?"

"I've never paid more than five hundred. But Stella's got connections, as in major connections. I'd be happy to share some names with you if you'd like."

Adeline's lips split, revealing the kind of smile that Delilah was sure would charm the judges of any pageant she entered. "That would be amazing. I'd be so grateful."

As long as she was trying to get to the bottom of things, Delilah decided to test that gratefulness with a question. "Can I ask you something?"

"Anything." Adeline scooted closer to the table.

"Did you put crickets in my trailer?"

"What?" Her eyes rounded. "Why, I'd never do something as disgusting as that. What would make you think that?"

Either she'd majored in lying in college or she was telling the truth. "Someone filled my trailer with crickets on my second night in town. Are you sure you didn't have anything to do with that?"

"I swear on the lives of my sorority sisters." Adeline did some complicated hand gesture, then plastered her palm over her heart. "I'd never use bugs against a fellow woman."

"Okay then." Delilah had been sitting on the vinyl booth so long that when she tried to stand, the backs of her legs stuck to the surface. She pulled a business card out of her purse and handed it to Adeline. "I need to go. But send me a text with your contact info and I'll follow up with some introductions to some people you probably ought to meet."

Adeline bounced out of the booth and pulled her into a hug. She hadn't been lying about that pineapple shake; Delilah could smell it on her. With a final squeeze, Delilah peeled herself away. She needed to find Jasper. He was the only one who might be able to help her sort out the mess swirling around in her head.

twenty-three

Jasper finished installing the swing Abby had picked out as the sun began to set. He was used to putting in a full day's work at the orchard, but something had been eating at him all day, making each task seem monumental as he went through the motions of getting things ready for the Fall Festival.

Everything he'd been working for over the past several weeks was coming to an end. Within a week, the contest would be over, Delilah would move back to Dallas, and he'd be left here, still trying to pick up the pieces. They had to win. If Ido didn't earn the title, he wasn't sure what he'd be able to do to keep the world from crashing in on his family and losing the farm.

"I like it." Abby hopped on the swing to test it out. "I think Delilah will like it, too."

"I hope so." Jasper set down the drill he'd been using and sat down next to his sister.

"What happens if we don't win the contest? Will the

bank really take away the orchard? Will we really have to move?" Abby leaned her head on his shoulder.

"I hope not, Little Bug." He pushed off the ground with his feet, setting the swing in motion. "No matter what happens, things will probably change."

"I know. The only constant in life is change."

He drew back to look at her. "That sounds pretty deep for a twelve-year-old. What are they teaching you in school nowadays?"

She pushed into his shoulder. "I didn't make that up. It's from Heraclitus. He was a Greek philosopher."

"You're studying philosophy now? What else did Heraclitus say?"

"You're teasing me."

"No, I really want to know."

"Okay. He said, 'A man's character is his fate.'" She gave him a smug grin.

"And what does that mean to you?" He had to give his little sister some major credit. She just might grow up and be the smartest one out of all of them.

She screwed her lips up. "I think it means that your future depends on the kind of person you are inside."

"I think you're right." He leaned into her, nudging her to the side. "What do you think about driving by the Dairy Dell on our way home? I probably owe you an ice cream cone for all of your help today."

"A double scoop?"

"Maybe even a triple if you help me load all of this stuff back into the truck."

When he dropped Abby off at home, he grabbed the to-go pint he'd picked up at the Dairy Dell for Delilah. The lights were on in the trailer. Even though every inch of his skin craved a shower, he couldn't wait to see her.

She answered after a few short knocks. But instead of the smile he was hoping for, her eyes were red, and she held a wad of tissues in her hand.

"Are you okay?" He immediately held out his arms, pulling her in close.

She clung to him, her nose running, her eyes watering, her heart pounding against his chest so hard he could feel it.

"My mom left. And Helmut's my dad. It's been a rough day." She mumbled the words into his chest.

"I'm sorry, Helmut's your what?" He pulled back just far enough to make sure he'd heard her clearly. "Did you just say Helmut's your dad?"

"Yes. He and my mom dated in high school. I think your aunt Suzy knew. My whole life has been a lie."

"Can I come in?" He held up the brown bag. "I brought ice cream."

Fifteen minutes later she'd relayed the events of the morning, including the news that Adeline denied being involved in the cricket infestation.

"I believe her." Delilah slipped another spoonful of turtle cheesecake ice cream into her mouth. "She did some weird hand thing and swore on the lives of her sorority sisters that she was telling the truth."

He'd never vouch for Adeline since he'd been on the receiving end of so many of her lies, but swearing on the lives of her sorority sisters did seem like a big deal. At least in her convoluted world.

"Have you heard from your mom?"

"No. I'm sure she had her reasons, but I don't care what they were. Lying to someone you love, that's inexcusable, no matter what. Don't you think so?"

He wanted to say yes. But how could he when that's exactly what he'd been doing to his own family for the past three years?

"Jasper?" She'd dipped the spoon into the quickly disappearing pint and held it out to him. "You agree, don't you?"

"Of course." Inwardly, he cursed himself for not taking the opportunity to tell her the truth about his own situation right then and there.

"I knew I was right to believe in you." She finished the last bite of the ice cream then left his lap to toss it in the trash. "When this contest wraps up, I'm done. I've been thinking about what you said."

"Hmm?"

"About me being so much happier when I'm working with the girls I want to support. I'm going to talk to Monique about finding a different spokeswoman for the cosmetics line."

"Are you sure?" He spread his legs as she stepped between them.

"I'm surer than sure." She wrapped her arms around his shoulders, and he nestled his cheek against her chest. "Coming here was the best decision I've ever made. What would you think about me becoming a permanent resident?"

His heart squeezed tight. "You want to stay in Ido?"

She lowered herself to perch on his thigh. "I want to stay with you."

With the contest coming to a close, Delilah didn't want to risk someone seeing her and Jasper together and thinking she was playing favorites, so as much as she wanted to go all in with him, she forced herself to keep her distance over the next few days. She hadn't heard from Stella except for a text saying she'd made it home and was hoping they could get together when Delilah got back to Dallas and sort through everything that had happened between them.

With a little free time on her hands, she decided she'd take the opportunity to try to get to know Helmut a little bit better. At first glance they didn't seem to have much in common. But she wanted to know more about her past and her own history, so she put her reservations aside and accepted his invitation to hang out for a little bit.

They met at the Burger Bonanza. If Jasper had been

impressed with the dually pickup she'd been tooling around in, she wondered what he'd have to say about Helmut's truck. It sat high above the ground on jacked-up tires and she had to use both hands to pull herself into the cab.

"Thanks for being willing to spend some time with me this morning." Helmut gave her a shy smile, a far different look than the one he usually wore when he was slinging burgers behind the grill.

"I want to get to know you. At least as much as I can while I'm still in town." She clipped her seat belt in place and faced forward. "Where are you going to take me today?"

He put both hands on the wheel. "I figured I'd take you on a tour of where your mother and I grew up. Try to give you a sense of our history together."

"I'd like that."

"Then let's get started." While he navigated through Ido, he pointed out places she hadn't necessarily spotted on her own yet. Told her about the people who'd lived there all their lives. Like Jojo, who'd been working at the Burger Bonanza since high school and had recently started making wedding cakes for Lacey's brides. And Kirby, who'd been an eclectic recluse for decades, but wanted to do his part in revamping the town, so he'd started a transportation company and now had a small fleet of unique limos.

"It sounds like the town really pulled together to make Lacey's dream come true."

"But it's not just Lacey's dream. I guess we all needed it, it just took her to prod us into realizing it." Helmut passed through Swynton, pointing out places he and Stella used to hang out way back when.

Then he drove into Bellsview. Tall trees lined the narrow residential street. Cookie-cutter houses sat close to each other, the color of their shutters the only thing that distinguished one from the next.

"There's the house I grew up in." Helmut brought the

truck to a stop in front of a small white house with dark blue shutters. "My bedroom was that front window right there."

Delilah took in a deep breath as she gazed out the window. "Who lives there now?"

He licked his lips and shifted in his seat. "My folks."

"You mean . . ." Her heart seemed to stop beating for a moment.

"You've got kin, Delilah." He put his hand on hers and gave it a squeeze. "I don't expect you're ready to meet them yet, but when you are, I know they'd love to get to know you."

Tears welled up in her eyes, threatening to spill over. "Why didn't Stella go to them when she found out she was pregnant? Why leave? Why keep a secret from so many people when it seems like she had people here who loved her and would be willing to help?"

"Let me drive you by your mama's old place." He shifted into gear and headed out of town.

Delilah took in steady, even breaths, trying to regulate her erratic pulse. By the time Helmut slowed the truck again, she'd almost gotten her breathing back to normal.

"Here we are." He'd stopped on the side of a two-lane highway.

Delilah's gaze swept over the sparse plot of land, stopping when she eyed a rusted-out trailer sitting in the middle of some tall grass. Part of the roof looked like it had caved in. As hard as she tried, she couldn't picture her mother within five hundred yards of a place like this.

"I know it doesn't look like much now, but when your grandmother was alive, she did the best she could." He pointed to a spot by a thick stand of trees. "Over there's where we had our first kiss. Your granddad hung a tire swing, and Estelle used to love it when I pushed her on it."

Delilah could hear the emotion in the way his voice trembled. "I'm sorry."

"What are you sorry for? None of this was your fault." His lips quivered as he gave her a shaky smile. "I thought showing you a bit of our history might give you a better understanding of your mother."

"Thank you. It has."

"Now, let me drive you by the high school, then how about we end back at the restaurant? I'd love to make you some lunch."

"That sounds wonderful, but there's something I probably ought to tell you." She thought of Jasper's warning that Helmut might not be able to handle her being a vegetarian. But no more secrets, no more lies. "I'm a vegetarian."

Helmut's eyes grew wide. "A what?"

She grinned at the mock horror in his tone. "I don't eat meat."

Smiling back at her, he shook his head. "I'm not sure I know what to do with that."

"Maybe we can learn together."

"I'd like that."

twenty-four

Jasper woke early on the day of the Fall Festival. He'd made his lists, checked them twice, and couldn't wait to get through the last event on the calendar before he could have that heart-to-heart with Delilah that he'd been waiting for.

It was so obvious to him what she ought to do. Leave her mom in Dallas, move to Ido, and spend the rest of her life working with the kids she so desperately wanted to help, and loving on him.

But with all of the other curveballs life had thrown at her lately, he wasn't about to add another. So he'd vowed to wait until the contest was over before asking her about the future. Maybe she'd even be willing to help him with the wedding barn if Ido won the title.

"Ready for today?" Dad asked as Jasper entered the kitchen.

"I hope so."

"Weather looks good." Dad lifted his head from his habitual scan of the morning paper. "Did you see this bit about that damn dog-fighting ring? Says they think they're getting close again to finding out who's behind it."

"Oh?" Jasper tried to come off nonchalant. He hadn't heard from Colin in almost two weeks, not since the day he'd disappeared. With any luck he was long gone again, hopefully for at least another three years. "I thought that whole thing had settled down?"

Dad thumped the paper. "Says here there's been some new activity. You'd best be careful out there tonight. Fall Festival can bring a lot of squirrels out looking for nuts, if you know what I mean."

Jasper eyed his dad, not really sure what he meant, but also not willing to ask for clarification. "We will."

He'd promised to pick Delilah up and take her on a quick run-through of the day's events. It was hard to believe that she'd be leaving the next day. He didn't want to think about that yet. One day, one hour at a time, that's how he'd get through.

She was sitting in one of the chairs in front of the trailer when he stepped out onto the front porch. He'd filled a thermos with coffee and wrapped up a few of the blueberry muffins his mom made. With a day packed full of events, he wanted to have her to himself for a bit before everything got underway.

"Good morning." He would have swept her up in a kiss right then and there if they hadn't promised to keep things on the down low. That was another reason he was ready to put the contest behind them. He wanted to be able to hug her and kiss her in public, not always be wary of who might see them.

She grinned up at him. "Good morning. Are you ready for today?"

"I'll be more ready for the day after that gala."

"I know. But it's only another week away. We can keep up pretenses until then, can't we?" She stood and brushed off her backside. "What's in the bag?"

"Blueberry muffins."

Her tongue darted out and swept along her lip. "For me?"

"Maybe."

"What do you want for one?"

"What will you give me?"

Her eyebrows rose. "How do you do with delayed gratification?"

"Recently, I've been handling it fairly well, I think." He held up the thermos. "I've got coffee if you want to walk with me for a bit."

"Sure."

He led her down, past Tie Dye's pen, past the old barn where they'd relocated Abby's horses, to the big barn he wanted to turn into an event venue.

"You brought me to the barn for breakfast?" she asked.

"I wanted to get your opinion about something." He slid the big door open. "After you."

They walked into the dim interior. He glanced around. It was going to take a hell of a lot of work to transform the interior, but it would be worth it.

"Smells like manure. Is that what you wanted my opinion on?" She held out her hand, beckoning for the brown paper bag.

"Not exactly. But you do have a valid point. Maybe we should wait on the muffins until we're done here."

Her eyes rolled and her hip bumped his. "What kind of opinion did you want?"

"What would you think about us turning this place into a wedding barn?" He bit down on his lip while he waited for a response.

She didn't answer right away, but took her time, letting her gaze drift up to the high peak of the ceiling and along the thick rafters that had held the barn up through years of daily use, hundreds of storms, and generations of Taylors.

"I think it could be lovely."

"Really?"

"Really. Is that what you've been working on with Lacey?" She arched a brow. "I know the two of you have been up to something."

He nodded. "Yeah. She thinks it would be a good complementary business to the Phillips House. She's getting so many requests, she's had to turn some away."

"It could be beautiful in here." She reached for his hand. He shifted the bag into the same hand as the thermos and twined his fingers with hers.

"Is this the kind of place you might want to have your wedding someday?"

Her eyes sparked. "My wedding? What makes you think I'm the marrying kind?"

"I don't care what kind of kind you are, as long as you'll be mine." He pulled her against him and pressed a kiss to the top of her head. "I can't wait for this contest to be over."

"You and me both." She held tight, wrapping her arms around him.

A soft whimper made him pull back. "Was that you?"

"No." Delilah held perfectly still.

The noise came again.

"Is there some kind of wild animal in here?" Delilah asked.

"Hold on a sec." Jasper moved to the very back of the barn, to one of the stalls they hadn't cleaned out yet. He peered over the edge. Six kennels sat inside the stall.

"What is it?"

Jasper flipped on his flashlight app. "Oh, hell."

Delilah sucked in a breath as she looked down on the crates filled with dogs. "What are they doing here?"

Jasper turned her toward the door they'd come through. "You know what? I bet Trent or Mitchell is helping Zina out again. Sometimes they deliver dogs for her when they get adopted out of state."

"I thought Zina said she only adopted to local families. She told me she likes to meet them and make sure they know what they're in for before they take one of her dogs."

"Yeah, I think that's how she usually does it. But if she gets a lot of dogs, sometimes she works with rescues in other states to do the legwork for her." He pulled the door shut behind them as soon as they walked through. "Did you want one of these muffins?"

"Sure. Do I get some of that coffee, too?"

"You know what? Why don't you take it? I'm going to follow up with Trent to make sure everything's okay with those dogs and see how long he expects them to stay in the barn. I'll meet up with you later?"

"But you wanted to walk me through the events for today, didn't you?" He'd handed her the bag and the coffee. It wasn't like him to seem so flustered. Maybe he was feeling just as off as she was. With the contest coming to an end, her time in town would be over. They'd both talked around the idea of her moving to Ido, but hadn't had time to work out the details or make real plans.

"How about I drop you off in town and have Suzy walk you through things? There are a few last-minute details I need to work on and then I'll meet up with you before it's time to go?"

"I think you're working too hard on this festival." She cupped his cheek. "You know you've already impressed me, don't you?"

"I didn't know for sure until you just told me." He rubbed his cheek against her palm.

"I'm not saying you've got the win in the bag, but if it gets you out of work so we can spend my last night in town together, I can tell you, you've got a really good shot at the title."

"Shh." He silenced her with a kiss. "We promised we

wouldn't let the contest come between us. I don't want to get us disqualified because you're falling for me."

"Falling for you?" She sidled up against his chest, wishing her hands weren't full of breakfast so she could use them for other things, more important things in the moment.

"Aren't you?" His arms wrapped around her, his hands resting against the sliver of skin between her shirt and the pair of jeans she'd slipped on.

"I think I've already fallen." Rising on her tiptoes, she touched her lips to his.

He deepened the kiss, slipping his tongue into her mouth. The man sure knew how to kiss. And someday soon, hopefully her lips would get a lot more action from his.

"We'd better get back." He let his arms drop from her sides.

She fell into step beside him, appreciating the way he always seemed to adjust his longer stride to match hers, wishing they had a little more time together.

About twenty minutes later, Jasper pulled up in front of the gazebo in the town square. Delilah popped the last of the muffin into her mouth and drained her coffee. Rows of white tents lined the sidewalk. Vendors were setting up their wares and Delilah spotted everything from fresh produce to homemade apple butter to midway games. Jasper had filled her in on what to expect at the Fall Festival, but he hadn't told her it was more like a carnival.

Suzy rushed over when she saw them, her arms full of miniature pumpkins. "Am I ever glad to see you!"

"You need some help with that?" Delilah made a move to stabilize the pile of pumpkins.

"I'm good for now. But I could use some help with the pumpkin bowling station. I promised Lacey I'd finish setting it up before I can run home and get ready."

"I was hoping you'd be able to take Delilah around and show her how everything's going to go today," Jasper said.

Delilah didn't miss the surprise in Suzy's eyes.

"Um, sure. Do you have other plans?"

"There's something I need to follow up on with Mitchell and Trent. I'll be back before you know it. An hour, maybe two at the most." Jasper put a hand on Delilah's shoulder and squeezed. "I'll see you later, Miss Lovin' Texas."

Then he climbed into his truck and backed out of the space, not even waving as he sped off down the street.

"Is it just me or did he run off faster than shit off a shovel?" Suzy glanced toward the empty spot where Jasper's truck had been.

"He seemed a little off this morning," Delilah admitted.

"How so?"

"After we found those . . ." Jasper had asked her not to mention it to anyone, at least until he had a chance to check with his brothers. As odd as that seemed, she trusted him completely. He had to have a good reason.

"Those what?" Suzy eyed her with suspicion.

Delilah wouldn't lie. After what Stella had done to her . . . stringing her along all those years . . . she'd never tell another lie as long as she lived.

"Dogs. He found a few dogs in the barn and said he needed to check in with Trent, or maybe he mentioned Mitchell. I still can't keep all of them straight." Delilah shrugged. "What's left to do for pumpkin bowling?"

Suzy screwed her mouth into a frown. "I just remembered I've got to run an errand. Think you can handle this on your own?" She began to pass the pumpkins to Delilah, losing several in the transfer.

"But, I don't know what you have in mind. I've never even been bowling, much less pumpkin bowling." Delilah's protests fell on deaf ears.

Unencumbered by the pumpkins, Suzy spun her around and pointed to a tent. "Just draw some faces on those bowling pins and stack the pumpkins over there. I'll be back in just a bit."

Delilah stood by, helpless, while Suzy stalked down the sidewalk and disappeared around the corner. Something was going on in Ido. Something she needed to figure out, and fast.

twenty-five

Jasper tried dialing the last number he had for his older brother. A recorded voice came on the line saying it had been disconnected. Colin had to be the one who'd left those dogs in the barn. But why?

If what his dad read in the paper that morning had any merit to it, the dog-fighting ring Bodie had been chasing around for the past couple of years might be closer than they thought. And Jasper had a fairly good idea how to find out for sure. The whole way back to the barn, he tried to figure out how to handle it.

He needed things to go well tonight. For Lacey, for Ido, for his family. There was no guarantee Colin would be back for the dogs soon. Maybe they'd make it through the Fall Festival and he could confront his brother tomorrow. Once Delilah was safely on her way back to Dallas.

But if Jasper knew his brother at all, he had a sinking feeling in his gut that whatever Colin had planned for those dogs would be happening tonight. Like Dad said, there would be plenty of people around for the festival, so if there was something going on with the dogs, it would be hard to tell with all the extra activity.

He couldn't let him get away with it. Colin had done nothing but lie, steal, and cheat. Jasper had looked the other way once and it had cost him. He didn't have a choice but to try to get to his brother before someone else did.

Abby wasn't in her room when he got back to the house. She'd be performing later on that afternoon and had probably already left for practice. Jasper searched through her drawer for the old phone he'd given her. Mom and Dad wouldn't let her have one of her own yet, so he'd taken out the SIM card and let her use it for apps.

She'd loaded an app that could track her device and he synced it with his own phone. It would have been much easier asking Bodie for help, but Jasper couldn't afford the risk.

He headed back to the barn, a tiny part of him hoping that Colin had come back for the dogs in the short time he'd been gone. Then he could let himself off the hook, tell himself he'd tried but it was too late.

But there they were. Jasper wasn't sure what kind of temperament they might have so he picked the one that looked to be the friendliest and opened up the cage. The dog let out a low growl, its ears flattening against its head.

"I'm not going to hurt you." Jasper held out a cookie he'd grabbed on his way through his mom's kitchen.

The dog sniffed at it. After a few good whiffs of his mama's homemade snickerdoodle, the pup gave it a lick. As it cautiously nibbled, Jasper secured the old phone to the inside of the plastic kennel. Odds were his plan wouldn't work. But he had to try.

"I wish I had something for all of you." Jasper broke off several small bites of cookie and handed them out to the other dogs. "Don't worry. I'm going to get you out of this mess. Just hang tight until later tonight, okay?"

With phase one of his plan complete, he stood, brushed off his jeans, and headed back to his truck. No matter what his asshole brother was up to, Jasper needed to show Delilah the time of her life tonight. He had to secure the win.

Two hours later he'd checked in with his brothers, changed into a nicer pair of jeans, and was letting his gaze drift over the gorgeous woman in the seat next to him. She wore her sash over a deep red dress that matched the color of her lips. Jasper hadn't been able to keep his eyes off her, even almost drove them off the road when she'd pulled his hand into her lap and tangled her fingers with his.

"You ready for this?" He held her door while she climbed out of the truck. The smell of apple turnovers and simmering apple cider reached his nose.

"What's that smell?" She turned, her nose in the air, and inhaled.

"That's the scent of Ido's Fall Festival. Get ready to have your senses overloaded. Do you want to start with apples or pumpkins?"

"What does that mean?" She wrinkled her nose, making her eyes crinkle at the edges.

"There are two schools of thought around town. You love fall for either the apples or the pumpkins. Before we go any further, I'm going to need to know which side you're on." It might sound ridiculous to an outsider, but that's the way they'd celebrated in Ido for as long as he could remember.

"Which side are you on?" Her brow furrowed like she was afraid of making the wrong decision.

"I can't tell you that." He smiled as she rubbed her lips together.

"Apple strudel is the best. But I can't imagine Thanksgiving without pumpkin pie."

He lifted a shoulder. "What's it going to be?"

"I don't know. Can I try a little bit of everything and give you an answer at the end?"

"Why not?" Jasper directed her to the first tent, where Jojo had set up a table holding several types of muffins, cakes, and breads.

"Help yourself to samples." Jojo pointed to the handwritten signs. "I've got pumpkin bread, mini apple turnovers, and much more."

Delilah took a sample of each. "Thank you."

Then she moved on to the next table, where she picked up a pumpkin spice cookie and a cup of spiced cider. "You didn't tell me the festival was all about eating."

"How else will you figure out if you're team pumpkin or team apple?" he joked.

She was giving the question her full consideration. He could tell by the way she evaluated the samples from each table. She'd take a bite, pause, chew, pause, swallow, pause. Then repeat the process all over again.

After they'd visited the food vendors, they made their way to the activity area. Kids and adults carved pumpkins donated by Milkweed Farms while others engaged in a friendly match of pumpkin bowling.

"I helped with that." Delilah pointed to where Lucas guided Maggie to roll the pumpkin toward the pins. When her pumpkin didn't knock any down, she toddled over and kicked them.

"That's my niece." Jasper let out a whistle. "Way to go, Mags!"

"Are you going to win me something?" Delilah tucked her arm through his.

He should have pulled away, but he enjoyed the way her hand felt on his arm, the way he could catch that heady scent of lemons and sunshine when the slight breeze blew past her hair.

"What should we play?" He evaluated the options. "How about knocking the milk jugs off the stand?"

"Let's see it." She dropped his arm as they neared the tent.

Jasper handed over the cash and the kid behind the table—Jojo's oldest son—passed him three beat-up softballs. The first one went wide, and the second one knocked the bottle over, but not off the stand.

"So close." Delilah groaned next to him.

He fired the last one toward the bottle and it slid to the edge of the platform before tumbling to the ground.

"You did it!" Delilah jumped up and down, her excitement contagious.

The kid brought over the basket of prizes . . . some trinkets the town probably inherited when the stationery and imports business shut down.

"This one." Delilah held up a cheap silver-tone chain that had a butterfly dangling from the center.

"You know that's probably going to turn your neck green."

"I don't care." She leaned close. "It's going to remind me of you."

Warmth spread through his limbs, like he'd just taken a shot of whiskey that burned through his veins.

"Can you help me put it on?" She held her hair up and turned her back toward him.

His fingers fumbled with the tiny clasp but somehow, he managed to secure it.

"Thank you. Now, what do you think?" She spun to face him, her eyes reflecting the same kind of emotion he felt toward her.

"I think you look beautiful." He wanted to lean down and capture her mouth with his. But he couldn't. Not here. Not now. "You ready for the big surprise?"

"Can't wait." She let him lead her past the edge of the tents toward the tunnel two of his brothers had installed. One of them had used pink chalk to draw a series of hearts down the sidewalk. "What's that?"

"Read what it says," Jasper prompted.

Delilah stepped close to the front of the tunnel, where a

framed note was attached. "'Welcome to the Pucker-Up Path.' Did you have something to do with this?"

He checked to make sure no one was around, then wrapped his hand around hers. "You have to follow the hearts to find out where your next kiss will take place."

"Really?"

He took a few steps, then tugged on her hand to get her to move closer. "Come here. This is the Pucker-Up Path picture spot number one. We're supposed to grab a selfie, then hash tag it and post on the town's page."

"You up for it?" She held out her phone.

"You're not going to post it, are you?"

"Of course not. But that doesn't mean I can't take them for me." She stood in the middle of the tunnel, the twinkling lights making the highlights in her hair shimmer and the rhinestones on her tiara sparkle. "Pucker up, Jasper."

As they touched lips, he forgot he was standing in the middle of the Fall Festival. He forgot all about the rule of not kissing in public. And whatever trouble his brother had gotten himself into was the farthest thing from his mind.

Until his phone buzzed in his back pocket. The makeshift tracker he'd installed in one of the dog crates had just moved.

"I've got to go." Jasper backed away, a smear of red lipstick on his lips.

"What do you mean you've got to go?" Delilah squinted at him through a warm curtain of desire. The tunnel, the thousands of sparkly twinkle lights . . . the man couldn't have picked a more romantic place to take her on her last night in town.

"I'm sorry. Something's come up with one of my brothers."

"Is everyone okay? Let me come with you."

He peeled her hand off his arm and gave it a squeeze.

"Not this time. I'll be back before you know it. I've still got to take you on the rest of the Pucker-Up Path."

"But . . ." Something was off. If one of the boys was hurt, he wouldn't even bother with an explanation, they'd already be in the truck, heading to whatever crisis had come up. She knew him well enough by now to tell that family came first with him, no matter what. If he was willing to walk away from the biggest night they'd shared, whatever was going on had to be serious.

He put his hand at the small of her back and led her out of the tunnel. Lucas and Maggie stood nearby, snacking on apple cider donuts.

"Hey, Lucas. Can you show Delilah around for a bit? I've got to run and take care of something that just came up."

Delilah didn't want to be pawned off on another brother. But she also didn't want to cause a scene.

Lucas glanced over, his surprise at being roped into hanging out with her evident in the way his eyebrows rose halfway up his forehead. "Uh, sure, we can do that for a bit, right, Mags?"

Maggie laughed, spraying donut crumbs down his shirt.

"I promise not to let her get near you." Lucas shifted his daughter to his other hip. "We were just about to decorate a pumpkin for the pumpkin float. Want to come with us?"

Delilah's gaze bounced from Lucas's smile to Jasper's frown and back again. Didn't seem like she had much of a choice.

"Sure." But even as she stepped away from Jasper, it felt like she was making the wrong choice.

"I'll be back in a bit," Jasper promised. Then he disappeared into the crowd, swallowed up by the other festivalgoers.

"The pumpkin tent is right this way." Lucas took a few steps and she reluctantly followed.

Jasper had taken the magic with him. But she'd never shirk her responsibilities. So, she pasted a smile on her face and took a seat across the table from Lucas and Maggie.

"Did Jasper say why he had to leave in such a hurry?" Lucas asked.

Delilah chose a pumpkin and began to draw a face on its smoothest side with one of the markers that sat between them. "No. He just said something about one of your brothers needing some help."

"Hmm." Lucas checked his phone. "Whoever it is, they must not be in too much of a jam. We've got a family group text and no one's sent out an alert."

That calmed Delilah's nerves enough that she could focus on the project at hand. Lucas seemed to be a loving dad to Maggie. She wondered if that's how Helmut would have treated her if he'd been given the chance.

Lucas picked out a tiny pumpkin and let Maggie cover it with marker scribbles and stickers while he worked on the one he was carving.

"So, this is where all the fun's happening." Trent sat down and picked up his niece. "Nice job, Maggie. Mom keeps saying she's going to be an artist."

"That would be better than working retail at the auto parts store," Lucas commented.

Delilah hadn't spent much time around the brothers, especially without Jasper present, so she kept quiet and figured she'd see what kind of information she could glean from their exchange.

"That won't be for forever." Trent bumped his shoulder into Lucas. "Once we get that wedding barn fixed up, we'll all be back to working at the orchard."

"Jasper showed me the barn this morning. It has real potential." Finished with her drawing, she started to cut out the top of the pumpkin.

"He did? I thought he was going to keep that to himself

until after you awarded Ido the title. But once we get that title, Lacey said she'll send plenty of business our way." Lucas's grin slipped as Trent elbowed him in the ribs.

"What?" Lucas asked.

Something passed between the brothers, some nonverbal communication that Delilah picked up on enough to know that Lucas wasn't supposed to mention that.

"You've got a lot riding on this win," she commented.

Neither man responded.

"I guess this is where the party's happening," Mitchell said as he and Davis entered the tent, followed by their parents and Abby. "Are you making me a pumpkin, Maggie?"

Maggie reached for her grandmother, who picked her up and snuggled her in her arms.

"Where's Jasper?" Mr. Taylor asked.

Seven pairs of eyes turned to her. Everyone except Maggie, who was too busy playing with her grandma's apple-shaped earrings.

"He had to go do something." She felt like she was shrinking under their collective gaze.

"He said one of us needed help," Trent said.

Mrs. Taylor's gaze swept over her children. "But we're all here except Jasper."

"Unless it's Noah." Davis pulled out his phone.

Suzy joined them, toting Helmut behind her. "Well aren't y'all a sight for sore eyes. They're about to put the pumpkins in the river, you don't want to miss that."

Helmut moved close and gave Delilah a half hug. She was still getting used to the fact that she had family beyond Stella. It might take her a little while to get comfortable, but as her gaze drifted over everyone surrounding the table, her heart warmed.

This could be her life. Siblings, a dad, a niece with the potential of more nieces and nephews on their way, brothers and a sister whom she adored. For once in her life, she felt secure in her own skin. Like she was exactly where she was supposed to be with exactly whom she was supposed to be with. Except for Jasper.

"Where's Jasper?" Suzy asked. "He's the one who pulled this together. Did he head down to the river to start on the pumpkin float?"

"No. He left Delilah here with Lucas because he said one of his brothers was in trouble," Trent said.

Davis held up his phone. "Noah said he's studying at the library tonight."

"So, if he's helping one of his brothers but everyone's accounted for, where do you think he is?" Helmut was the first to voice the question aloud.

"If y'all will excuse me . . ." Suzy ducked out of the tent.

"Where do you think she's going?" Mitchell asked.

"I don't know," Trent said. "But I'm sure as hell going to find out."

"I'm coming with you." Delilah was tired of other people trying to tell her what to do. If Jasper was hiding something from her, something big that might threaten what they'd been building together, she had a right to find out what it was.

"Me, too," Mitchell said.

Davis nodded. "And me."

"You call us when you know something." Mr. Taylor stopped Trent on his way out with a hand to the shoulder.

"Will do, Dad." Then he stalked toward the parking lot with Delilah, Davis, and Mitchell hot on his heels.

twenty-six

Jasper silenced his phone. Suzy had called three times so far. He couldn't afford the distraction. He was close to the dogs. The dot on his screen confirmed it.

If he was right about where Colin had taken them, he'd be coming in behind the abandoned Jericho homestead. He hadn't been out that way in years, but once upon a time, he and Colin used to hang out with the Jericho kids. That was before they lost their ranch and had to move away. The place had been sitting there for years now, boarded up and forgotten.

He'd left his truck behind a clump of trees, preferring to cover the rest of the distance on foot. As he cleared a small hill, the old barn appeared. Light filtered through the cracks between boards. He'd bet the pecan orchard there was something suspicious going on down there. He just needed to figure out what it was.

Silently, he crept toward the building. About a dozen vehicles sat behind the barn. Jasper touched his hand to the hood of a big black Chevy truck. It was still warm.

He thought about calling Bodie and turning his brother in once and for all. But he needed proof. With every inch of his heart, he hoped he was mistaken about Colin. For his sake. For Colin's sake. But especially for the sake of his parents and the rest of his family.

Plastering himself against the worn boards, he peered through a knothole in the wall. A small crowd circled around a ring of hay bales. They cheered as they glanced down at something inside the ring.

Barks, growls, and a whimper came from the barn. Jasper's stomach clenched before it dropped into his boots. Whatever was going on inside, he needed to put an end to it right the hell now. But first, he needed to see if his brother was there.

He brought his eye to the wall again, searching for Colin. Jasper vaguely recognized a few faces, but most of the men were strangers. He let out a sigh. Colin wasn't there. It didn't explain the dogs in the barn, but knowing his brother wasn't part of what was happening tonight, right under their noses, brought him some relief.

With every intent of calling Bodie and letting him know what was going on, he pulled his phone out of his pocket, ready to retreat to the safety of his truck to make the call.

As he stepped away from the barn, something poked into his back. "Going somewhere?"

Delilah bounced in the passenger seat as Trent navigated the truck over ruts in the narrow dirt road. Her fingers wrapped tight around the handle over her head. The brothers argued back and forth as Davis kept an eye on the dot on his screen.

"Now where?" Trent asked. They'd reached a dead end.

"It says he's close." Davis held out his phone.

Delilah couldn't tell from the screen, but the dot representing Jasper didn't seem to be terribly far from where Davis's own dot blinked.

"I guess we walk from here." Trent shifted into park.

"Walk where?" Delilah glanced out the window. Nothing but tall grass and clumps of trees surrounded them.

"Aren't we out by the Jerichos' old place?" Mitchell leaned into the front seat.

"Sure are. Just beyond that ridge over there." Trent pointed out Delilah's window.

She strained, trying to make out some sort of landmark in the darkness but all she could see were waves of tall grass and weeds shifting in the slight breeze. "We're going up there?"

"Why don't you wait in the truck?" Trent suggested.

"Hell, no." She'd rather take her chances with Jasper's brothers than wait around in the truck for something bad to happen.

"You can't go traipsing around in that." Mitchell nodded toward the formfitting dress she had on.

"Just watch me." She climbed out of the truck and her heel immediately sank into the ground.

"At least put these on." Trent handed her a pair of rubber boots.

"Thanks." She left her heels in the truck and slipped her feet into the oversized boots.

They set off up the hill, Davis checking his phone every so often to make sure they stayed on track. She knew the Taylor family was close, but never imagined they kept track of one another's whereabouts with an app.

Davis had explained it was their mother's idea. She'd insisted on it when they were younger, and the brothers had kept it up so they could keep tabs on one another. Whatever the reason, hopefully it would pay off.

The four of them cleared the top of the small hill and looked down at an old barn. Light streamed through one of the doors. Muffled yells and cheers drifted up the hill.

"You're sure he's in there?" Delilah asked. Looked like there was some sort of party going on.

"I sure as hell hope not." Mitchell's jaw was set. Besides Jasper, he was the biggest of the brothers. If he felt uneasy, Delilah ought to be shaking in her borrowed rubber boots.

"Shit." Trent scrubbed his hands over his barely there hair. "Please tell me this isn't what I think it is."

"What?" Delilah looked over the dozen or so trucks and SUVs parked outside the barn, a bad feeling starting to take root in her chest.

"Let's not go making shit up. Jasper deserves the benefit of the doubt until we know for sure what he's up to." Davis slid his phone into his pocket. "I'm going closer."

Delilah made a move to follow. "You'd better stay here." Mitchell put a hand out to stop her. Then he nudged his head toward her as he looked at Trent.

"I'll keep an eye on her." Trent put his arm in front of her, like that barrier would keep her from following the other two. "Let's wait it out up here."

She wanted to argue, but she also had enough sense to realize that if they thought it was bad, there was probably something horrible going on inside that barn. "What do they think's happening in there?"

"I don't even want to say." Trent grabbed a tall piece of grass and focused on ripping it to small pieces.

Delilah pursed her lips, her heart squeezing so tight, she couldn't stand to be still. When Trent didn't expand, she figured she'd have to take matters into her own hands, and took off down the hill after Davis and Mitchell.

"Dammit." Trent followed, cursing as he caught up. "Jasper's going to kill me if you get hurt. Can you please stay back?"

"I'll stop at the edge of the grass. How's that?" She needed to witness what was happening with her own eyes.

"I can see why he likes you so much." He attempted a smile, but Delilah could sense the worry underneath his grin.

She ducked down in the grass, her skin tingling with the

sensation of bugs and other creepy things crawling all over her. Not wanting to find out if it was just her vivid imagination or if a variety of critters covered her skin, she shook her arms and tried to be quiet while Davis and Mitchell edged toward the open barn door.

Mitchell moved fast, darting from the cover of the grass to press himself against the boards. He turned slightly, peeking into the barn. Her pulse ticked up while she waited.

After what felt like eons, he scrambled across the gravel and squatted down next to them. "It's bad. Jasper's in there, along with about a dozen dogs and a big group of huge assholes. I think we need to bring Bodie in on this. We can't take 'em all, not by ourselves."

"What do you mean Jasper's in there with dogs?" Delilah put a hand on Mitchell's arm, drawing his attention.

"I'm sorry, you might not want to be here when this all goes down." He cocked his head. "Davis, you want to take her back to the festival?"

"I'm not going anywhere until this is sorted out. Somebody better tell me what the hell's going on before I head in there to see for myself."

The brothers looked at one another, then shifted their eyes to the ground.

Delilah had enough of everyone trying to protect her. She stood, hiked up the skirt of her long dress, and headed toward the barn. "Jasper Taylor! I know you're in there."

"Oh, shit!" Trent sprang from where he'd been hunkered down, wrapped his arms around her, and tried to pull her back.

"Let go of me." She struggled against him, her elbow connecting with his gut. He let out an *oof*, and his arms fell away as he doubled over.

Two men came out of the barn. "Who's there?"

Delilah forged ahead, just one thought in her mind. She had to get to Jasper. He'd tell her what was going on.

* * *

Not even two minutes later she regretted her questionable act of bravery as she stepped into the light of the barn. Jasper stood in the center of a ring of hay bales. Crates of dogs spread around the perimeter. The men around him stepped back.

"Delilah, what are you doing here?" He rushed toward her, his gaze racing over her. "Are you okay?"

The men who had caught her outside came in, prodding Jasper's brothers along with the barrel of a rifle. "Caught this group sniffing around outside. Somebody want to tell me what the hell's going on?"

Jasper stepped toward her, his hands up, palms out. "Let's all keep our cool. What are y'all doing here?"

"You told her you had to go help one of your brothers in trouble," Davis said. "Didn't make sense to any of us since we were all at the festival, getting ready for the pumpkin float."

"He did have to help one of his brothers." A man stepped out from the shadows.

Delilah squinted. There was something familiar about him, but she knew she'd never seen him before.

"Colin?" Trent stepped toward him, his arms wide. "What are you doing here?"

The two men embraced as Jasper pinched the bridge of his nose.

Colin. That was Jasper's older brother. The one who'd moved away. Delilah glanced back and forth between the brothers. Besides Trent, the other two didn't look quite so happy to see their sibling.

"What the fuck's going on?" the guy with the rifle asked.

"It's okay, they're with me." Colin's voice was steady.

Jasper edged close enough to pull Delilah into his side.

"The fuck we are." Mitchell's glare could have burned

the whole place down. "Please tell me you're not involved with this. I'm outta here."

"Not so fast." The guy with the rifle tapped it against Mitchell's leg. "We didn't know we were having a family reunion of sorts going on."

"Let them go." Jasper motioned for Davis to move next to Delilah. "Colin and I will stay. If the others don't get back to the festival, they're going to be missed. You don't want Mayor Cherish sending her husband out with a search party looking for the missing guest of honor, do you?"

The men murmured among themselves and Delilah slid her gaze over the roughly constructed ring of hay, noticing several splatters of something red. She immediately glanced back to Jasper. He didn't appear to be injured, making her wonder whose blood it was.

"We'd better scram." One of the men ran in through the door. "Cops are on their way. I can see the lights headed this direction."

"What did you do?" Jasper yelled at his brothers.

The men gathered the crates, scattering like ants abandoning a flooded anthill. Engines rumbled, tires scraped on gravel, and Delilah stood there the whole time, wondering what in the world she'd gotten herself involved with this time.

twenty-seven

“Come here.” Jasper moved toward Delilah, his only goal to protect her, to shield her from the sheer hell they’d found themselves in.

“Stay away.” Her green eyes, usually a place of refuge where he could forget his worries and hide for a while, held a world of fear.

“I’m not going to hurt you. I want to keep you safe.” He held out an arm, desperate to guard her from the chaos.

“I think you’ve done enough.” Mitchell slung an arm around Delilah’s shoulders.

Jasper’s heart cracked. Then, as Delilah turned her back on him, taking comfort in his brother’s arms, it shattered. What had he done?

“It’s not what you think.” How could he explain? As he tried to come up with the right words to defend himself, Bodie came through the door of the barn. The sheriff walked in behind him, followed by a few other men.

“What’s going on?” Bodie moved toward Jasper, his

hand ready to grip his service weapon. "Somebody needs to fill me in, fast."

Jasper's brothers began to talk at the same time.

Bodie held up a hand. "Delilah, what did you see when you got here?"

She looked Bodie in the eye, her lip trembling. Jasper would have given anything in that moment to wrap her in his arms and reassure her that what she saw wasn't the truth of the situation.

"I saw Jasper, standing in the middle of all of those bales of hay. All of these men surrounded him. And the dogs." Her voice cracked.

Bodie's eyes closed for a long beat. "We need to sort this out, but my wife tells me you're expected to shut down the Fall Festival. If you promise you'll be available for questions later if I need you, I'll have someone run you back downtown if you're up for it."

Delilah bit her lip and nodded. Jasper tried to catch her attention before she turned her back and walked away. It was important for her to know that he wasn't the bad guy in all of this. Before he could say a word, Bodie stepped in front of him, blocking his view.

"I actually can't believe I'm about to say this to you." He reached for Jasper's arm. "But you have the right to remain silent . . ."

Jasper tuned him out. He let himself be cuffed and led outside, hoping Delilah didn't see him being stuffed into the back of the car, his arms behind him.

Bodie and his team were able to round up several of the men who'd been at the barn. Jasper hoped Colin would be one of them, but it looked like his older brother might have gotten away. He'd messed up. Bad. He never should have tried to handle Colin by himself tonight. If he'd been the one to call

Bodie, he'd probably be kissing Delilah on the swing he and Abby built right about now.

Instead he sat on a metal bench in the holding cell at the sheriff's office, waiting for a chance to set things right.

"Come on, it's your turn to talk." One of the other deputies took him into a small office where Bodie waited.

"Want to fill me in on what the hell you were doing at a dog fight tonight? You ought to know better than that. Just being a spectator is a felony in all fifty states." Bodie crossed his arms over his chest.

"I messed up." Jasper raked his fingers through his hair. "Colin came back in town recently. Said he'd gotten in over his head and wanted to get out. I was trying to help him. When I found those dogs in the barn today, I knew he had to be involved."

"And you decided to take matters into your own hands?" Bodie's lips twisted into a frown. "What did you think you'd accomplish by tracking him down to a dog fight? You know you could have gotten yourself killed?"

Jasper scrubbed a hand over his chin. He hadn't thought about the consequences for himself, he'd been so focused on trying to get to his brother and force a change of heart. "I'm sorry."

"You sure as hell ought to be. Not only did you put my entire operation at risk, you also dragged your brothers and Delilah into this. Do you have any idea how pissed my wife is going to be? You really think Ido is going to be voted the most romantic small town in Texas when they find out Miss Lovin' Texas followed you to an illegal dog fight?"

Jasper shook his head. "If anything had happened to her . . ."

Bodie didn't respond, just let the reality of the moment hang in the air. The weight of it pressed down on Jasper to the point where he felt like he couldn't take in a breath. He thought he'd been doing the right thing by protecting his family from Colin's misdeeds. But what he'd really done was put everything he loved at risk.

He hung his head, letting his forearms rest on his thighs while he focused on a spot on the floor just in front of the toe of his boots. "I didn't mean for it to turn out this way."

Bodie reached across the table and clapped him on the shoulder. "There's no doubt in my mind you weren't involved in the dog fighting. One of my guys picked up your brother trying to hot-wire a truck and skip town. He confessed to everything and we've got enough evidence to put him away for quite a while. I don't owe that piece of scum a fucking thing, but he wants to talk to you."

Jasper lifted his head. "You believe me?"

"I never thought you were caught up in that. But if you stand in the way of me doing my job again, I'm not going to be so forgiving."

"I understand." Jasper glanced toward the door where Colin stood, his hands cuffed, his face a mixture of fear and regret.

"I'm going to give the two of you a few minutes before we book him." Bodie nodded toward Colin as he slid his hat back on his head and closed the door behind him.

Colin perched on the edge of a chair, his wrists cuffed together in front of him.

Jasper leaned back. "What happened?"

"I fucked up." Colin wouldn't meet his gaze.

"You fucked up because you really fucked up, or you fucked up because you got caught?" There was a world of difference in those two statements and Jasper needed to know which way Colin intended it.

"Does it matter?" The sneer on his brother's face told him everything he needed to know.

Why had he let so many years go by trying to protect his brother and cover up his crimes? He'd wanted to shield his parents, keep his brothers out of harm's way, and not spoil their image of his older brother. But for what?

Colin didn't appear to regret his actions, just that he got caught.

"When you showed up on my doorstep saying you wanted out, did you mean it?" Jasper's heart had been shattered twice already tonight. Once at the look in Delilah's eyes and again when he realized he'd probably ruined everything for everyone he loved.

"I got left behind. Needed somewhere to hide out for a few hours. And I was injured. Damn dog caught me right on the arm."

Jasper glanced at the scar on Colin's arm, left behind by the stitches he'd put in himself. "You're not even sorry about what happened, are you? Do you even care that Mom and Dad are going to be devastated when they find out what you've been up to?"

"Let me fix it." Colin moved closer, his voice shaky. "You can take over for me. You get to the right people and you can be pulling in thirty grand a month."

"No." Jasper stood and moved toward the door. "I'm done. You've made your decision on how you want to live your life. I can't protect them from it anymore."

"You're making a huge mistake. None of this would have happened if you hadn't brought that chick around. I thought she would have left when she got freaked out by those damn crickets. But no . . . you had to save the day."

Jasper turned back to face his brother. "You're responsible for the crickets in the trailer?"

"You know what happens if Ido wins that stupid title?"

His eyes narrowed, Jasper clenched his fists and waited for Colin to continue.

Colin ground his molars together. "It's already bad enough with that bitch mayor bringing in all kinds of wedding traffic. If Ido managed to get themselves declared the most romantic small town in Texas, we'd have so many tourists crawling around this part of the county that the dog ring would be done."

"So you tried to make sure that wouldn't happen." Jasper thought back to all the things that had taken place since Delilah had been in town. "The movie?"

"Come on, I can't believe anyone still hangs out watching movies at the Hampton barn. It was a piece of cake to make a few cuts in the film. How was I to know they'd have another one ready to throw on though? And a butterfly wedding without butterflies sure ain't very romantic, is it?" With his lips curled up in an ugly smirk, Colin glared at him. "At least she won't be giving you the title now. Not after the crappy time you've shown her."

Jasper saw red. Anger flared, his hands fisted at his sides, and he took a swing at his older brother, connecting with his chin.

Colin backed up, a wild shine to his eyes. "It didn't have to go down like this."

"You're right about that. I should have turned you in years ago when I had the chance." With that, he opened the door and stepped to the side while one of the deputies went in to finish dealing with Colin.

He'd fucked up. But unlike his brother, he was more upset about the choices he'd made that had brought him to this moment than he was about getting caught. Hopefully his family would be able to forgive him. He'd not only failed the people who counted on him, like Lacey, but he'd failed the people he loved the most. His parents, his siblings, and Delilah.

It was failing her that hurt the most.

"I'm headed down to wrap up at the festival. You need a ride?" Bodie asked.

Jasper nodded. Hopefully he'd have a chance to get to her. Before it was too late.

twenty-eight

Delilah smiled and nodded, even though her heart wasn't in it, waving at the small crowd from the steps of the gazebo. It was hard to believe that this was where it had all started just thirty days ago. She'd borrowed a spare outfit from Lacey after arriving back at the festival with grass stains all over her dress and rubber boots on her feet.

Looking out over the group, she tried to keep her emotions in check. Her time in Ido had come to an end, and not a moment too soon. Watching Jasper get arrested had ripped her to pieces. She thought she'd found a safe place with him, free from the lies and betrayals she'd lived with her whole life at the hands of her mother.

Truth was, she couldn't count on anyone. It was just too bad that she'd had to learn that lesson the hard way. The one man she thought she could trust, to be there for her through thick and thin, had been leading a whole other life.

Lacey turned off the mic and pulled Delilah into a hug. "Thank you so much for being here. I just wish Jasper was here to say a few words, too."

Numb, Delilah nodded. Obviously, Lacey hadn't heard the news yet that the hospitality host had proven to be less than hospitable.

"You want to meet up for breakfast tomorrow? I wasn't sure what time you'd be leaving."

"I've got so much to do back in Dallas. I figured I'd head out tonight. I'm eager to get home and sleep in my own bed for a change." Delilah didn't even bother trying to force another smile. Her job was done.

"You sure?" Lacey squeezed her hands. "Don't you want to get a good night's sleep and leave in the morning?"

"No." Her original plan for the night had been to spend the evening in Jasper's arms, joined together in every way that mattered. But that had been dashed as she watched him get put into the back of a squad car. "I think it's best to get on the road tonight."

"If you're sure . . ."

"I am." Delilah let go and turned to scan the departing crowd. She'd been looking for Jasper's family, but they all seemed to have disappeared. It was best that way. She hadn't been looking forward to saying good-bye, especially to Abby. This would make it easier.

She caught a ride back to Taylor Farms with one of the volunteers. All the lights in the house were out. The long driveway usually held at least two or three cars, but thankfully, no one had come back yet. She didn't want to be there when they did.

Jasper had hooked her trailer up for her earlier that day in preparation for her trip home. At the time he'd planned on going with her, saying he wanted to make sure she got back to Dallas safely and that he didn't want her to have to face Stella alone.

So much for that.

She didn't even bother to change out of the borrowed clothes. Just got behind the wheel, turned over the ignition, and slowly pulled out of the drive.

* * *

Jasper glanced around the circle of people surrounding him. His mom and dad stood to his left. His brothers fanned out on his right. Even Suzy had come to the station and stood next to Abby, who hadn't stopped crying since he'd exited the sheriff's office a full five minutes before. He'd been doing his best to explain himself to everyone, with mixed results.

"You're telling me you've been lying to us for the past three years?" Dad's cheeks always got red when he was pissed off, and now they looked like two bright, ripe apples as he whipped his hat off his head and tossed it on the ground.

"Frank, calm down. You're going to give yourself a heart attack." Mom bent down to pick up the hat while Jasper tried to hold his ground against the withering gazes of his brothers.

"So, you're not running the dog-fighting ring." Trent nodded. "That's good to know. I didn't want to believe it but when I saw you standing there . . ."

"I'm sorry. I owe all of you a huge apology and I hope you can forgive me." Jasper shuffled his feet. "All I ever wanted to do was protect you. I figured if you thought Colin was just mad at me, it would be easier than having to tell you he'd gotten himself mixed up in all of this."

Mom put a hand on his shoulder. "You should have told us the truth."

He met her gaze, only able to hold it for a moment before looking away. The disappointment in her eyes mixed with motherly love, and he was afraid to see which one was stronger. "I know that now."

"What's going to happen to Colin?" Mitchell asked.

Jasper shook his head. "I don't know."

"I'm going to find out." Dad pulled the door open and disappeared inside the building. Mom gave Jasper's hand a squeeze, then followed right behind him.

Davis checked his watch. "Fall Festival just wrapped up. Do we need to clean up now or can we take care of it tomorrow?"

Jasper swallowed, hard. He'd let so many people down tonight, especially Delilah. The horror on her face when she'd realized what she'd walked in on kept playing through his mind. He'd never forget the look of sheer terror in her eyes. If she never wanted to speak to him again, he deserved it.

"I'm going to head that way now. See if I can catch Delilah and try to explain what happened."

"Good luck, bro." Trent clapped a hand on his shoulder. "Come on, I'll give you a ride."

Jasper shook hands with Davis and Mitchell before pulling Abby into a hug. "I'm sorry, Little Bug. I didn't mean to mess things up so bad."

"Remember what I said about Heraclitus?"

"Hera who?" Trent asked.

"Abby's a budding philosopher." Jasper tucked her head under his arm and rubbed his knuckles over it. "What's the latest, wise one?"

She pushed against his side. "The road up and down is one and the same. He said that, too."

"What the hell is that supposed to mean?" Trent asked.

"Jasper knows." Abby stood there, a girlish grin on her face.

"It means I got myself into this mess, so I ought to be able to find my way out."

"That works." Abby skipped over to Davis's truck. "Can we stop at the Dairy Dell on the way home?"

"Here"—Jasper peeled off a twenty from the bills in his wallet—"get her whatever she wants. My treat."

Trent had already started his truck when Jasper slid into the front seat. "Thanks for the ride."

"Thanks for not being the asshole I was afraid you might

be when I saw you standing in that barn tonight." Trent shifted into gear and pulled out onto the main road.

"You're welcome?" Jasper let himself return Trent's smile. It might be rocky for a bit, but things were going to be okay with his family. They understood why he'd done what he did, and even though none of them seemed to agree with how he'd handled things, at least they'd be willing to forgive him. Eventually.

With any luck, Lacey and Delilah would feel the same way. If not, he may as well ask Bodie to book him.

twenty-nine

Delilah woke and for several moments had no idea where she was. When she'd arrived back in Dallas last night, she'd parked the truck and trailer in the lot of her condo and somehow managed to make her way inside. Her phone had buzzed and constantly pinged the first hour of her drive, so she'd turned it off.

She wasn't ready to talk to Jasper yet. A tiny part of her wondered if she ever would be. All she wanted to do was sleep.

A quick glance at the clock on her nightstand showed her she'd done just that. It was after three o'clock in the afternoon. She'd been gone for so long that her refrigerator was as bare as the first time she'd seen Jasper's.

She pulled a can of organic lentil soup out of the cabinet and heated it on the stove. Even though she didn't feel like eating, didn't appear to have any feelings about anything at all, she figured she should put something in her stomach before she turned on her phone again.

After finishing the soup and scrubbing away any remnants of her time in Ido with a hot shower, she sat down at her kitchen table and faced her phone.

The first voice mail was from Jasper.

"D, hey, it's me. I'm so sorry about tonight. I just need a chance to explain. Please call me. We need to talk before we leave tomorrow."

Her heart squeezed at the hope in his voice. He could have the best reason in the world for doing what he did, but it wouldn't change the fact that he'd lied to her.

She pressed play on the next message.

"It's me again. I came by the Fall Festival to find you, but Lacey said you headed out already. I'm on my way back now. I'll be there in twenty minutes. Please give me a chance to make this up to you."

Her heart lodged in her throat. She tried to force a swallow past it as the next message began.

"Where are you, Delilah? The trailer's gone, your truck's gone. I thought we were going to head back to Dallas tomorrow. Together. I need to talk to you. We can work this out."

She couldn't handle any more. As she stared at the phone, it rang, vibrating against the table. Her mother's number flashed on the screen. Feeling like she was trading one evil for another, she picked up.

"Hello?"

"Darling, are you home? I got a call from Jasper and he was worried sick about you. I know we've had our differences over the past couple of weeks, but I need to know, are you okay?"

Hearing her mother's voice seemed to loosen the cork on the emotions she'd been trying to bottle up. "Jasper and I broke up. Can you come over?"

"I'll be there in ten."

Stella disconnected, and Delilah turned off her phone.

* * *

Jasper didn't know what to do. He'd been trying to reach Delilah for three days. He was tempted to drive to Dallas to try to talk to her in person, but Lacey had forbidden him to go after her. At least until after the big gala celebration this weekend. Since he'd probably be the reason Ido lost their chance at the title, he felt obligated to honor her request. Even though every part of him urged him to do it anyway.

At least he'd put all of that nervous energy to good use. The barn had been cleared out and he'd made a list of everything they'd need to do if Dad decided to move forward on the wedding barn idea. He'd cleaned up after the Fall Festival, except for the Pucker-Up Path. Lacey thought it made a nice addition to the town and had started incorporating the hashtag into her marketing materials for the wedding business.

Abby even showed him a picture his mom and dad posted. They were sitting in the swing under the flowery arbor he and Abby had built together. Maybe something good would come out of all of the bad, even if he hadn't been able to talk to Delilah.

He'd even spent a few days over at For Pitties' Sake. Thanks to Mitchell calling Bodie when Jasper still thought he could handle things himself, they'd managed to rescue the dogs that had been in the barn that night and were getting close to issuing warrants on several other locations that had come to light during interrogations. Zina had her hands full with almost fifteen new dogs and possibly dozens more on the way.

That should have made him feel better, but nothing seemed able to pull him out of the black hole he'd fallen into.

He'd finished feeding Tie Dye and was heading to the

big house to wash up before dinner when he spotted Suzy and Abby sitting on the porch.

"There's double trouble waiting to happen." He stopped at the railing and watched Suzy trying to pull Abby's hair back into some kind of braid.

"How are you holding up?" Suzy asked.

He shrugged. "I've been better."

Abby sighed. "I don't know why you can't just go to Dallas and talk to her."

Jasper missed Delilah like a hole in his heart, but Abby missed her, too. He hadn't been kidding when he told Delilah that Abby had taken to her like the sister she'd never had. Knowing he'd broken Abby's heart, too, only made him feel worse.

"Lacey won't let me. I promised her I'd wait until after the big party in Houston to go talk to her. Lacey's holding out hope that there might be a slim chance of Delilah choosing Ido."

"Slim to none and Slim left town." One corner of Suzy's mouth ticked up. "I'm sorry, sugar, but I think the writing's on the wall with that one."

"Dad said we might have to sell the horses." Abby hugged her arms to her stomach.

Jasper cringed. "I'm so sorry, Little Bug."

"It is what it is."

"You know what? These fingers aren't made for braiding hair. I'm sorry, honey, but I think Delilah's the only one who can tame these unruly locks." Suzy smoothed her hand over Abby's hair.

Abby let out a sigh as she slumped farther into the chair. "I wish she'd come back."

"You and me both, kiddo." Jasper squatted down next to his sister. "I'm going to do my best to talk to her before it's too late."

Abby's eyes sparked. He'd seen that look. Right before she'd insisted he add the swing to the arbor.

“I’m almost afraid to ask, but what’s on your mind?”

“It would suck to have to sell the horses, but I wouldn’t mind.”

“No?” He had the feeling that wasn’t all.

“Not if you bring Delilah back. I think you ought to go to that fancy party and tell her you love her.”

“Just like that?”

“Well, no. You should bring her some pretty flowers and get dressed up, too.”

“Thing is, I don’t think she likes me anymore.” Sooner or later he’d have to make peace with the fact that he’d done the worst thing he could have done when it came to Delilah. “I lied to her, Little Bug. If I go to Houston, all she’s going to do is turn me down.”

“She might turn you down, but do you think she’d be able to say no to all of us?” Suzy bent over and put an arm around Abby’s shoulders just as Trent and Mitchell stepped onto the porch.

“What’s going on?” Mitchell asked.

“We’re figuring out how we can help Jasper win back Delilah.” Abby looked at Trent. “Go get Lucas and Davis. They need to be part of this, too.”

“Abby, it’s not going to work.” Jasper couldn’t fault his little sister for wanting to try. She was still young enough to believe that true love could conquer all and that everyone deserved a happily-ever-after.

“Wait a minute.” Trent tapped his lip. “You’ve been protecting us, trying to keep us all from getting hurt all this time.”

“Yeah, and look how that turned out,” Jasper said.

“The whole reason you were such a jerk was because you love us so much. I know that’s why you were trying so hard to help.” Abby seemed so much older, so much wiser than he was at her age. Who was he kidding . . . than he was even now.

“What’s done is done.” Jasper shrugged.

"Be ready at five o'clock on Saturday. Wear something nice and leave the rest to me." Abby got up and made her way to the front door. "By the way, I'm not just talking to Jasper. All of us are going. We're a family. We're all going to win her back together."

thirty

Delilah held Stella's hand as she waited in the wings to go onto the stage. She'd managed to bail on the dinner portion of the evening. Stella lied for her and said she'd been battling a migraine. The last task she had to complete to fulfill her contractual obligation was to announce the winner at the final gala. With her heart thundering in her chest, she trained her gaze on Mr. Plum while he talked about all the criteria that went into selecting the winner of the Most Romantic Small Town in Texas competition.

Lacey was in the crowd. Delilah had caught a glimpse of her and Bodie when she'd arrived. Although she'd removed Jasper's name from the guest list, she still wasn't looking forward to seeing anyone from Ido. Her feelings were still too raw, too painful.

She'd had to relive all of them over the past week while she sorted through the time she'd spent in each town. Her decision had been a difficult one, even more so due to the circumstances, but she was comfortable with her choice and couldn't wait to put the past few months behind her.

"Without further ado, let me introduce the contest judge to announce the winner. Please welcome the reigning Miss Lovin' Texas, Delilah Stone, to the stage." Mr. Plum clapped his hands while he waited for her to meet him onstage.

"This is it, go on." Stella gave her a tiny nudge.

Delilah took a deep breath in through her nose and held it for a count of three before letting it out in a slow exhale. Then she pasted on the biggest, brightest smile she could muster, and stepped into the spotlight.

"Thank you, Mr. Plum. It's been my pleasure being involved in such an exciting competition. All three towns put their best foot forward, making my decision an incredibly difficult one." Delilah smiled into the crowd, her gaze drawn to Lacey, who sat at a table right in front of the stage.

Bodie had moved his chair right next to his wife's and held her hand. They both looked so hopeful, it almost made Delilah forget her next line.

"Ms. Stone?" Mr. Plum blinked a few times. "Would you do us the honor of announcing the third-place winner?"

Her attention snapped back to the laptop sitting on top of the podium. She clicked the mouse and a picture of East appeared on the screen. "Coming in third, I'd like to congratulate the town of East, Texas."

A polite smattering of applause came from the crowd.

"I had a fantastic time getting to know the folks in East. If you're ever in the mood for a romantic trail ride or date night at the most charming barbecue joint west of the Mississippi, East is where it's at." Delilah stepped back from the podium as Mr. Plum welcomed East's mayor and his wife to the stage. They snapped a few photos and he handed them a small trophy in the shape of Texas with a heart placed over East's location on the map.

"I'll be honest, I had a hard time choosing the second-place winner. Both Hartwood and Ido welcomed me with open arms." She paused, glancing down to see Lacey grip Bodie's fingers and sit up straighter in her seat.

"Both towns have tons of personality. The residents were so friendly and welcoming. But a decision had to be made, so I'm thrilled to announce the second-place winner is Hartwood." Delilah posed for pictures with Mr. Plum and the mayor of Hartwood, who was clearly annoyed at the perceived snub.

Mr. Plum took the mic. "As you've all figured out by now, we have a winner. But before we make it official, Ms. Stone was kind enough to go above and beyond her official duties to prepare a slideshow of some of her favorite moments in Ido."

The lights dimmed as a screen lowered behind the stage. Music filtered from the speakers, and the tune "Cowboy Take Me Away" began to play. Images of Ido flashed on the screen. First, the kickoff celebration where she'd had her first taste of Helmut's cooking, then heard the musical magic of Kirby and the rest of the Wicked Washboarders. There were photos from the vineyard tour, her luncheon with the ladies' group, and the speech she'd given at Abby's school.

Delilah managed not to cry until the picture she'd taken of Jasper and Buster on the blanket at the Hamptons' movie barn appeared on-screen. She dabbed at her cheeks with a tissue. Even though she'd chosen waterproof mascara because she was afraid she wouldn't be able to hold it together, she still didn't want to have streaks running down her cheeks.

Light from the hall spilled into the room as the ballroom door opened. The slideshow froze, a picture of her and Jasper covered in butterflies and mud stuck on the screen.

"That right there was the moment I knew I'd fallen in love with you," Jasper's voice boomed from the back of the room.

Delilah's heart pounded in her chest as she squinted into the darkness. All she could see were the silhouettes of the people who were coming through the door.

He wound his way through the sea of tables, each step bringing him closer to the stage. "Although I was pretty sure you were going to steal my heart the very first time I set eyes on you."

Delilah closed her eyes, the tears free-falling down her cheeks. She tapped on the mouse, desperate to get the slide-show playing so she could leave the stage. The next picture showed her and Abby with the crazy goat, then faded into the shot she'd captured of the butterflies being released into the air.

"Delilah." He stood at the foot of the stage, his hair tamed, his cheeks freshly shaved, his broad shoulders en-cased in what looked like a brand-new dark gray suit coat. His tie was yellow, her favorite color.

"You can't do this now, Jasper," she whispered. "It's too late."

Lacey made a move to get out of her chair but Bodie put his arm around her and muttered something in her ear. Any chance of being saved by the mayor disappeared.

"I love you, Delilah Stone. Someone once told me it's never too late to do the right thing. Please, tell me you meant it. Say you'll give me a chance to explain myself and prove I'm the man you fell in love with."

Mr. Plum gasped and grabbed for the mic. "Lights, please. We're thrilled to congratulate the town of Ido . . . the most romantic town in Texas."

Jasper's eyes went wide. "You picked Ido?"

She moved to the edge of the stage and squatted down as best she could in the tight yellow dress she'd picked to wear that night. "You missed it. I did pick Ido. You could have saved yourself the trip."

"Delilah, what you saw in the barn that night, it's not what you think. I was trying to save my family from finding out the truth about my brother. I should have come clean when I'd had the chance but I didn't want my folks to get their hearts broken."

Her mouth went dry and she tried to swallow but the emotion welling up in her chest made it almost impossible. "I know."

"How?" Jasper's gaze searched hers.

She took in a breath, trying to stabilize her pulse. "My dad called and told me."

"Helmut." Jasper's shoulders rose and fell. "But why, after everything I put you through, why would you pick Ido?"

She didn't want to look at him, didn't trust herself not to lose it when she saw the hope and love shining in his eyes. But then he put his finger under her chin and nudged her head up, forcing her to meet his gaze.

"Because that's where I fell in love. And what's more romantic than that?"

"Come here." He reached out and swept her off the stage, cradling her against his chest before he set her down on her feet in front of him.

"Ask her, Jasper." Abby came close and Delilah slowly shifted her gaze from Jasper to see his family had joined them.

"What are all of you doing here?"

Suzy stood next to Abby, her hands covered in those black lacy gloves she'd been wearing the first day Delilah met her. Mitchell, Trent, and Davis had all cleaned up. She almost didn't recognize Jasper's brothers without their cowboy hats and jeans. And there was an extra. She assumed that was Noah, the only Taylor brother she hadn't met in person yet. He must have driven down from college. He stood next to Lucas, who held little Maggie in his arms.

"Yeah, ask her." Helmut stepped next to Mr. and Mrs. Taylor, who smiled like they'd just won the lottery.

Jasper got down on one knee in front of her. "Delilah Stone, I know I'm not an easy man to love, but I'm also not a man who love found easily. That's why I know in my heart we're meant to be together. You bring out the best in me and I hope you'll let me do my very best, every single day for the rest of our lives, to bring out the best in you."

"Get to it," Stella said. She'd joined Helmut at the edge of the circle, her eyes taking on a kind of shine Delilah had never seen before.

"That's why I'd like to ask you . . ." Jasper looked up at her. The light in his eyes shut out everything else in the room.

"Will you marry us?" Abby shouted, jumping up and down.

"Abby!" Jasper jerked his head toward his sister.

"What? You were taking too long." She shrugged, her cheeks flushing pink.

"Us?" Delilah asked.

Jasper stood and took both of her hands in his. "Yes, us. You told me once you'd always wondered what it would be like to have a big family."

She nodded. "That's true."

"Well, here we are." He glanced around at his brothers, his sister, his parents, and his aunt. "If you say yes, you'll be getting more than a husband. You'll be getting all of us."

It was too much. She'd never known the kind of love that seemed to pour from the Taylors, wrap around her and Jasper, and fill her so full of happiness she felt like butterflies were beating their wings against the walls of her chest.

She looked straight into his eyes. "Yes."

He immediately caught her lips in a kiss while his family clapped and shrieked around them.

Delilah had gone into the contest with no expectations, but she was leaving with everything she'd ever wanted.

Ido may have won the title, but there was no doubt in her mind that she was the real winner.

epilogue

Delilah stood at the back of the newly renovated Taylor Farms Event Barn. She'd spent the past six months working with a handful of young girls from the surrounding area, the pilot group for the program she and Monique would be launching soon. By this time next year they'd be able to offer a summer camp program as well, which would match the girls with one of the dogs from For Pitties' Sake, something she'd been wanting to do since the first time she'd visited the rescue shelter.

"How do you think they're going to do?" Jasper came up behind her and circled her in his arms. His hands came to rest on her stomach and she leaned into him.

"I don't know. I'm so nervous right now I feel like I could puke."

His breath brushed against her ear as he let out a soft laugh. "You've done what you could. It's up to them now."

Stella had arrived the day before, insistent on being the

one to emcee the competition, and now walked across the temporary stage Jasper and his brothers had constructed. "I'd like to welcome you to the first annual Pucker-Up Pageant, a competition that recognizes the hard work these young women have done, working with their canine partners for six months, training them in the areas of agility, behavior, and following basic commands."

Delilah turned her head to whisper into Jasper's ear. "She looks like she was made for this, doesn't she?"

He nodded, the scruff of his cheek rubbing against her skin. "Poor Adeline. I almost feel sorry for her, don't you?"

Biting back her smile, Delilah squeezed her fiancé's hands. Stella and Adeline were a match made in pageant heaven. They'd only been working together for a few months and with Stella's coaching, Adeline had already been crowned Mrs. Blushing Bluebonnet. Stella had her sights set on a state title next, and based on Adeline's level of enthusiasm, Delilah had no doubt they'd be successful.

Jasper stood straighter as Abby walked across the stage. She'd been matched with the shy pup Delilah met the day she'd toured the rescue. There was nothing shy about Chantilly now. Under Abby's constant care and attention, the pup had come out of her shell. Abby put Chantilly through her paces, stopping as they reached center stage.

"Smile. That's it. Now let the dog give you a kiss." Franco stood right in front, snapping photos.

Delilah had scrapped the cosmetics line Stella had been working on and decided to develop something that would be 100 percent vegan, and cruelty-free. Fifty percent of their profits would go to charity: 25 percent to For Pitties' Sake and 25 percent to the program she'd be running that would empower girls.

Franco surprised them all by offering to donate his time and skills, and the pictures he was shooting today would be part of their new "Beauty Isn't Only Skin-Deep" campaign, which would promote their line while raising awareness about the evils of dog fighting.

"Have I told you how proud I am of you?" Jasper nibbled at her ear, causing ripples of goose bumps to pebble her skin.

"Well, I'm proud of you right back." She meant it, too. He'd busted his butt to turn the old barn into the beautiful building they stood in today.

"I told you we make a good team."

"And you were right."

Franco finished snapping photos and Stella introduced the next pair. Today's run-through was supposed to get the girls comfortable onstage. Tomorrow the real pageant would take place and the seats would be full. Just thinking about it made Delilah's knees go weak.

"What do you think about making it official?" Jasper's chin rested on her shoulder.

"Making what official?"

"Us." He ran his thumb over the engagement ring he'd given her. "The barn's ready. I figured we ought to be the first ones to get married here."

She shivered at the idea of standing in a gorgeous white dress and saying her vows in front of all their family and friends. "Weddings take a long time to plan. We've both been so busy, I haven't given it a ton of thought yet."

"I'm sure our families will want to help. I figure we'll need about a thousand butterflies."

"Oh, at least. And it's probably best if we catch them ourselves." She smiled as she remembered the day they'd spent covered in mud by the creek.

"I bet Zina would break down and let us incorporate some of the rescue dogs. Lacey's been trying to get her to do it for years, but I'm sure she would if you asked."

Delilah nodded. "Buster will be the ring bearer."

"Of course. Hopefully that new food you started him on

will cut down on his gas." Jasper swayed back and forth. "Kirby will be devastated if we don't ask the Wicked Washboarders to play the reception."

"And Helmut will have to do the food. He's been working on a whole vegetarian menu. I can't wait to see what he comes up with."

"What do you say, Ms. Stone? Seems like we've got a good handle on the plans. Want to pick a date?"

Delilah closed her eyes and took in a deep breath. "September thirtieth. That's the first day I laid eyes on you. It can be the first anniversary of the day we met. I think that will be perfect."

"I'm glad we got that settled." His arms tightened. "There's one more thing I think we need to discuss."

"What's that?"

"When do we get to go on a honeymoon?"

Her belly fluttered. "If you'll stop yapping in my ear so I can pay attention, we can start practicing for that in about forty-five minutes."

"You don't have to entertain your mom while she's in town tonight?"

Delilah shook her head. "She's got a date with Helmut."

Stella held her hand to her forehead, shading her eyes against the spotlights Davis had rigged from the rafters. "If you can't keep it down back there, why don't you go do something more productive?"

Jasper bit down on his lip, though Delilah could feel the laugh bubbling up in his chest.

"You heard her." Delilah shrugged. "It'll be more fun to watch the competition live tomorrow anyway."

"Does that mean you want to head back to our place?"

Our place. She loved the sound of that. "I thought you'd never ask."

Jasper pinched her behind, making her squeal and earning her a scowl from Stella. But it was worth it. Delilah twirled out of his arms and tugged him by the hand toward the big barn door.

She was going to officially become a Taylor.

And she couldn't think of a better way to celebrate than at their place, with the love of her life wrapped in her arms.

acknowledgments

Huge thanks to the entire team at Berkley for all of the behind-the-scenes work to bring my books and so many others to life. Special thanks to my editor, Kristine Swartz, for continuing to believe in my stories. To my agent, Jessica Watterson, I'm so grateful to have you in my corner.

A special shout-out to Crushin' It Crew member Megan Hiesterman for providing the name for the Wicked Washboarders. After hearing that suggestion, I don't see how Kirby's band could ever be called anything else.

To all of my fellow authors who inspire and encourage me every day to keep doing this crazy thing called writing. There are too many to name but know that your enthusiasm lifts me up, and I wouldn't be able to survive the world of publishing without you having my back (and making me laugh).

To my reader group, the Crushin' It Crew, thanks for showing up for me. We're in this together, and you put a smile on my face every freaking day. I do this for you!

And finally, to my family . . . it's been a year full of challenges and loss. Despite the ups and downs, you're still and will always be my why. Love and hugs to Mr. Crush, Honey Bee, Glitter Bee, and Buzzle Bee. XOXO

KEEP READING FOR AN EXCERPT FROM
THE FIRST BOOK IN THE
TYING THE KNOT IN TEXAS SERIES . . .

the cowboy says i do

AVAILABLE IN PAPERBACK FROM JOVE!

one

"I do."

Lacey Cherish blinked multiple times, trying to see through the obnoxious fake eyelashes her assistant had talked her into wearing at the last minute. Her fingers fiddled with the microphone in front of her as she silently willed the reporter from the television station in Houston to give it a rest. Not even forty-eight hours into her term as the newly appointed mayor of the little town of Idont, Texas, and she already had a full-blown crisis on her hands.

The reporter didn't back down. Instead, she got up from the metal folding chair, causing the legs to scrape across the linoleum. Lacey squinted as she fought the urge to cover her ears. Her upper and lower eyelashes tangled together and she struggled to peer through the dark lines barring her vision.

"Let me rephrase that." The reporter cocked a hip while she consulted her notebook. "You expect us to believe you're going to find a way to put a positive spin on this?"

Lacey inhaled a deep breath through her nose in an attempt

to buy some time and answer with what might sound like a well-thought-out response. The problem was, she was winging this. No one had been more shocked than she was to find out the biggest business in town, Phillips Stationery and Imports, had closed their doors. The company had made their headquarters in Idont for over a hundred years, starting as a printing press then moving into manufacturing, and importing all kinds of novelties from overseas.

"I'm sure Mayor Cherish will have more to say as the situation unfolds." Leave it to Deputy Sheriff Bodie Phillips to bully everyone back into line. He was part of the problem. Granted, he wasn't the ogre who decided to shut down the warehouse, but he did share DNA with the two men in charge.

"I'll have a statement to the press by the end of the week," Lacey promised.

Her assistant stepped to the microphone as Lacey moved away. "Thanks, everyone, for coming. As Mayor Cherish said, she'll be prepared to address the closing by the end of the day on Friday."

"You okay?" Bodie appeared at her side. He angled his broad chest like a wall, as if trying to protect her from the prying eyes of the people who'd turned out for the press conference at city hall. All six of them.

"Yes. No thanks to you." She summoned her best scowl, ready to chastise him for interfering in her business. It didn't matter that much when they were kids, but he needed to see her in a different light now. She was the mayor, after all, not the same scrawny, bucktoothed little girl who used to follow him everywhere.

"I'm just as surprised as you." The look in his eyes proved he was telling the truth. She'd never seen that particular mixture of anger and frustration, and she was pretty sure she'd been exposed to all of his moods. "Dad didn't say a word to me about this and I spent the holidays over at their place, surrounded by the family."

"Well, you and your dad aren't exactly bosom buddies, now, are you?" She gathered her purse and shrugged on her jacket before heading down the hall to the back door of the building.

Bodie followed, taking one step to every three of hers. Damn heels. She would have been much more comfortable in a pair of ropers, but her new assistant never would have let her step in front of a microphone without looking the part of mayor. Which was precisely what Lacey paid her to do.

"Hey, you can't punish me for something my dad and my pops decided to do." Bodie stopped in front of her, his muscular frame blocking the door, his head nearly touching the low ceiling.

Lacey clamped a hand to her hip, ready for a throw-down. "I'm not trying to punish you. I just don't understand how all of a sudden, after a century in business, they decided they can't make a go of it anymore. And breaking the news right after the holidays?"

Bodie shrugged. "I don't know, Sweets."

"Stop calling me that. I'm the mayor now." She pursed her lips. Why couldn't he take her seriously? She'd figured the childhood nickname would have disappeared, along with her aggravating attraction to the man who'd been her big brother's best friend all her life. But here she was, back in Idont where nothing had changed, especially the way her traitorous body reacted to Bodie Phillips.

"Aw, come on, Lacey. You'll always be Sweets to me." He grinned, dazzling her with his million-dollar smile. Well, maybe not million-dollar, but she'd been there when he had to go through braces twice, so it had to be worth at least five or six grand.

She resisted the pull of his charm. He'd always been able to tease her back into a good mood when hers had gone sour. But this was different. The only reason she'd run for mayor was because her dad had been forced out of office after a particularly embarrassing public incident. In which he drove a golf cart into a pond. A stolen golf cart. While drunk.

His stunt earned him his third DWI and twenty-four months of house arrest. During her tenure as mayor, she hoped she could polish off the tarnished family name and turn the tide of public opinion about the Cherish family. That, and she couldn't find a real job. Evidently a degree in communications wasn't worth much more than the paper her diploma was printed on.

"What am I going to do, Bodie?" She shook her head, her gaze drawn to a section of chipped linoleum on the floor. The whole town seemed to be falling apart.

"Maybe it's time to consider merging with Swynton."

Lacey jerked her head up, causing one of her fake eyelashes to flop up and down. "Please tell me you didn't just suggest we wave good-bye to our roots and hand our town over to that obnoxious man." She tried to reattach the line of lashes against her eyelid.

Bodie didn't bother to suppress his smile. "Come on, Lacey. You've got to admit, their economy could run circles around ours. I know you don't care for Buck, but he's doing something right over there."

She pressed her lips together. The only thing Mayor Buck Little was doing was turning the once-semicharming town of Swynton into a hot pocket of cheap housing and seedy businesses. "Have you seen how many building permits they've issued in the past three months? If he had it his way, we'd end up with empty strip malls and low-rent apartment buildings all over town."

"At least that would create jobs and give people some affordable housing options." Bodie leaned against the wall. "My family's business was our biggest employer."

"I know." Lacey gritted her teeth, wishing with all her heart she had someone to talk to about this. Someone who might be able to offer a realistic option, not just confirm everything she already knew about what a sorry situation they were in. "I need to think."

Bodie pushed open the door leading to the back parking lot and swept his arm forward, gesturing for her to go first. "You want to grab lunch over at the diner and talk?"

"I can't now. I'm late for my shift at the Burger Bonanza." She jammed her sunglasses on her face, crushing them against the stupid lashes as she brushed past him through the door into the sunny, but chilly, February day.

"When are you going to quit that job, Lacey Jane? The mayor shouldn't be flipping burgers and mixing milk shakes."

She turned, jabbing a finger into Bodie's chest. "I'll do what I have to do to pay the bills." She jabbed harder. "And I'll do what I have to do to keep this town afloat."

Despite her effort, the concrete plane of his pecs didn't budge. Damn him.

He grabbed her hand, twirling her around like they were doing a two-step instead of sparring about the future of their hometown. "That's one thing Idont has going for it that Swynton never will."

"What's that?" Lacey stumbled as he released her, not sure if she was dizzy from the spin or off-balance because of the way her hand had felt in his.

"You." Bodie tipped his cowboy hat at her as he walked away. "You're determined, I'll give you that, Mayor."

She adjusted her purse strap and tried to compose herself as he climbed into his pickup and drove away. Bodie wasn't one to dish out compliments, especially to a woman he'd considered a pesky nuisance most of his life. Either that was the nicest thing he'd ever said to her or he wanted something. Knowing him, it was the latter.

That would give her two things to think about while she worked her shift at the Burger Bonanza . . . how to save the town of Idont, and why in the world Bodie was trying to butter her up like a fresh-baked biscuit.

* * *

"You're late." Jojo stood at the counter, loading her arms with blue plate specials. "Watch out for Helmut, he's on a bender."

"Thanks." Lacey slipped off her heels and slid her feet into her flats before tying an apron around her waist. "Where do you need me today?"

"Why don't you start on the floor and take over the grill when Helmut leaves?" Jojo had been waiting tables at the Burger Bonanza since she and Lacey started high school. If Helmut had taken the time to name a manager, Jojo would be the natural choice. But instead he paid her the same as the rest of the waitstaff and expected her to keep everyone in line.

"Sounds good." Lacey grabbed her order pad and made her way to the front of the restaurant.

"Table twelve just got seated." Jojo nodded toward the corner booth.

"Got it." Lacey headed that way, her eyes on her notebook. "Hey, can I get y'all something to drink?"

"Well, look who it is." The voice that had squashed a thousand of Lacey's childhood dreams drifted across the table.

Lacey lifted her gaze to stare right into the eyes of her high school nemesis—Adeline Monroe. "Oh, hi, Adeline. It's been a long time." And thank God for that. Adeline lived over in Swynton. It used to be the only reason she'd cross the river that divided the two towns was if she was on the hunt for some too-good-to-pass-up gossip. What was she after now?

"It sure has. And look at you. I heard you came back." Adeline leaned over the table, lowering her voice, that familiar glint in her eye. "Is it true you got yourself elected mayor?"

Lacey nodded. "Yep, sure did. Now, what will it be? A round of Burger Bonanza Banzai Shakes? Or can I start you off with a basket of buffalo bites?" She tried to pull a smile from deep down, but it seemed to stick on the way to her face. Half of her mouth lifted, the other half slid down, probably making her look like an undecided clown, especially with the damn lashes still glued to her eyelids.

Adeline turned to the man next to her. A quick glance at the giant rock on her left hand confirmed he was probably her fiancé. What happened to the curse Lacey had cast at graduation? Adeline was supposed to be hairless and withered by now, or at least well on her way. Instead she looked like she'd just stepped out of a salon. Every highlighted hair was in place. Her eyebrows were plucked to perfection and there was no sign of premature aging.

"Lacey, I'd like you to meet my fiancé, Roman." Adeline put her hand on Roman's arm, obviously staking her claim. As if Lacey were going to try to hump the man right there at table twelve.

"Congratulations. Nice to meet you, Roman." She managed to correct her awkward expression and forced a smile. "Are you ready to order?"

Adeline's smirk faded. She ran a manicured nail down the side of the menu. "We'll take two Burger Bonanza baskets with fries. Diet for me."

"Do you have iced tea?" Roman asked.

Lacey nodded. She'd been afraid the man couldn't speak. She wouldn't have put it past Adeline to marry a man incapable of talking back to her. He probably didn't get a word in edgewise most of the time. "I'll be back in a minute with your drinks."

She tucked her order pad into the front of her apron. First the news of the Phillips business closing, now an unexpected visit from Adeline. Bad news usually came in threes. What would happen next?

It took less than a minute to find out. As she approached the soda station to grab two cups, someone grabbed her arm.

Bodie.

"Mayor Cherish, you'll need to come with me." His voice was all business. The commanding tone sent a shiver straight through her. But his lips twitched. A hint of humor shone in those deep gray eyes. She'd spent way too much of her life thinking about what it would feel like to lose herself in those depths.

"What are you doing here? I've got a shift."

"I'm aware of that." His fingers closed around her elbow, eliminating any argument, propelling her toward the door. "But we've got a problem that needs your attention. Now."

two

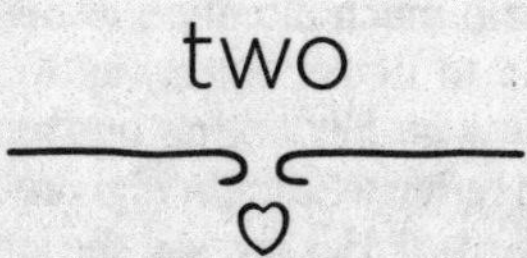

Bodie gripped Lacey's elbow a little tighter as he led her outside. He wouldn't admit it, but he kind of enjoyed spending time with Idont's new mayor—much more than he expected, and a lot more than he should.

"Stop, Bodie. I'm not taking another step until you tell me what's going on." Lacey planted her feet as she wrapped her arms around her middle. It was chilly, even for Texas. He should have grabbed her coat, but now he didn't want to take the time to go back inside.

"Here." He slid his jacket off then draped it over her shoulders.

"I don't want your jacket." She shrugged it off and tossed it back at him. "I want to know why you dragged me out here during my shift. Helmut's going to pop a blood vessel over this. What's so important?"

"There's a protest down at the warehouse. Seems Jonah Wylder has chained himself to the front doors. Says he's not leaving until someone gives him his job back."

"You've got to be kidding me." She tilted her head back,

giving him a full-on glimpse of the smooth ivory column of her neck.

When did the little girl who used to bug the hell out of him turn into such a beauty? Seemed like she'd always been underfoot as a kid. He and her big brother, Luke, couldn't go anywhere without her tagging along. Since she'd been back he hadn't paid much attention to her—he'd been too focused on trying to figure out a way to get out of Idont himself. But now with her taking on the doomed role of mayor, he started to wish he hadn't ignored her for so long.

"So what do we do?" Her jaw set, she leveled her gaze on him. "I suppose I need to try to talk some sense into him."

Bodie tried to suppress a smile. "Good luck with that. Jonah's not exactly known for keeping a level head."

"Let's go. I'll ride with you so we can talk on the way." She didn't give him much choice but to follow behind her as she crossed the parking lot to his truck.

Should he try to open the door for her or let her handle it on her own? He wavered as they got closer. He'd never treated Lacey as anything but a kid. But now, there was no trace of the freckle-faced teen. He increased his pace to make it to the passenger door before her.

"Thanks." She barely glanced at him as he held the door while she climbed into the truck.

While he waited for her to get settled, he couldn't help but notice the way her skirt rode up on her thighs. Rubbing a hand over the scruff on his chin, he chastised himself. This was Luke's sister he was undressing in his mind. He needed to shut that shit down. Fast. He closed the door and stomped around the truck to get behind the wheel.

They rode in silence for the first few minutes, giving him a chance to sort out his thoughts.

"So how do you suggest I handle Jonah?" Lacey swiveled in her seat to face Bodie.

"Let him sit out there and freeze his ass off." Bodie took a sip of water from his travel tumbler. "Jonah's a hothead.

He'll make a scene but once everyone goes home and the excitement wears off he'll slink back to the rock he lives under."

"That's one of my constituents you're talking about." Lacey adjusted the vent on the dash.

"Yeah, I feel sorry for you about that. He was an asshole when he was younger and he's grown into an even bigger asshole now."

"Great. How long is my term again?" She twisted a strand of hair around her finger as she gazed out the front window.

"Four years. But as long as you don't get arrested, you'll probably get reelected." He meant that as a joke, a little bit of humor at her dad's expense, but Lacey didn't smile. Bodie glanced back and forth from the road in front of him to Lacey's profile. Her pulse ticked along her jaw as she drummed her fingers on her knee. "You know I didn't mean anything by that, right?"

Her breath came out on a long sigh. "I know. Wish I knew what Dad was thinking when he decided to go on a joyride."

"If it's any consolation"—Bodie gave her an apologetic grin—"I really didn't enjoy arresting your dad that day." Her dad had been more of a father figure to him growing up than his own flesh and blood.

"Nope." Her mouth quirked into a half smile. "That doesn't make me feel any better. I don't know why I thought it would be a good idea to run for mayor. What was I thinking?"

"You want me to answer that?" He could tell her if she really wanted to know. Lacey was a fixer. Always had been and always would be.

"No." She closed her eyes and let her head roll from side to side, like she was trying to ease some tension. "I just wish I'd thought it through. Seemed like the thing to do when Dad had to step down."

"Idont is lucky you stepped up. If you hadn't, can you imagine where we'd be right now without a mayor?" He slowed the truck to make a right.

"Probably annexed into Swynton by now. I've heard Mayor Little works fast."

He'd heard that, too, and even experienced it firsthand. The mayor of Swynton had definite ideas about how things should be done. They'd had their fair share of run-ins during the few years he'd been working as deputy sheriff. Mayor Buck Little wasn't someone to cross.

"Have you had time to think about what you're going to do yet?" he asked.

"You mean in the fifteen minutes I had in between my dealings with you?" Lacey shook her head, sending her wavy, shoulder-length hair bouncing.

He caught a whiff of something flowery. Had to be her. Although he didn't recall her ever smelling like anything but horses when they were younger. Horses and the butterscotch candy she always seemed to have in her mouth. That's what earned her the nickname of Sweets in the first place. "You warm enough?"

"No." She clamped her arms around her middle. "But I'll be fine. What should we do with Jonah? A little 'good cop, bad cop' routine?"

"Sure, I'll rough him up then you sweet-talk him into going home." He slid his gaze her way to catch her reaction.

"Really? Does that kind of stuff work?"

"Only on TV."

She let out a groan. "Maybe I should just let you handle it, then. I can wait in the truck while you take care of Mr. Wylder."

"And miss out on the fun?" He'd known her all her life and had seen her in action time and again. She'd no more be able to step aside in a moment of crisis than he'd be able to ignore someone purposely breaking the law. The only difference was, he got paid to maintain law and order while she spent her life trying to fix things whether it fell under her job description or not.

"Yeah, I suppose I ought to at least try to talk to him."

"That's the spirit." Bodie pulled the truck into the long, tree-covered drive leading to the warehouse. Once, the land had belonged to the founder of the town, his great-great-great-great-great-grandfather. He'd built the giant Victorian house first. When he decided to become a printer, he put up an outbuilding just down the drive. Over the years the Phillips family had expanded until the outbuilding became the warehouse it was today.

"You mean him and the mob he's got with him?" Bodie asked.

"What?" Lacey turned toward him. "I can't imagine Jonah inciting a mob."

As he eased the truck to a stop, Bodie pointed through the windshield. "Okay, maybe not a mob, but he did bring some friends."

"Oh, come on. When am I going to catch a break?" She opened the door and climbed down, looking out of place in her slim skirt and blouse among the flannel-and-denim-clad crowd.

Bodie grabbed his hat, prepared to provide backup.

"Well, if it ain't our new mayor." Jonah sized her up as she approached. He stood at the front door of the building, layers of metal chains wrapped around his torso.

"What can I do for you, Mr. Wylder?" Lacey offered her hand but must have thought better of it when Jonah struggled to work his arm free to take it.

"For starters you can reopen the warehouse." His eyes narrowed. A chorus of encouraging "yeahs" and "that's rights" floated up from the small crowd. "And then you can give us all a nice, fat raise."

Lacey crossed her arms over her chest. "I'm afraid I can't make that happen."

"Then figure out a way." Jonah nodded, his head being the only part of his body that he seemed to be able to move.

"Look, Mr. Wylder—"

"Jonah," he insisted.

"Okay, Jonah. I'd love nothing more than to open up the warehouse, give all of you your jobs back, and double your pay. But we both know that's not going to happen."

"Then I'll just stay here until you find a way." Jonah shrugged, making the chains clink together.

Bodie shifted his weight from one foot to the other, waiting to see how the situation would play out. Lacey looked like she was about to cry. Her bottom lip trembled and she tightened her grip around her middle. He couldn't let them get the best of her, not on her second day on the job.

"You're just going to stay out here all night, then?" Bodie asked.

Jonah nodded. "If that's what it takes."

"And I suppose you've got a permit for that?" He took a step toward Lacey, sensing her focus shift from Jonah to him.

Jonah glanced to one of his buddies. "I don't need a permit to stay out here."

"This land is private property. If you want to hold a demonstration or a public gathering, based on city code, you need to ask for permission from the owners first." Bodie shrugged his shoulders. "Unless you'd rather I arrest you and take you in."

"What are you doing?" Lacey whispered. "I'm handling this."

Bodie put a hand out, gesturing for her to be quiet. "Your call, Jonah, but I bet your wife will be real pissed if you end up with another offense."

Jonah gritted his teeth, then muttered something under his breath.

Lacey glared at Bodie. "I said I've got this."

"Fine." Jonah shook his head, the fight draining from him. "Boys, get me out of here. We'll have to find another way to settle our differences."

One of Jonah's friends fumbled with a set of keys. While he waited for the men to disperse, Bodie turned to Lacey, pretty damn pleased at the way he'd managed to break things up. No one got hurt, Lacey saved face, and it was a win-win all around.

But the look she gave him wasn't full of the thanks he expected—the thanks he deserved.

"What?" He held his hands out, wondering what he'd done to incite such an angry response. "You're welcome. Aren't you going to say something?"

Fire blazed in those bright baby blues, burning hot and icy cold at the same time. "Oh, I'm going to say something, all right."

Ready to find
your next great read?

Let us help.

Visit prh.com/nextread

Penguin
Random
House

WITHDRAWN